Vampire Game

JUDAL

Translator - Patrick Coffman
English Adaptation - Jason Deitrich
Associate Editor - Tim Beedle
Retouch and Lettering - Kristina Kovacs
Cover Layout - Anna Kernbaum

Editor - Nora Wong
Digital Imaging Manager - Chris Buford
Pre-Press Manager - Antonio DePietro
Production Managers - Jennifer Miller, Mutsumi Miyazaki
Art Director - Matt Alford
Managing Editor - Jill Freshney
VP of Production - Ron Klamert
President & C.O.O. - John Parker
Publisher & C.E.O. - Stuart Levy

E-mail: info@TOKYOPOP.com
Come visit us online at www.TOKYOPOP.com

A  Manga

TOKYOPOP Inc.
5900 Wilshire Blvd. Suite 2000
Los Angeles, CA 90036

Vampire Game Vol. 7

ISBN: 1-59182-559-8

First TOKYOPOP printing: July 2004

10 9 8 7 6 5 4 3 2 1

Printed in the USA

VAMPIRE GAME

Volume 7

by

JUDAL

Los Angeles • Tokyo • London • Hamburg

VAMPIRE GAME

The Story Thus Far...

This is the tale of the Vampire King Duzell and his quest for revenge against the good King Phelios, a valiant warrior who slew the vampire a century ago. Now Duzell has returned, reincarnated as a feline foe to deliver woe to... Well, that's the problem. Who is the reincarnation of King Phelios?

Equally as important, *where* is King Phelios? For quite some time, Duzell and Princess Ishtar have been looking for him in the kingdom of Ci Xeneth. As of yet they haven't found Phelios, but they *have* found a homicidal lord who would stop at nothing to obtain the Pheliostan throne for himself. They *have* found a dungeon full of monsters that have been kidnapped and mercilessly slaughtered to feed a dark obsession. They *have* found a young captain capable of unleashing some of the most destructive magic in Pheliosta. They *have* found a powerful sorcerer pulling the strings behind the scenes. A sorcerer who has revealed himself to be none other than the Vampire Sharlen, one of the most powerful vampires in Pheliosta.

Yes, Duzell and Ishtar have learned much about Ci Xeneth. Unfortunately, they still haven't learned how to stay out of trouble. Particularly Ishtar. Otherwise, she never would have freed all the monsters in the dungeon, spurring a rebellion that's sure to cost lives (and the castle's supply of Jell-O). She never would have angered her uncle Jened, who wanted her dead even before she turned his castle into a psychotic petting zoo. And she surely wouldn't have convinced Duzell to court the powerful Captain Illsaide, who's already confused about where his loyalties lie. Ishtar's meddling has caught up to her, and the punishment is likely to be severe, especially now that her beloved bodyguard has shown up to save the day. Darres has managed to keep Ishtar from harm so far, but with the demonic Sharlen determined to prevent their escape, the cost of Ishtar's actions just may be his life.

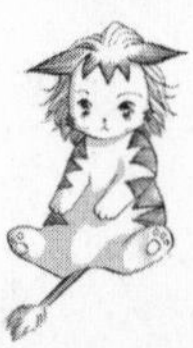

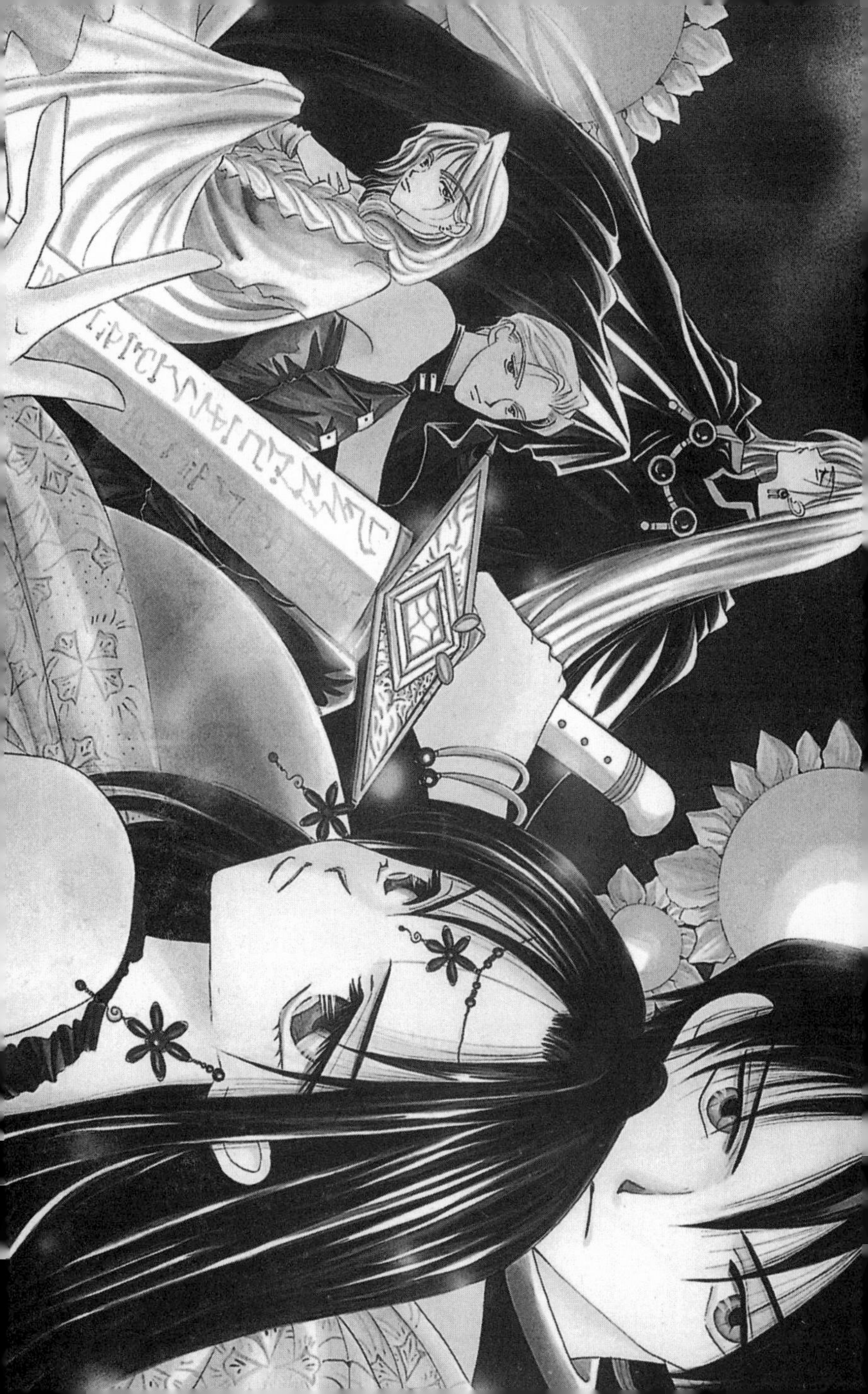

Table of Contents

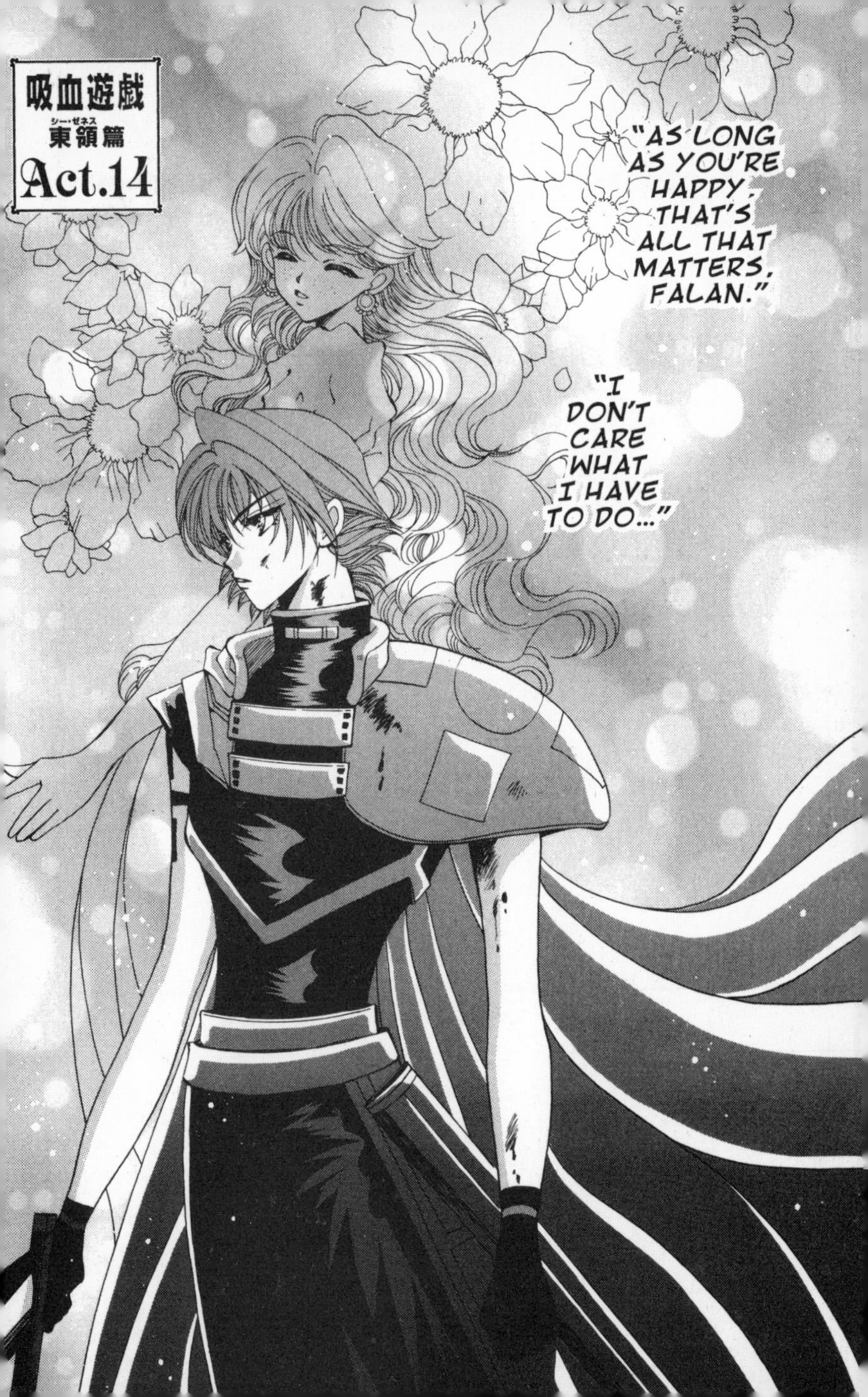
吸血遊戯
シー・ゼネス
東領篇
Act.14
"AS LONG AS YOU'RE HAPPY, THAT'S ALL THAT MATTERS, FALAN."
"I DON'T CARE WHAT I HAVE TO DO..."

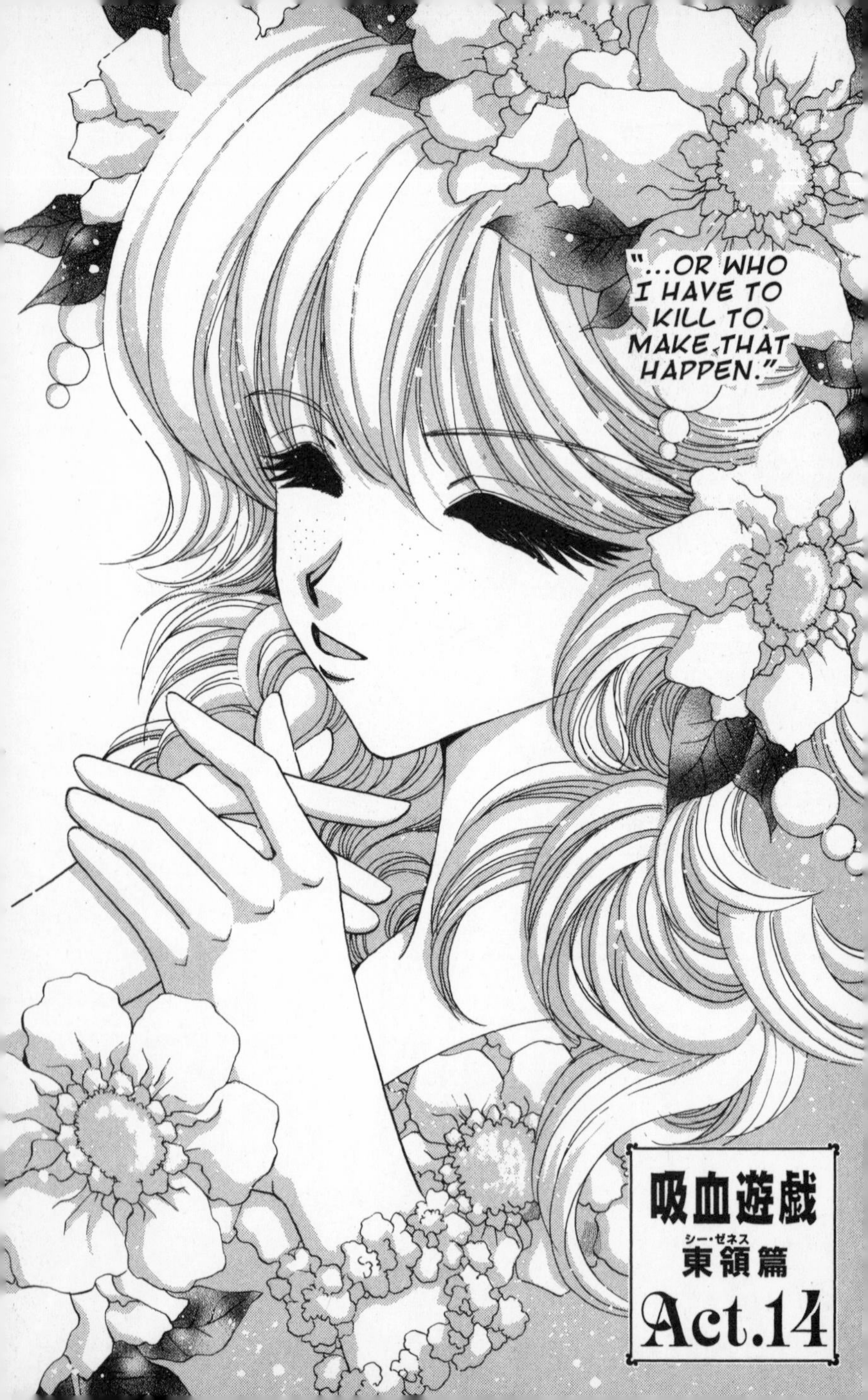
"...OR WHO I HAVE TO KILL TO MAKE THAT HAPPEN."
吸血遊戯
シー・ゼネス
東領篇
Act.14

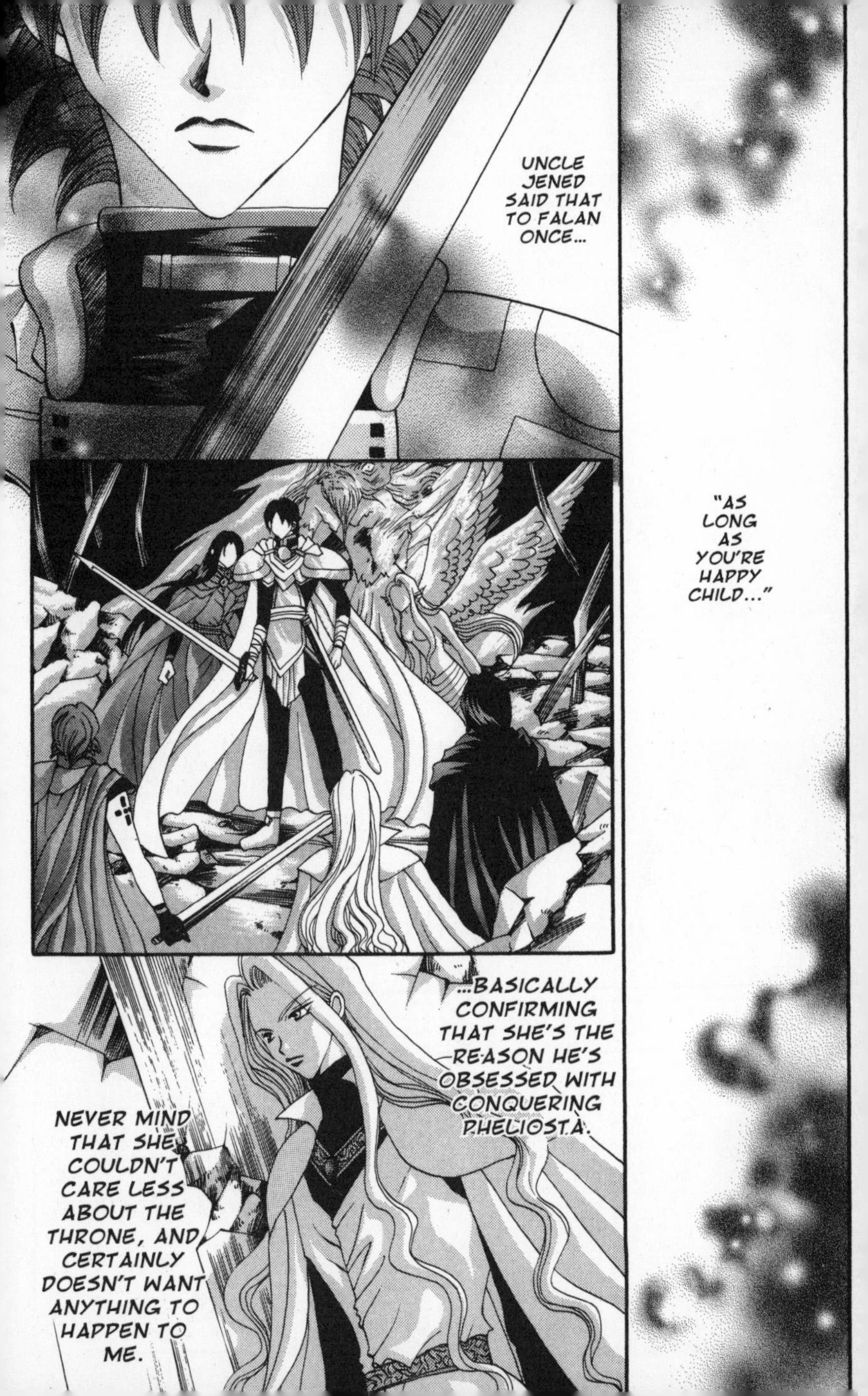
"AS LONG AS YOU'RE HAPPY CHILD..."
UNCLE JENED SAID THAT TO FALAN ONCE...
...BASICALLY CONFIRMING THAT SHE'S THE REASON HE'S OBSESSED WITH CONQUERING PHELIOSTA.
NEVER MIND THAT SHE COULDN'T CARE LESS ABOUT THE THRONE, AND CERTAINLY DOESN'T WANT ANYTHING TO HAPPEN TO ME.

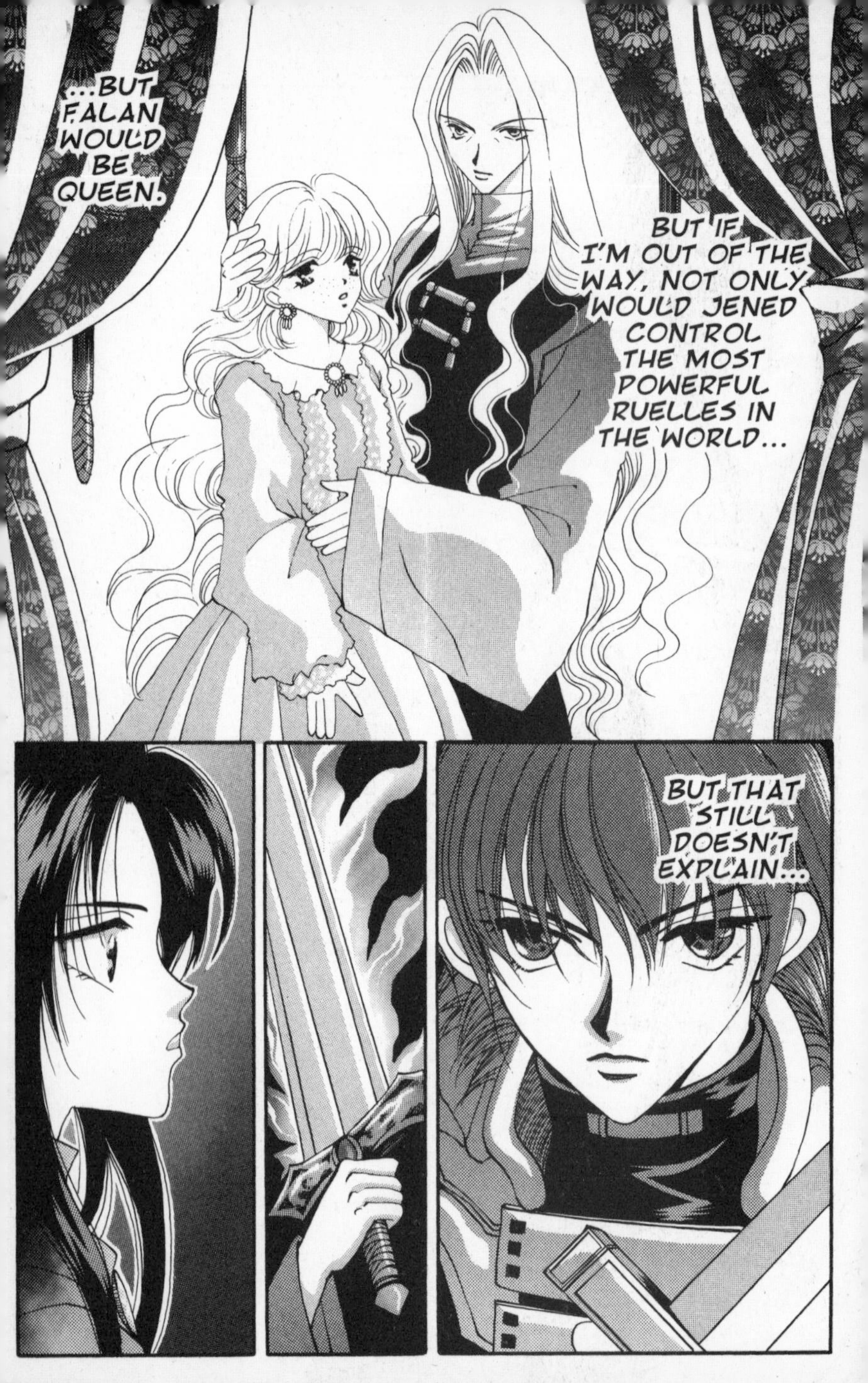
BUT IF I'M OUT OF THE WAY, NOT ONLY WOULD JENED CONTROL THE MOST POWERFUL RUELLES IN THE WORLD...
...BUT FALAN WOULD BE QUEEN.
BUT THAT STILL DOESN'T EXPLAIN...

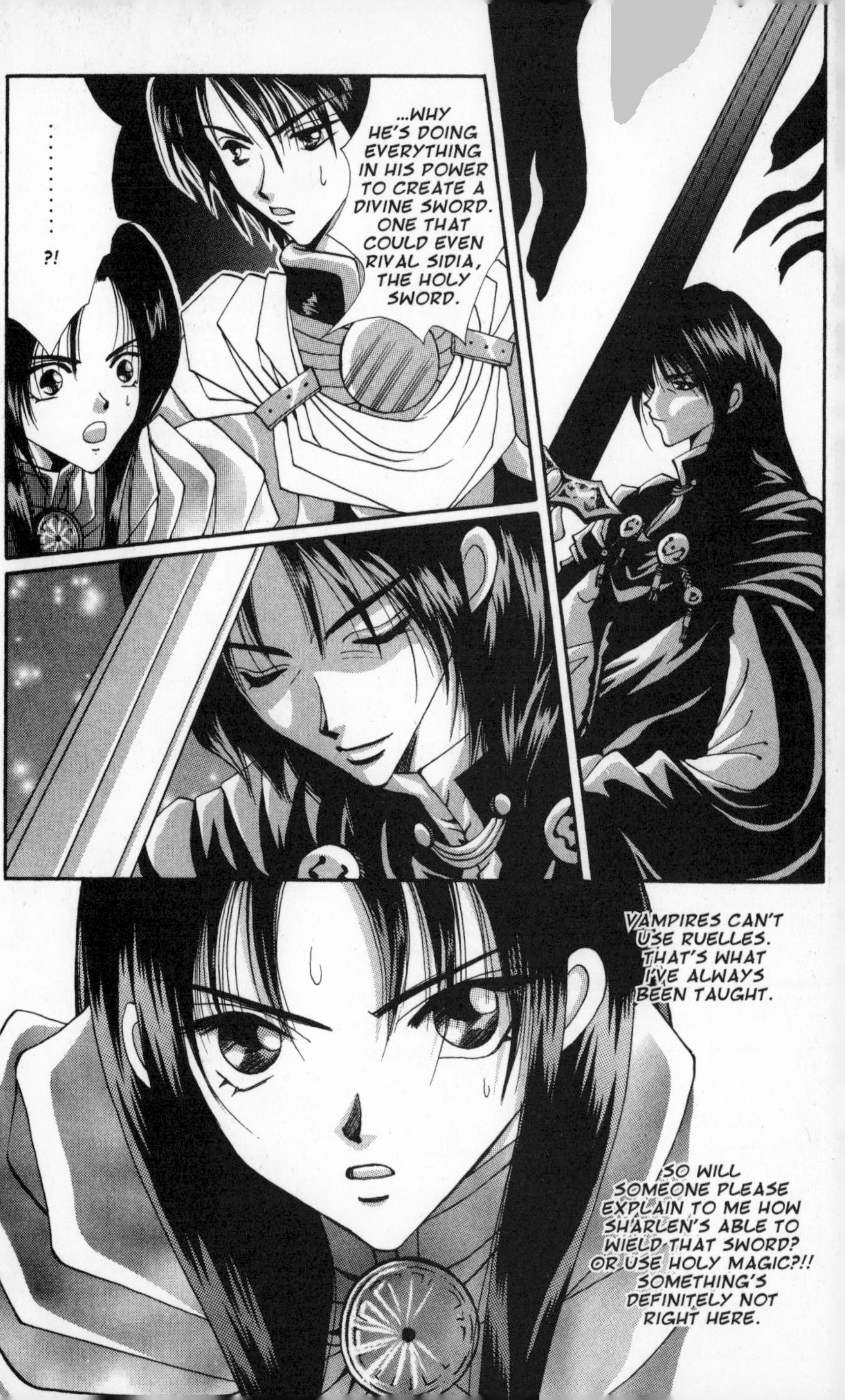
...WHY HE'S DOING EVERYTHING IN HIS POWER TO CREATE A DIVINE SWORD. ONE THAT COULD EVEN RIVAL SIDIA, THE HOLY SWORD.
......
?!
VAMPIRES CAN'T USE RUELLES. THAT'S WHAT I'VE ALWAYS BEEN TAUGHT.
SO WILL SOMEONE PLEASE EXPLAIN TO ME HOW SHARLEN'S ABLE TO WIELD THAT SWORD? OR USE HOLY MAGIC?!! SOMETHING'S DEFINITELY NOT RIGHT HERE.

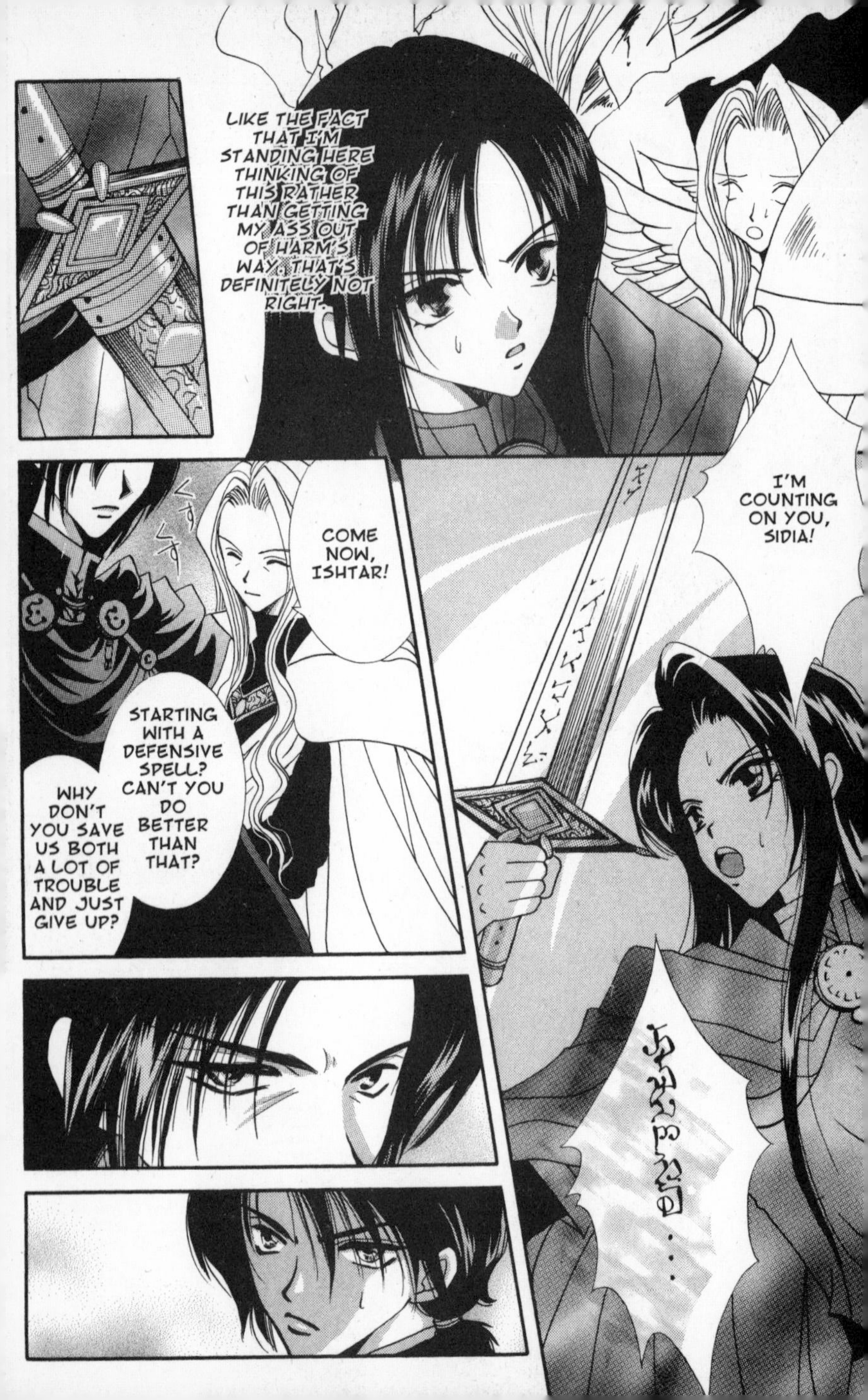
LIKE THE FACT THAT I'M STANDING HERE THINKING OF THIS RATHER THAN GETTING MY ASS OUT OF HARM'S WAY, THAT'S DEFINITELY NOT RIGHT.
I'M COUNTING ON YOU, SIDIA!
COME NOW, ISHTAR!
くすくす
STARTING WITH A DEFENSIVE SPELL? CAN'T YOU DO BETTER THAN THAT?
WHY DON'T YOU SAVE US BOTH A LOT OF TROUBLE AND JUST GIVE UP?

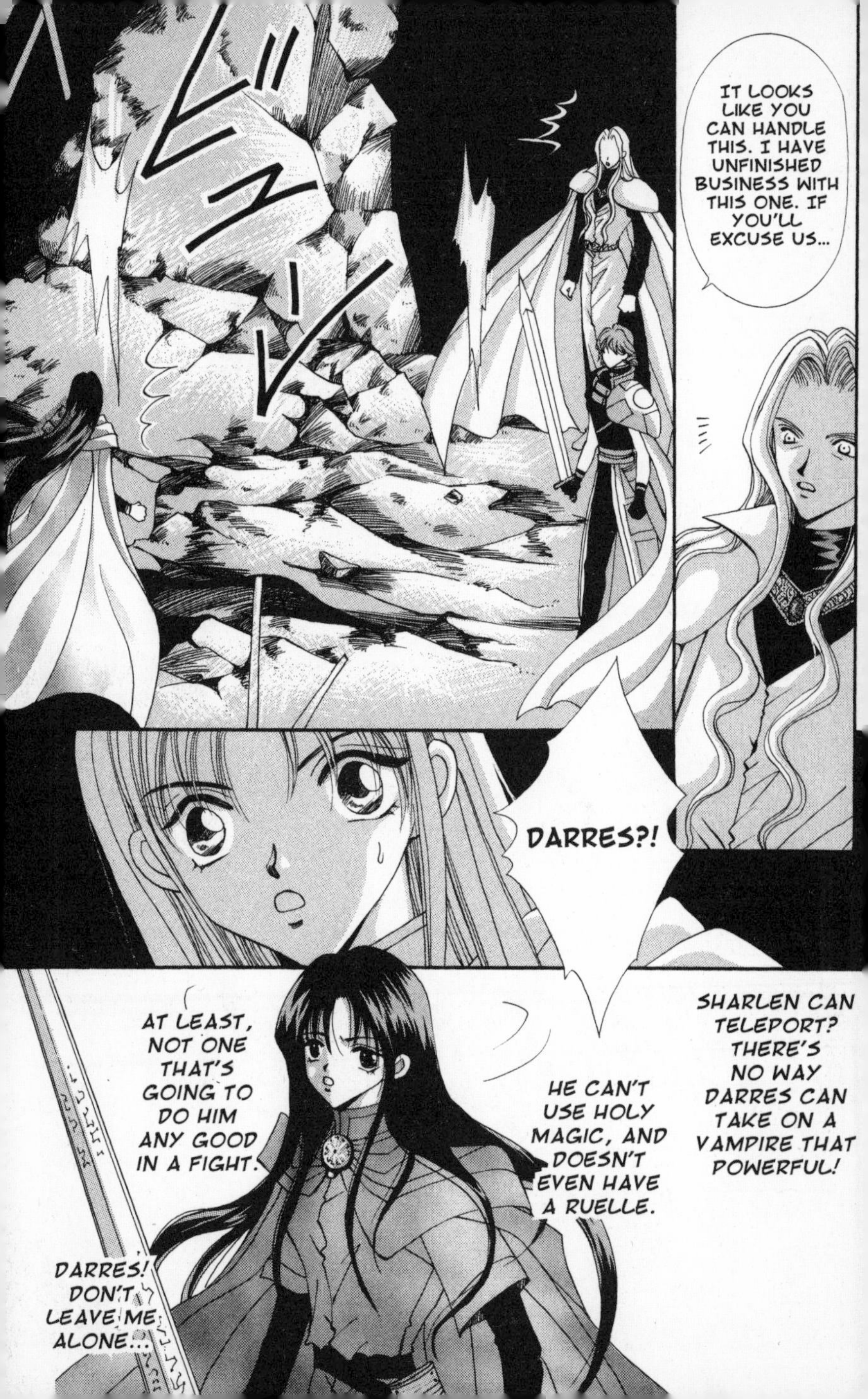
IT LOOKS LIKE YOU CAN HANDLE THIS. I HAVE UNFINISHED BUSINESS WITH THIS ONE. IF YOU'LL EXCUSE US...
DARRES?!
SHARLEN CAN TELEPORT? THERE'S NO WAY DARRES CAN TAKE ON A VAMPIRE THAT POWERFUL!
HE CAN'T USE HOLY MAGIC, AND DOESN'T EVEN HAVE A RUELLE.
AT LEAST, NOT ONE THAT'S GOING TO DO HIM ANY GOOD IN A FIGHT.
DARRES! DON'T LEAVE ME ALONE...

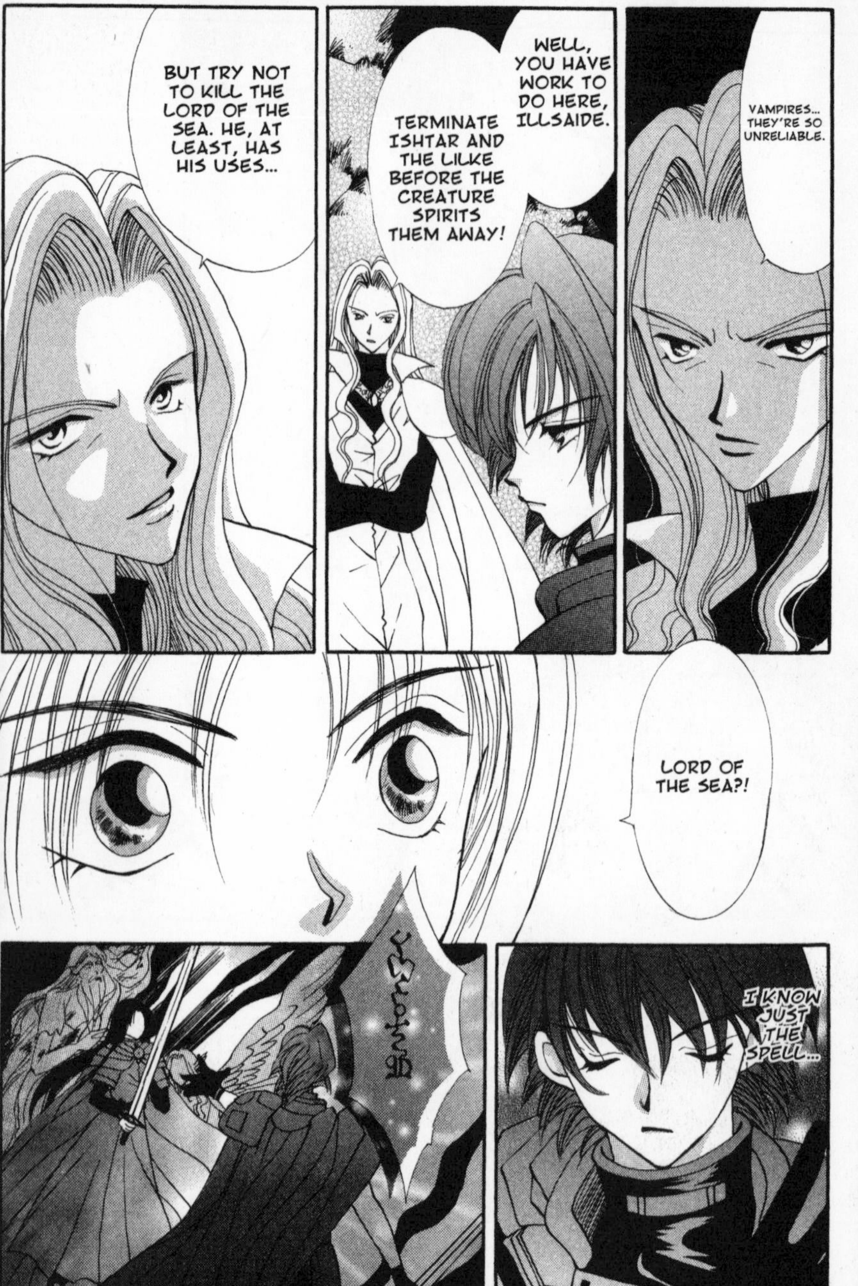
VAMPIRES... THEY'RE SO UNRELIABLE.
WELL, YOU HAVE WORK TO DO HERE, ILLSAIDE.
TERMINATE ISHTAR AND THE LILKE BEFORE THE CREATURE SPIRITS THEM AWAY!
BUT TRY NOT TO KILL THE LORD OF THE SEA. HE, AT LEAST, HAS HIS USES...
LORD OF THE SEA?!
I KNOW JUST THE SPELL...

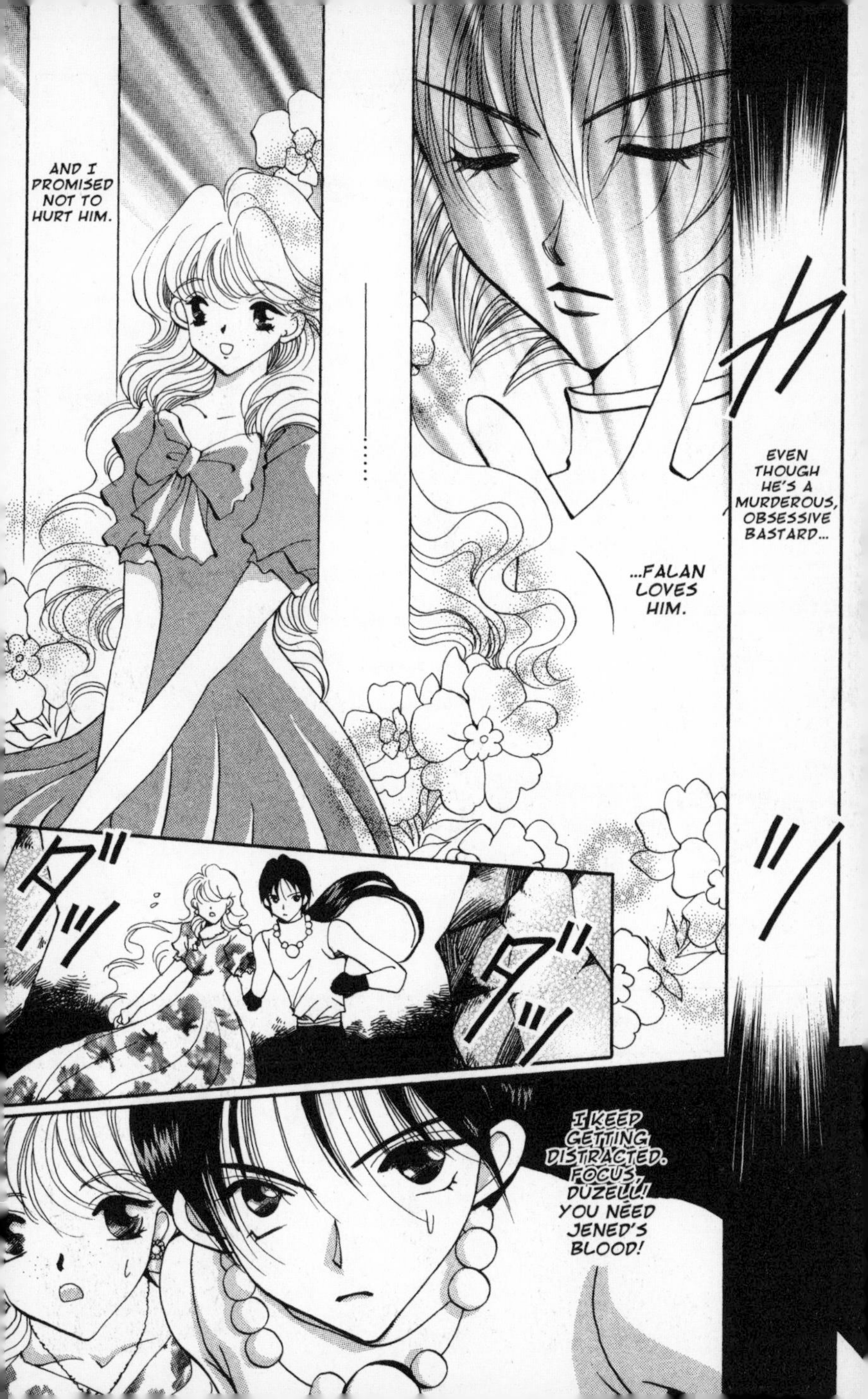

EVEN THOUGH HE'S A MURDEROUS, OBSESSIVE BASTARD...
...FALAN LOVES HIM.
......
AND I PROMISED NOT TO HURT HIM.
カツ
ダッ
ダッ
I KEEP GETTING DISTRACTED. FOCUS, DUZELL! YOU NEED JENED'S BLOOD!

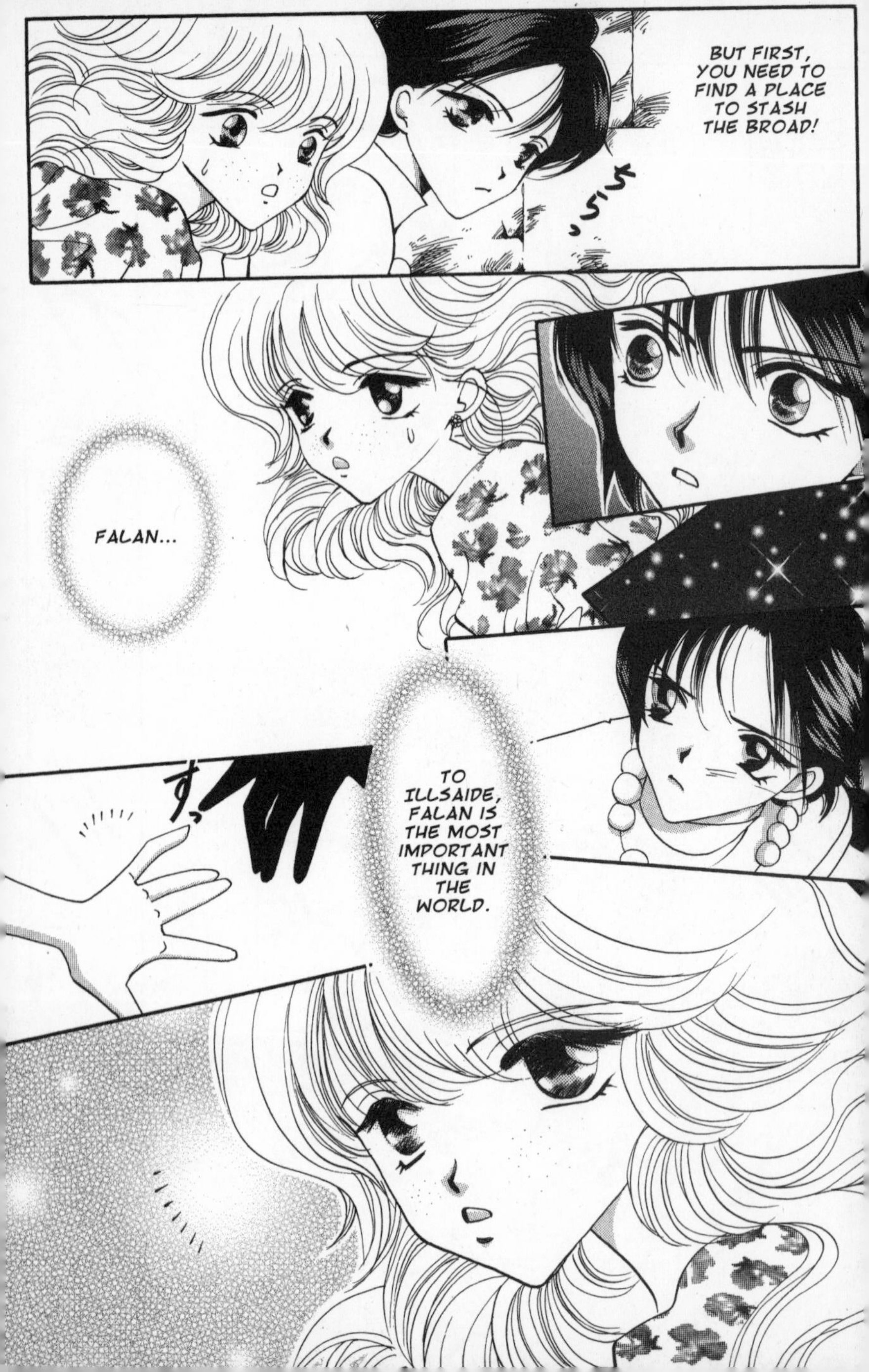
BUT FIRST, YOU NEED TO FIND A PLACE TO STASH THE BROAD!
FALAN...
TO ILLSAIDE, FALAN IS THE MOST IMPORTANT THING IN THE WORLD.
すっ

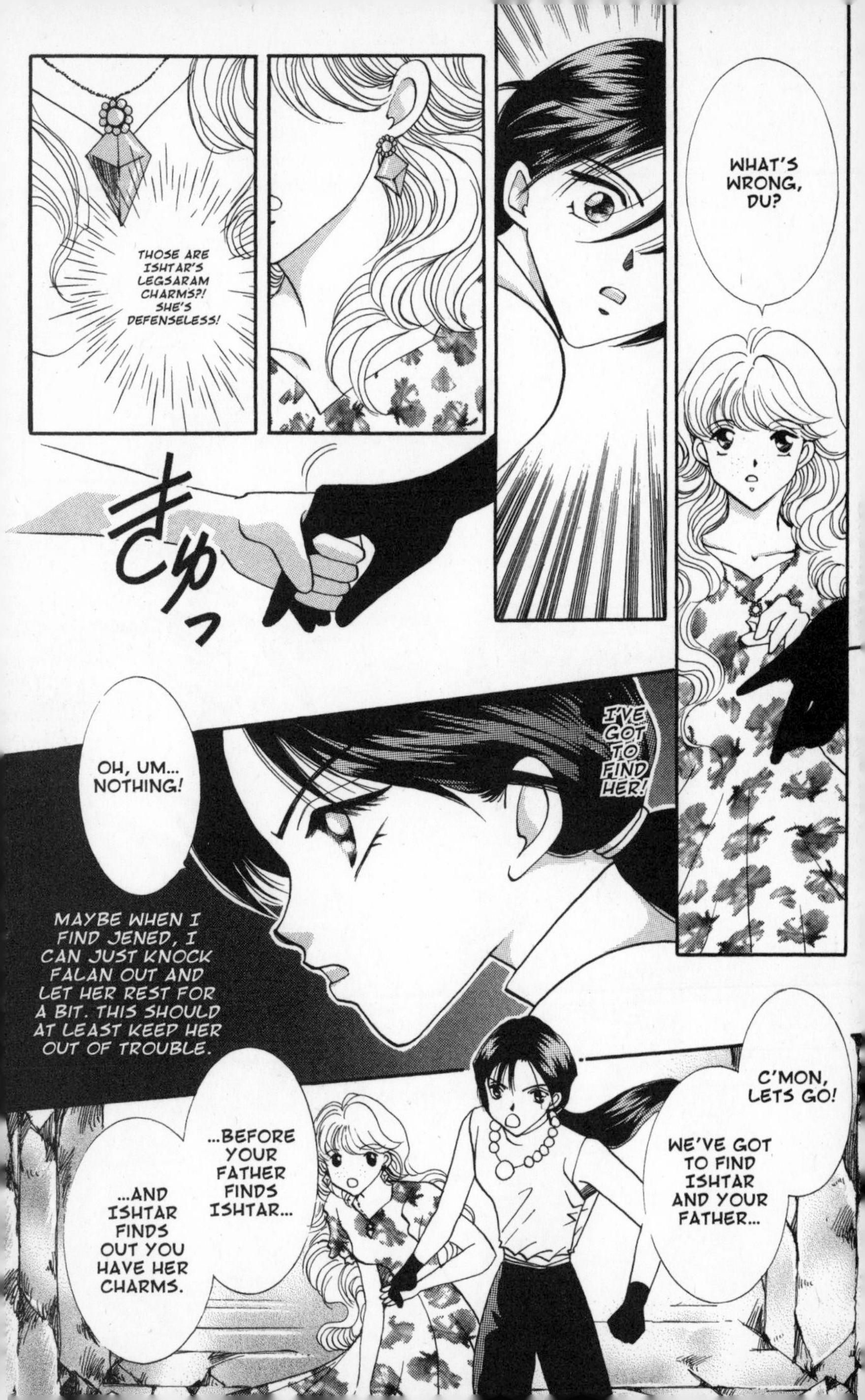
WHAT'S WRONG, DU?
THOSE ARE ISHTAR'S LEGSARAM CHARMS?! SHE'S DEFENSELESS!
きゅっ
I'VE GOT TO FIND HER!
OH, UM... NOTHING!
MAYBE WHEN I FIND JENED, I CAN JUST KNOCK FALAN OUT AND LET HER REST FOR A BIT. THIS SHOULD AT LEAST KEEP HER OUT OF TROUBLE.
C'MON, LETS GO!
WE'VE GOT TO FIND ISHTAR AND YOUR FATHER...
...BEFORE YOUR FATHER FINDS ISHTAR...
...AND ISHTAR FINDS OUT YOU HAVE HER CHARMS.

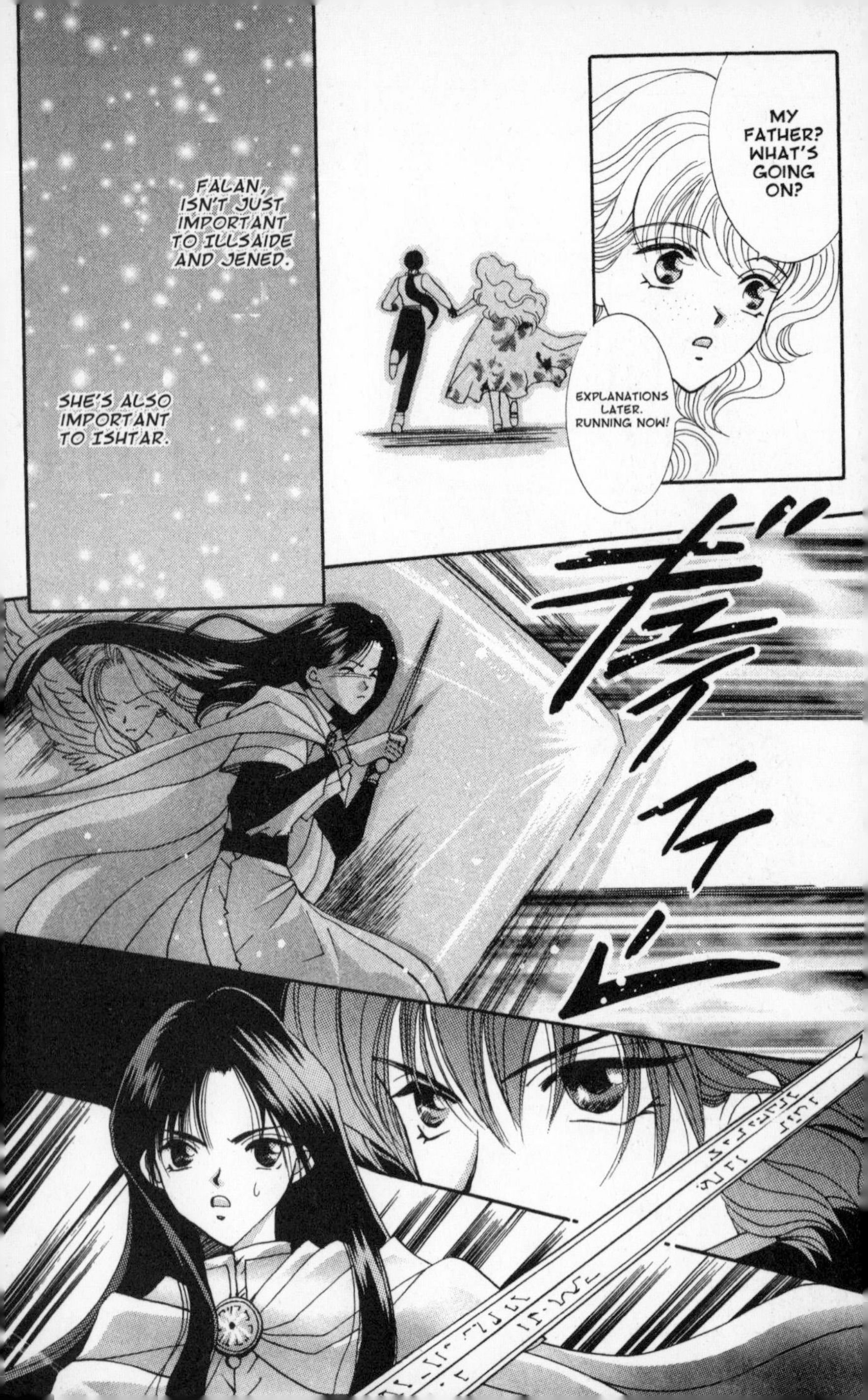
MY FATHER? WHAT'S GOING ON?
EXPLANATIONS LATER. RUNNING NOW!
FALAN, ISN'T JUST IMPORTANT TO ILLSAIDE AND JENED.
SHE'S ALSO IMPORTANT TO ISHTAR.
ギィィン

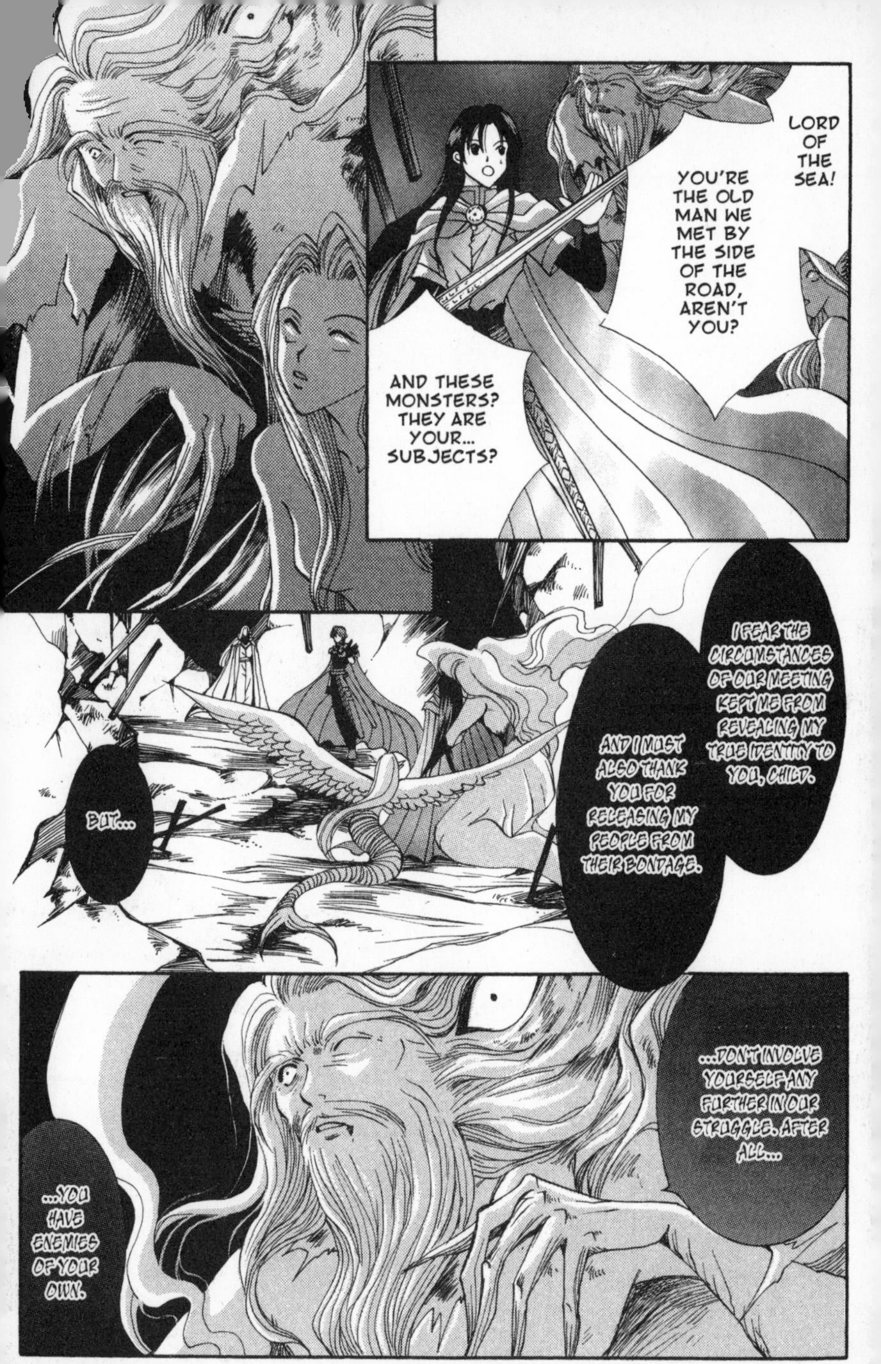
LORD OF THE SEA!
YOU'RE THE OLD MAN WE MET BY THE SIDE OF THE ROAD, AREN'T YOU?
AND THESE MONSTERS? THEY ARE YOUR... SUBJECTS?
I FEAR THE CIRCUMSTANCES OF OUR MEETING KEPT ME FROM REVEALING MY TRUE IDENTITY TO YOU, CHILD.
AND I MUST ALSO THANK YOU FOR RELEASING MY PEOPLE FROM THEIR BONDAGE.
BUT...
...DON'T INVOLVE YOURSELF ANY FURTHER IN OUR STRUGGLE. AFTER ALL...
...YOU HAVE ENEMIES OF YOUR OWN.

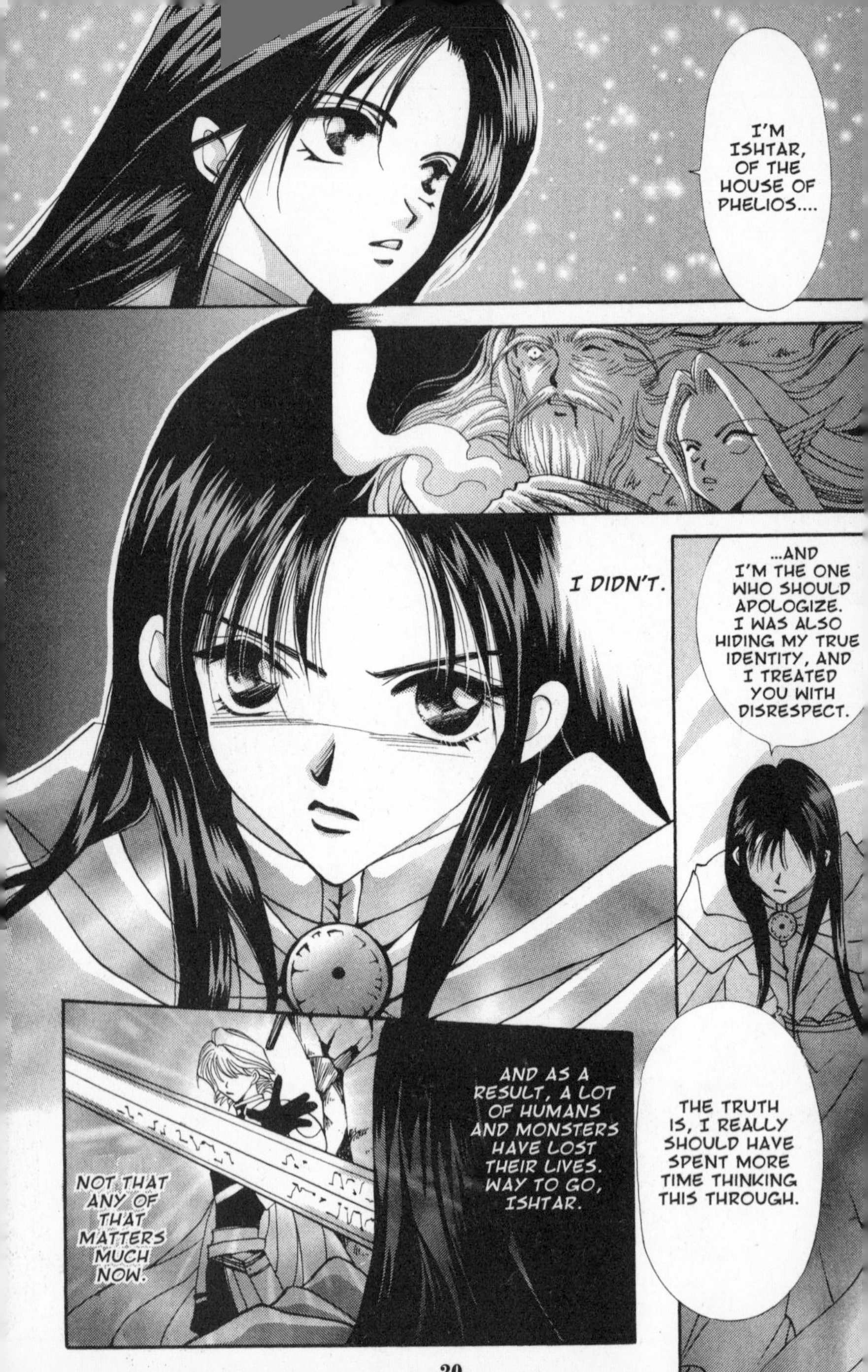
I'M ISHTAR, OF THE HOUSE OF PHELIOS....
...AND I'M THE ONE WHO SHOULD APOLOGIZE. I WAS ALSO HIDING MY TRUE IDENTITY, AND I TREATED YOU WITH DISRESPECT.
THE TRUTH IS, I REALLY SHOULD HAVE SPENT MORE TIME THINKING THIS THROUGH.
I DIDN'T.
AND AS A RESULT, A LOT OF HUMANS AND MONSTERS HAVE LOST THEIR LIVES. WAY TO GO, ISHTAR.
NOT THAT ANY OF THAT MATTERS MUCH NOW.

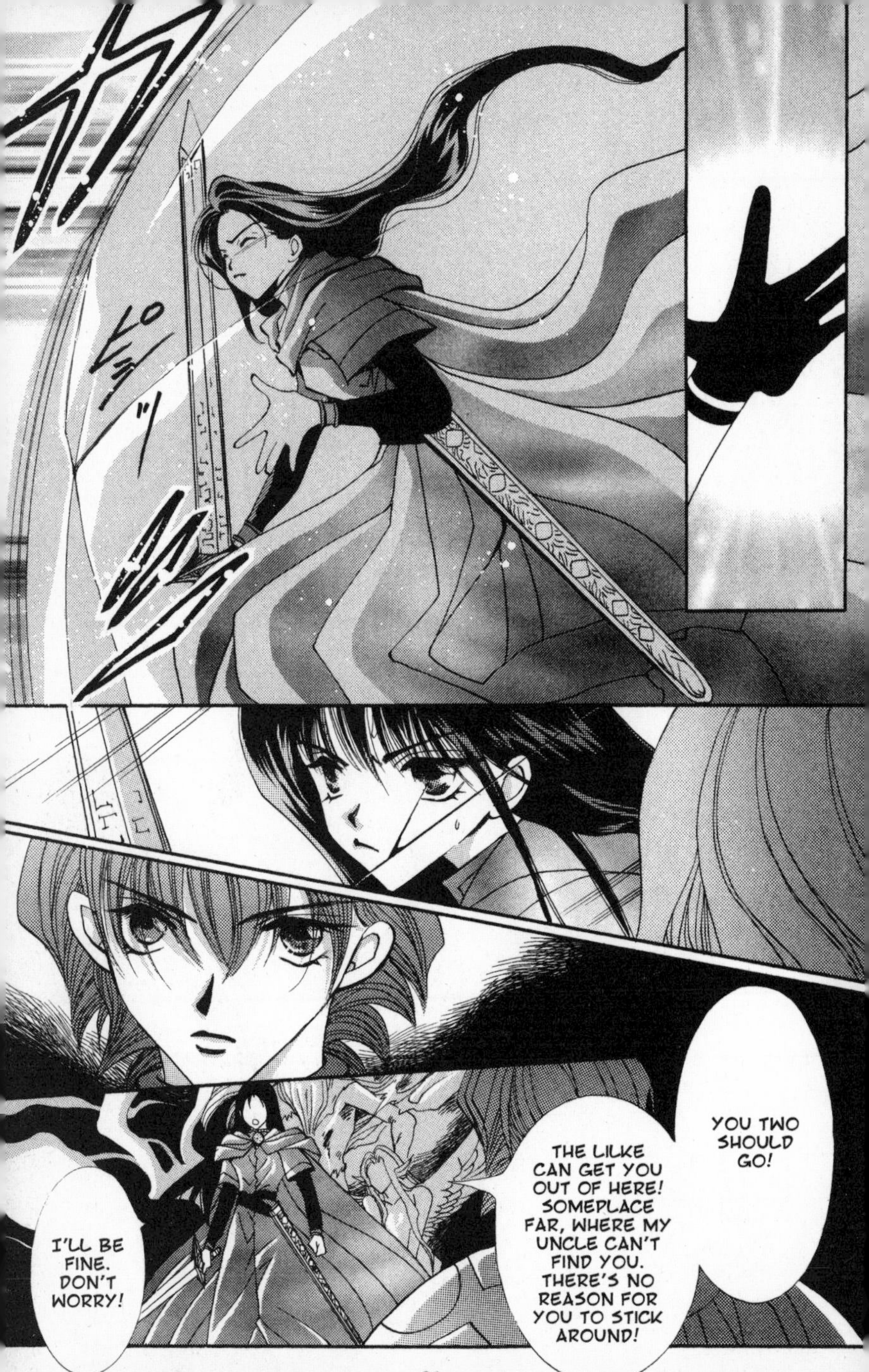
YOU TWO SHOULD GO!
THE LILKE CAN GET YOU OUT OF HERE! SOMEPLACE FAR, WHERE MY UNCLE CAN'T FIND YOU. THERE'S NO REASON FOR YOU TO STICK AROUND!
I'LL BE FINE. DON'T WORRY!

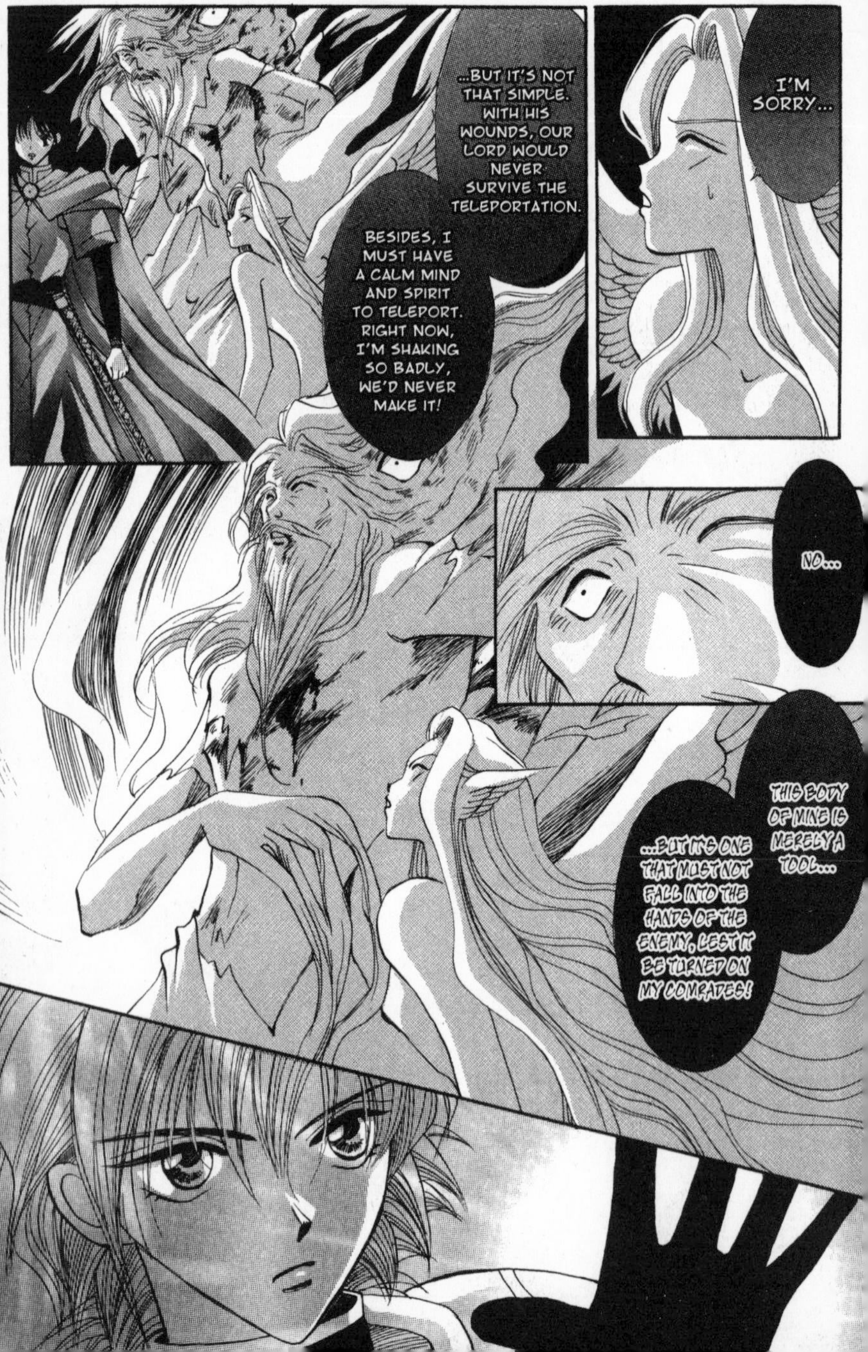
I'M SORRY...
...BUT IT'S NOT THAT SIMPLE. WITH HIS WOUNDS, OUR LORD WOULD NEVER SURVIVE THE TELEPORTATION.
BESIDES, I MUST HAVE A CALM MIND AND SPIRIT TO TELEPORT. RIGHT NOW, I'M SHAKING SO BADLY, WE'D NEVER MAKE IT!
NO...
THIS BODY OF MINE IS MERELY A TOOL...
...BUT IT'S ONE THAT MUST NOT FALL INTO THE HANDS OF THE ENEMY, LEST IT BE TURNED ON MY COMRADES!

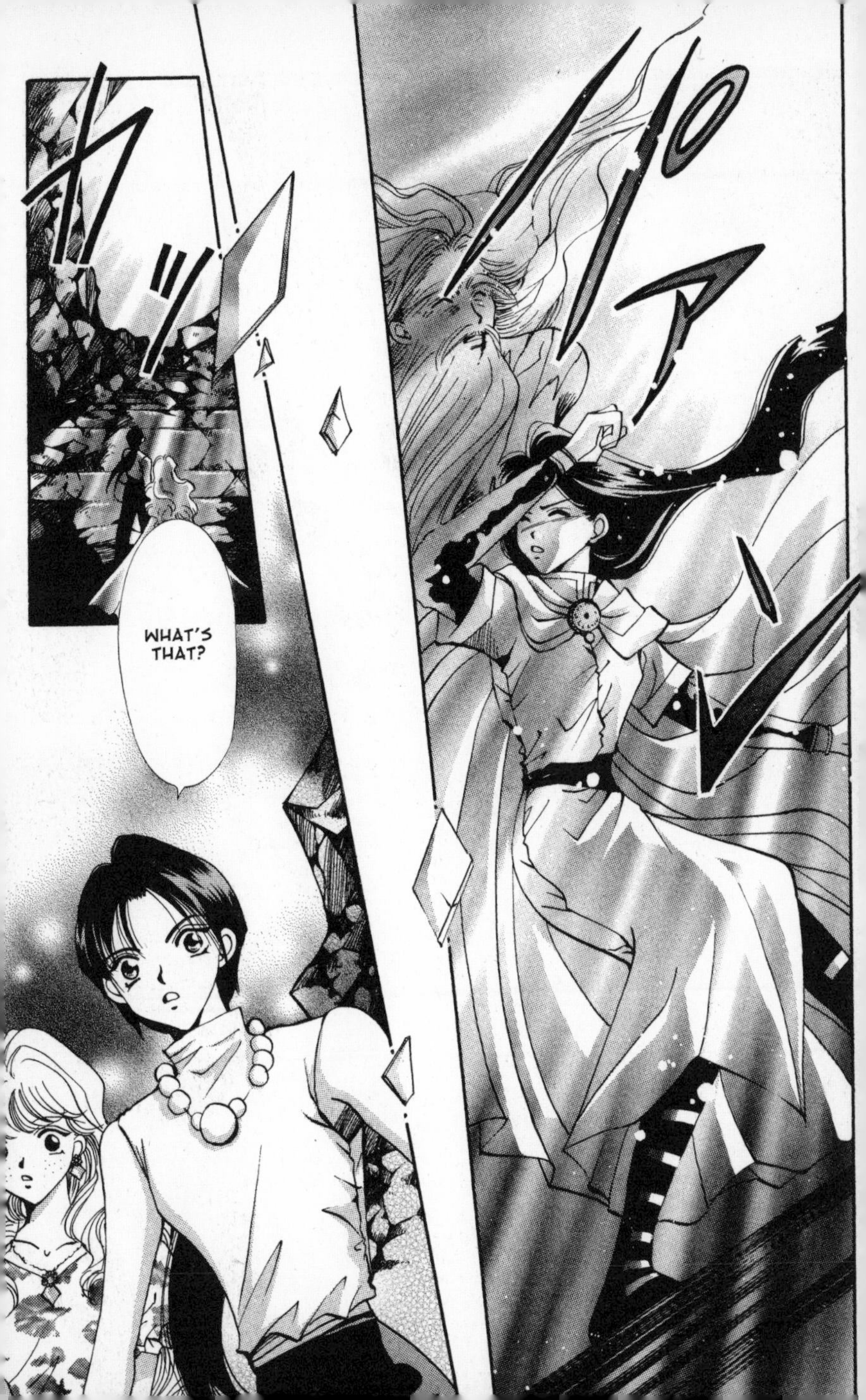
WHAT'S THAT?

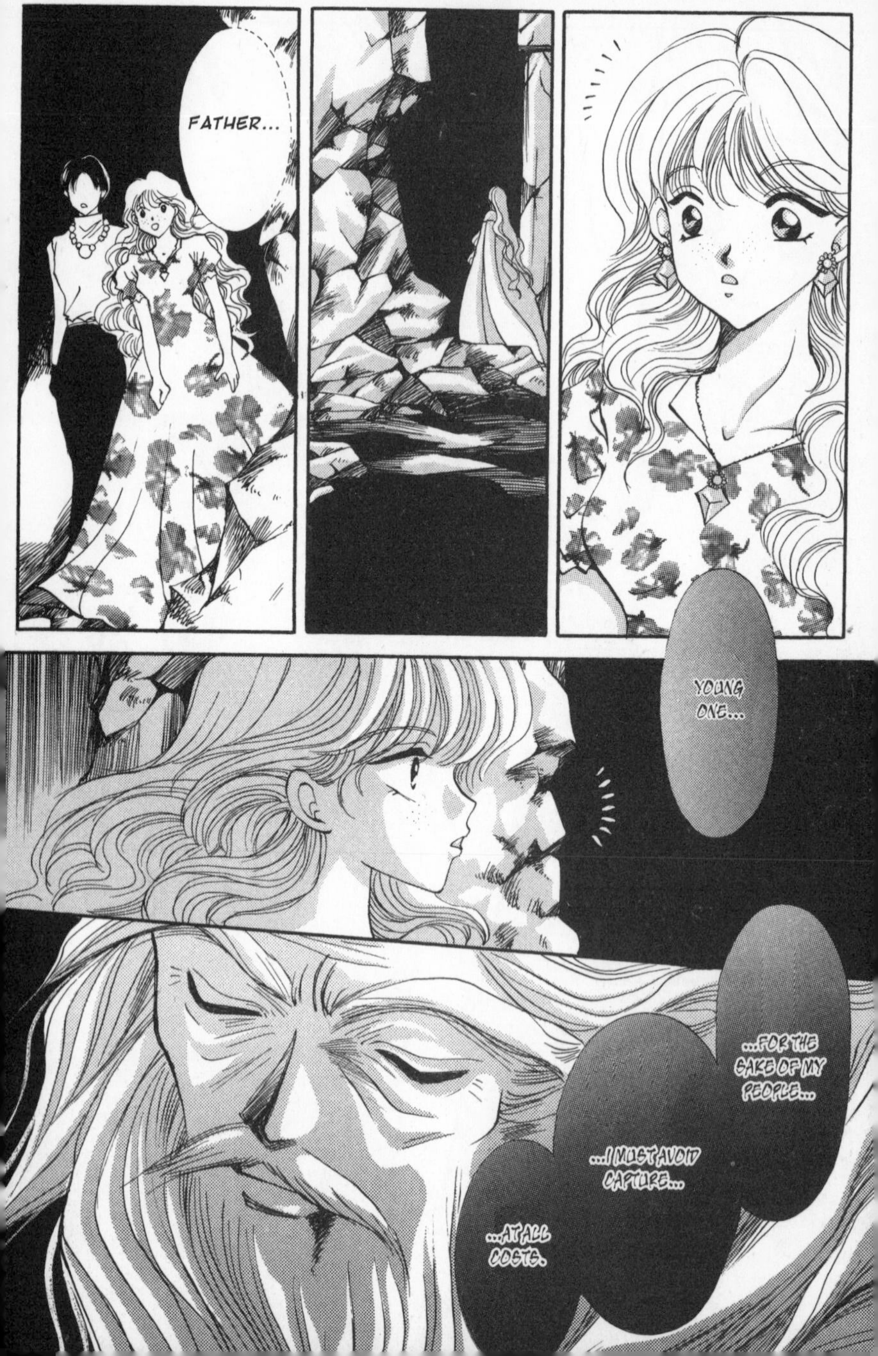
FATHER...
YOUNG ONE...
...FOR THE SAKE OF MY PEOPLE...
...I MUST AVOID CAPTURE...
...AT ALL COSTS.

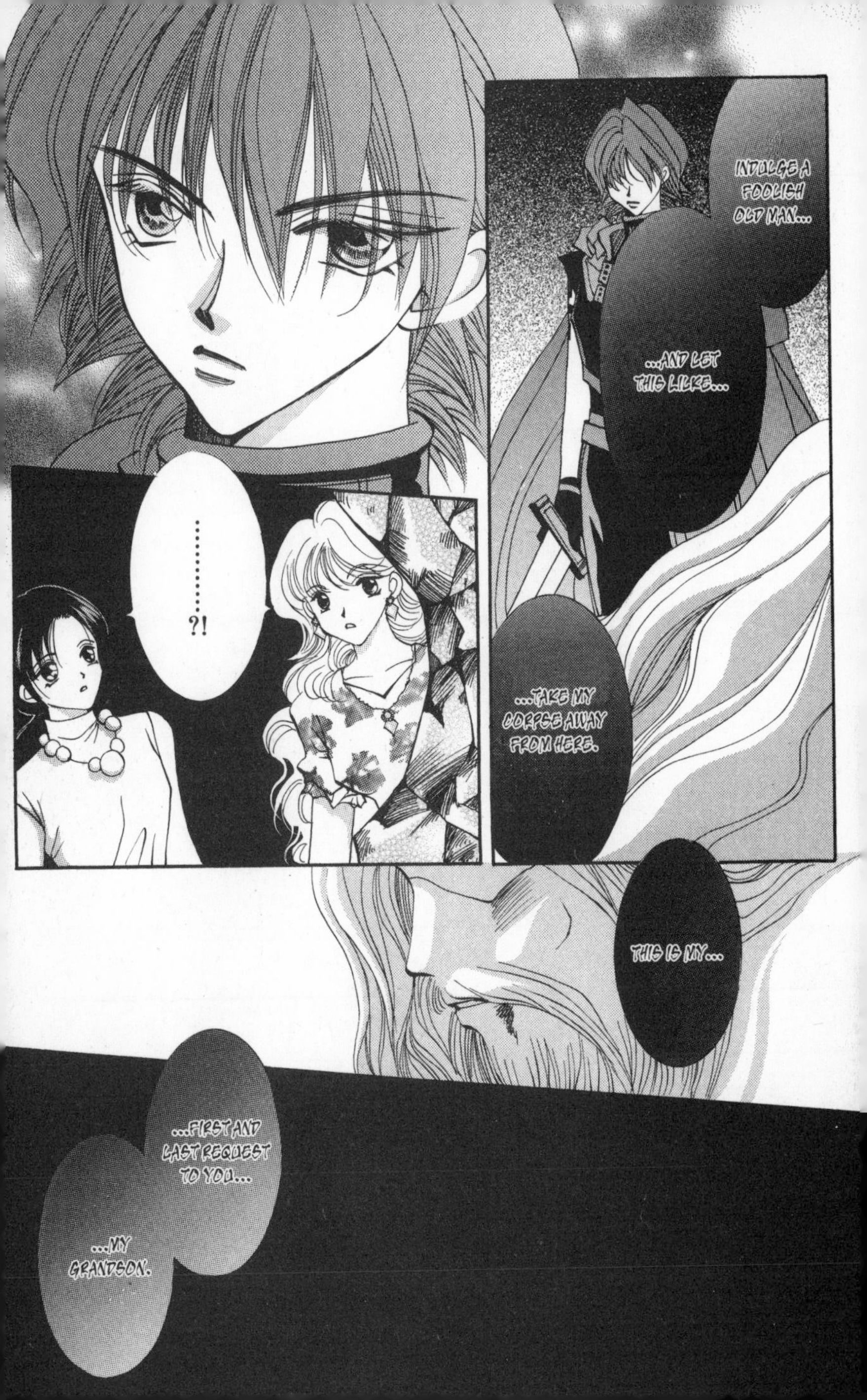
INDULGE A FOOLISH OLD MAN...
...AND LET THIS LILKE...
...TAKE MY CORPSE AWAY FROM HERE.
......?!
THIS IS MY...
...FIRST AND LAST REQUEST TO YOU...
...MY GRANDSON.

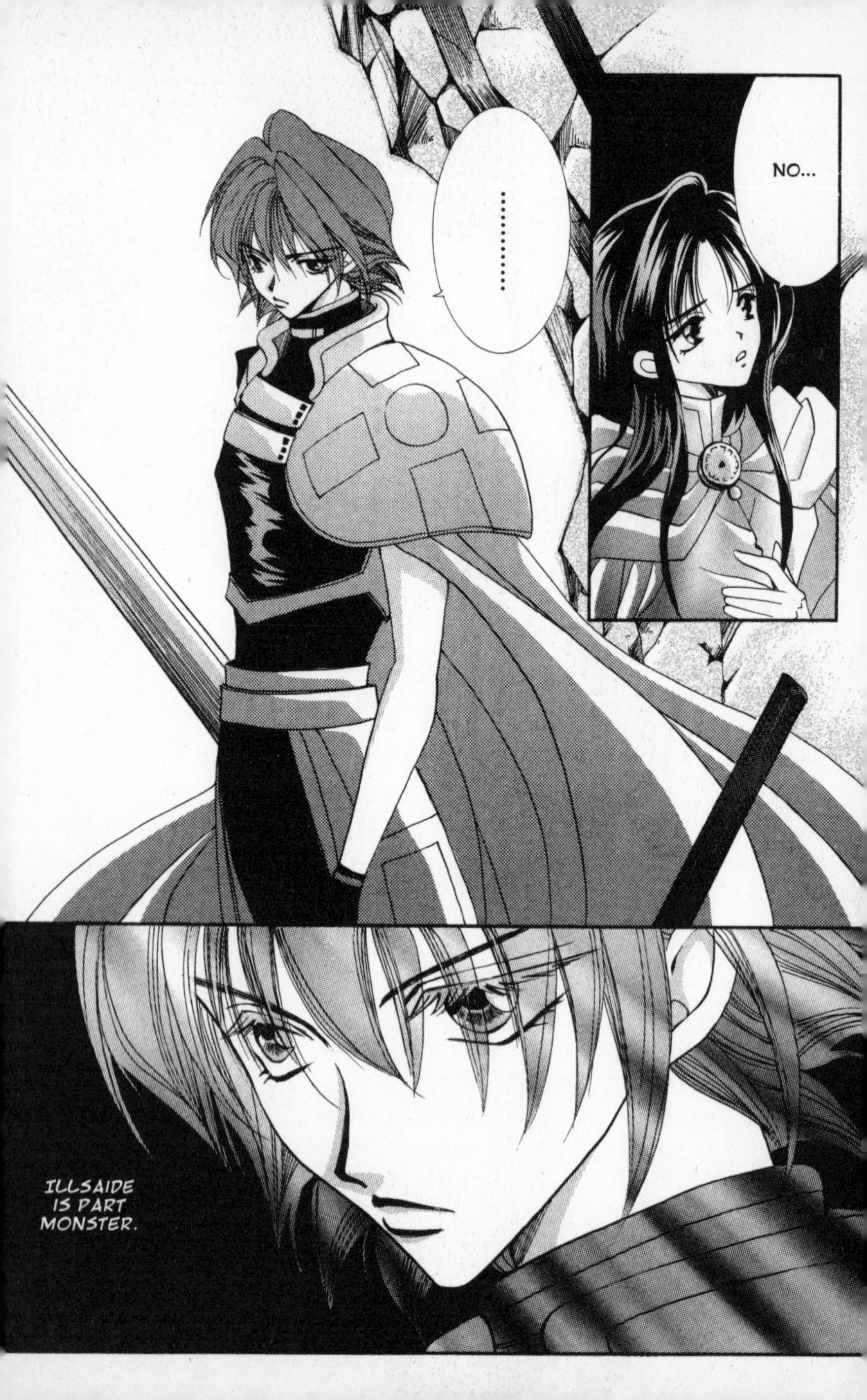
NO...
......
ILLSAIDE IS PART MONSTER.

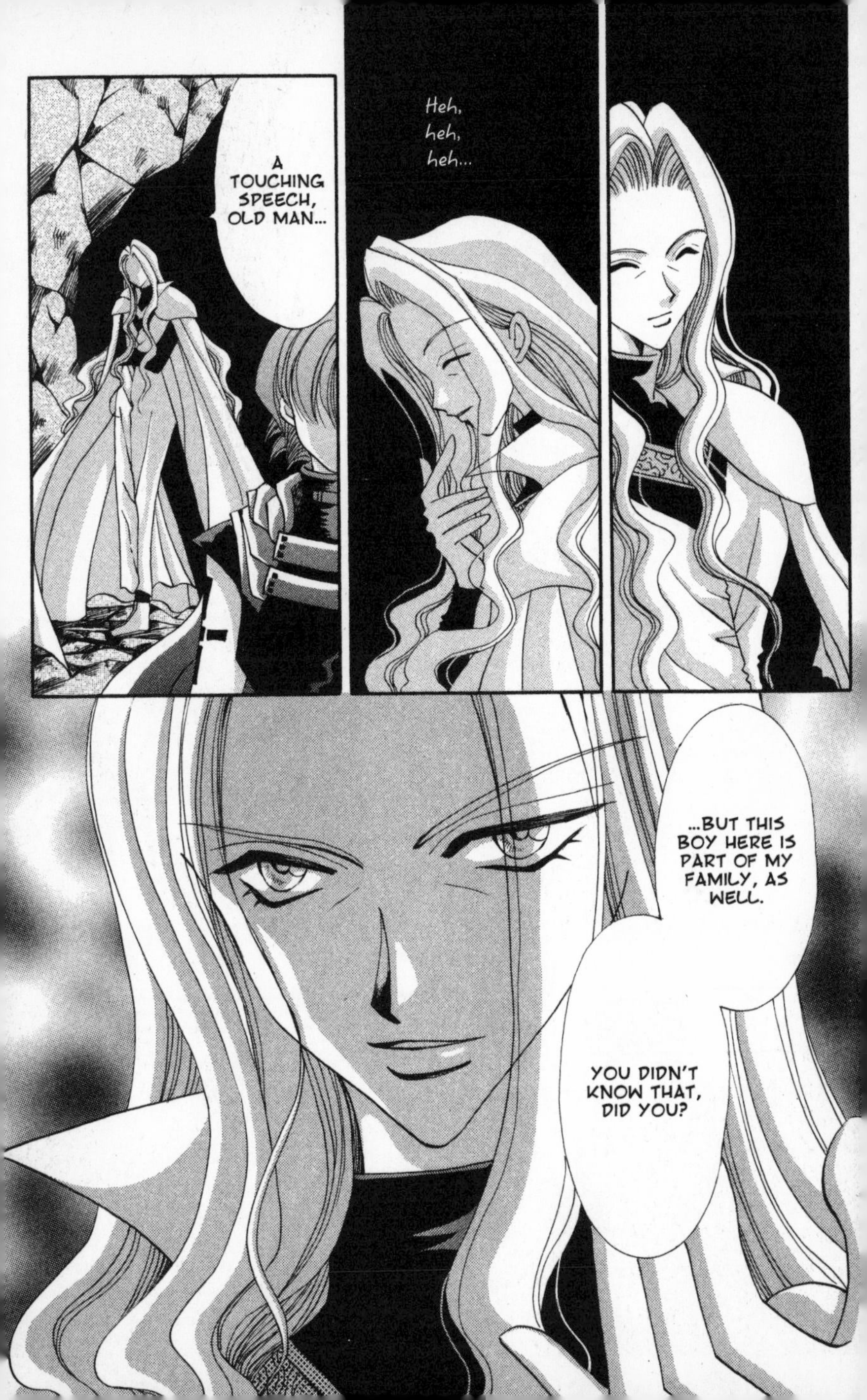
Heh, heh, heh...
A TOUCHING SPEECH, OLD MAN...
...BUT THIS BOY HERE IS PART OF MY FAMILY, AS WELL.
YOU DIDN'T KNOW THAT, DID YOU?

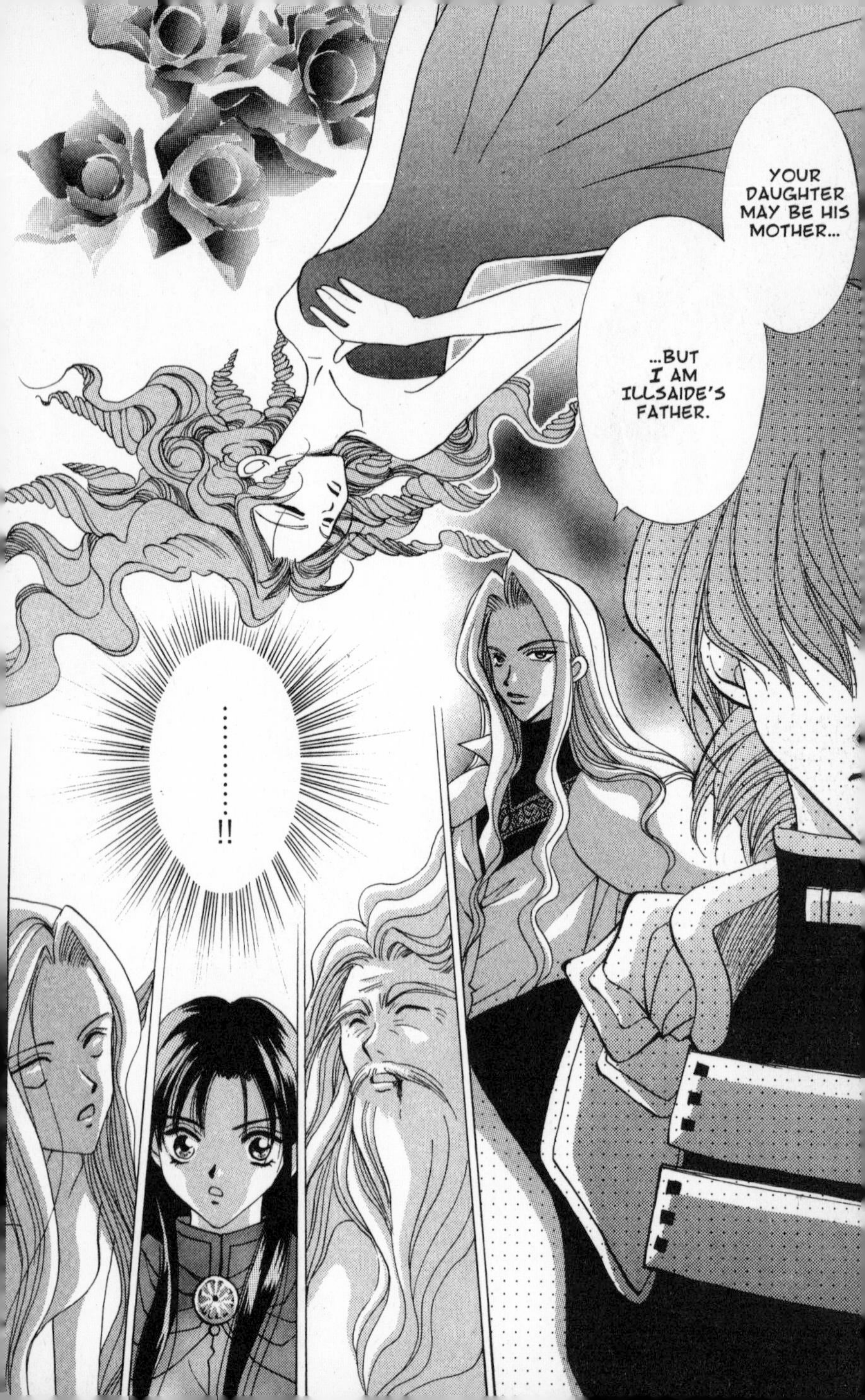
YOUR DAUGHTER MAY BE HIS MOTHER...
...BUT I AM ILLSAIDE'S FATHER.
..........!!

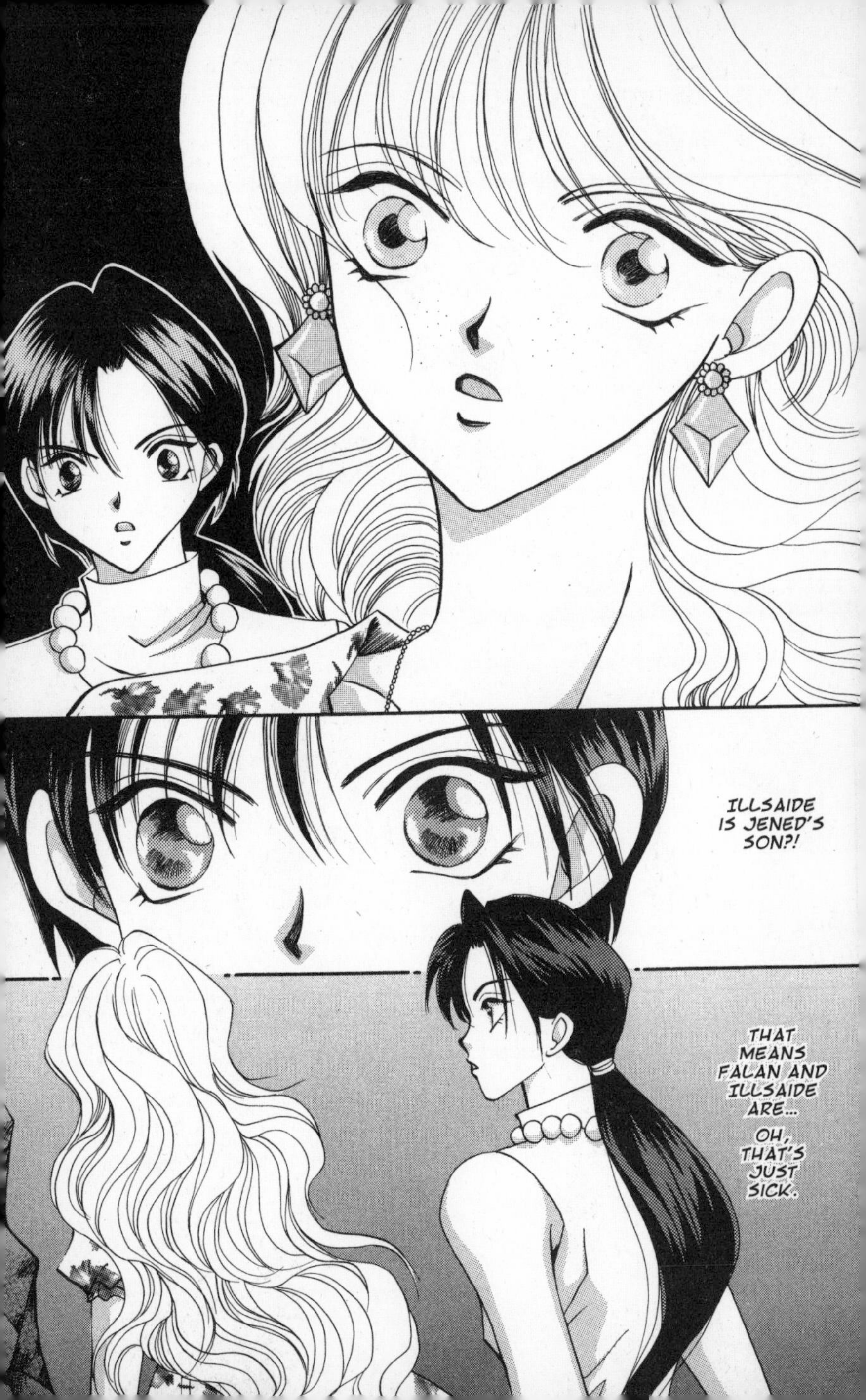
ILLSAIDE IS JENED'S SON?!
THAT MEANS FALAN AND ILLSAIDE ARE...
OH, THAT'S JUST SICK.

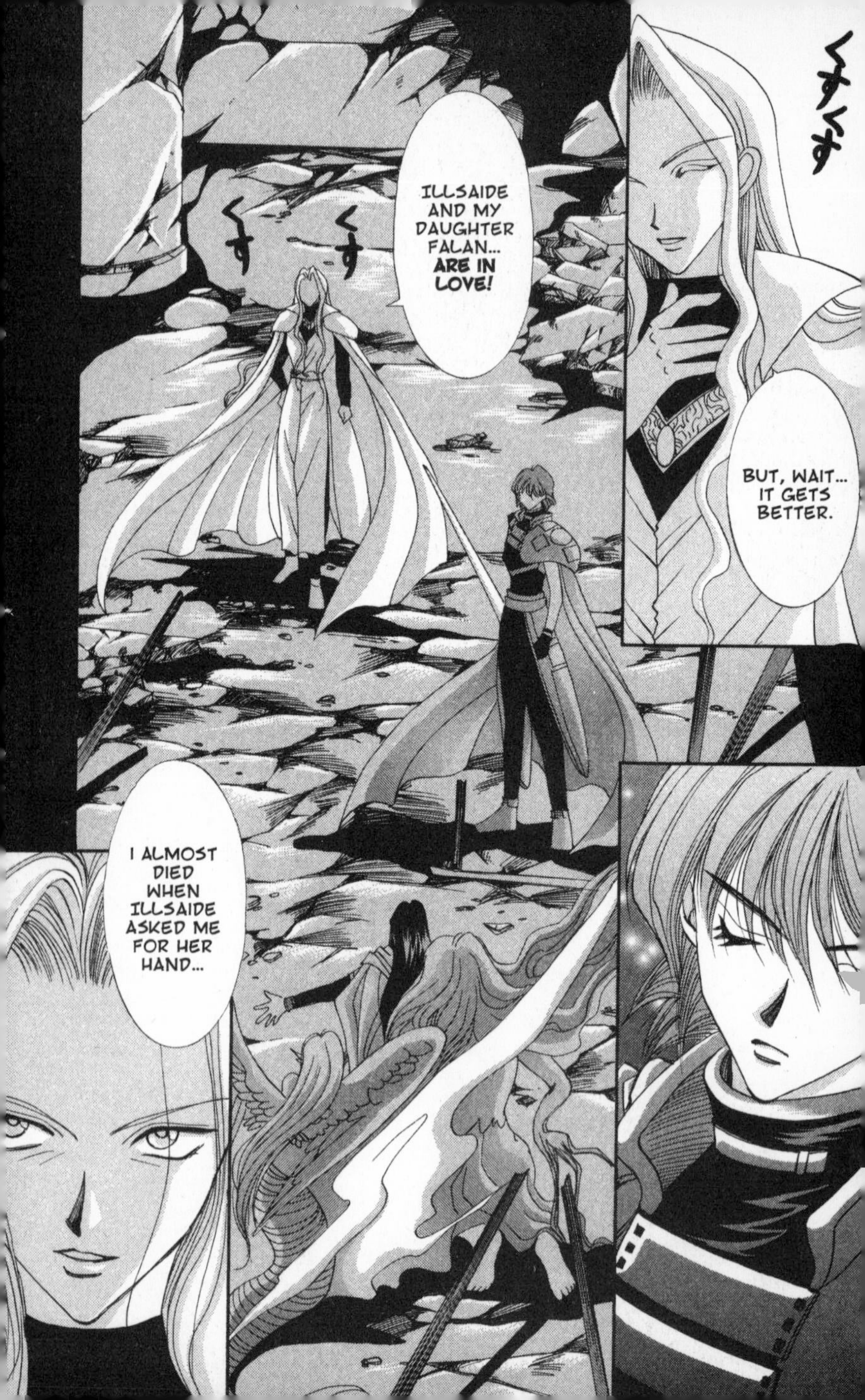
くすくす
BUT, WAIT... IT GETS BETTER.
ILLSAIDE AND MY DAUGHTER FALAN... **ARE IN LOVE!**
くす くす
I ALMOST DIED WHEN ILLSAIDE ASKED ME FOR HER HAND...

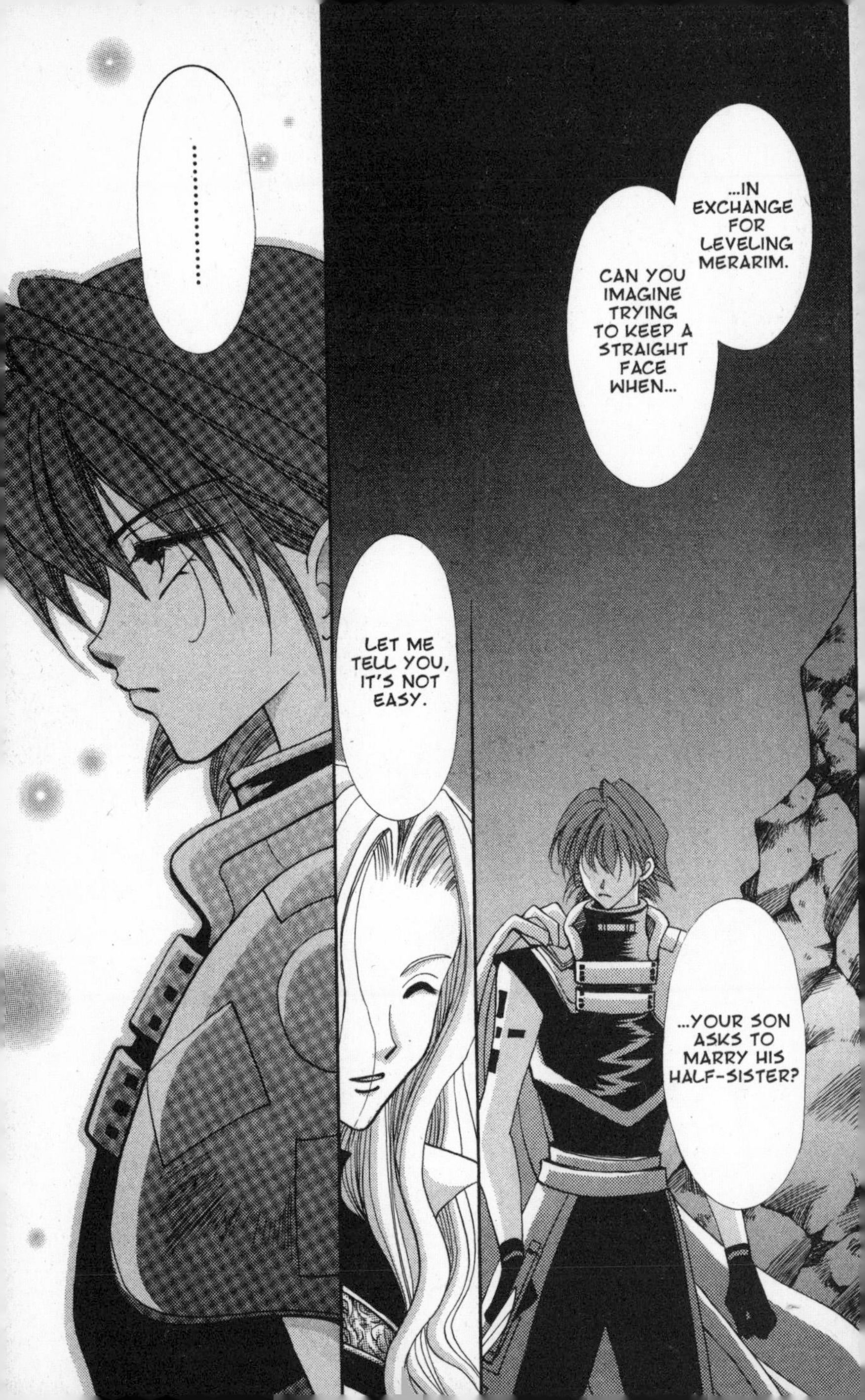
...IN EXCHANGE FOR LEVELING MERARIM.
CAN YOU IMAGINE TRYING TO KEEP A STRAIGHT FACE WHEN...
...YOUR SON ASKS TO MARRY HIS HALF-SISTER?
LET ME TELL YOU, IT'S NOT EASY.
....

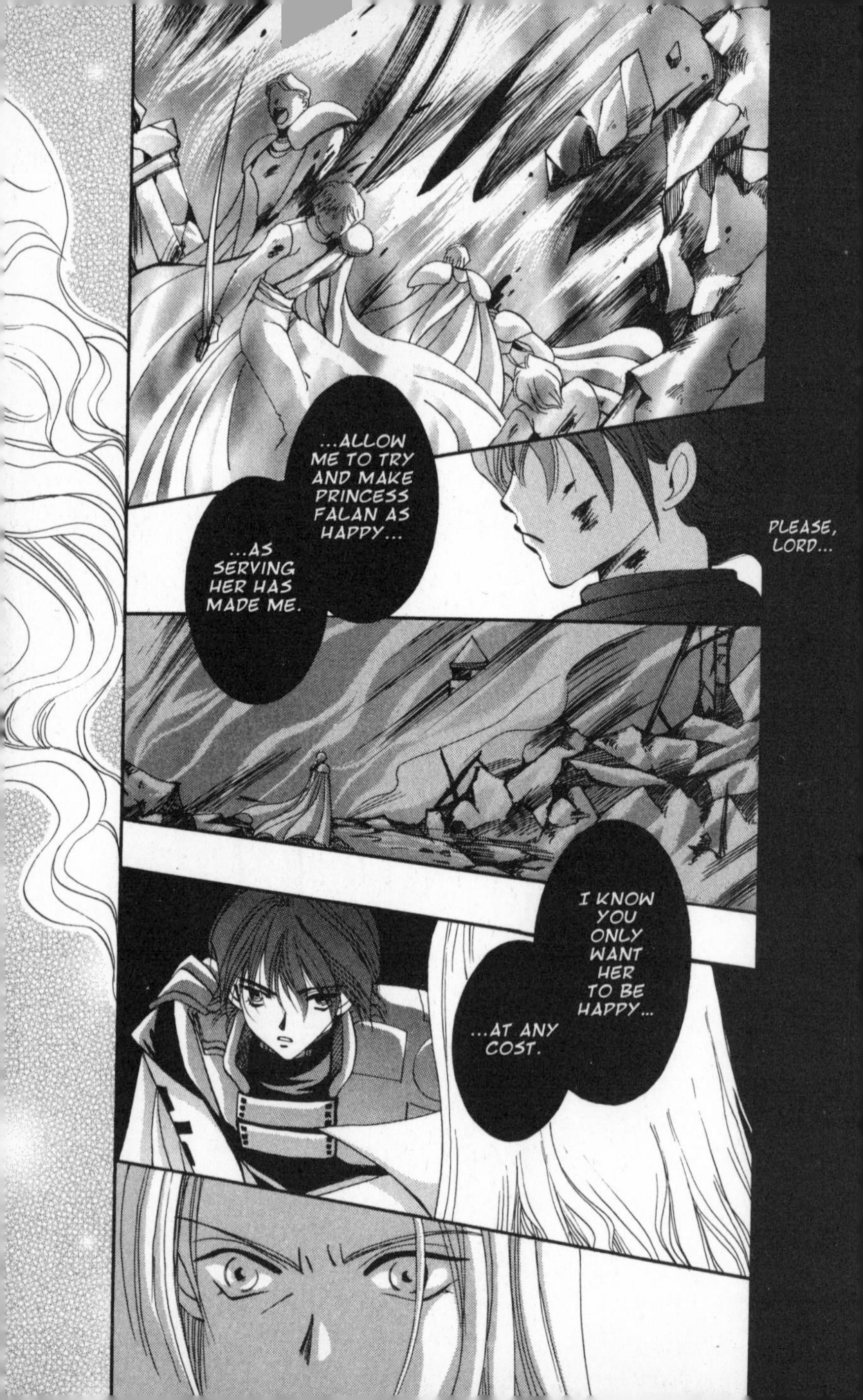
PLEASE, LORD...
...ALLOW ME TO TRY AND MAKE PRINCESS FALAN AS HAPPY...
...AS SERVING HER HAS MADE ME.
I KNOW YOU ONLY WANT HER TO BE HAPPY...
...AT ANY COST.

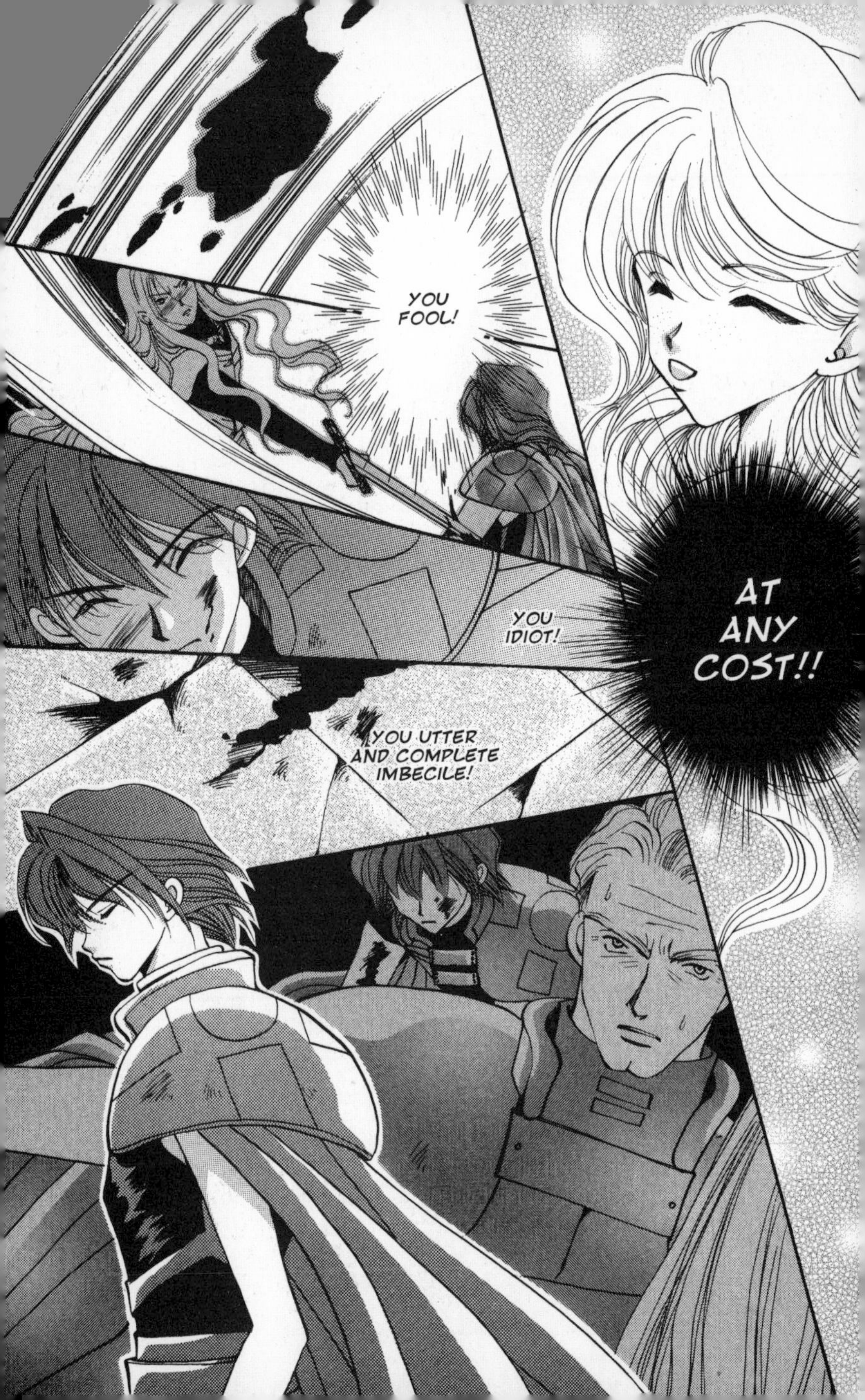
AT ANY COST!!
YOU FOOL!
YOU IDIOT!
YOU UTTER AND COMPLETE IMBECILE!

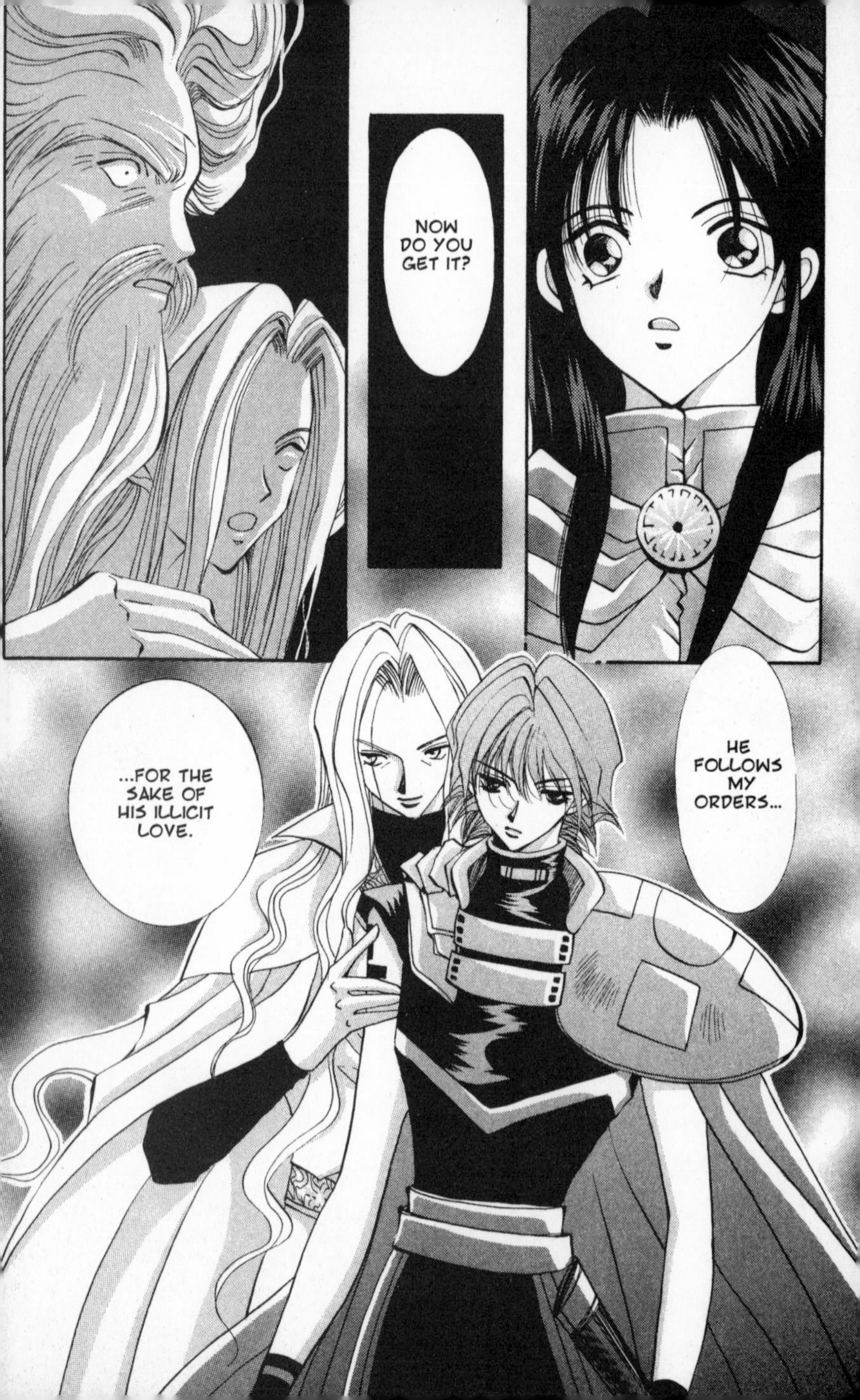
NOW DO YOU GET IT?
HE FOLLOWS MY ORDERS...
...FOR THE SAKE OF HIS ILLICIT LOVE.

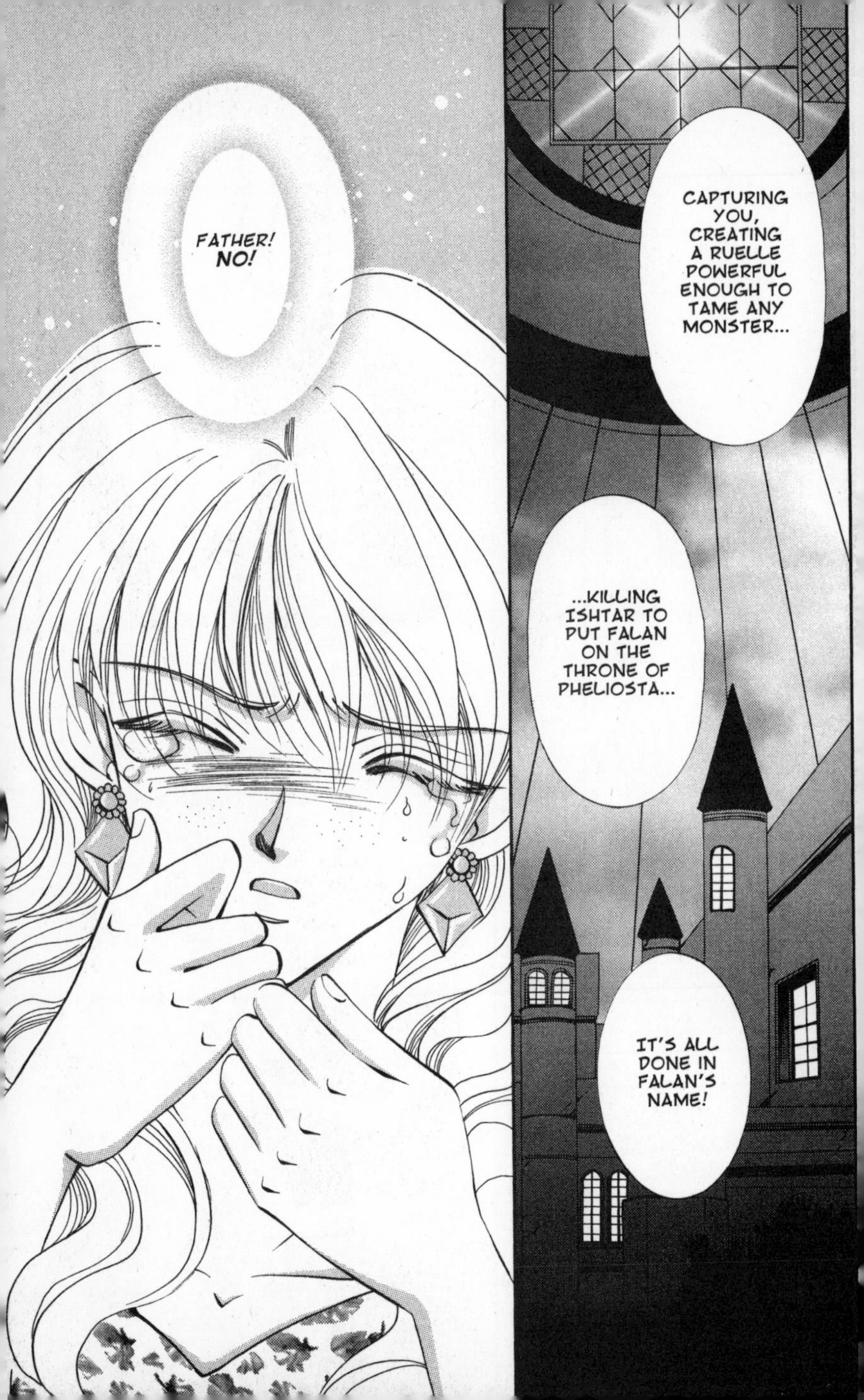
CAPTURING YOU, CREATING A RUELLE POWERFUL ENOUGH TO TAME ANY MONSTER...
...KILLING ISHTAR TO PUT FALAN ON THE THRONE OF PHELIOSTA...
IT'S ALL DONE IN FALAN'S NAME!
FATHER! NO!

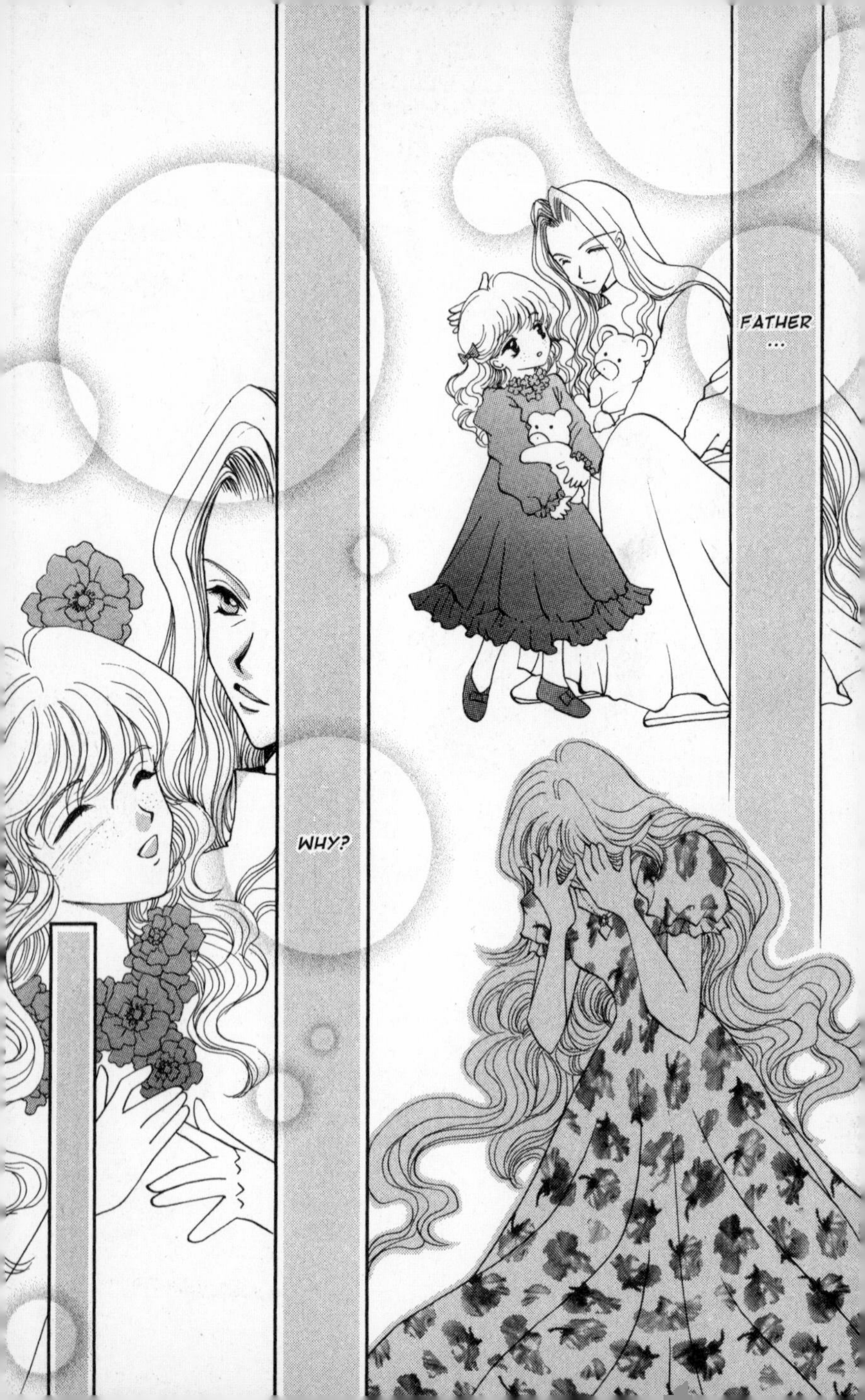
FATHER ...
WHY?

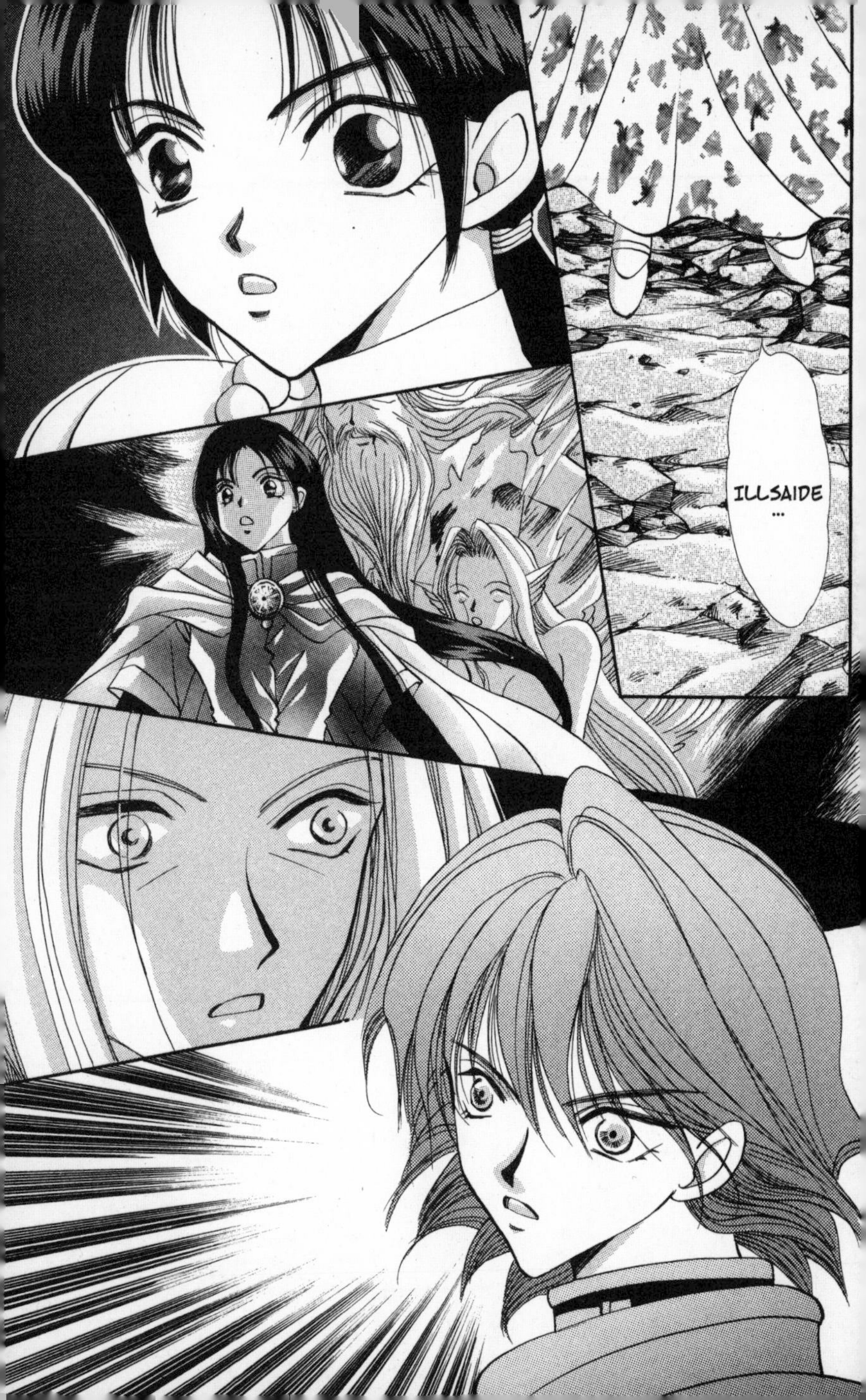
ILLSAIDE
...

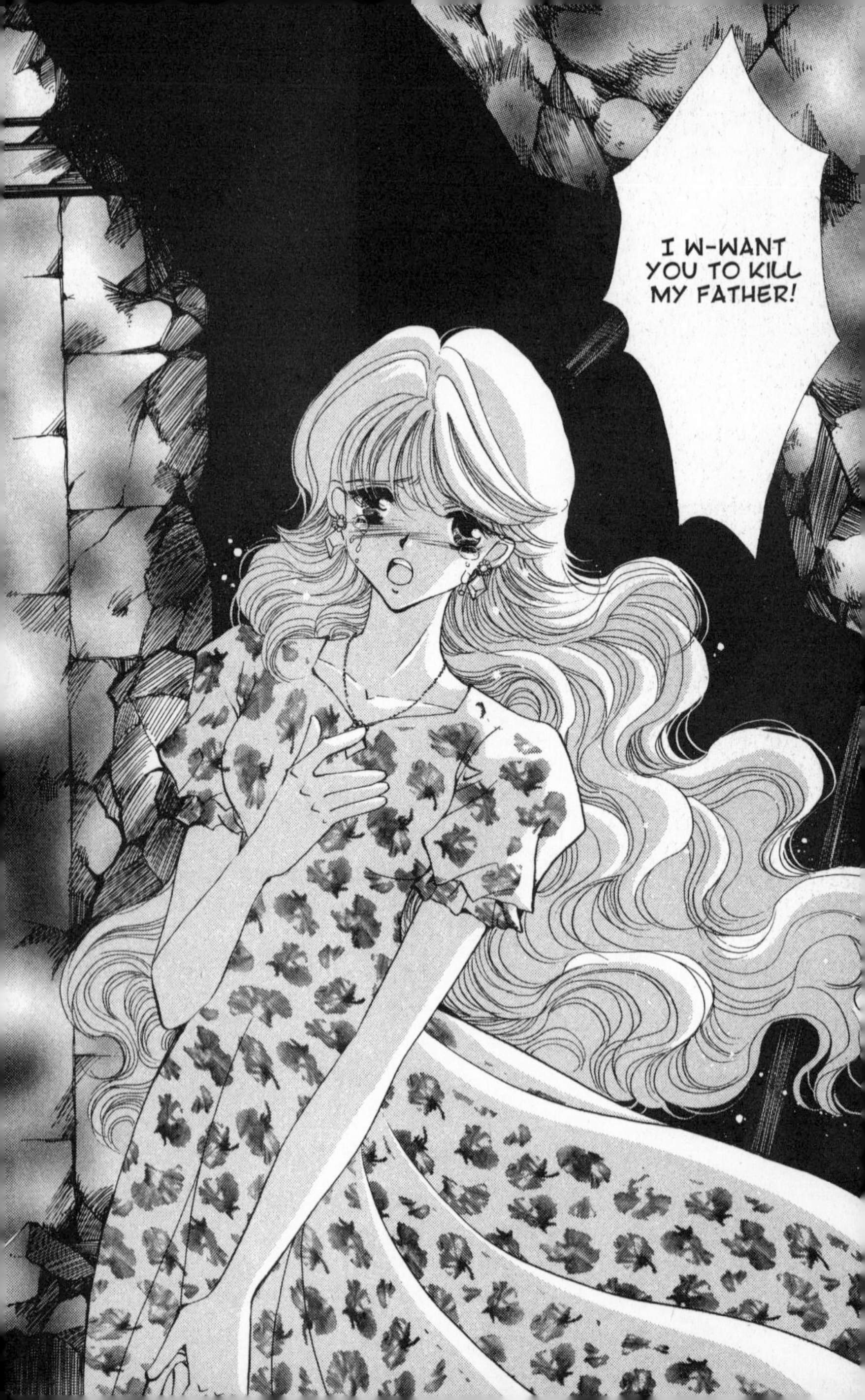
I W-WANT YOU TO KILL MY FATHER!

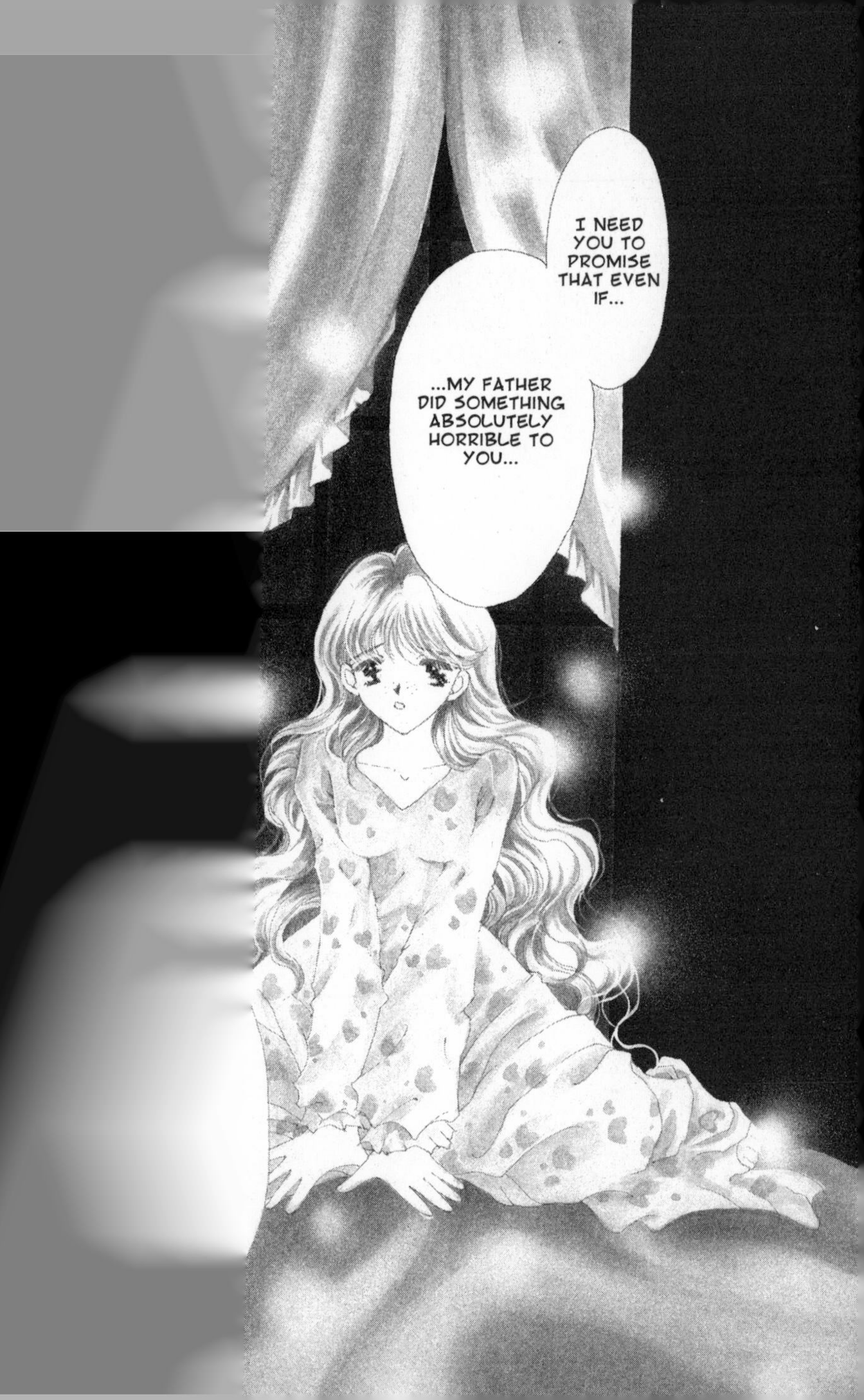
I NEED YOU TO PROMISE THAT EVEN IF...
...MY FATHER DID SOMETHING ABSOLUTELY HORRIBLE TO YOU...

吸血遊戯 東領篇 Act.15

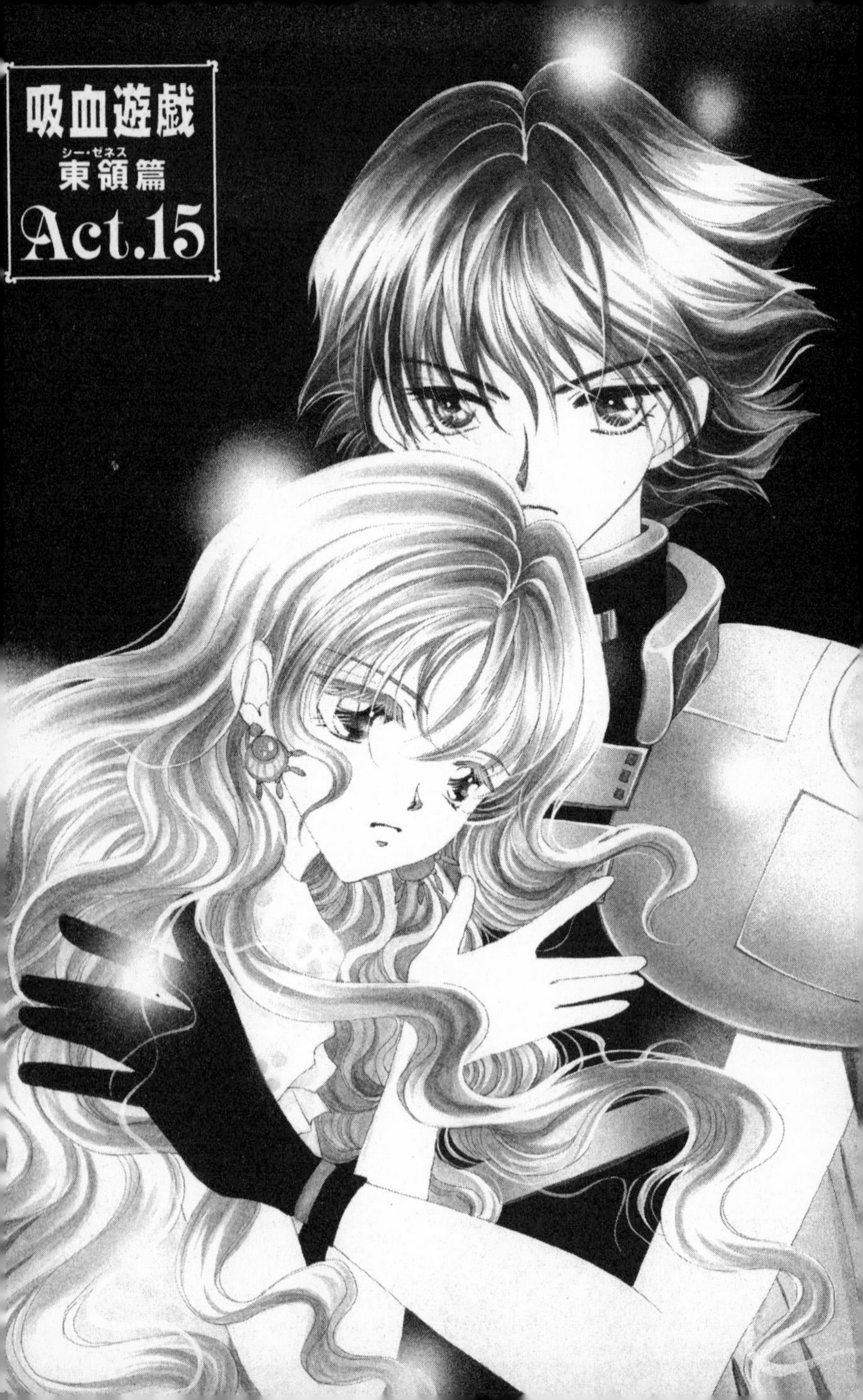
シー・ゼネス

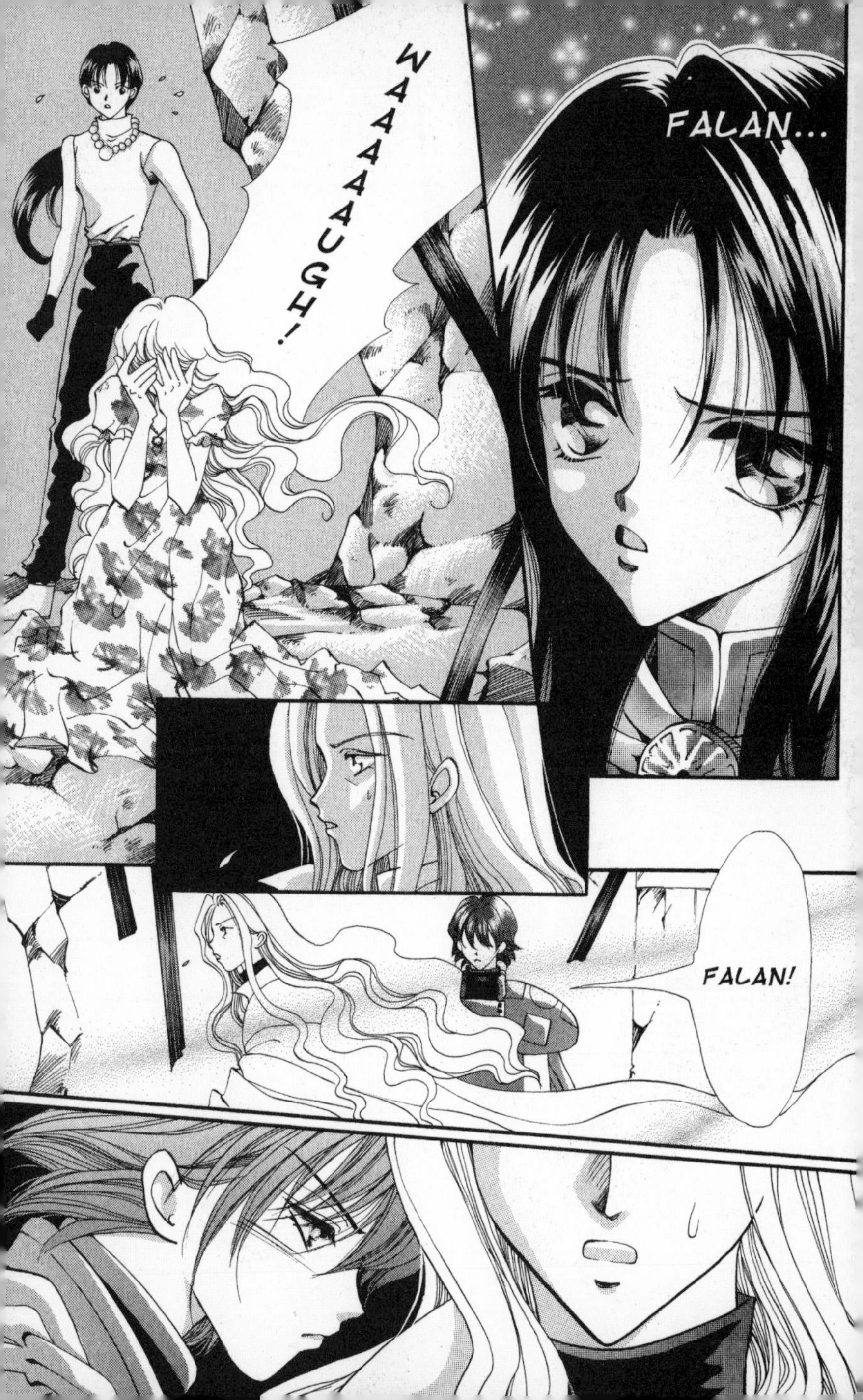
FALAN...
WAAAAAUGH!
FALAN!

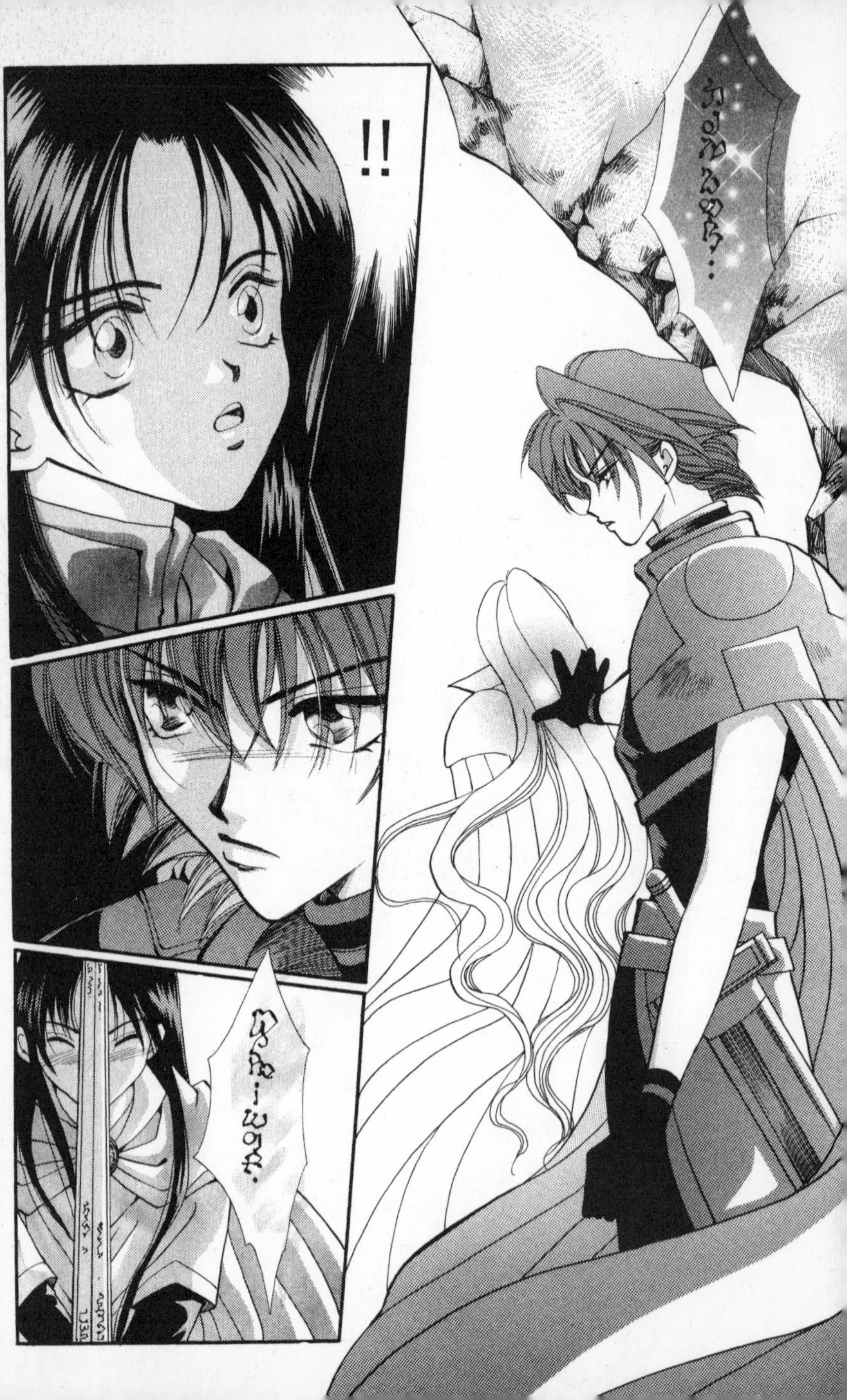
!!

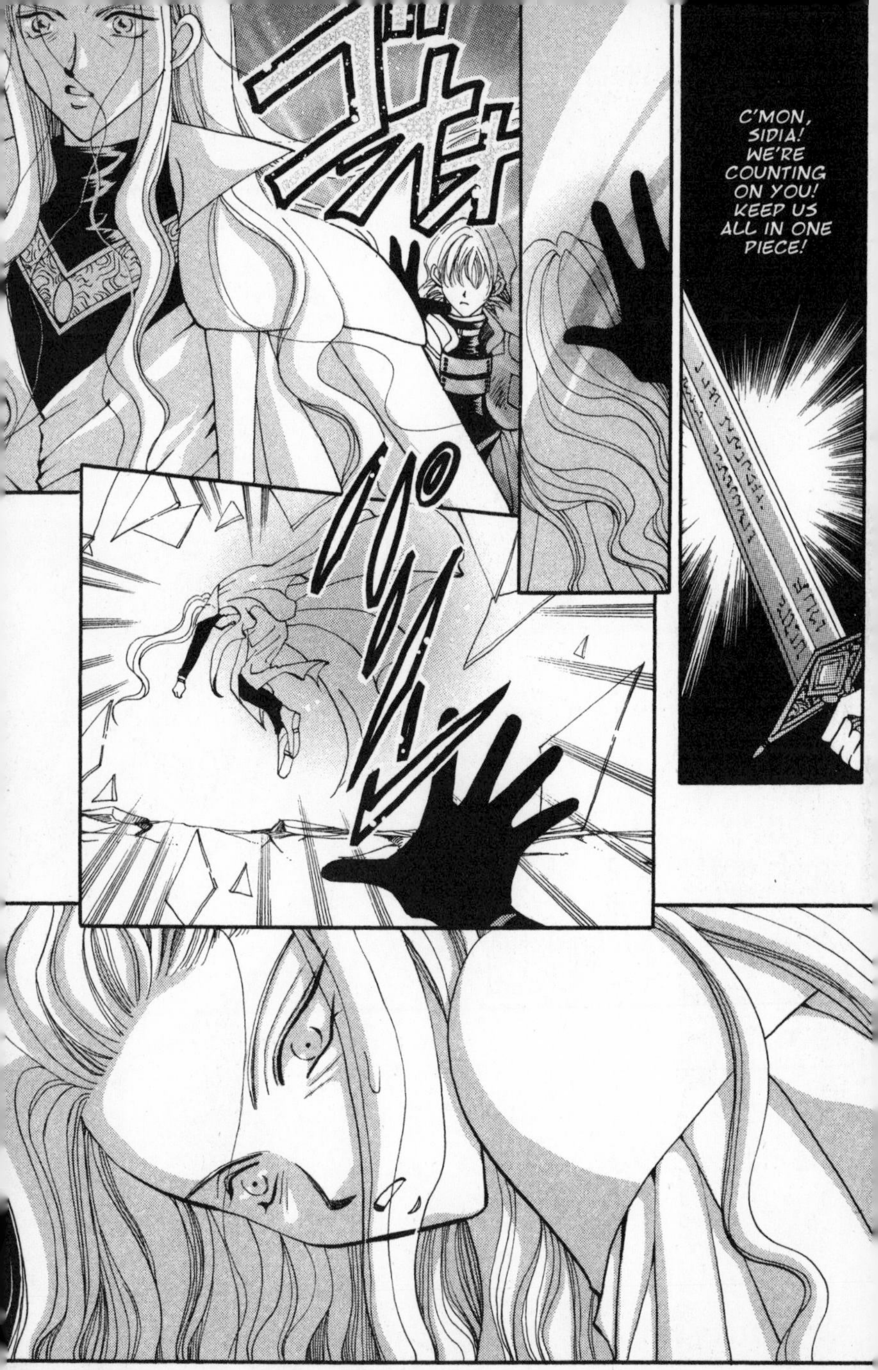
C'MON, SIDIA! WE'RE COUNTING ON YOU! KEEP US ALL IN ONE PIECE!

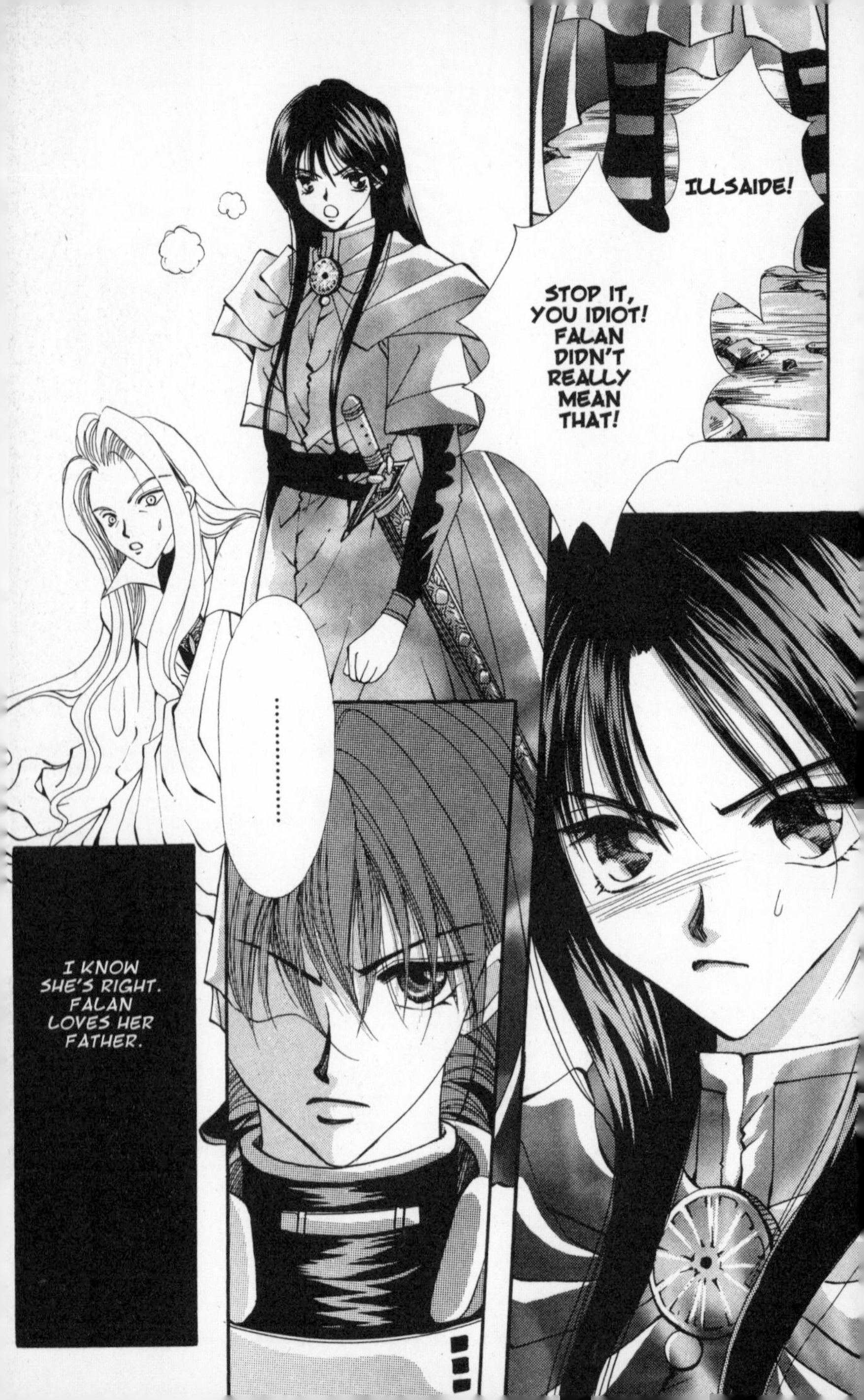
ILLSAIDE!
STOP IT, YOU IDIOT! FALAN DIDN'T REALLY MEAN THAT!
......
I KNOW SHE'S RIGHT. FALAN LOVES HER FATHER.

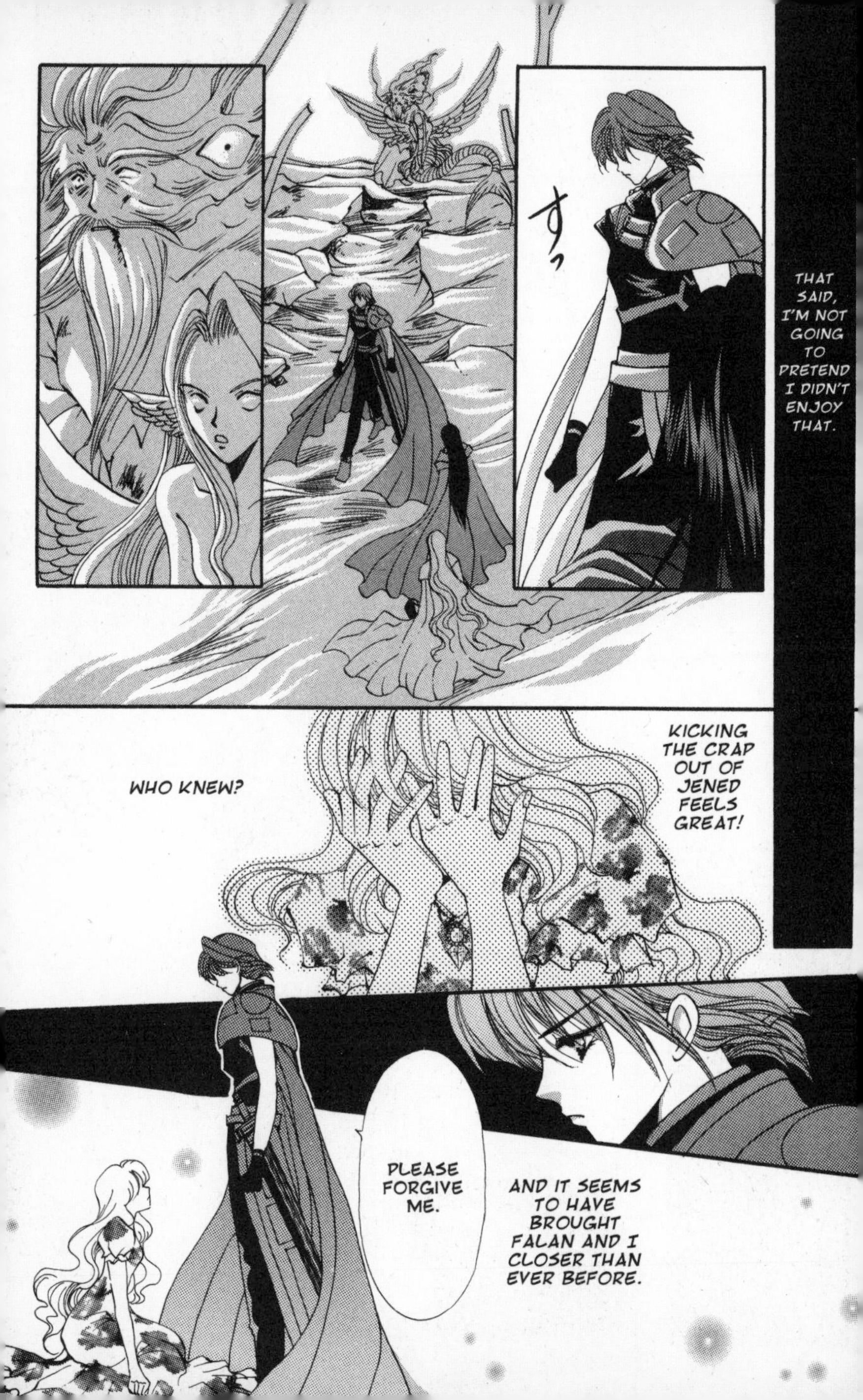
THAT SAID, I'M NOT GOING TO PRETEND I DIDN'T ENJOY THAT.
すっ
KICKING THE CRAP OUT OF JENED FEELS GREAT!
WHO KNEW?
AND IT SEEMS TO HAVE BROUGHT FALAN AND I CLOSER THAN EVER BEFORE.
PLEASE FORGIVE ME.

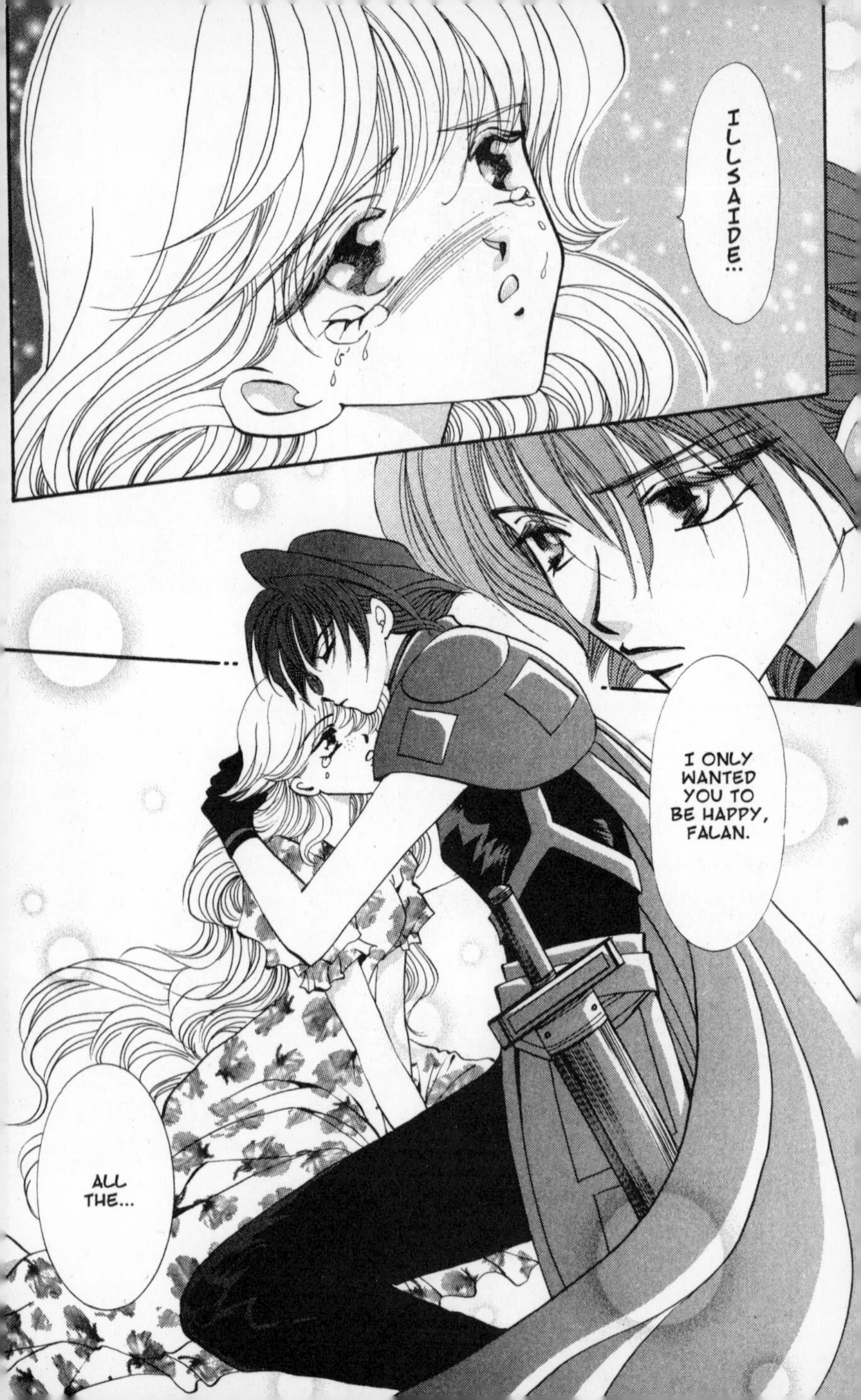
ILLSAIDE...
I ONLY WANTED YOU TO BE HAPPY, FALAN.
ALL THE...

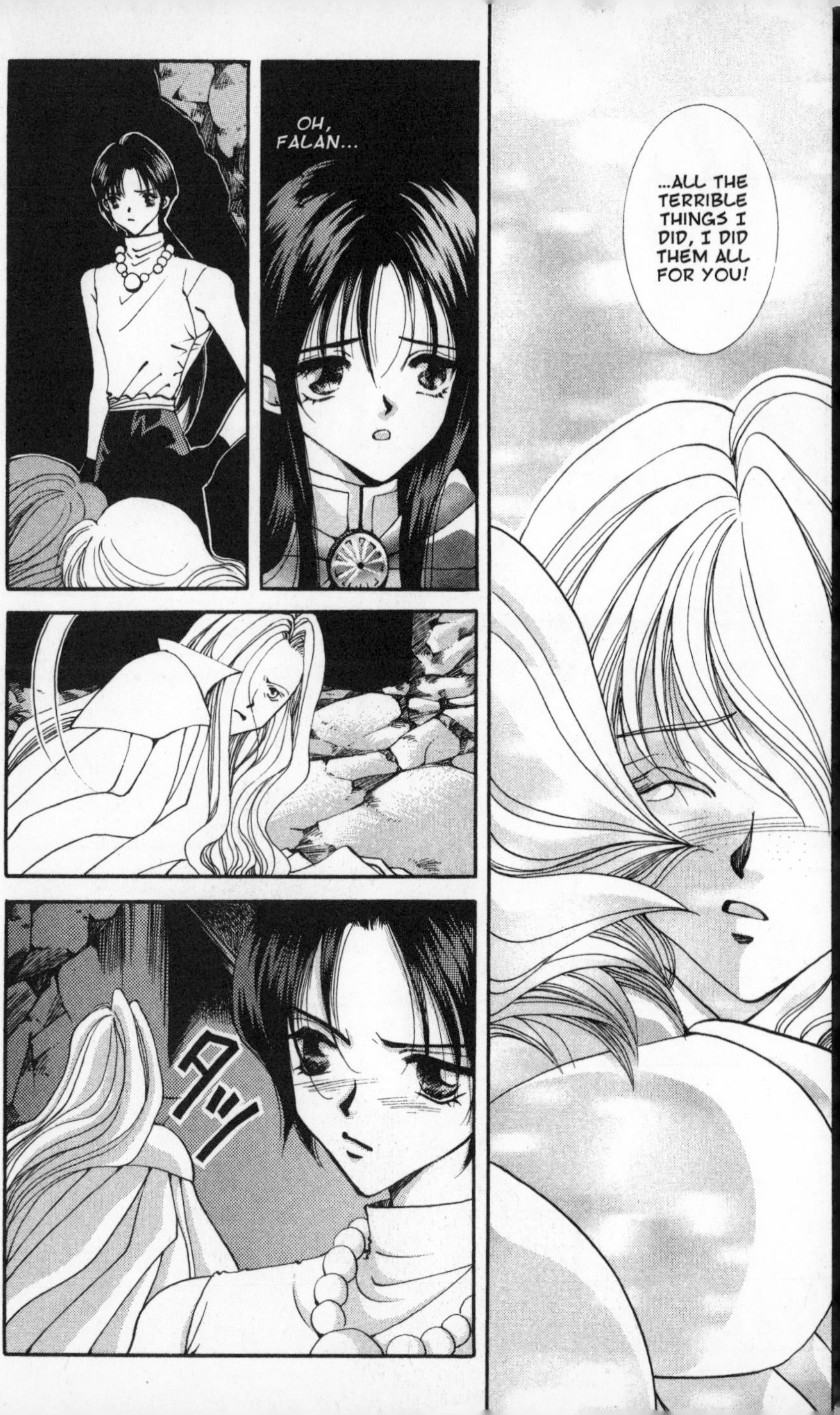
...ALL THE TERRIBLE THINGS I DID, I DID THEM ALL FOR YOU!
OH, FALAN...
タッ

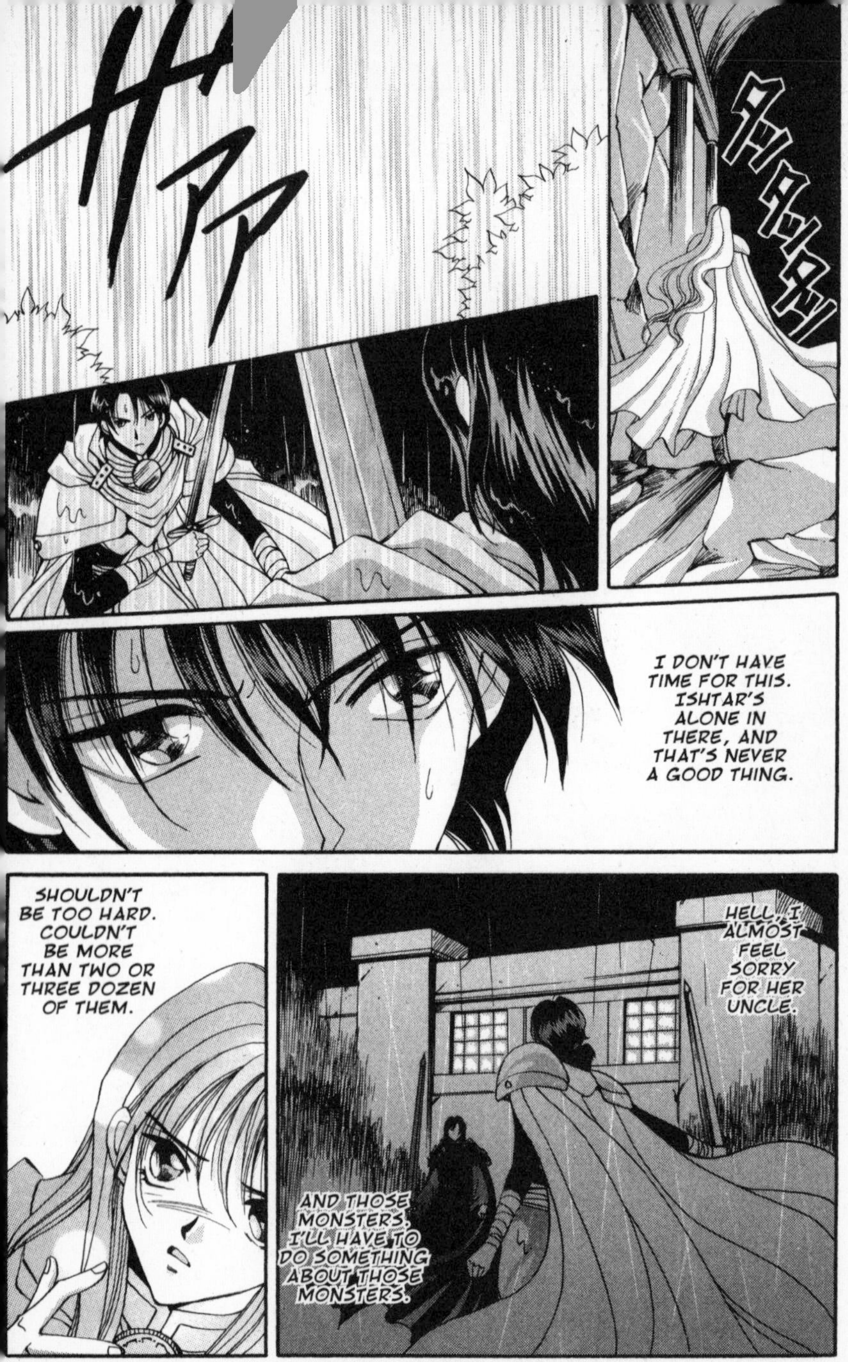
タッタッタッタッ
ザァア
I DON'T HAVE TIME FOR THIS. ISHTAR'S ALONE IN THERE, AND THAT'S NEVER A GOOD THING.
HELL, I ALMOST FEEL SORRY FOR HER UNCLE.
AND THOSE MONSTERS. I'LL HAVE TO DO SOMETHING ABOUT THOSE MONSTERS.
SHOULDN'T BE TOO HARD. COULDN'T BE MORE THAN TWO OR THREE DOZEN OF THEM.

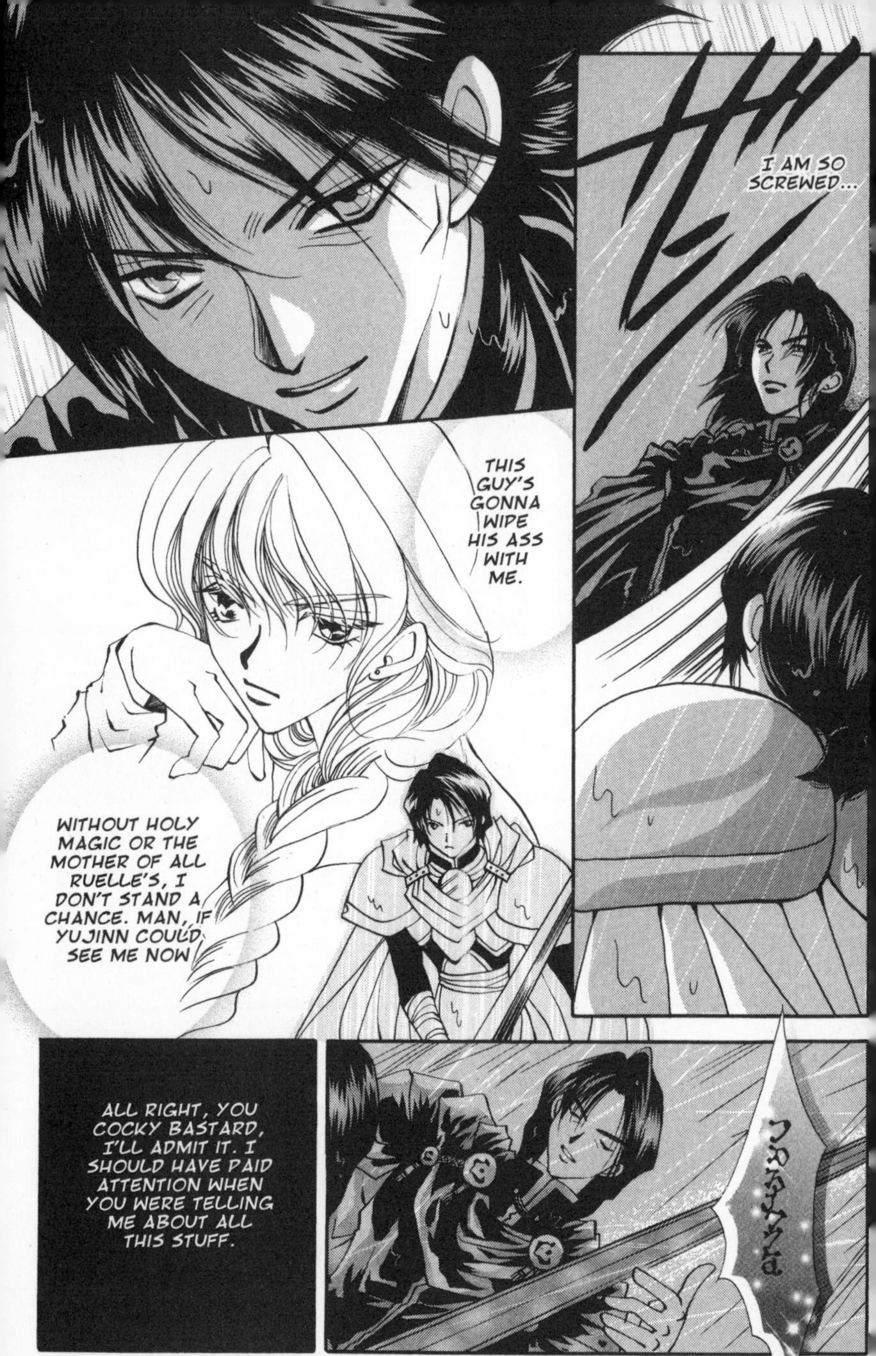
I AM SO SCREWED...
THIS GUY'S GONNA WIPE HIS ASS WITH ME.
WITHOUT HOLY MAGIC OR THE MOTHER OF ALL RUELLE'S, I DON'T STAND A CHANCE. MAN, IF YUJINN COULD SEE ME NOW
ALL RIGHT, YOU COCKY BASTARD, I'LL ADMIT IT. I SHOULD HAVE PAID ATTENTION WHEN YOU WERE TELLING ME ABOUT ALL THIS STUFF.

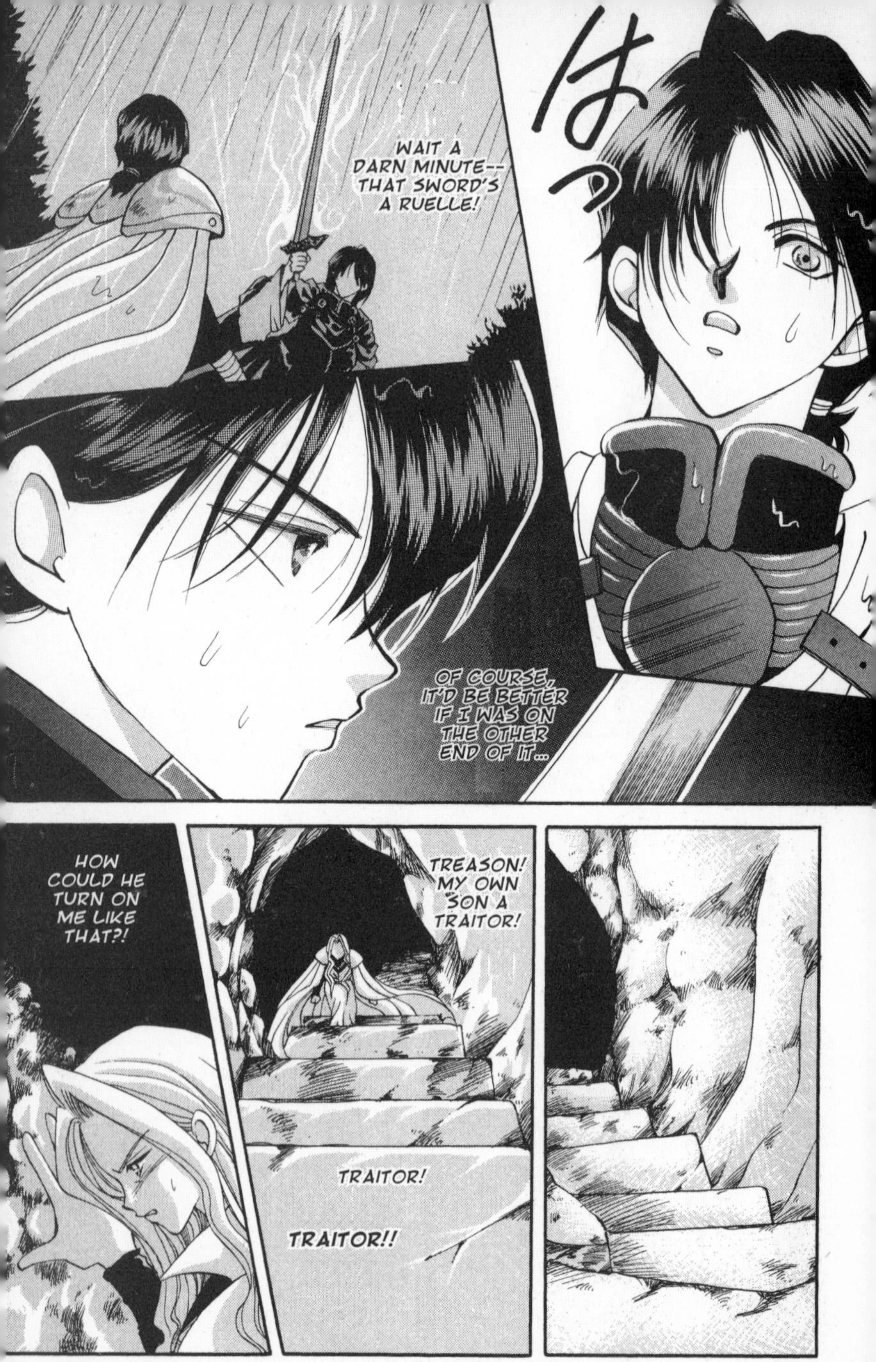
はっ
WAIT A DARN MINUTE-- THAT SWORD'S A RUELLE!
OF COURSE, IT'D BE BETTER IF I WAS ON THE OTHER END OF IT...
TREASON! MY OWN SON A TRAITOR!
TRAITOR!
TRAITOR!!
HOW COULD HE TURN ON ME LIKE THAT?!

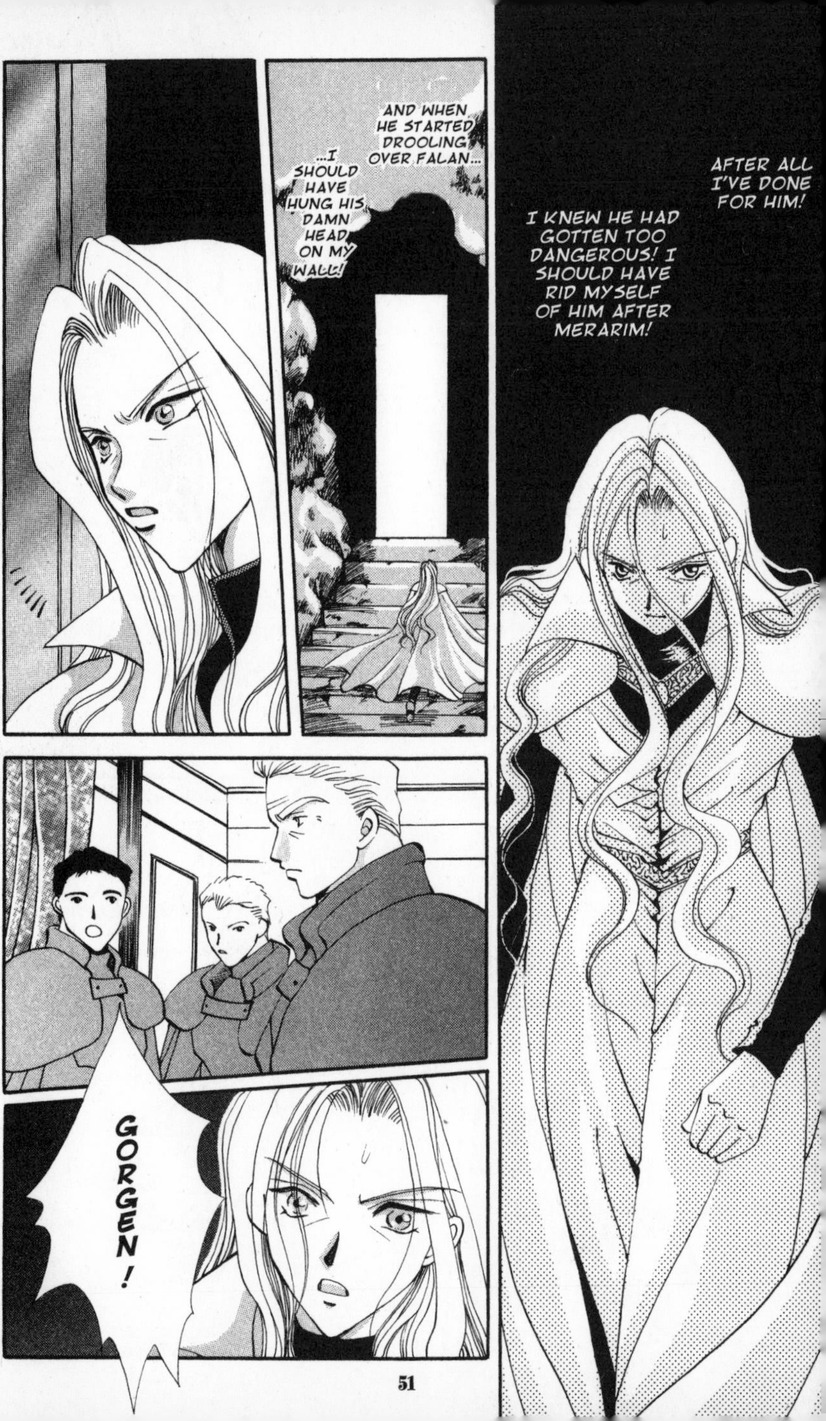
AFTER ALL I'VE DONE FOR HIM!
I KNEW HE HAD GOTTEN TOO DANGEROUS! I SHOULD HAVE RID MYSELF OF HIM AFTER MERARIM!
AND WHEN HE STARTED DROOLING OVER FALAN...
...I SHOULD HAVE HUNG HIS DAMN HEAD ON MY WALL!
GORGEN!

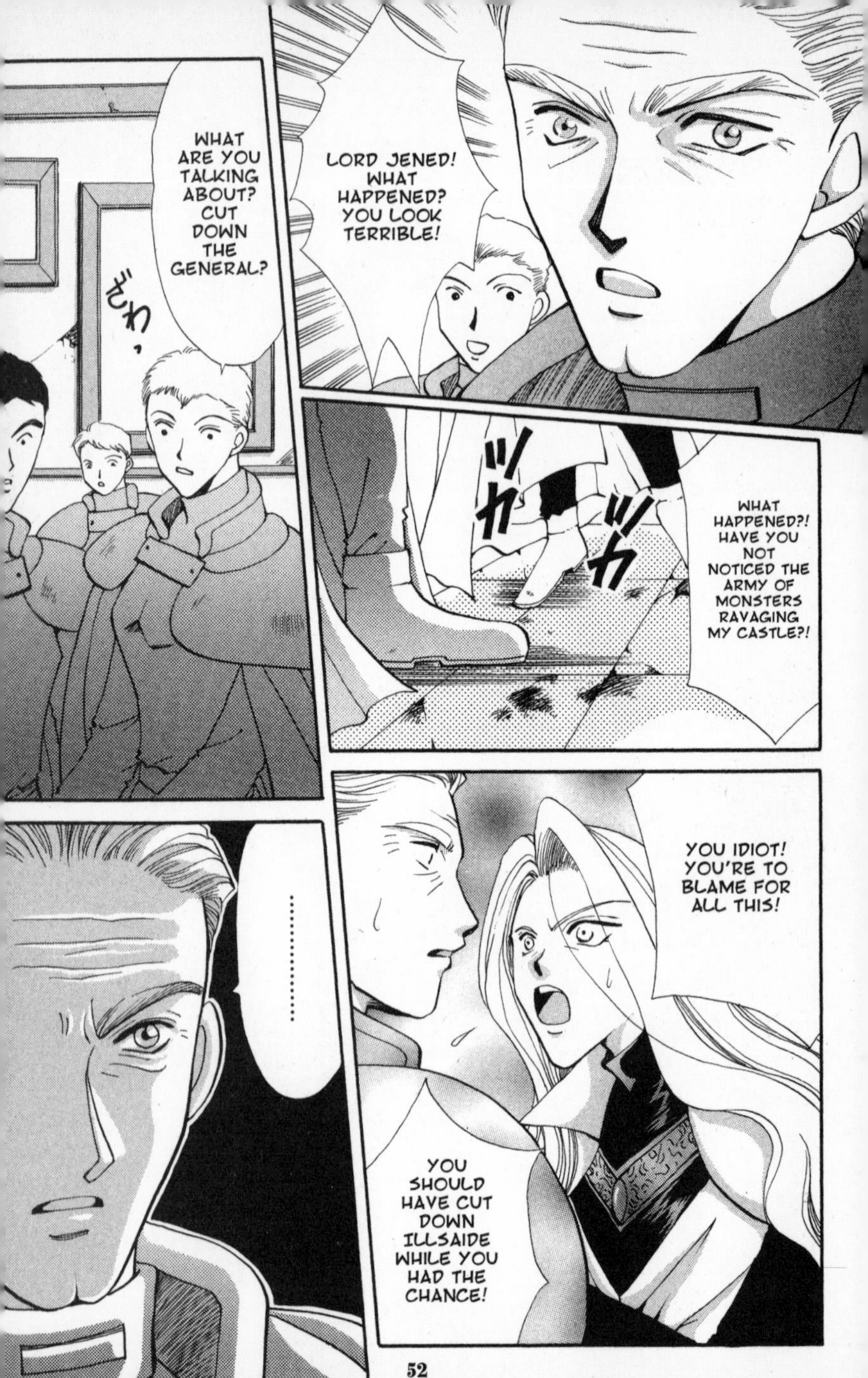
LORD JENED! WHAT HAPPENED? YOU LOOK TERRIBLE!
ツカ
ツカ
WHAT HAPPENED?! HAVE YOU NOT NOTICED THE ARMY OF MONSTERS RAVAGING MY CASTLE?!
WHAT ARE YOU TALKING ABOUT? CUT DOWN THE GENERAL?
ざわ
YOU IDIOT! YOU'RE TO BLAME FOR ALL THIS!
YOU SHOULD HAVE CUT DOWN ILLSAIDE WHILE YOU HAD THE CHANCE!
......

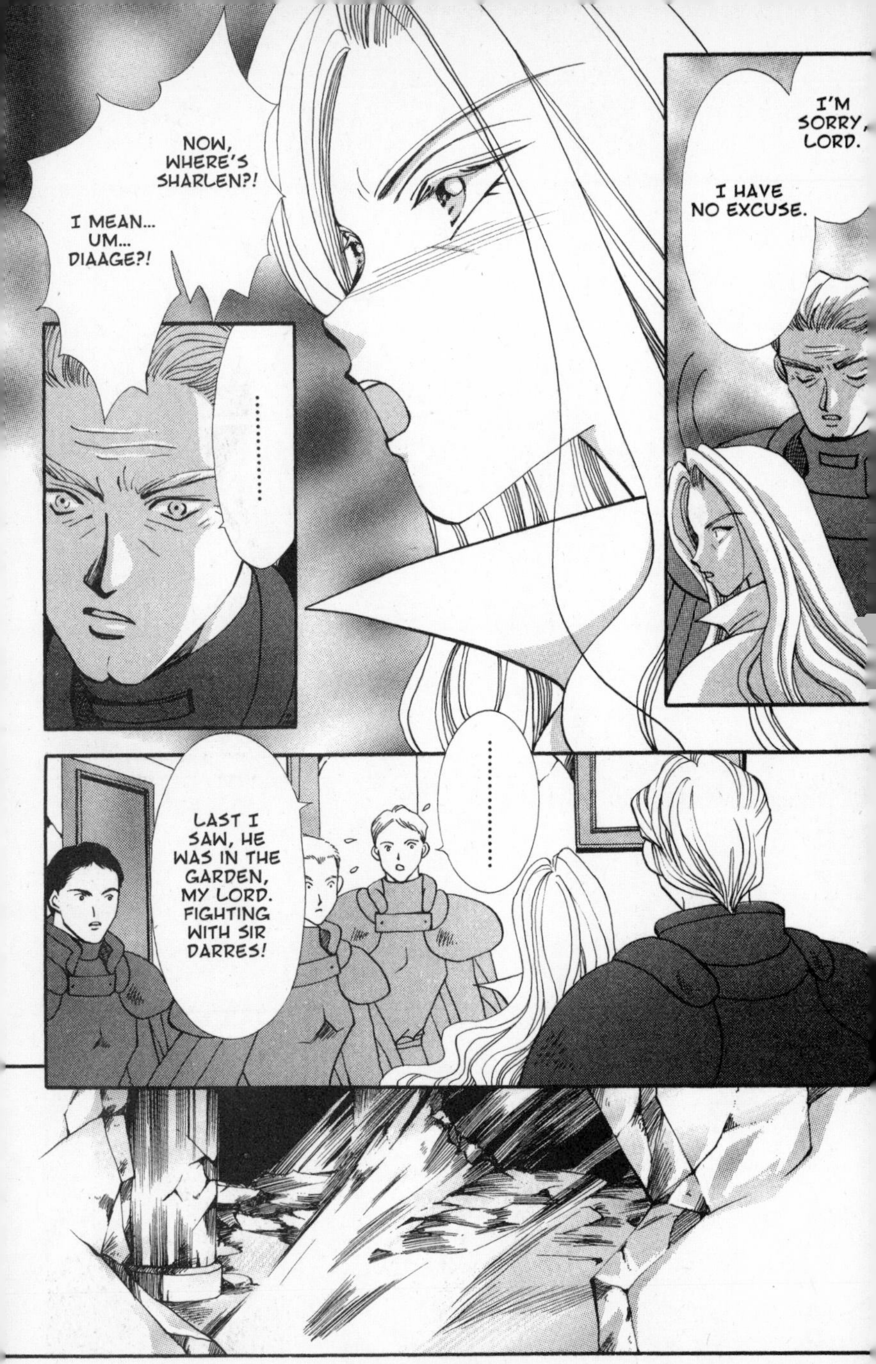
I'M SORRY, LORD.
I HAVE NO EXCUSE.
NOW, WHERE'S SHARLEN?!
I MEAN... UM... DIAAGE?!
....
....
LAST I SAW, HE WAS IN THE GARDEN, MY LORD. FIGHTING WITH SIR DARRES!

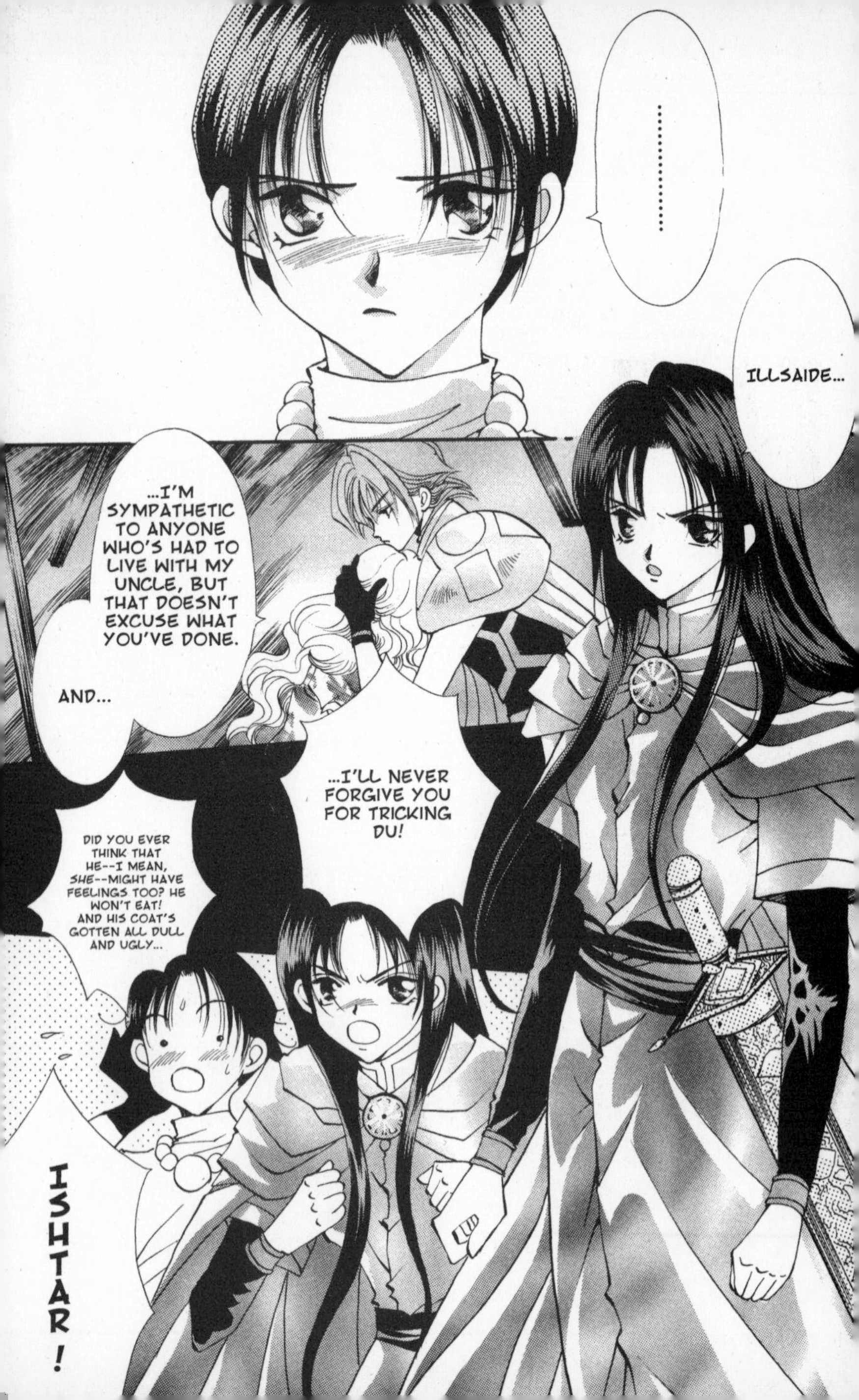
......
ILLSAIDE...
...I'M SYMPATHETIC TO ANYONE WHO'S HAD TO LIVE WITH MY UNCLE, BUT THAT DOESN'T EXCUSE WHAT YOU'VE DONE.
AND...
...I'LL NEVER FORGIVE YOU FOR TRICKING DU!
DID YOU EVER THINK THAT HE--I MEAN, SHE--MIGHT HAVE FEELINGS TOO? HE WON'T EAT! AND HIS COAT'S GOTTEN ALL DULL AND UGLY...
ISHTAR!

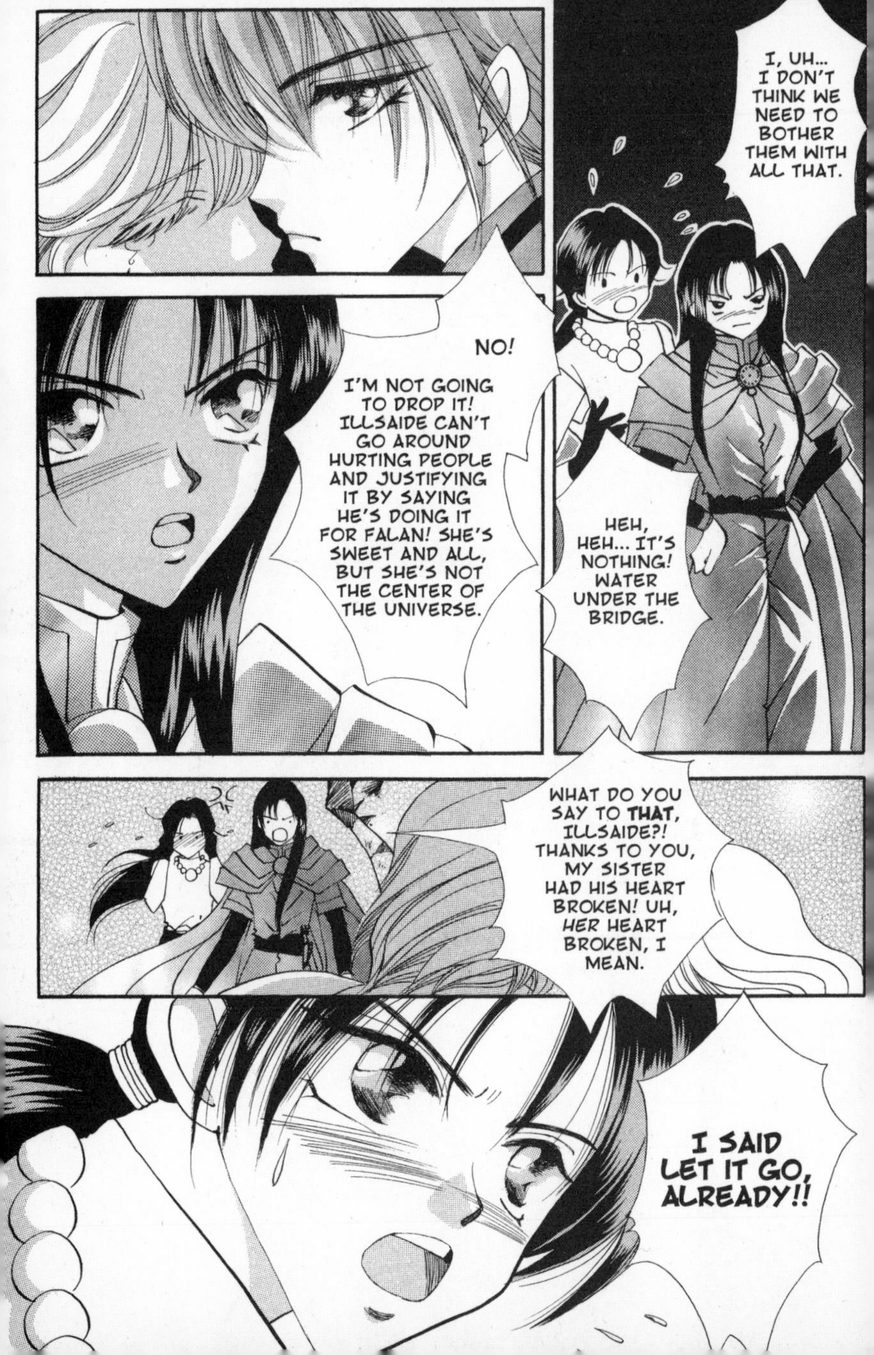
I, UH... I DON'T THINK WE NEED TO BOTHER THEM WITH ALL THAT.
HEH, HEH... IT'S NOTHING! WATER UNDER THE BRIDGE.
NO!
I'M NOT GOING TO DROP IT! ILLSAIDE CAN'T GO AROUND HURTING PEOPLE AND JUSTIFYING IT BY SAYING HE'S DOING IT FOR FALAN! SHE'S SWEET AND ALL, BUT SHE'S NOT THE CENTER OF THE UNIVERSE.
WHAT DO YOU SAY TO **THAT**, ILLSAIDE?! THANKS TO YOU, MY SISTER HAD HIS HEART BROKEN! UH, HER HEART BROKEN, I MEAN.
I SAID LET IT GO, ALREADY!!

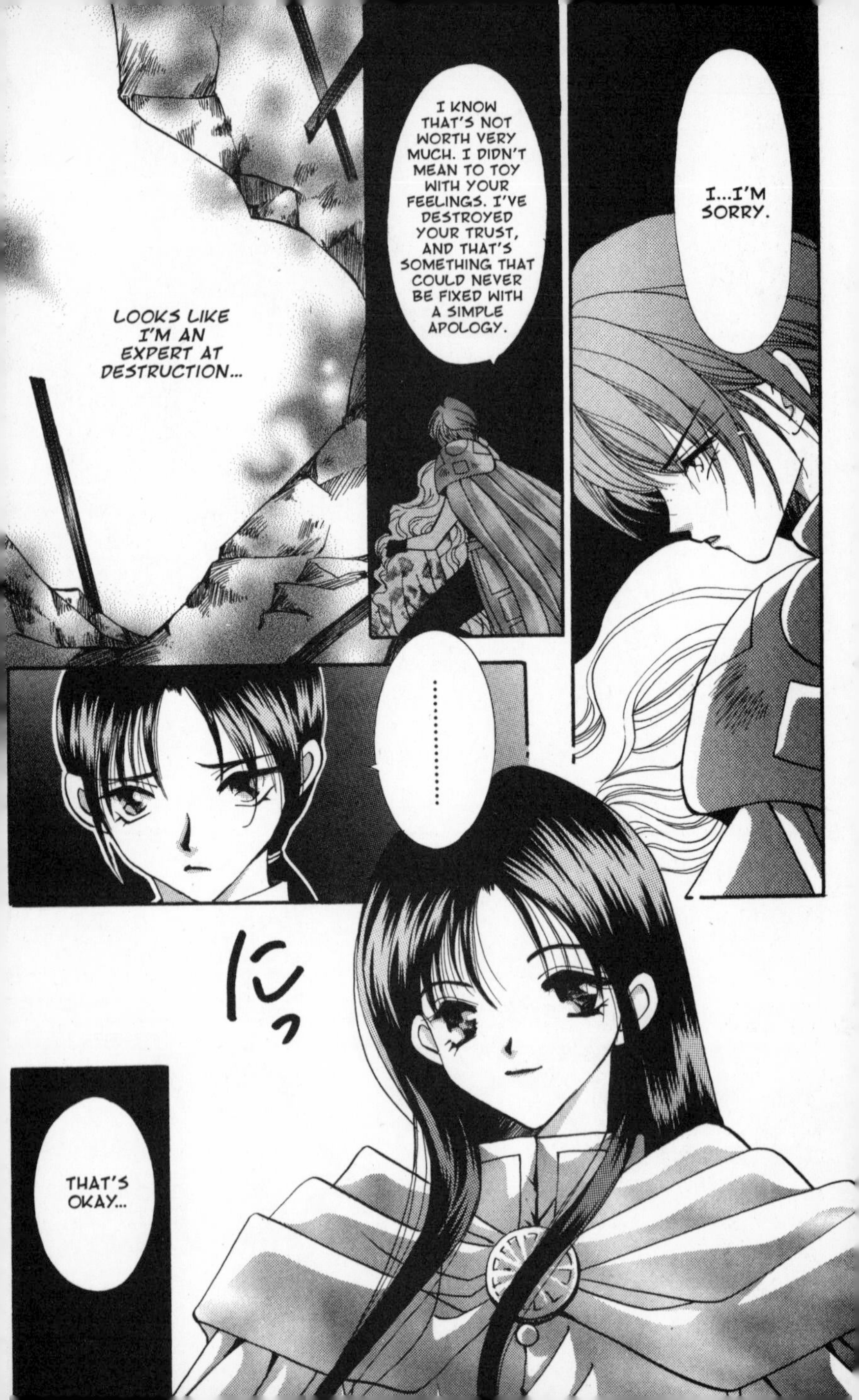
I...I'M SORRY.
I KNOW THAT'S NOT WORTH VERY MUCH. I DIDN'T MEAN TO TOY WITH YOUR FEELINGS. I'VE DESTROYED YOUR TRUST, AND THAT'S SOMETHING THAT COULD NEVER BE FIXED WITH A SIMPLE APOLOGY.
LOOKS LIKE I'M AN EXPERT AT DESTRUCTION...
......
にっ
THAT'S OKAY...

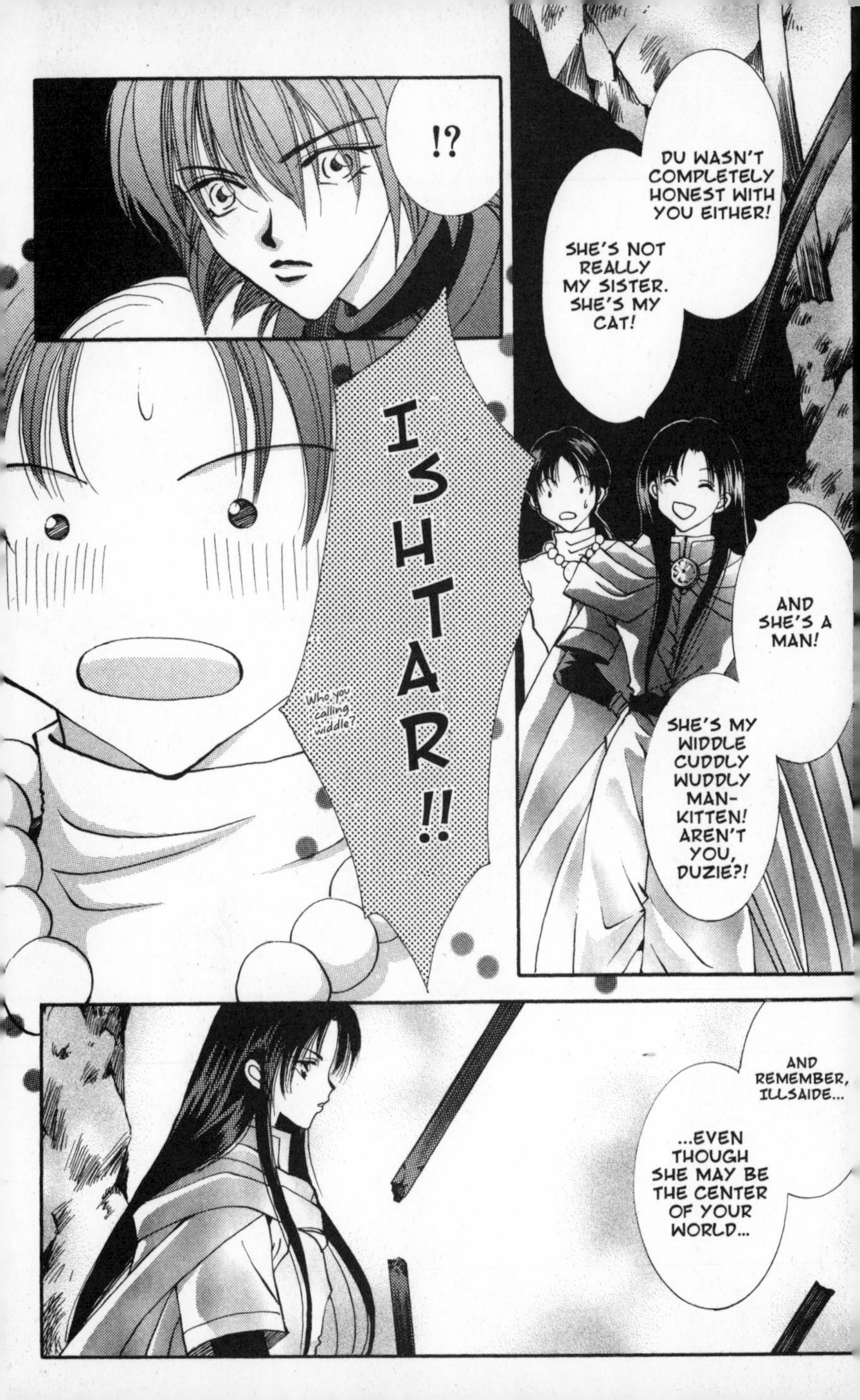
DU WASN'T COMPLETELY HONEST WITH YOU EITHER!
SHE'S NOT REALLY MY SISTER. SHE'S MY CAT!
AND SHE'S A MAN!
SHE'S MY WIDDLE CUDDLY WUDDLY MAN-KITTEN! AREN'T YOU, DUZIE?!
!?
ISHTAR!!
Who you calling widdle?
AND REMEMBER, ILLSAIDE...
...EVEN THOUGH SHE MAY BE THE CENTER OF YOUR WORLD...

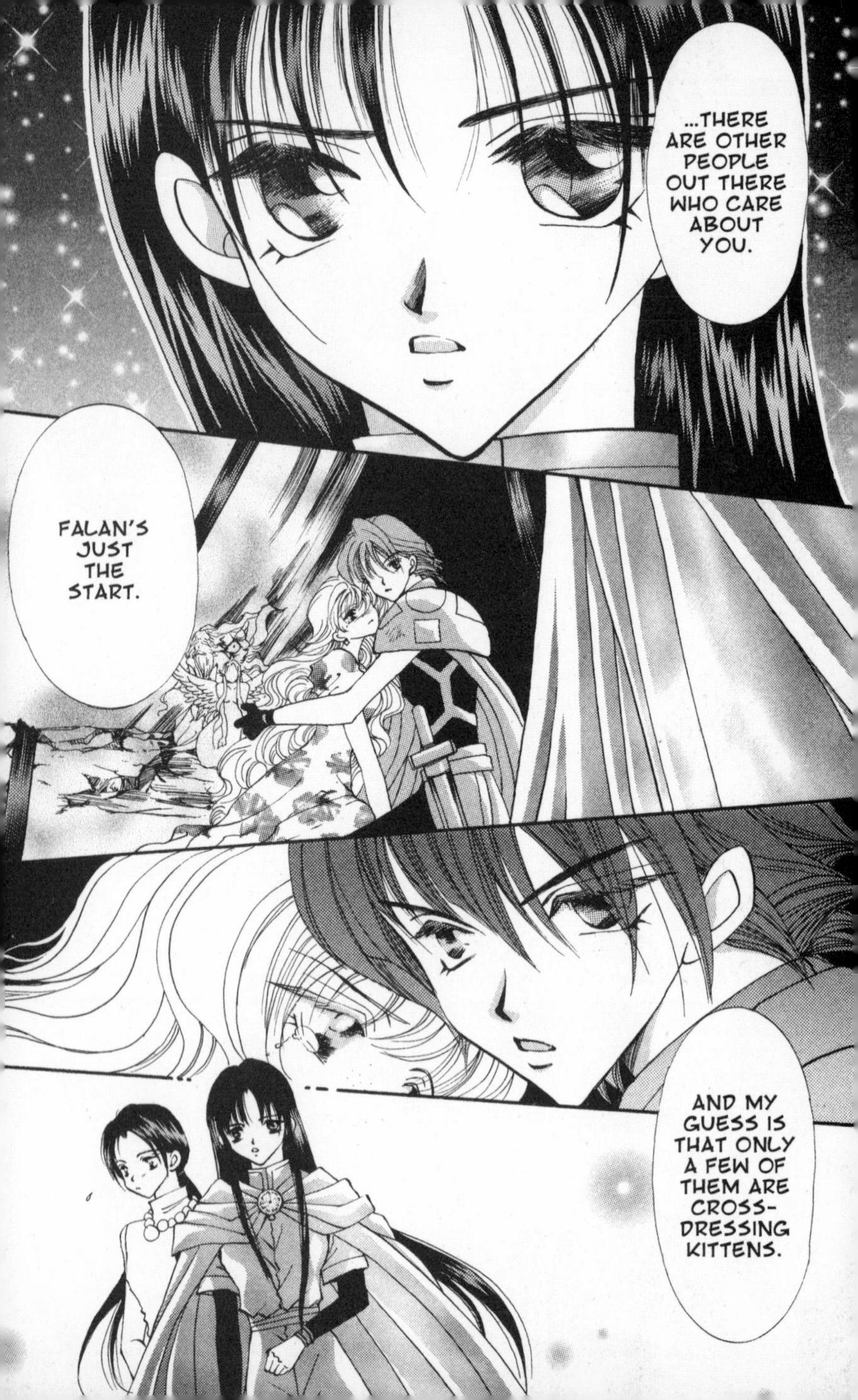
...THERE ARE OTHER PEOPLE OUT THERE WHO CARE ABOUT YOU.
FALAN'S JUST THE START.
AND MY GUESS IS THAT ONLY A FEW OF THEM ARE CROSS-DRESSING KITTENS.

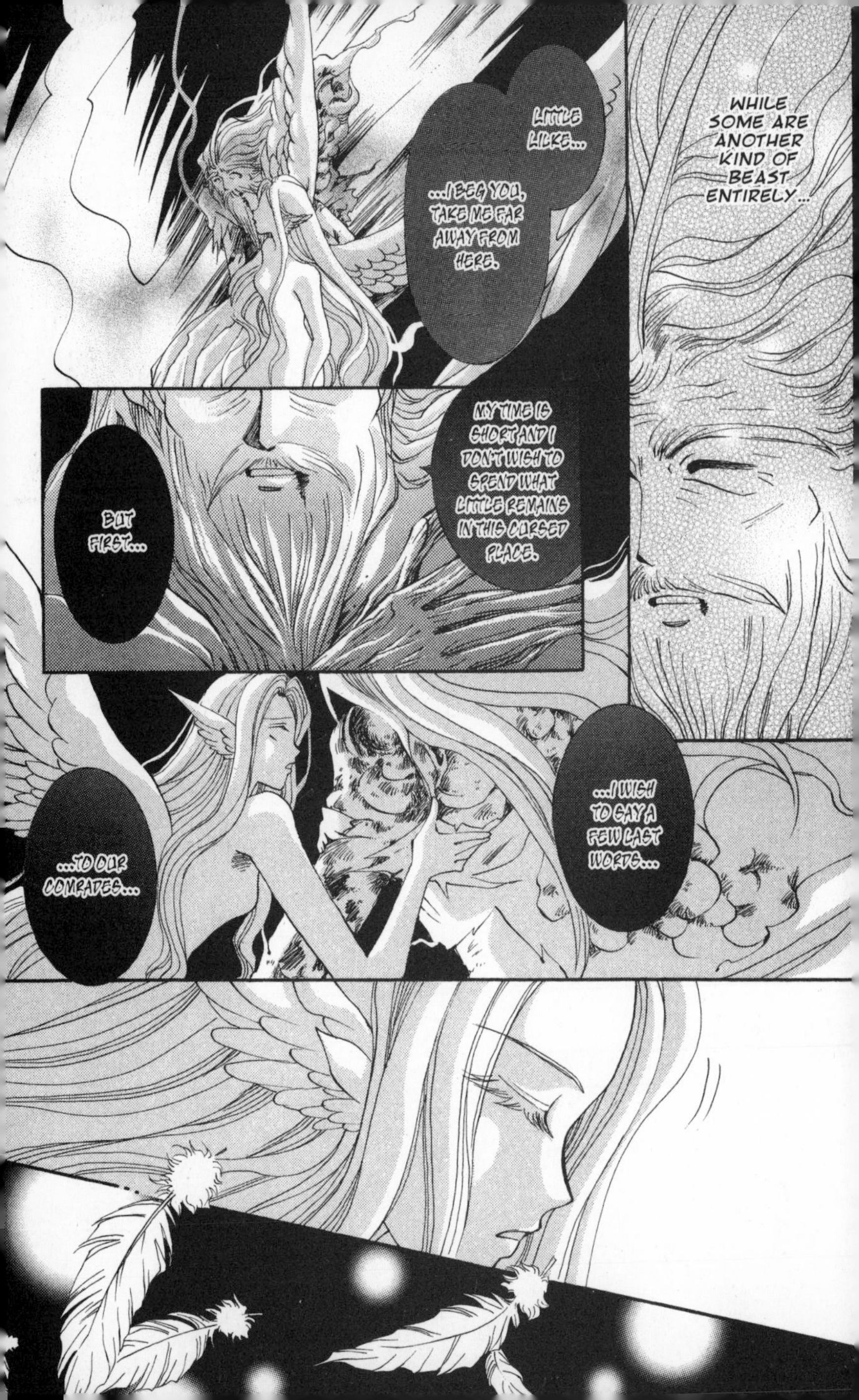
WHILE SOME ARE ANOTHER KIND OF BEAST ENTIRELY...
LITTLE LILKE...
...I BEG YOU, TAKE ME FAR AWAY FROM HERE.
MY TIME IS SHORT AND I DON'T WISH TO SPEND WHAT LITTLE REMAINS IN THIS CURSED PLACE.
BUT FIRST...
...I WISH TO SAY A FEW LAST WORDS...
...TO OUR COMRADES...

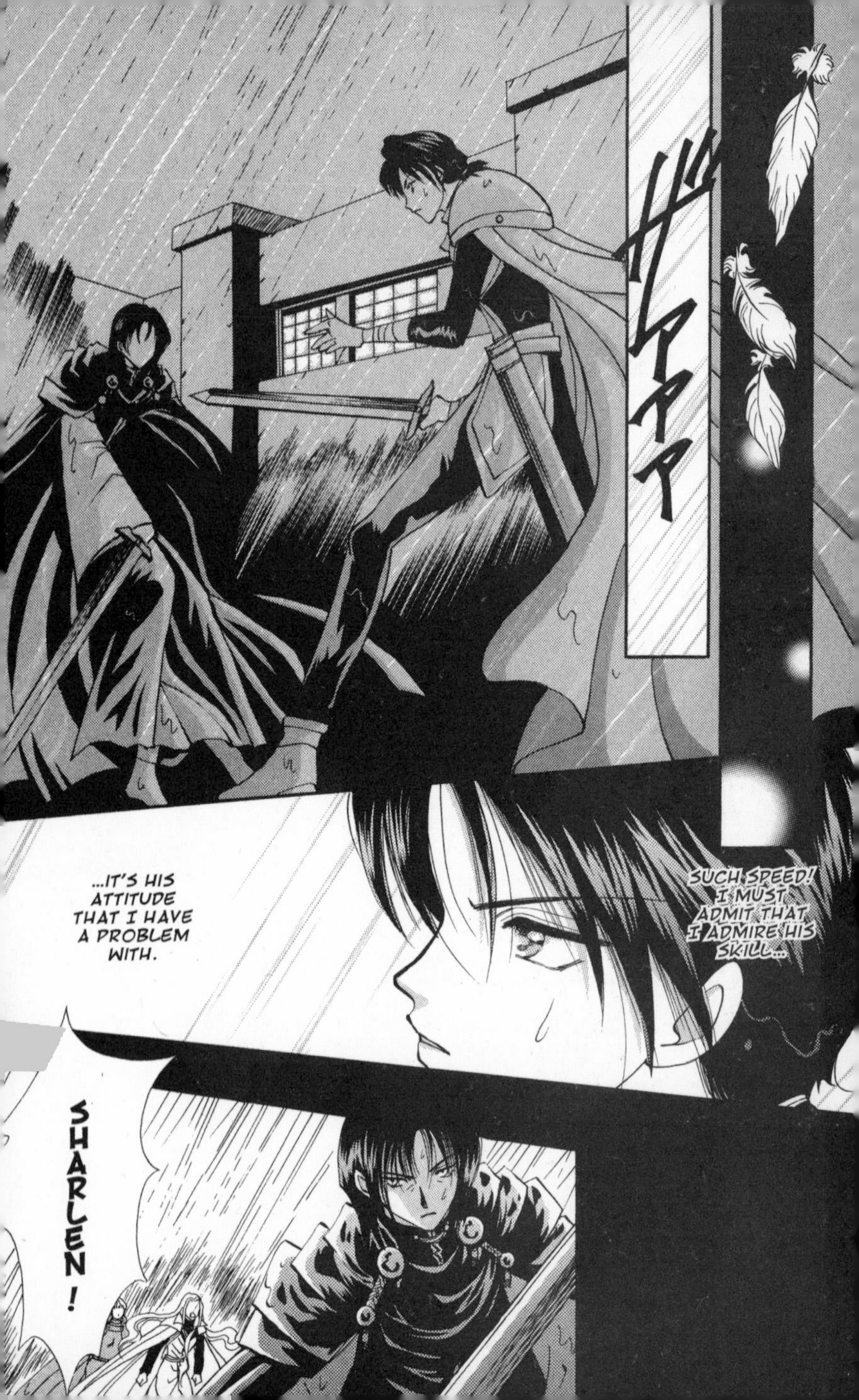
ザムァァ
SUCH SPEED! I MUST ADMIT THAT I ADMIRE HIS SKILL...
...IT'S HIS ATTITUDE THAT I HAVE A PROBLEM WITH.
SHARLEN!

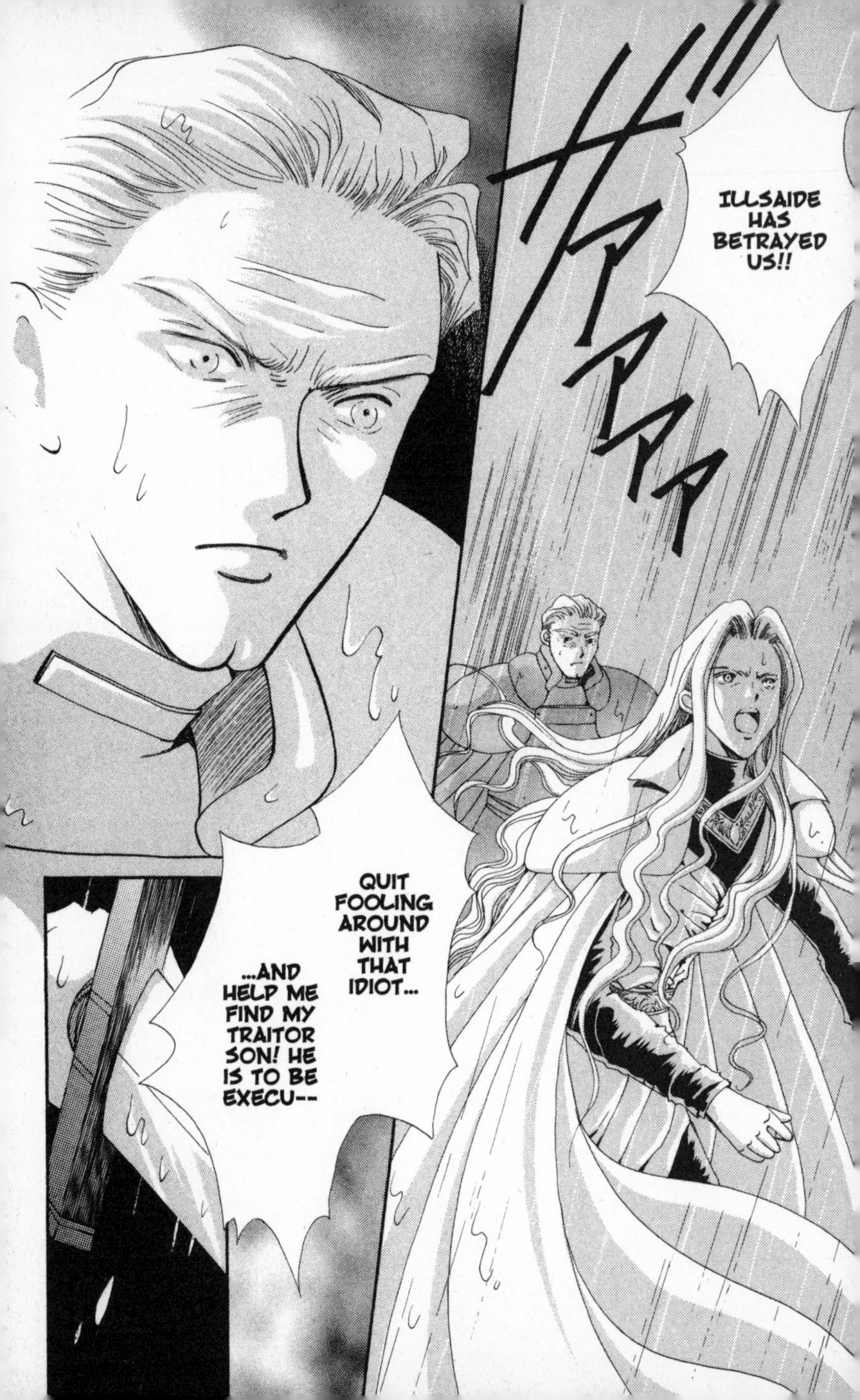
ILLSAIDE HAS BETRAYED US!!
QUIT FOOLING AROUND WITH THAT IDIOT...
...AND HELP ME FIND MY TRAITOR SON! HE IS TO BE EXECU--

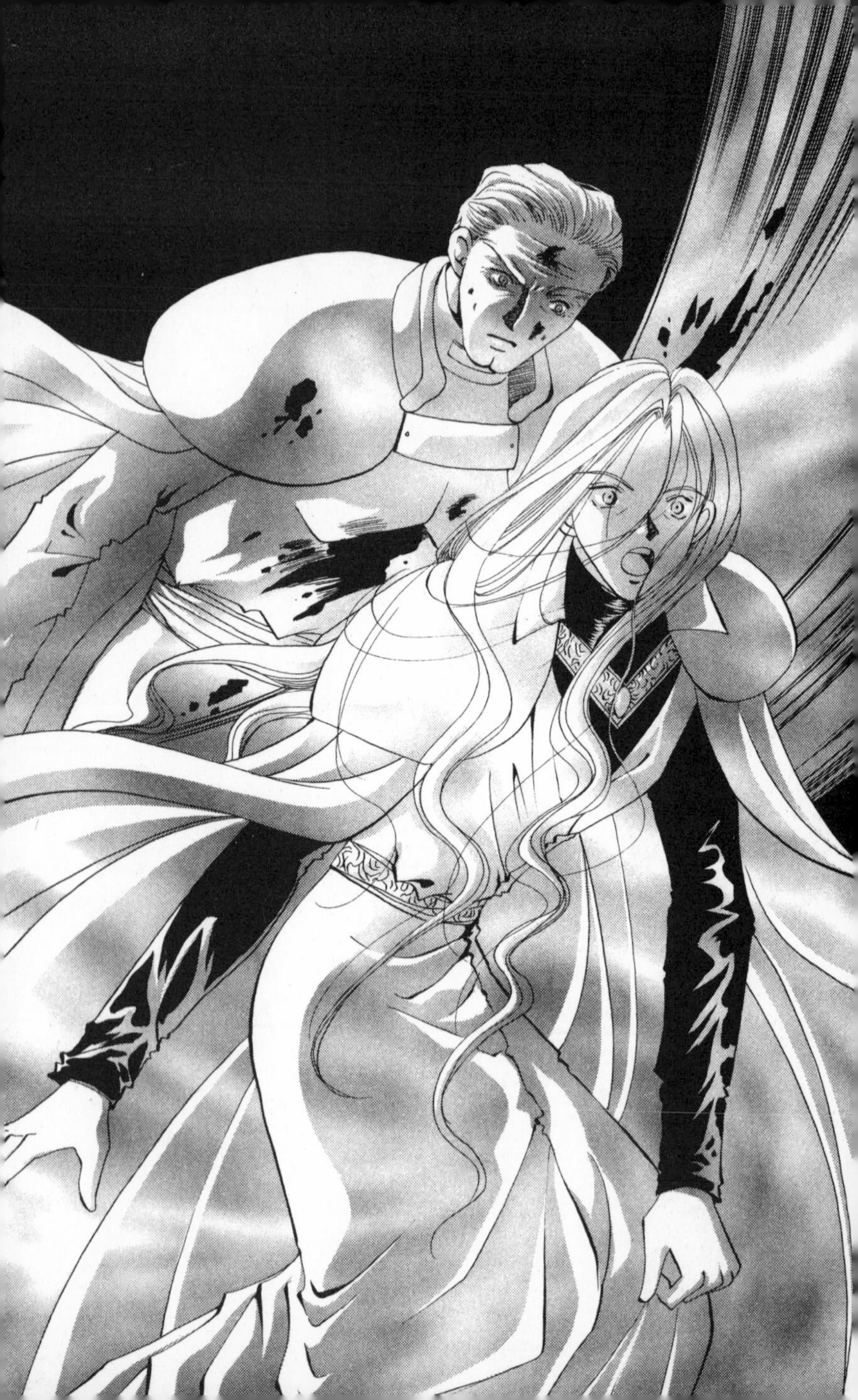

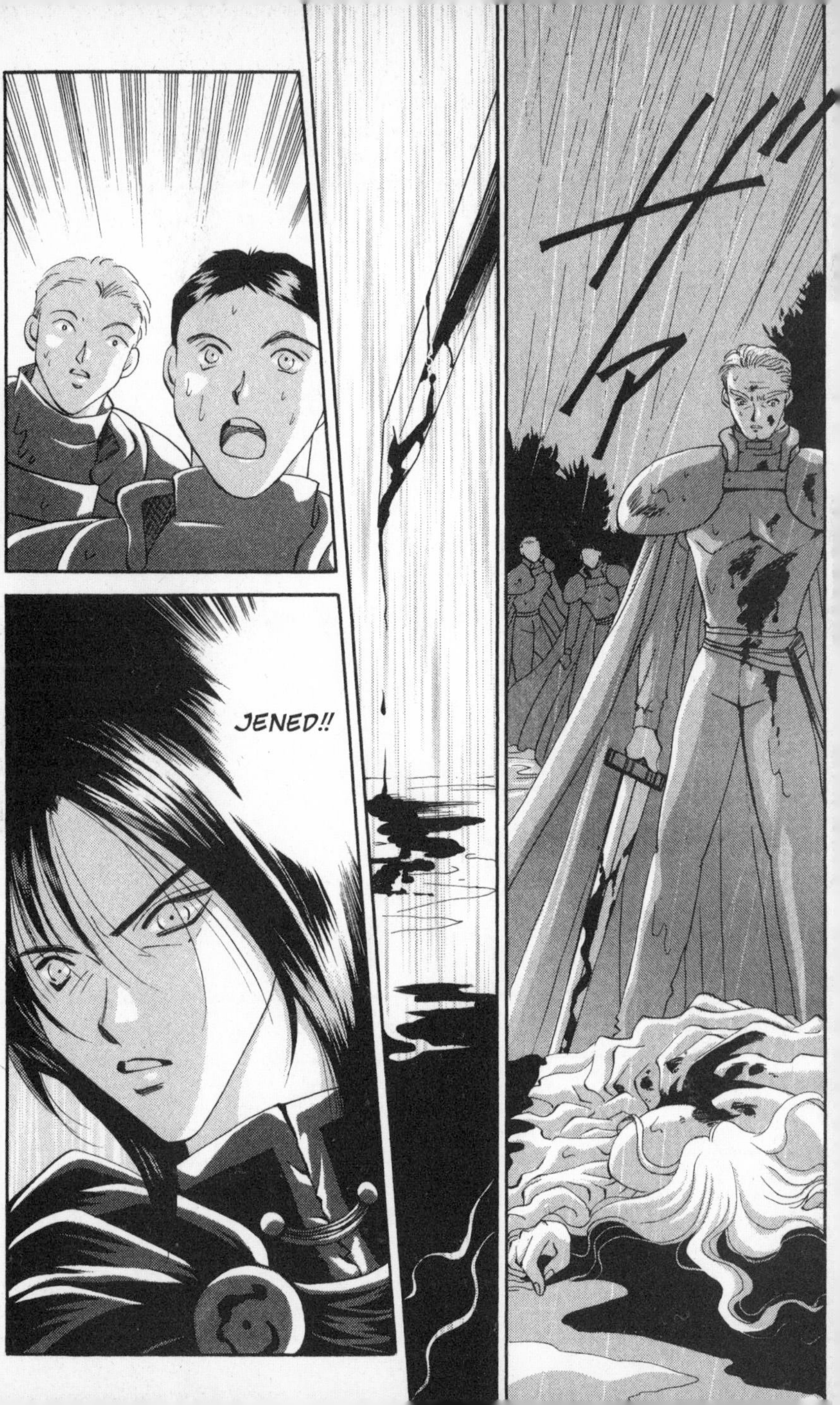
JENED!!

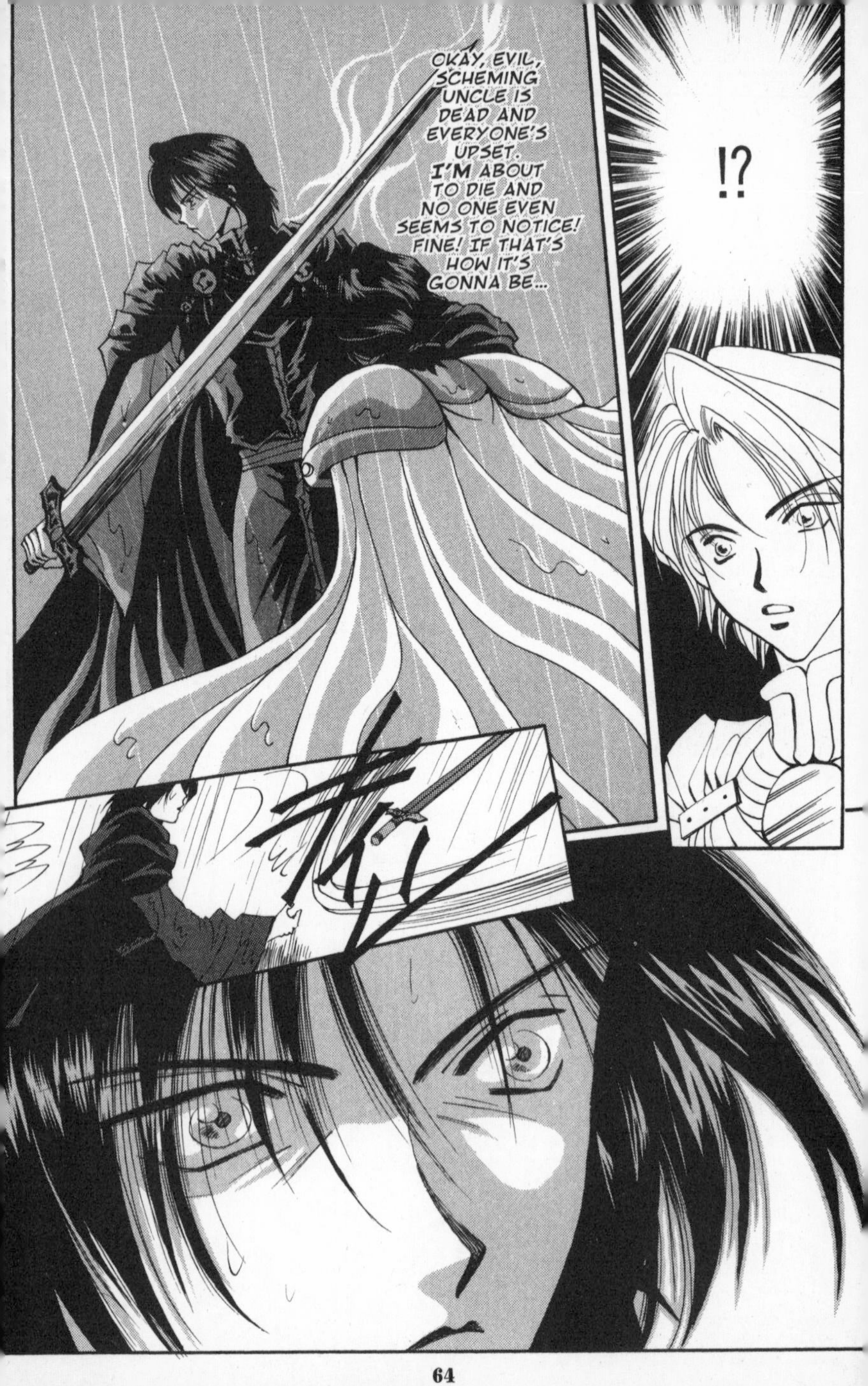
!?
OKAY, EVIL, SCHEMING UNCLE IS DEAD AND EVERYONE'S UPSET. **I'M** ABOUT TO DIE AND NO ONE EVEN SEEMS TO NOTICE! FINE! IF THAT'S HOW IT'S GONNA BE...

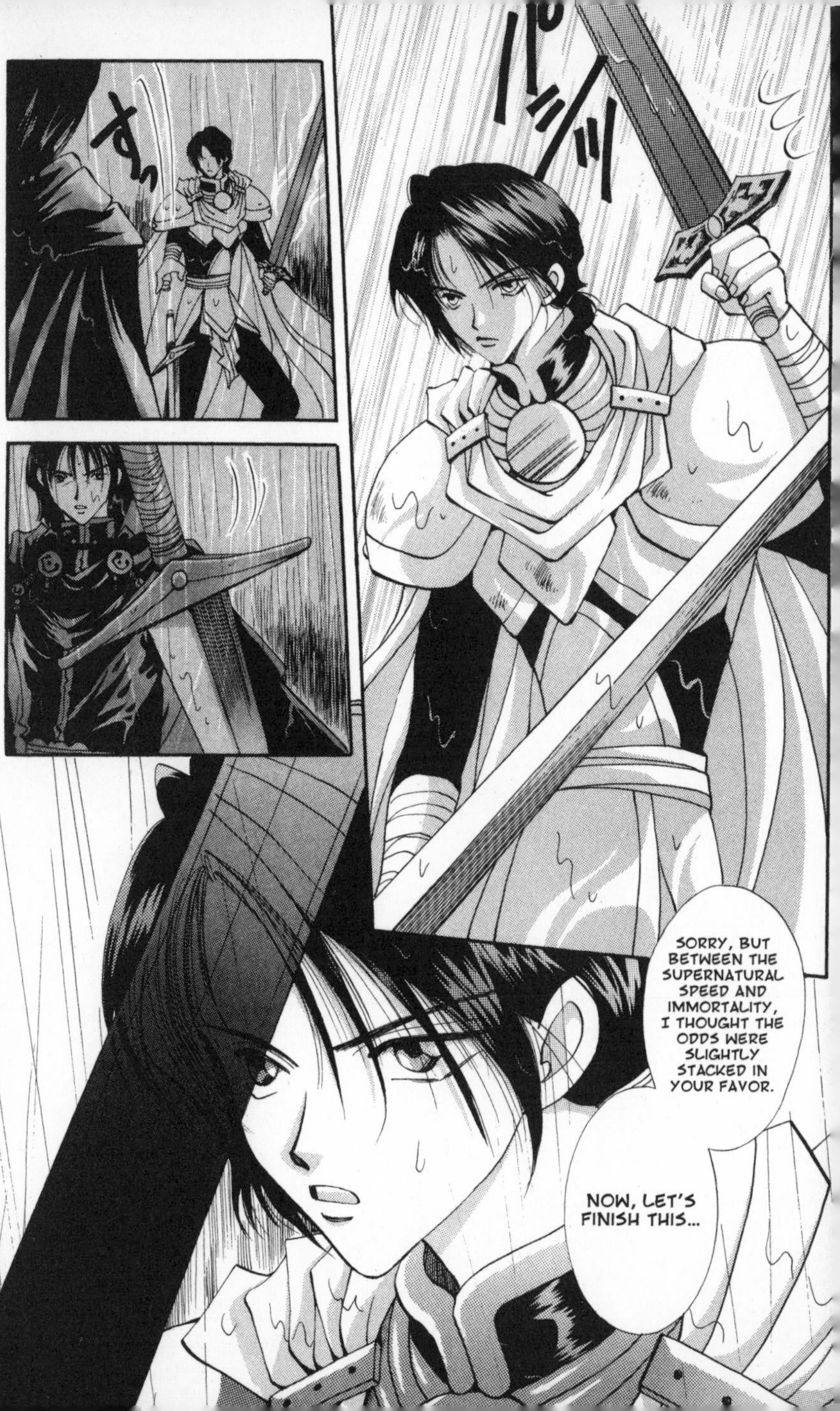
パシッ
すっ
SORRY, BUT BETWEEN THE SUPERNATURAL SPEED AND IMMORTALITY, I THOUGHT THE ODDS WERE SLIGHTLY STACKED IN YOUR FAVOR.
NOW, LET'S FINISH THIS...

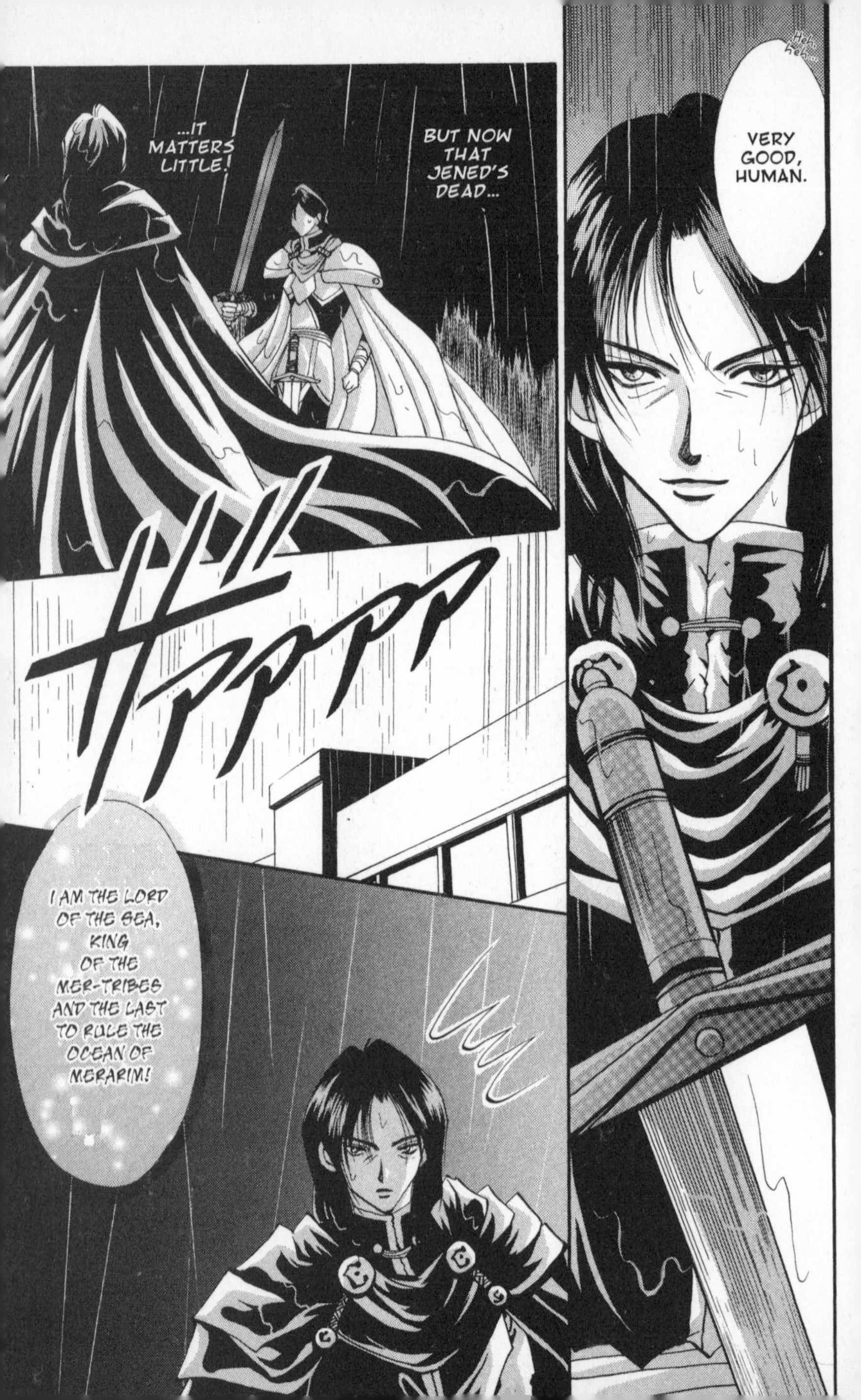
Heh heh...
VERY GOOD, HUMAN.
BUT NOW THAT JENED'S DEAD...
...IT MATTERS LITTLE!
HUPPPP
I AM THE LORD OF THE SEA, KING OF THE MER-TRIBES AND THE LAST TO RULE THE OCEAN OF MERARIM!

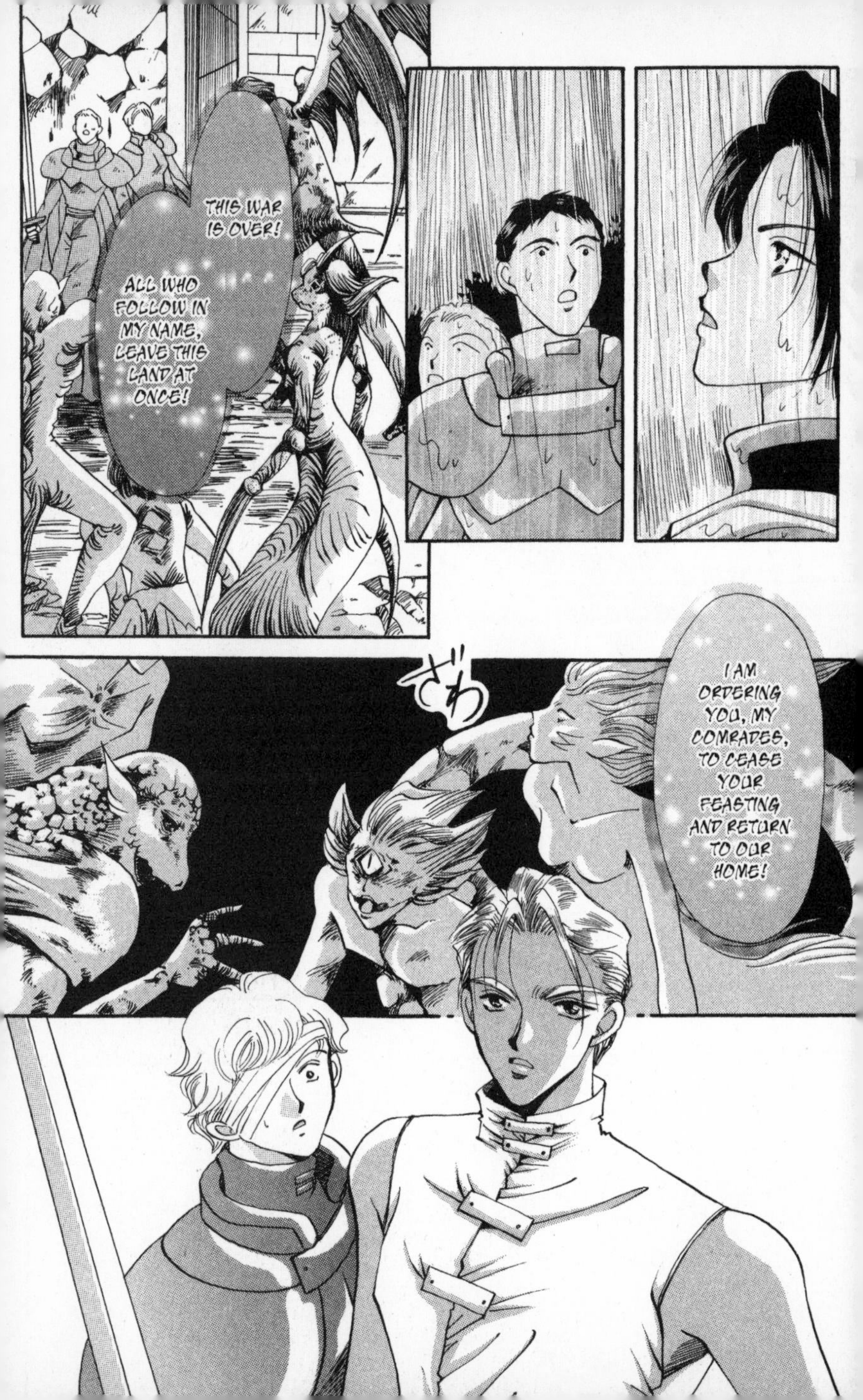
THIS WAR IS OVER!
ALL WHO FOLLOW IN MY NAME, LEAVE THIS LAND AT ONCE!
I AM ORDERING YOU, MY COMRADES, TO CEASE YOUR FEASTING AND RETURN TO OUR HOME!
ざわ

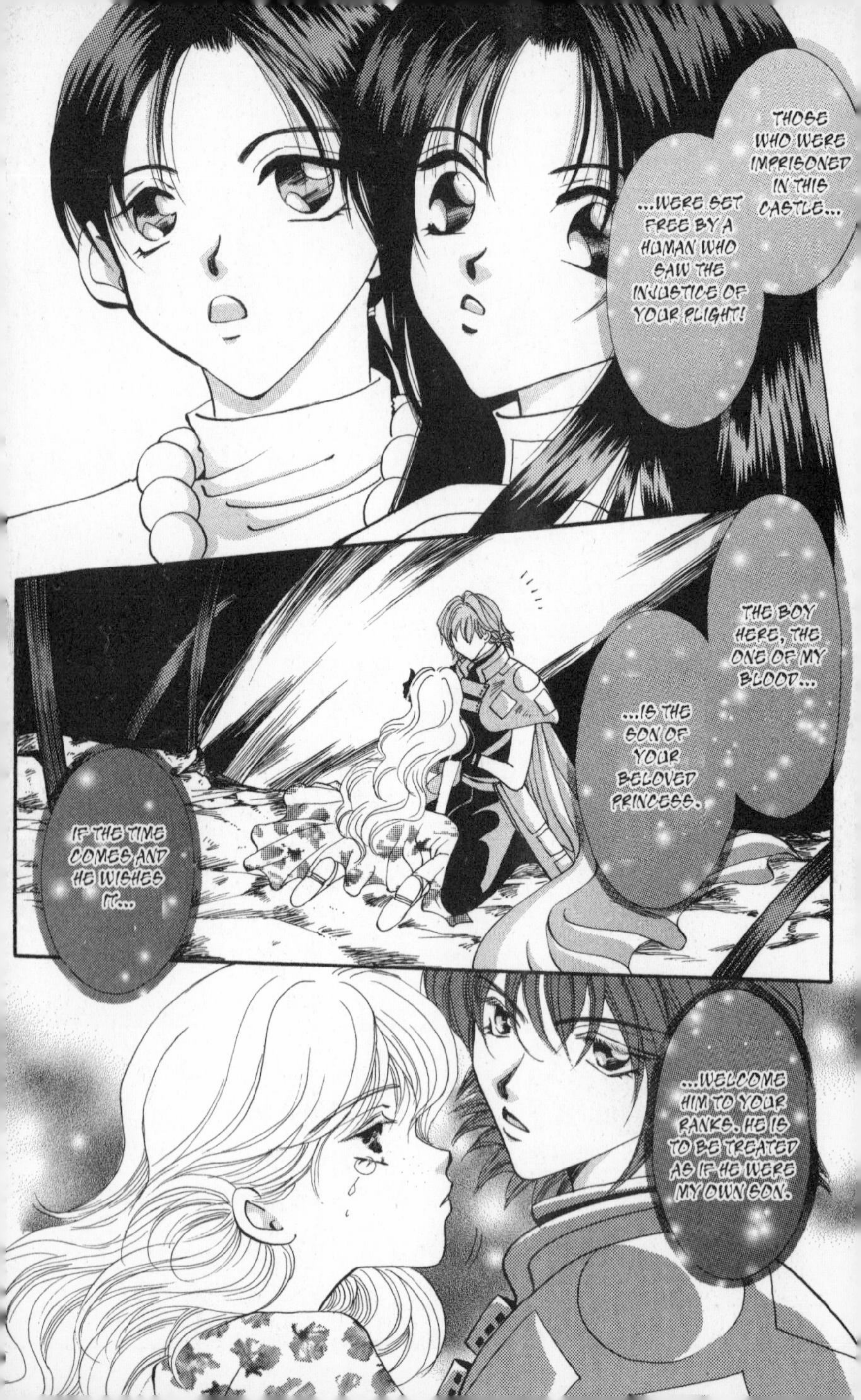
THOSE WHO WERE IMPRISONED IN THIS CASTLE...
...WERE SET FREE BY A HUMAN WHO SAW THE INJUSTICE OF YOUR PLIGHT!
THE BOY HERE, THE ONE OF MY BLOOD...
...IS THE SON OF YOUR BELOVED PRINCESS.
IF THE TIME COMES AND HE WISHES IT...
...WELCOME HIM TO YOUR RANKS. HE IS TO BE TREATED AS IF HE WERE MY OWN SON.

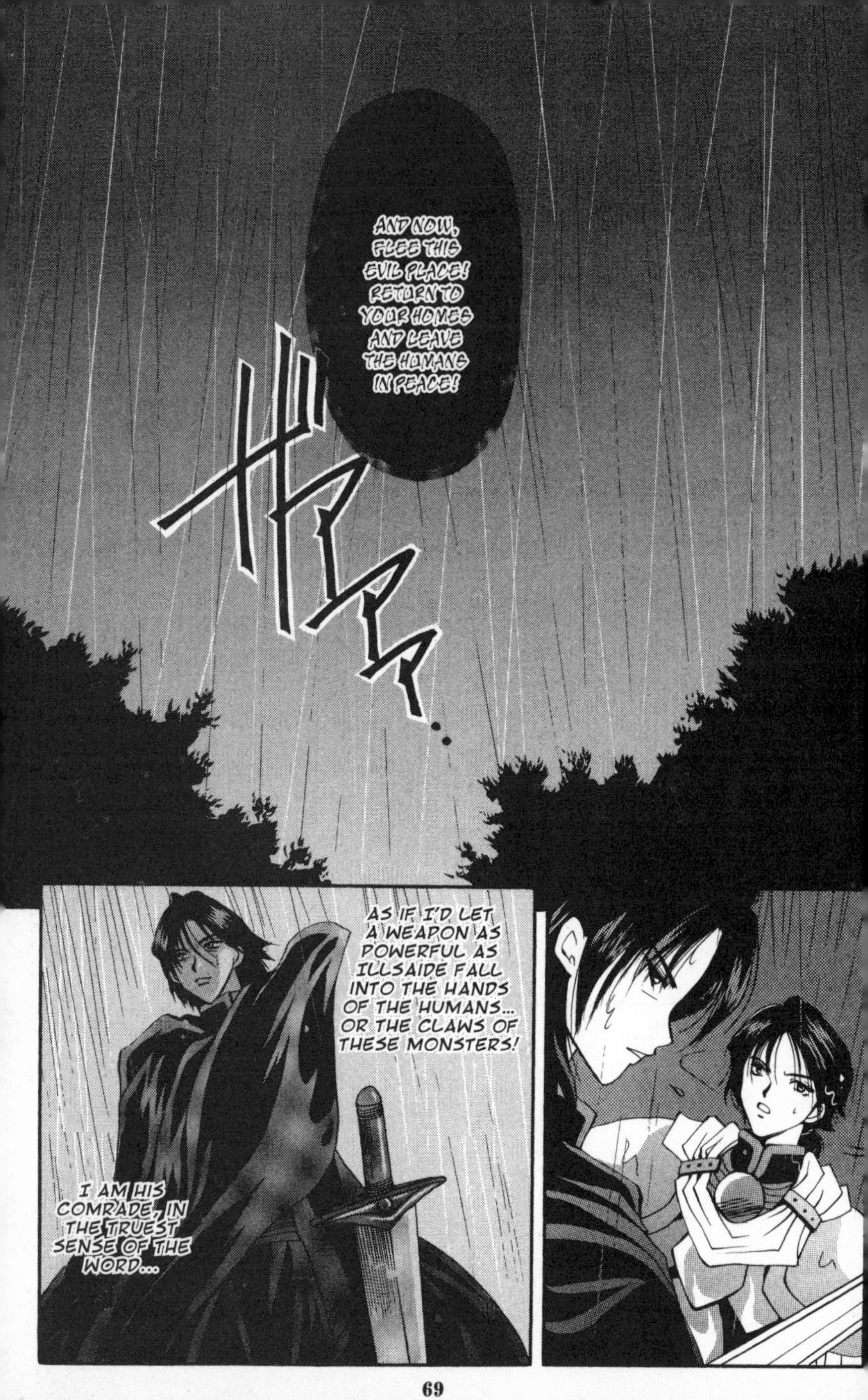
AND NOW, FLEE THIS EVIL PLACE! RETURN TO YOUR HOMES AND LEAVE THE HUMANS IN PEACE!
AS IF I'D LET A WEAPON AS POWERFUL AS ILLSAIDE FALL INTO THE HANDS OF THE HUMANS... OR THE CLAWS OF THESE MONSTERS!
I AM HIS COMRADE, IN THE TRUEST SENSE OF THE WORD...

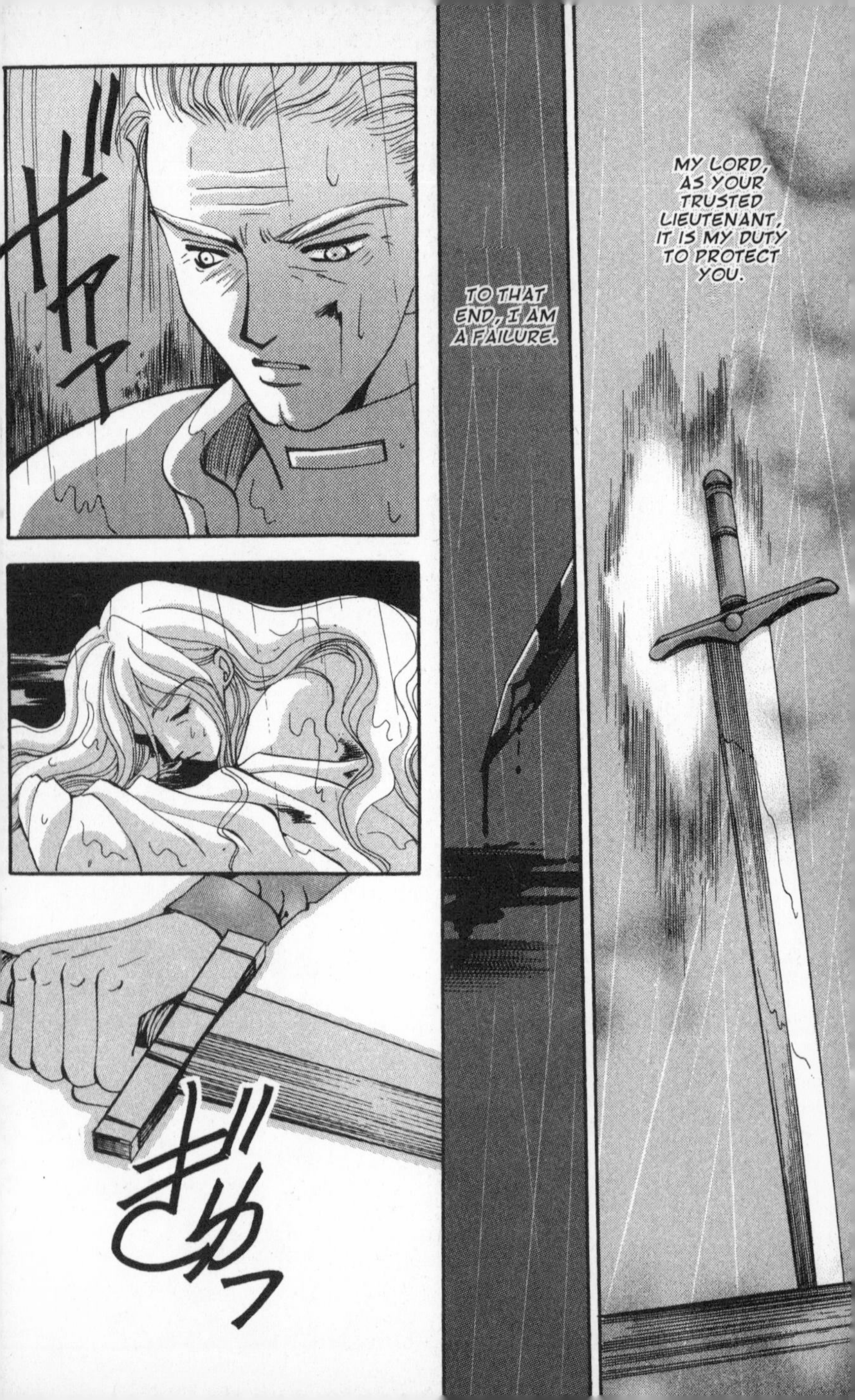
MY LORD, AS YOUR TRUSTED LIEUTENANT, IT IS MY DUTY TO PROTECT YOU.
TO THAT END, I AM A FAILURE.
ザァァ
ぎゅっ

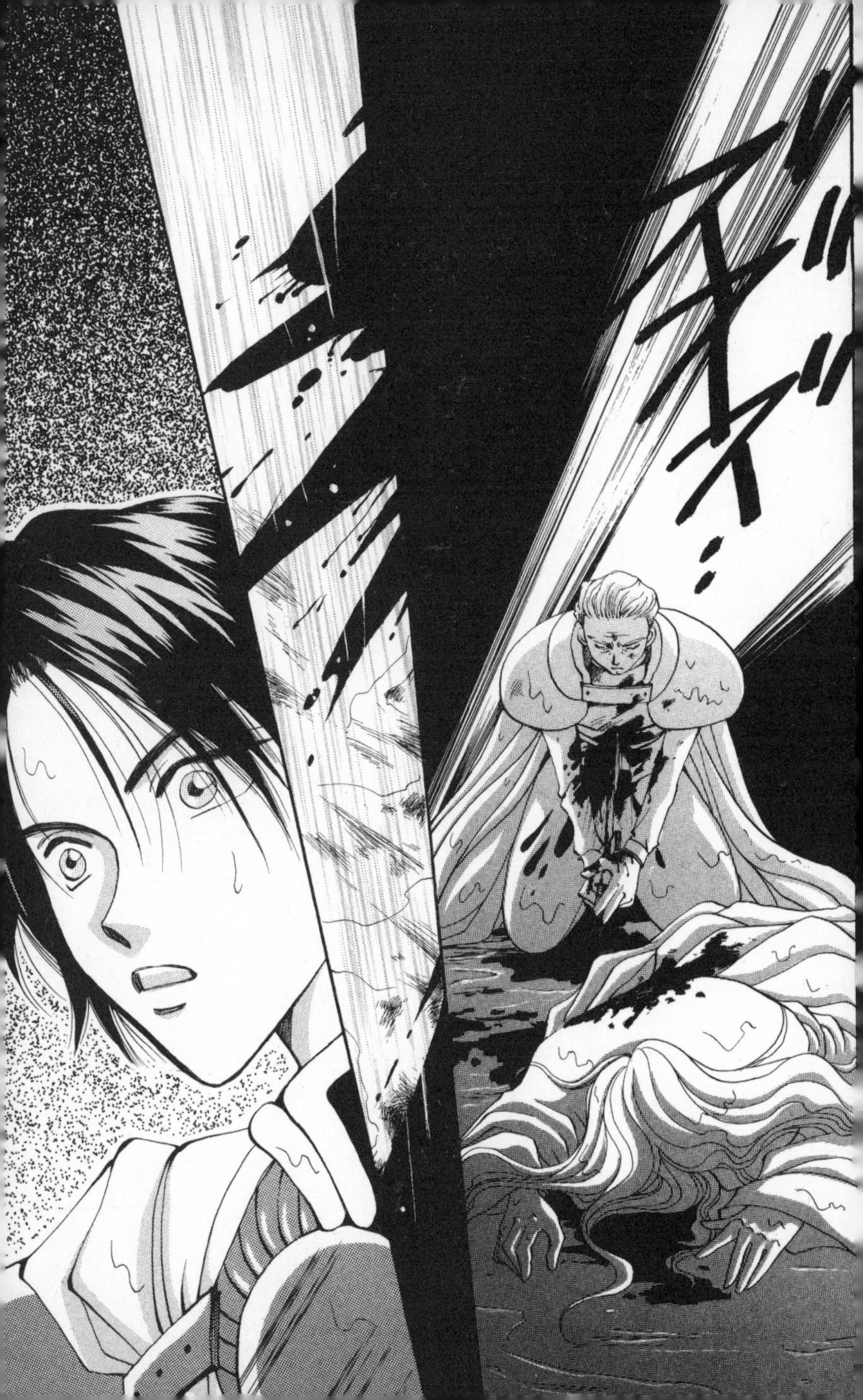
ズズズ…

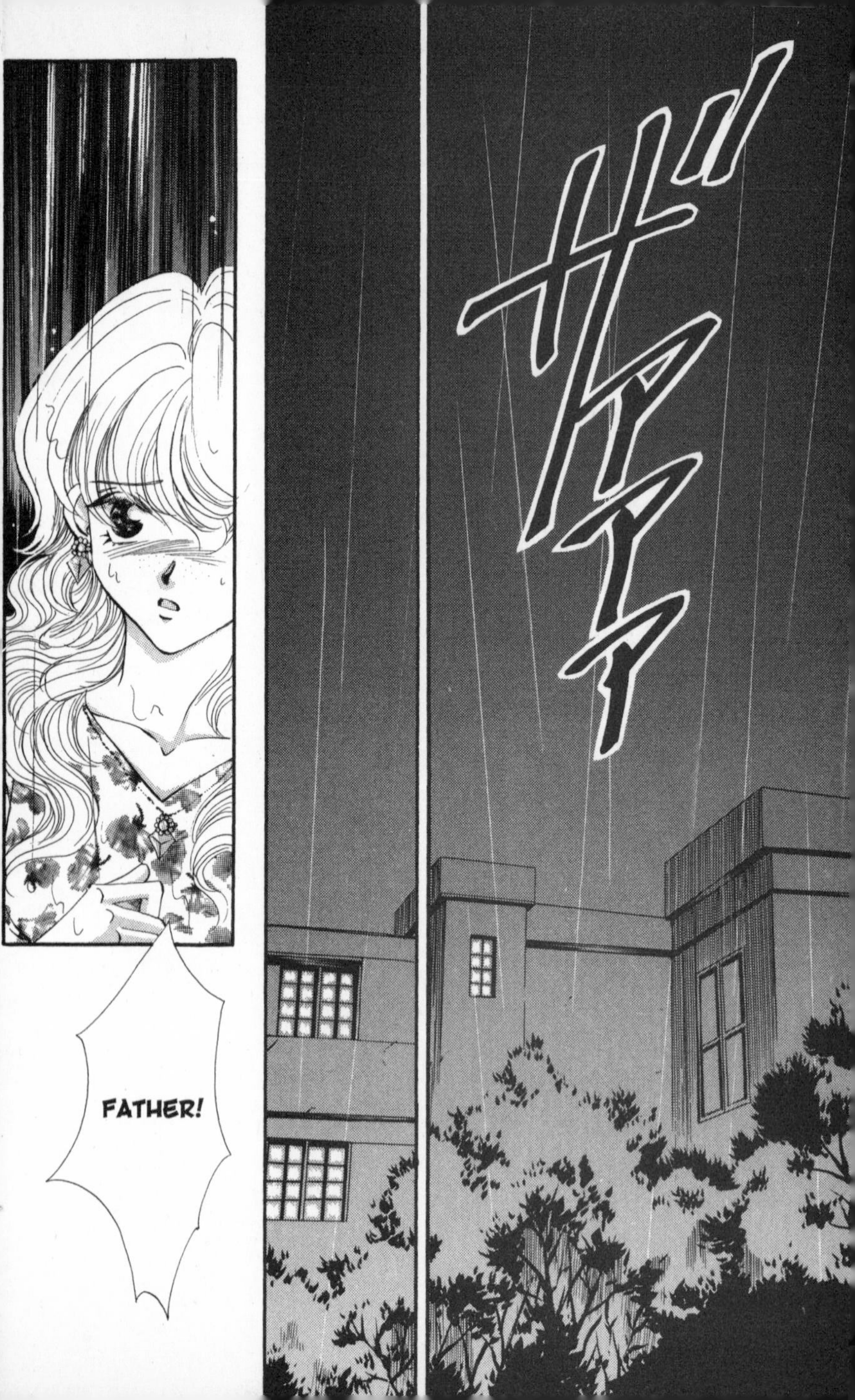
FATHER!

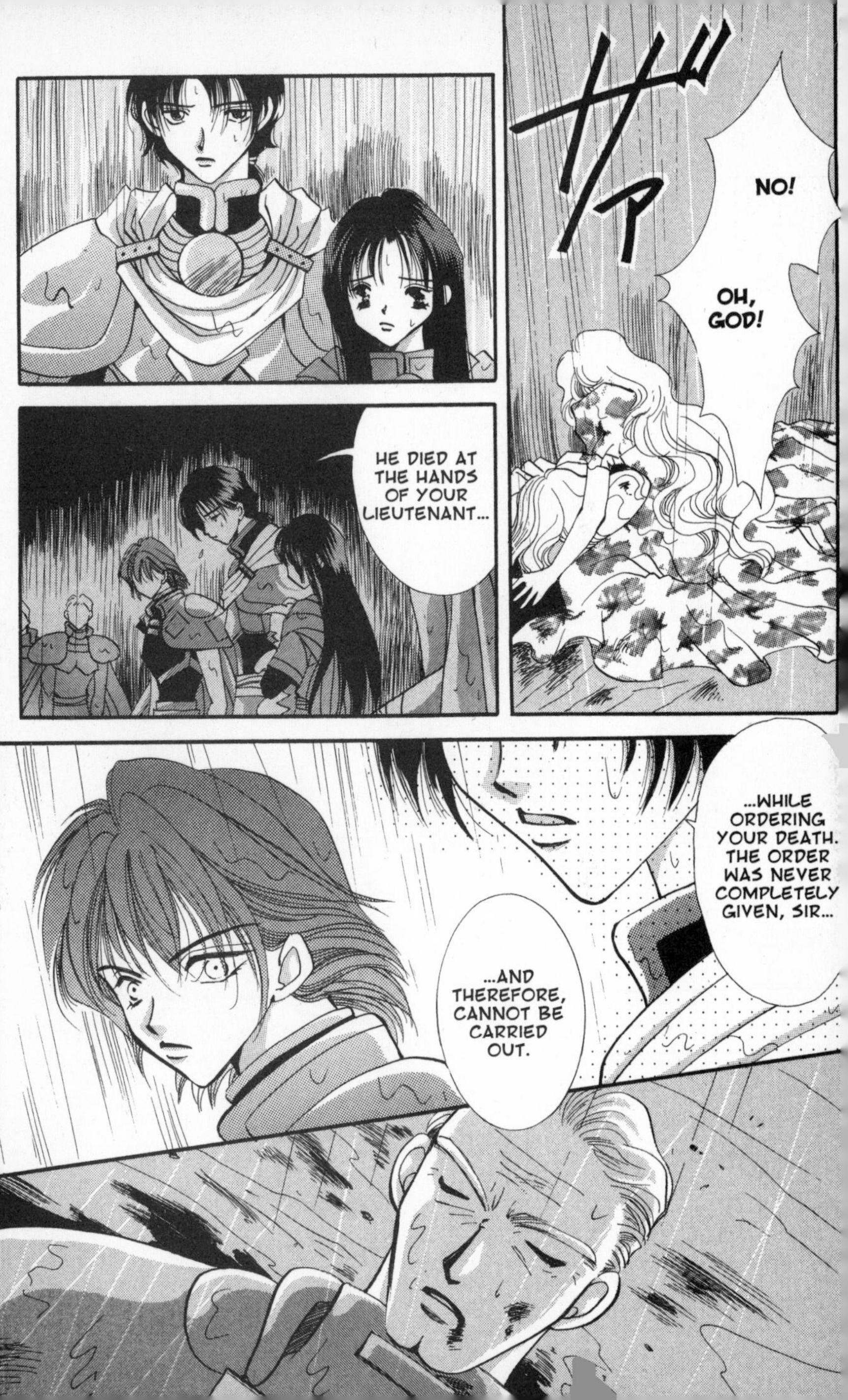
ザァ
NO!
OH, GOD!
HE DIED AT THE HANDS OF YOUR LIEUTENANT...
...WHILE ORDERING YOUR DEATH. THE ORDER WAS NEVER COMPLETELY GIVEN, SIR...
...AND THEREFORE, CANNOT BE CARRIED OUT.

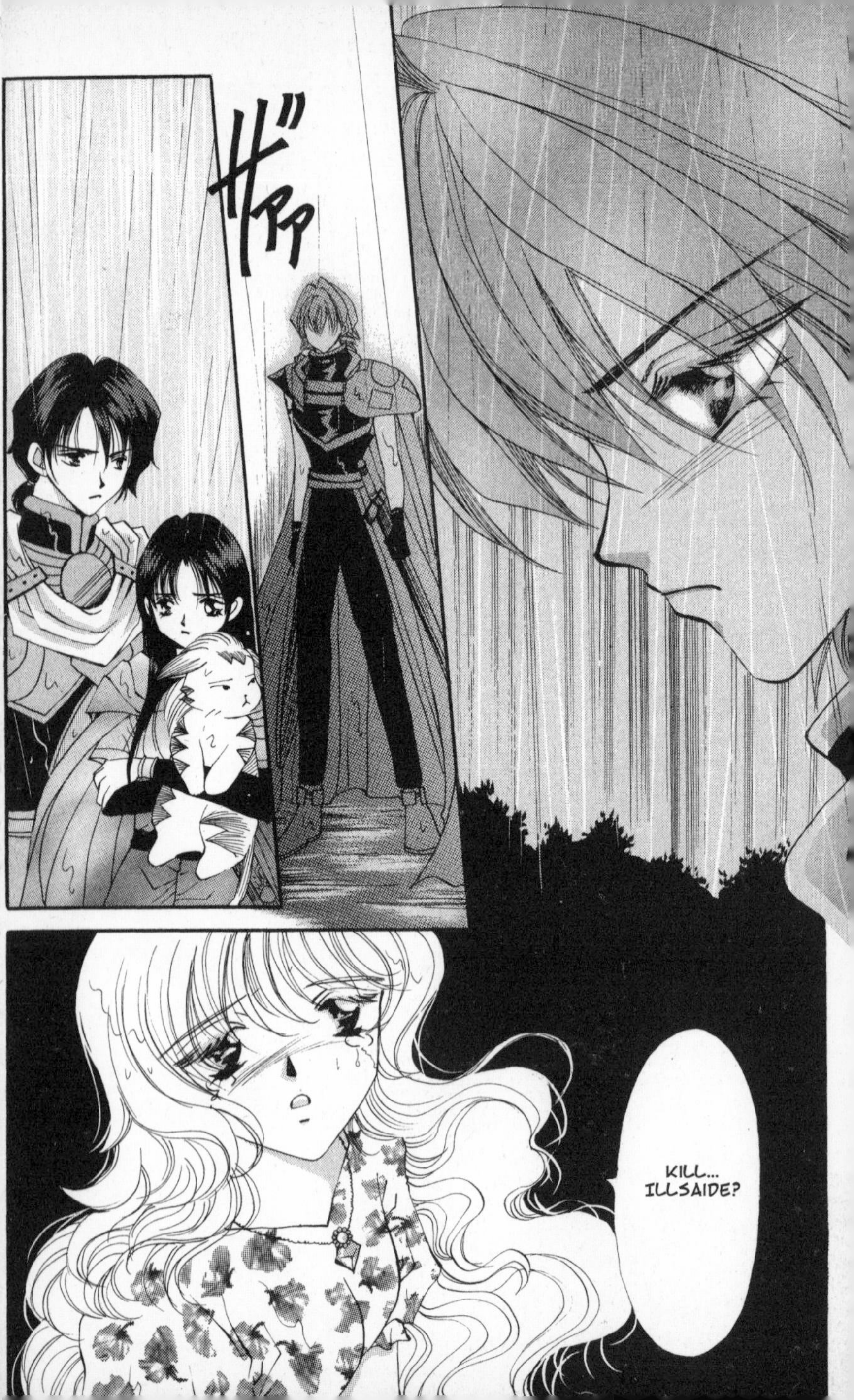
ザァァ
KILL... ILLSAIDE?

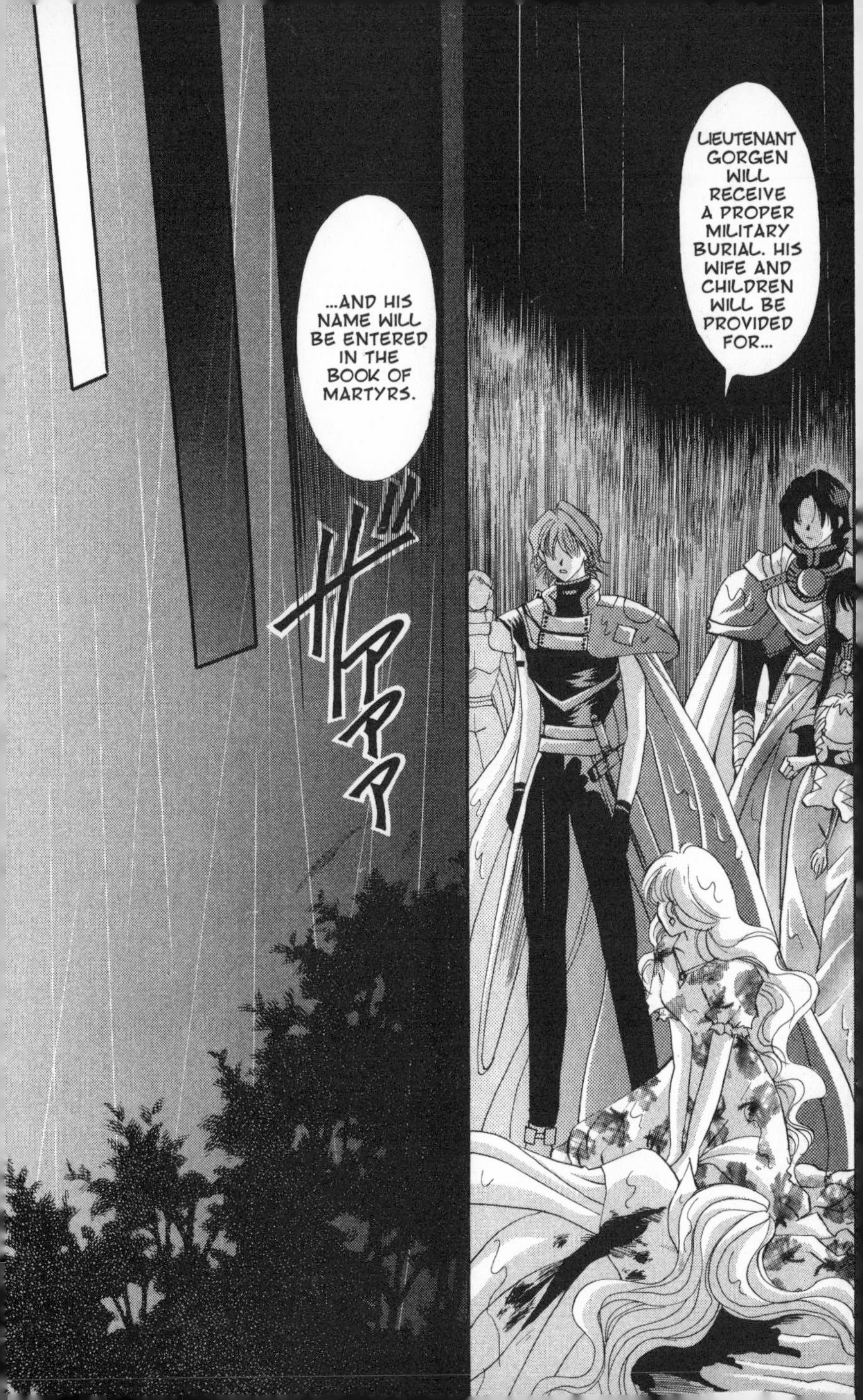
LIEUTENANT GORGEN WILL RECEIVE A PROPER MILITARY BURIAL. HIS WIFE AND CHILDREN WILL BE PROVIDED FOR...
...AND HIS NAME WILL BE ENTERED IN THE BOOK OF MARTYRS.

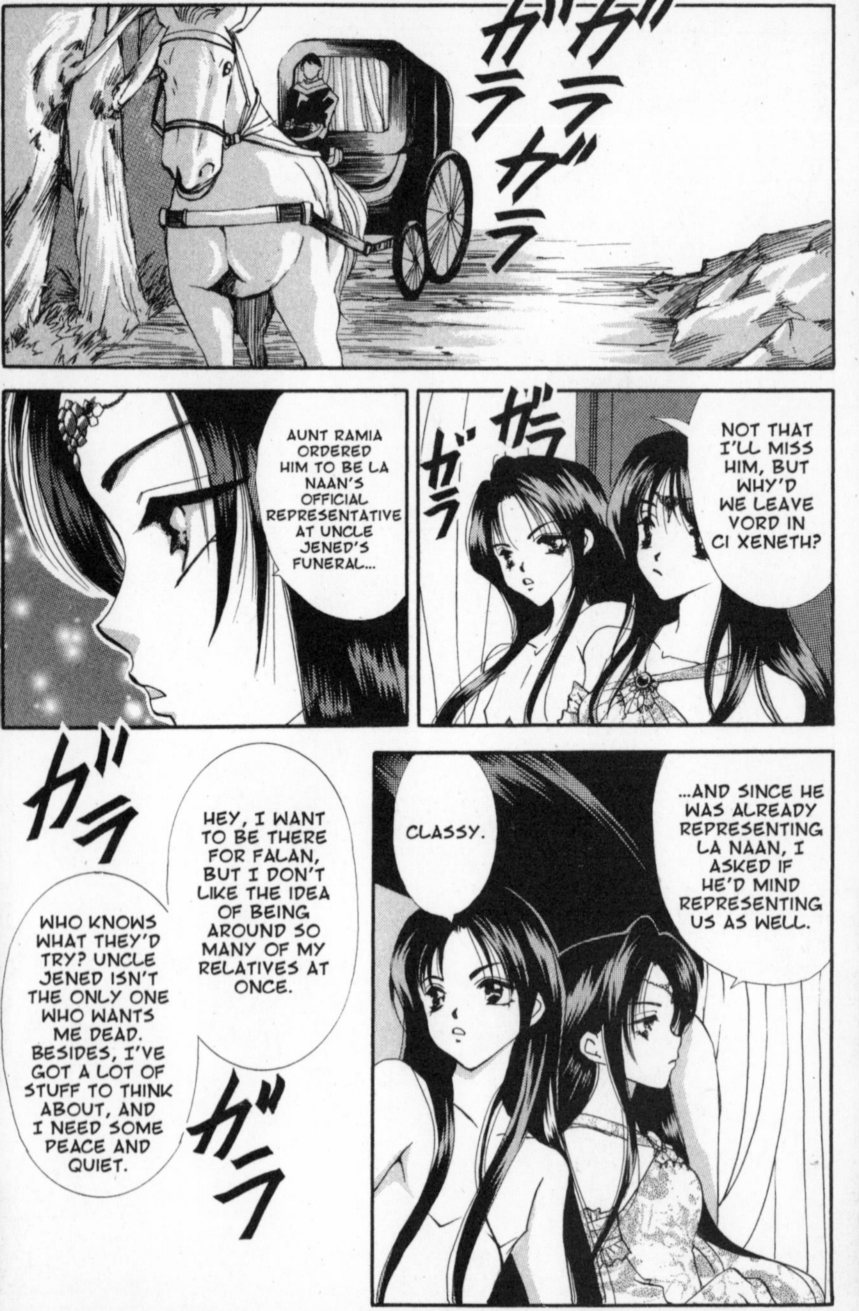
ガラガラ
ガラ
ガラ
ガラ
NOT THAT I'LL MISS HIM, BUT WHY'D WE LEAVE VORD IN CI XENETH?
AUNT RAMIA ORDERED HIM TO BE LA NAAN'S OFFICIAL REPRESENTATIVE AT UNCLE JENED'S FUNERAL...
...AND SINCE HE WAS ALREADY REPRESENTING LA NAAN, I ASKED IF HE'D MIND REPRESENTING US AS WELL.
CLASSY.
ガラ
HEY, I WANT TO BE THERE FOR FALAN, BUT I DON'T LIKE THE IDEA OF BEING AROUND SO MANY OF MY RELATIVES AT ONCE.
WHO KNOWS WHAT THEY'D TRY? UNCLE JENED ISN'T THE ONLY ONE WHO WANTS ME DEAD. BESIDES, I'VE GOT A LOT OF STUFF TO THINK ABOUT, AND I NEED SOME PEACE AND QUIET.
ガラ

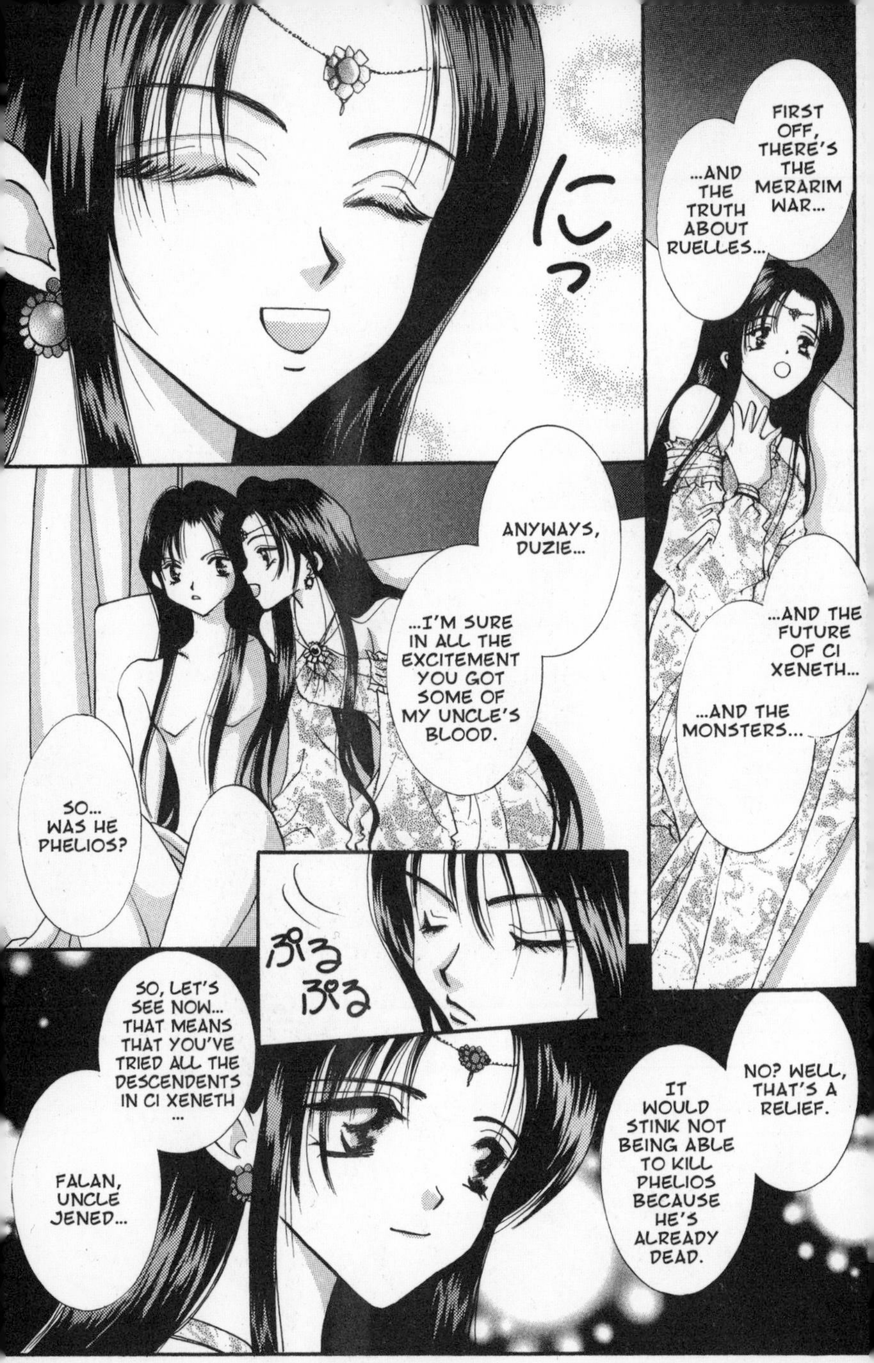
FIRST OFF, THERE'S THE MERARIM WAR...
...AND THE TRUTH ABOUT RUELLES...
...AND THE FUTURE OF CI XENETH...
...AND THE MONSTERS...
にっ
ANYWAYS, DUZIE...
...I'M SURE IN ALL THE EXCITEMENT YOU GOT SOME OF MY UNCLE'S BLOOD.
SO... WAS HE PHELIOS?
ぷるぷる
NO? WELL, THAT'S A RELIEF.
IT WOULD STINK NOT BEING ABLE TO KILL PHELIOS BECAUSE HE'S ALREADY DEAD.
SO, LET'S SEE NOW... THAT MEANS THAT YOU'VE TRIED ALL THE DESCENDENTS IN CI XENETH ...
FALAN, UNCLE JENED...

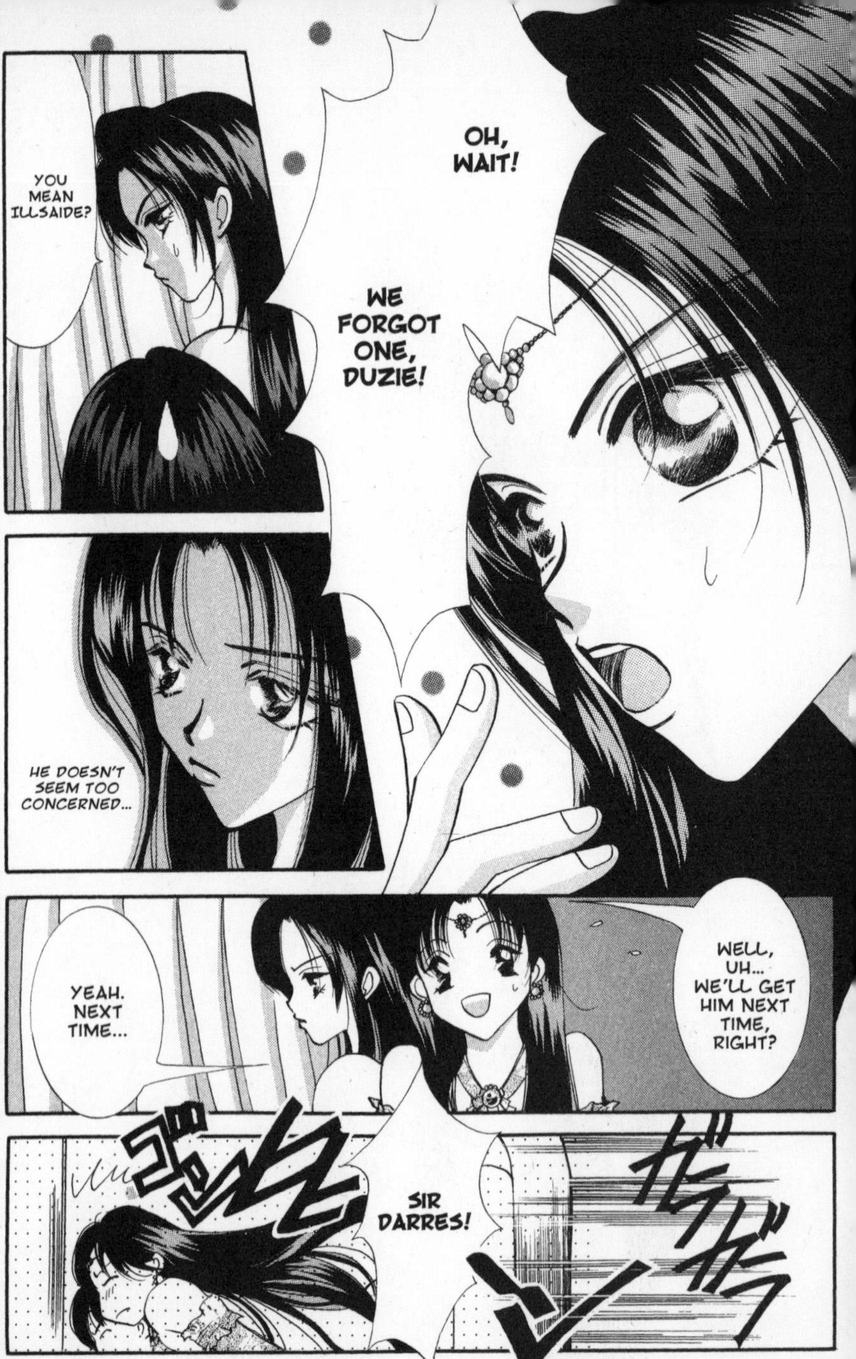
OH, WAIT!
WE FORGOT ONE, DUZIE!
YOU MEAN ILLSAIDE?
HE DOESN'T SEEM TOO CONCERNED...
WELL, UH... WE'LL GET HIM NEXT TIME, RIGHT?
YEAH. NEXT TIME...
SIR DARRES!

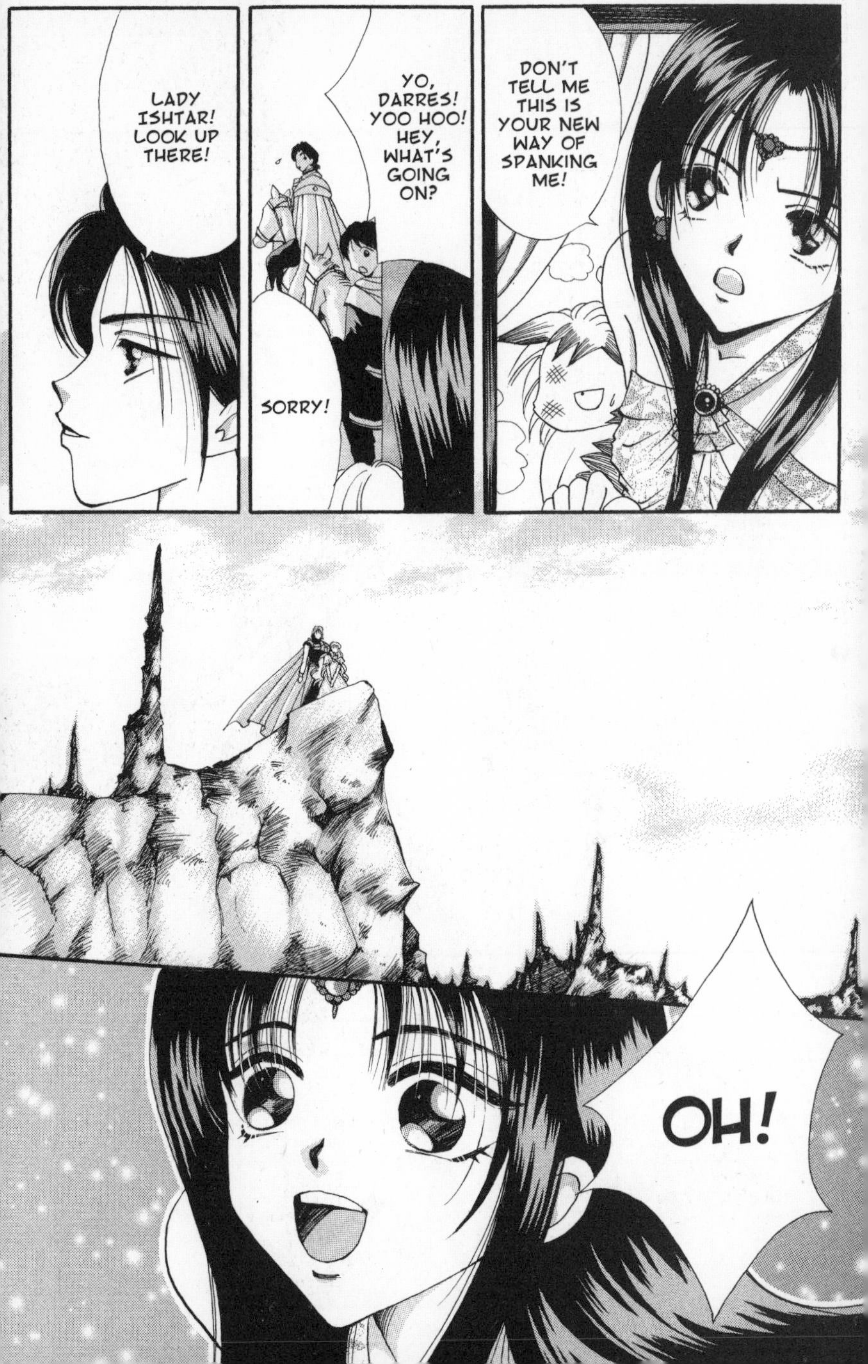
DON'T TELL ME THIS IS YOUR NEW WAY OF SPANKING ME!
YO, DARRES! YOO HOO! HEY, WHAT'S GOING ON?
SORRY!
LADY ISHTAR! LOOK UP THERE!
OH!

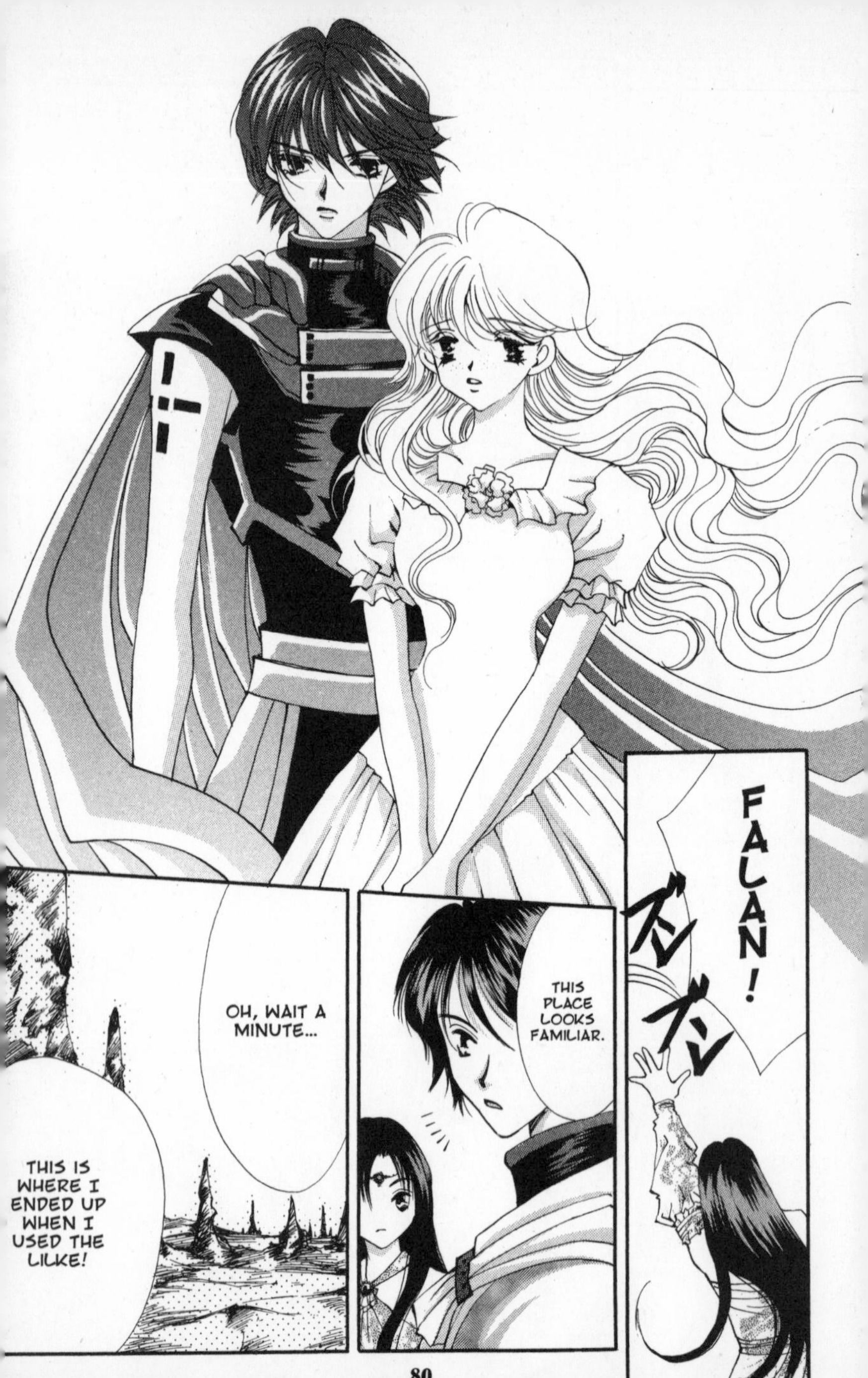
FALAN!
THIS PLACE LOOKS FAMILIAR.
OH, WAIT A MINUTE...
THIS IS WHERE I ENDED UP WHEN I USED THE LILKE!

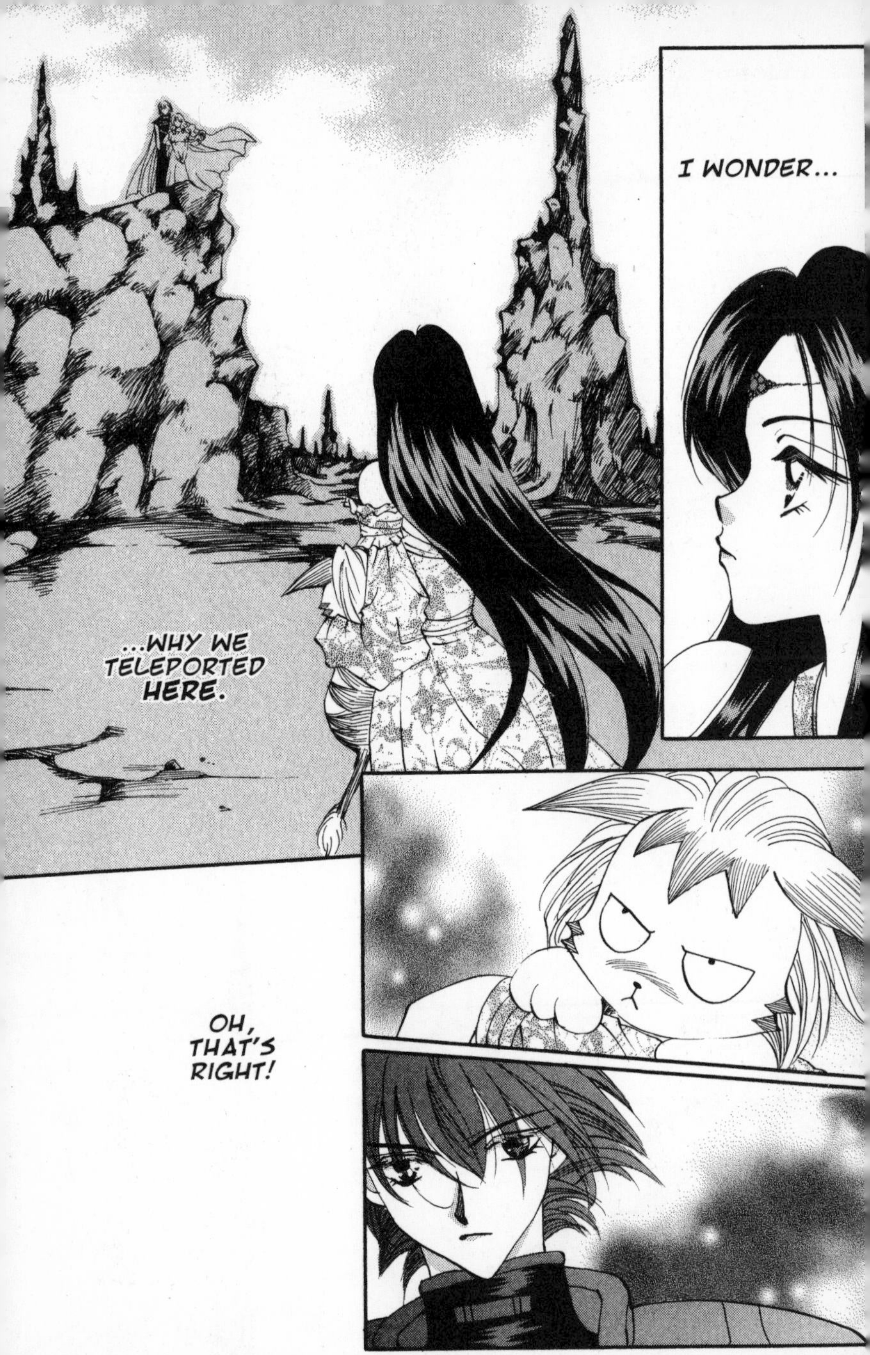
I WONDER...
...WHY WE TELEPORTED HERE.
OH, THAT'S RIGHT!

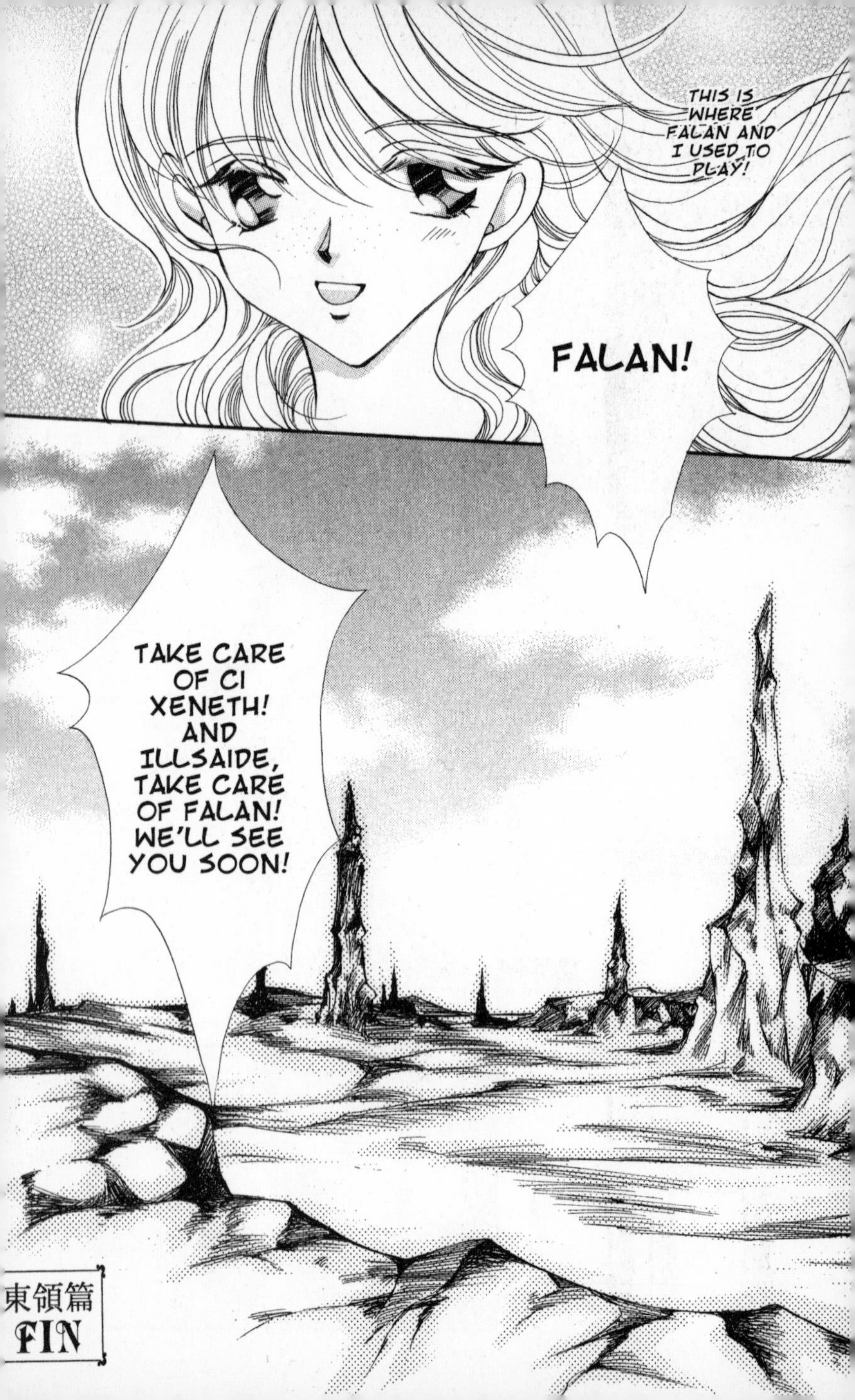
THIS IS WHERE FALAN AND I USED TO PLAY!
FALAN!
TAKE CARE OF CI XENETH! AND ILLSAIDE, TAKE CARE OF FALAN! WE'LL SEE YOU SOON!
東領篇
FIN

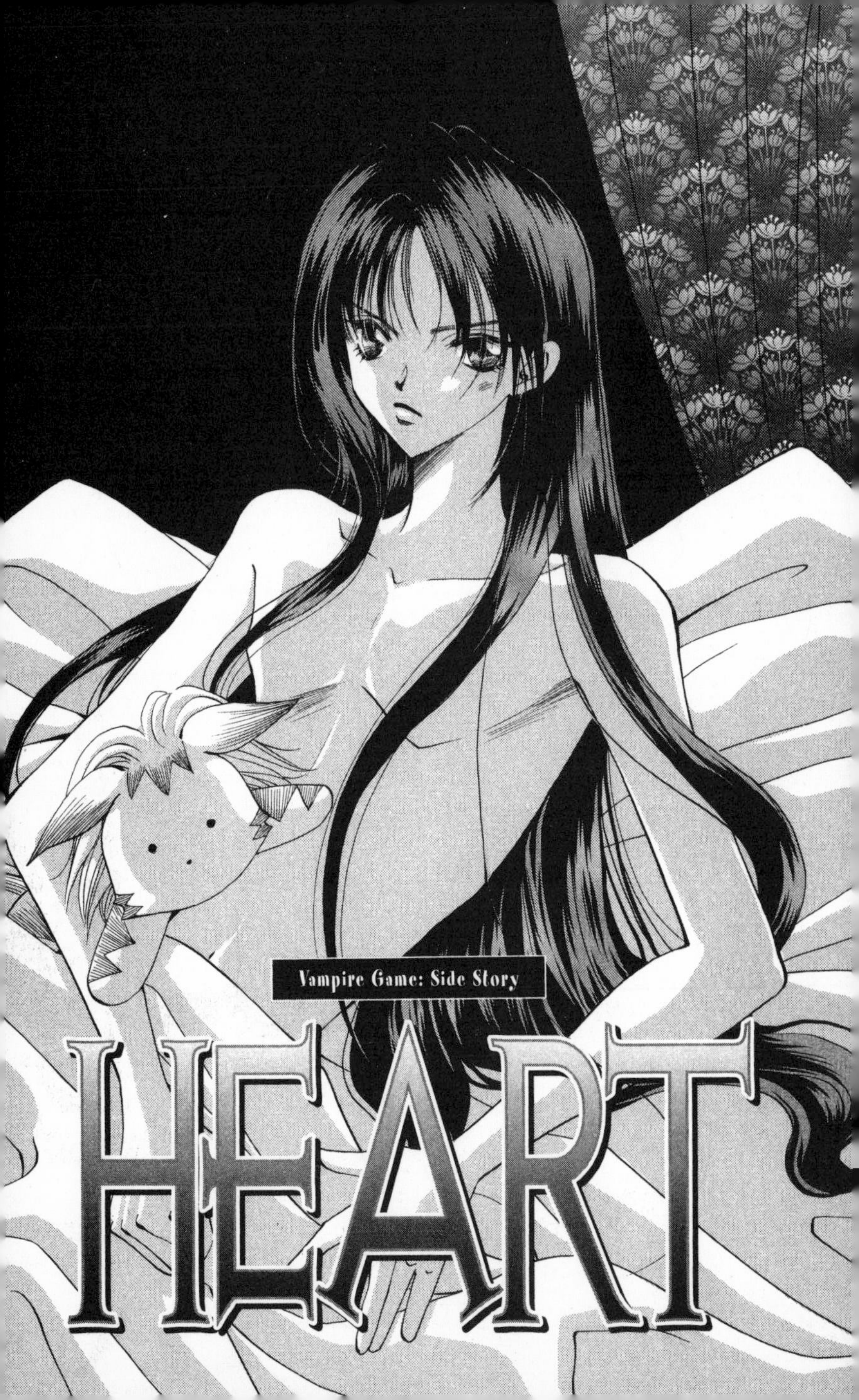
Vampire Game: Side Story
HEART

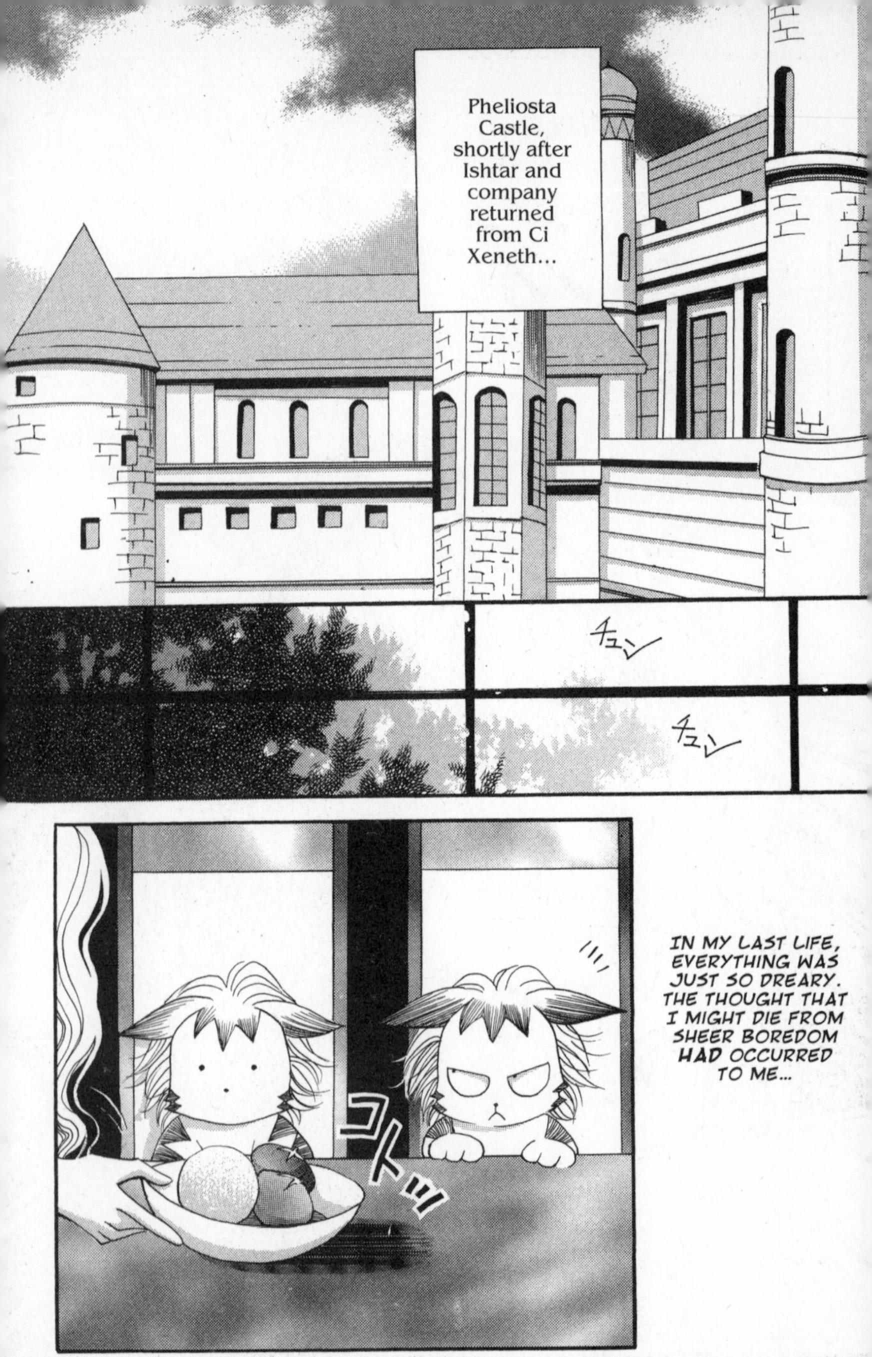
Pheliosta Castle, shortly after Ishtar and company returned from Ci Xeneth...
チュン
チュン
IN MY LAST LIFE, EVERYTHING WAS JUST SO DREARY. THE THOUGHT THAT I MIGHT DIE FROM SHEER BOREDOM HAD OCCURRED TO ME...
コトッ

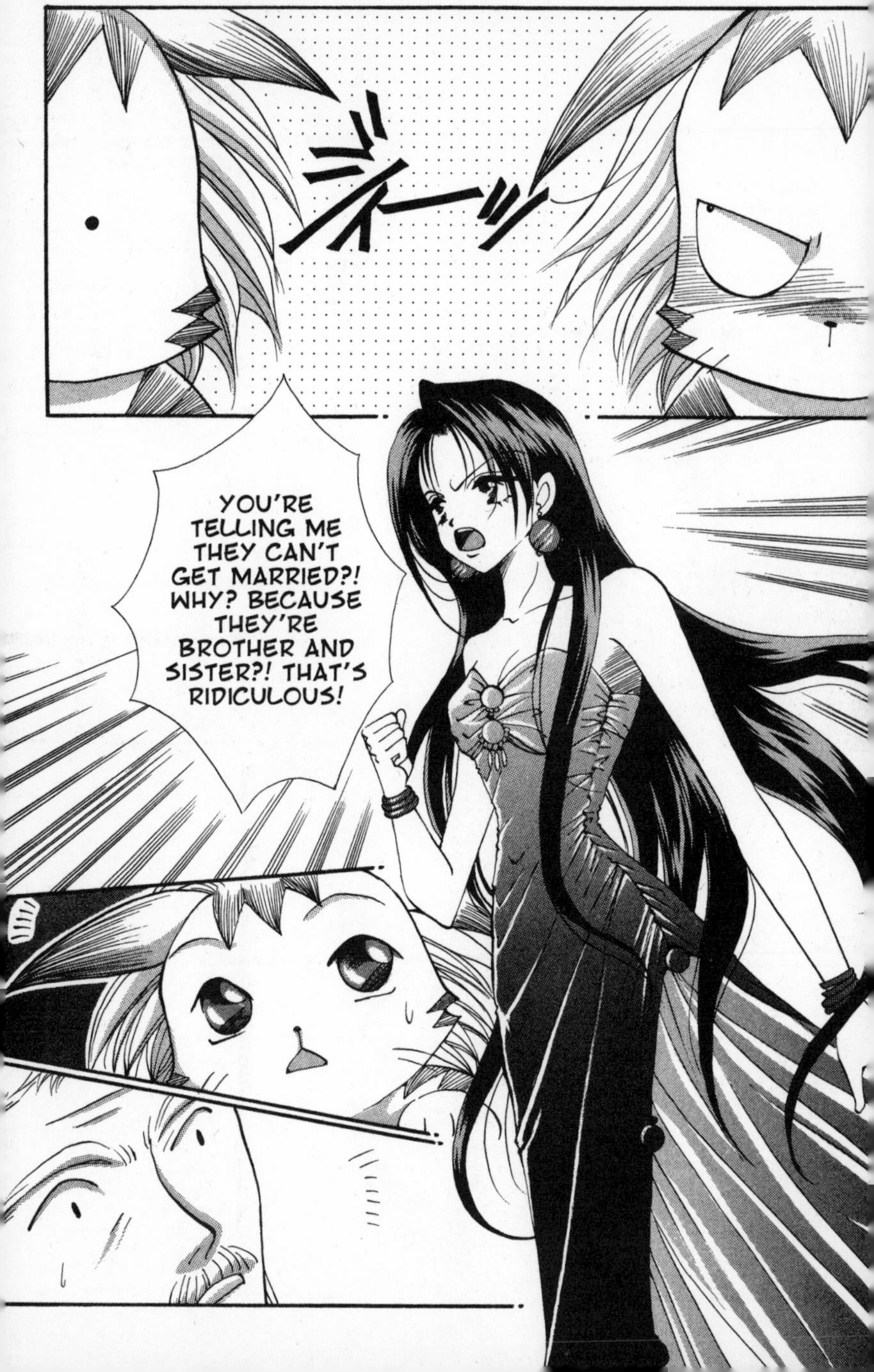
ジーッ
YOU'RE TELLING ME THEY CAN'T GET MARRIED?! WHY? BECAUSE THEY'RE BROTHER AND SISTER?! THAT'S RIDICULOUS!

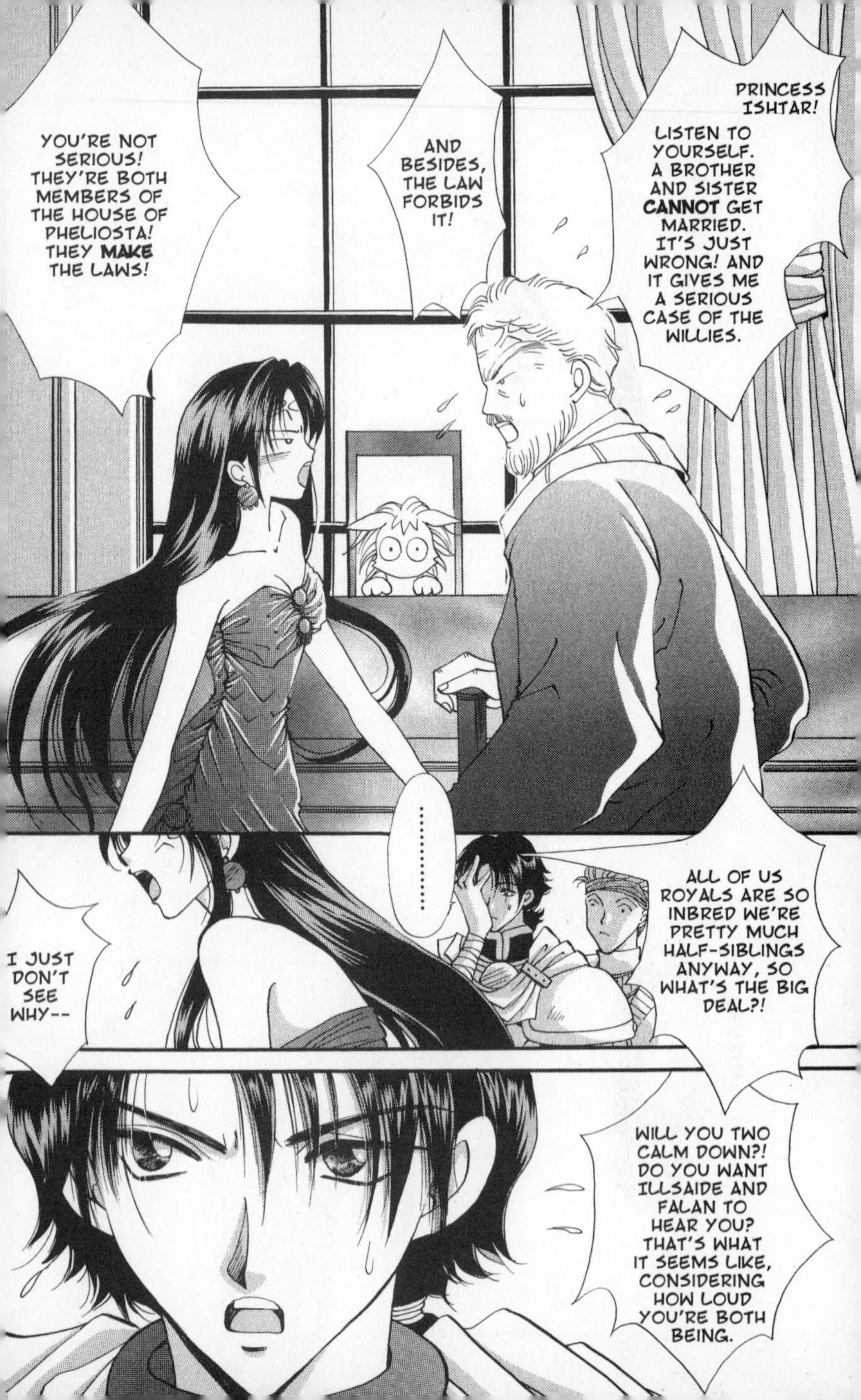
PRINCESS ISHTAR!
LISTEN TO YOURSELF. A BROTHER AND SISTER **CANNOT** GET MARRIED. IT'S JUST WRONG! AND IT GIVES ME A SERIOUS CASE OF THE WILLIES.
AND BESIDES, THE LAW FORBIDS IT!
YOU'RE NOT SERIOUS! THEY'RE BOTH MEMBERS OF THE HOUSE OF PHELIOSTA! THEY **MAKE** THE LAWS!
ALL OF US ROYALS ARE SO INBRED WE'RE PRETTY MUCH HALF-SIBLINGS ANYWAY, SO WHAT'S THE BIG DEAL?!
......
I JUST DON'T SEE WHY--
WILL YOU TWO CALM DOWN?! DO YOU WANT ILLSAIDE AND FALAN TO HEAR YOU? THAT'S WHAT IT SEEMS LIKE, CONSIDERING HOW LOUD YOU'RE BOTH BEING.

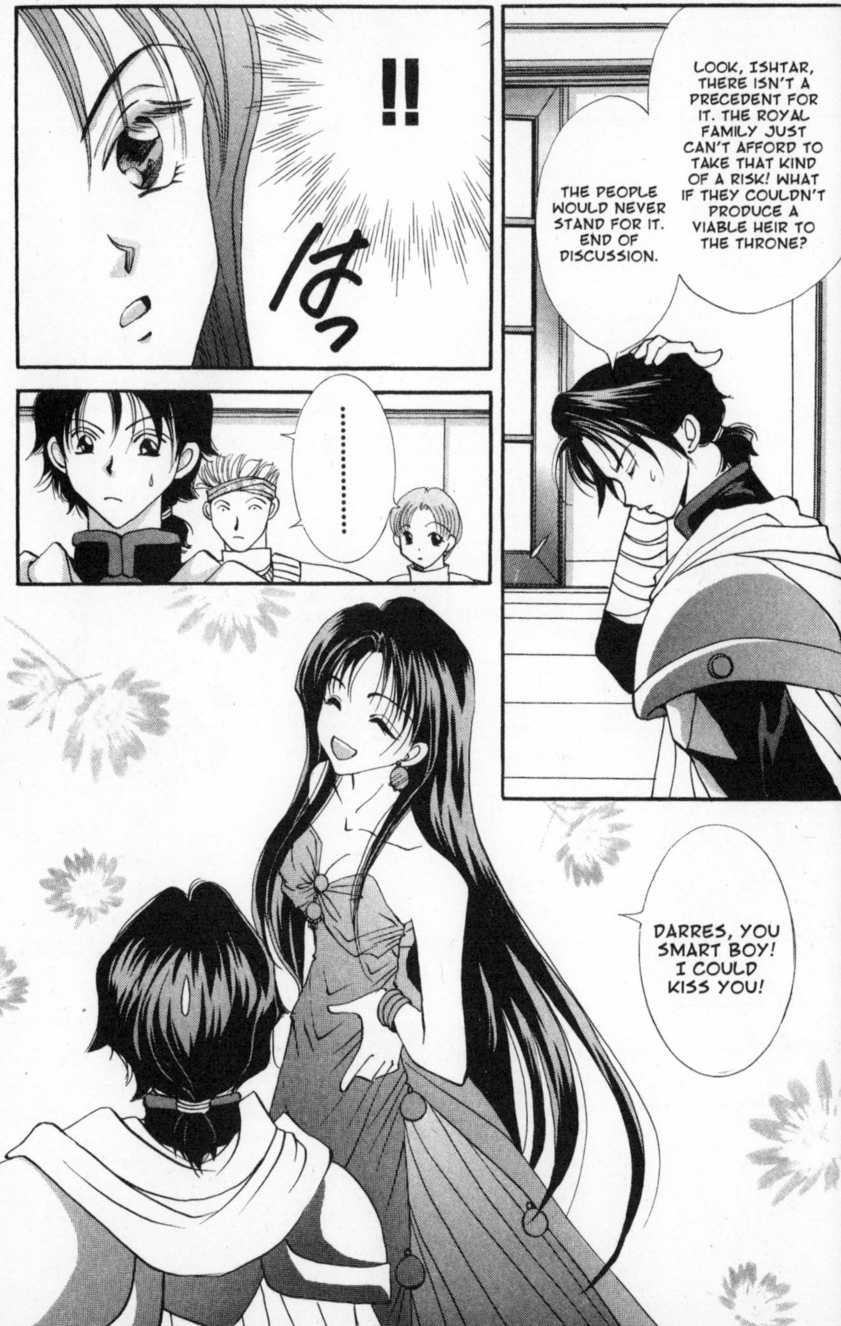
LOOK, ISHTAR, THERE ISN'T A PRECEDENT FOR IT. THE ROYAL FAMILY JUST CAN'T AFFORD TO TAKE THAT KIND OF A RISK! WHAT IF THEY COULDN'T PRODUCE A VIABLE HEIR TO THE THRONE?
THE PEOPLE WOULD NEVER STAND FOR IT. END OF DISCUSSION.
!!
はっ
....
DARRES, YOU SMART BOY! I COULD KISS YOU!

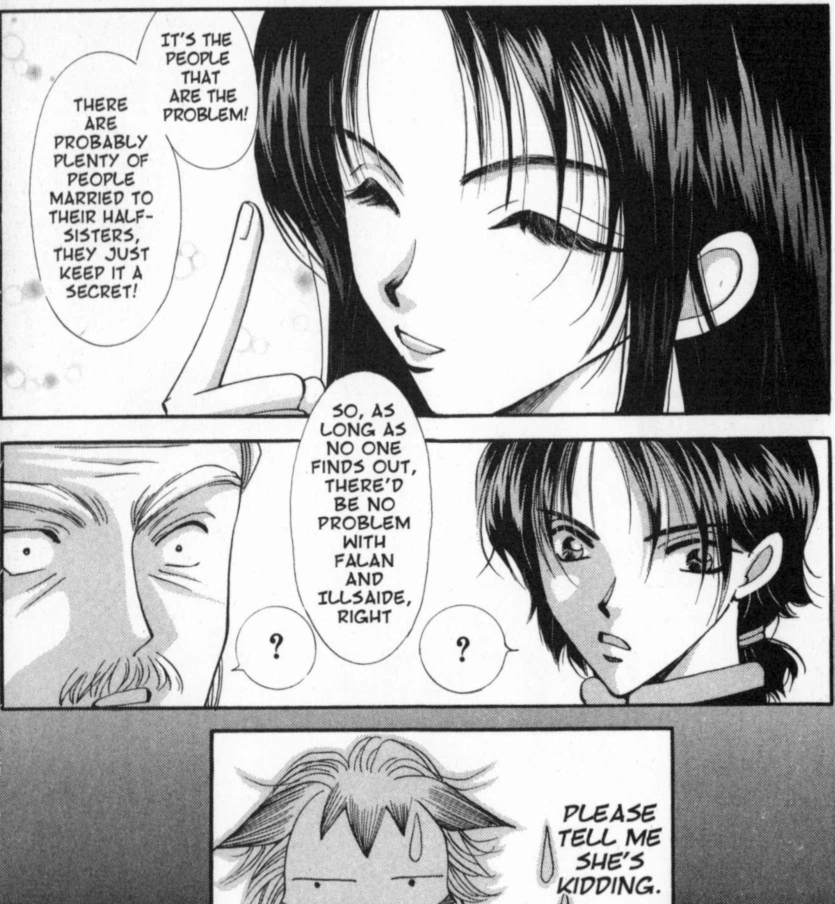
IT'S THE PEOPLE THAT ARE THE PROBLEM!
THERE ARE PROBABLY PLENTY OF PEOPLE MARRIED TO THEIR HALF-SISTERS, THEY JUST KEEP IT A SECRET!
SO, AS LONG AS NO ONE FINDS OUT, THERE'D BE NO PROBLEM WITH FALAN AND ILLSAIDE, RIGHT
?
?
PLEASE TELL ME SHE'S KIDDING.

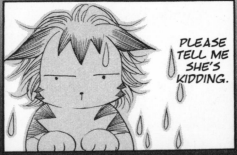

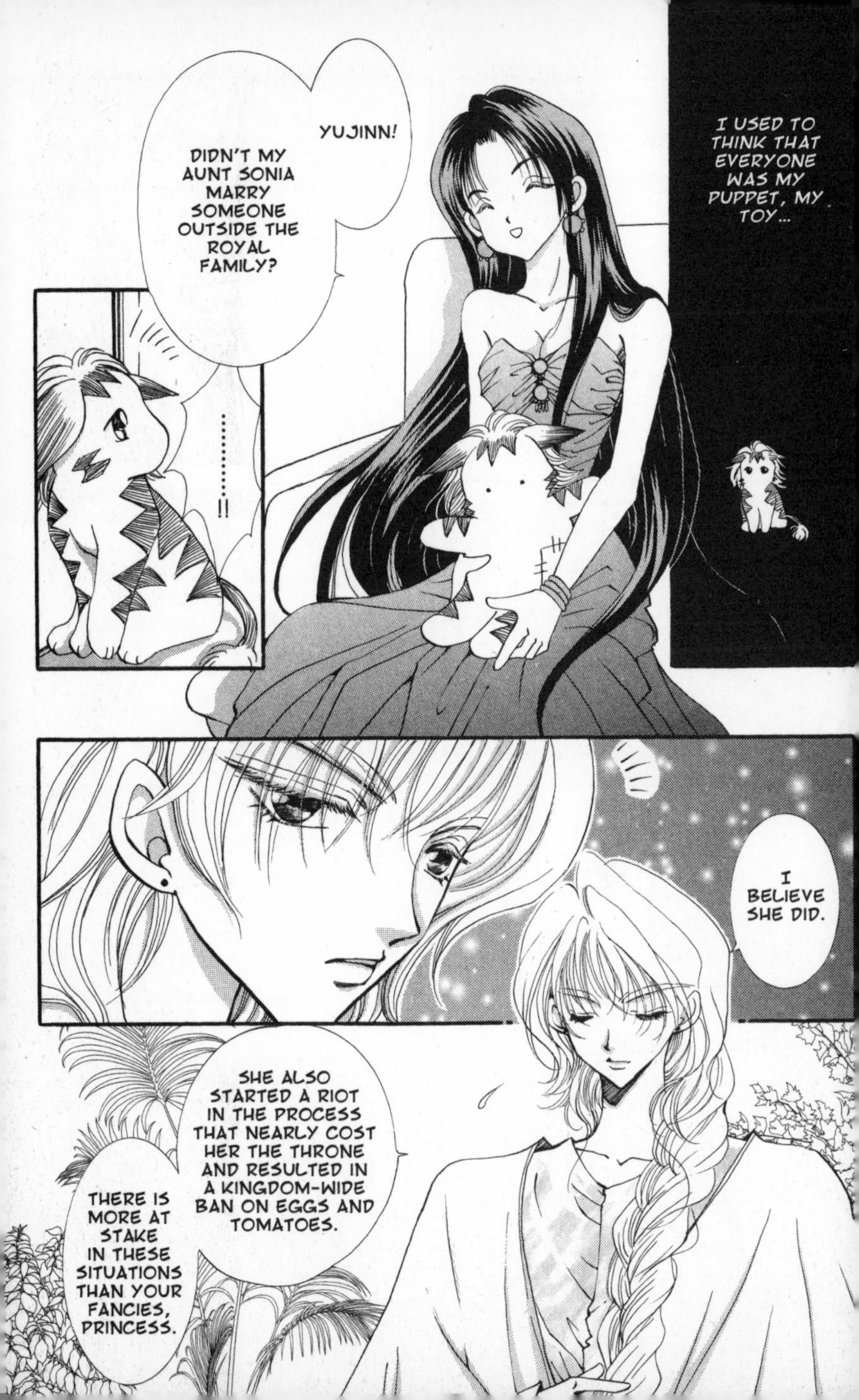

I USED TO THINK THAT EVERYONE WAS MY PUPPET, MY TOY...
YUJINN!
DIDN'T MY AUNT SONIA MARRY SOMEONE OUTSIDE THE ROYAL FAMILY?
........!!
I BELIEVE SHE DID.
SHE ALSO STARTED A RIOT IN THE PROCESS THAT NEARLY COST HER THE THRONE AND RESULTED IN A KINGDOM-WIDE BAN ON EGGS AND TOMATOES.
THERE IS MORE AT STAKE IN THESE SITUATIONS THAN YOUR FANCIES, PRINCESS.

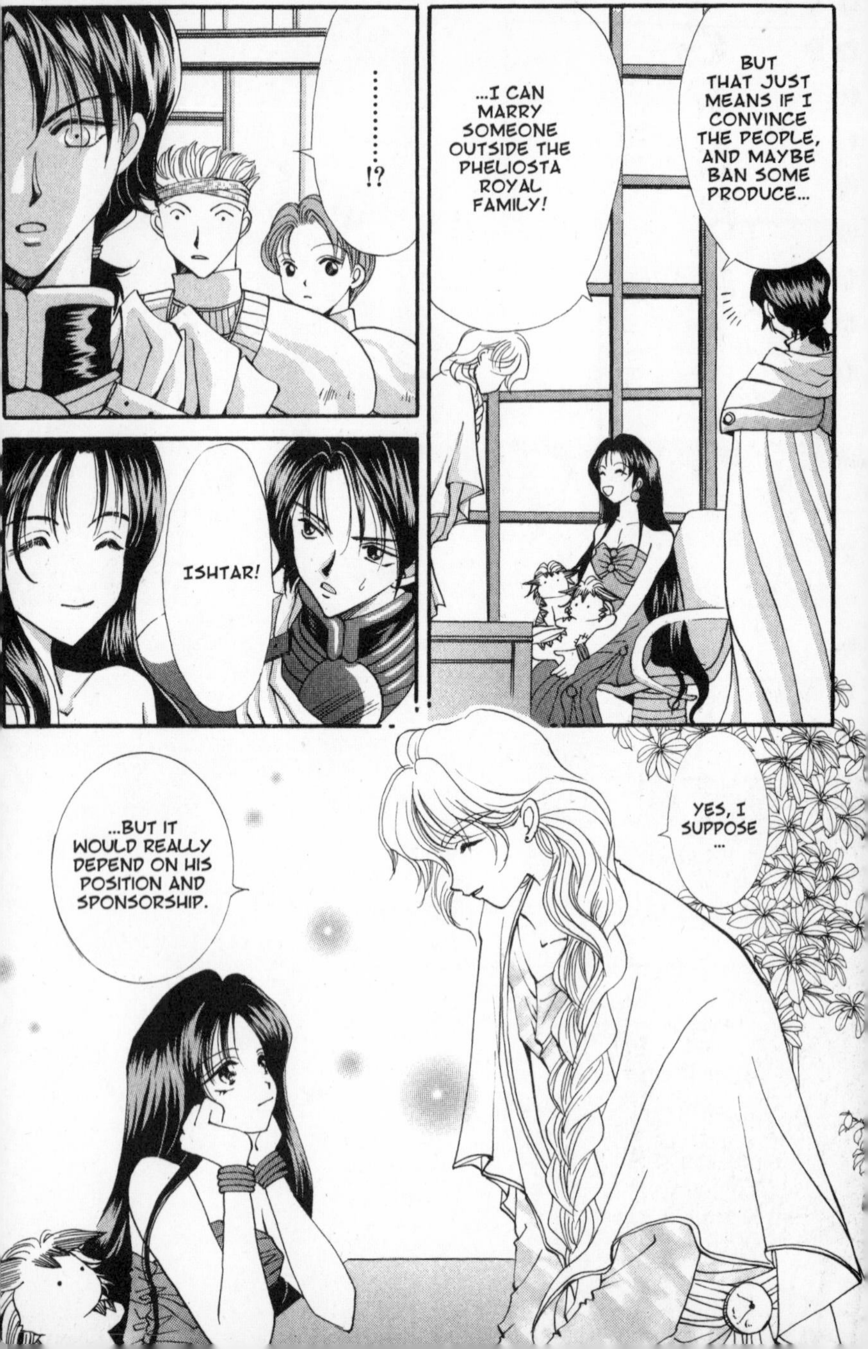
BUT THAT JUST MEANS IF I CONVINCE THE PEOPLE, AND MAYBE BAN SOME PRODUCE...
...I CAN MARRY SOMEONE OUTSIDE THE PHELIOSTA ROYAL FAMILY!
.........!?
ISHTAR!
YES, I SUPPOSE...
...BUT IT WOULD REALLY DEPEND ON HIS POSITION AND SPONSORSHIP.

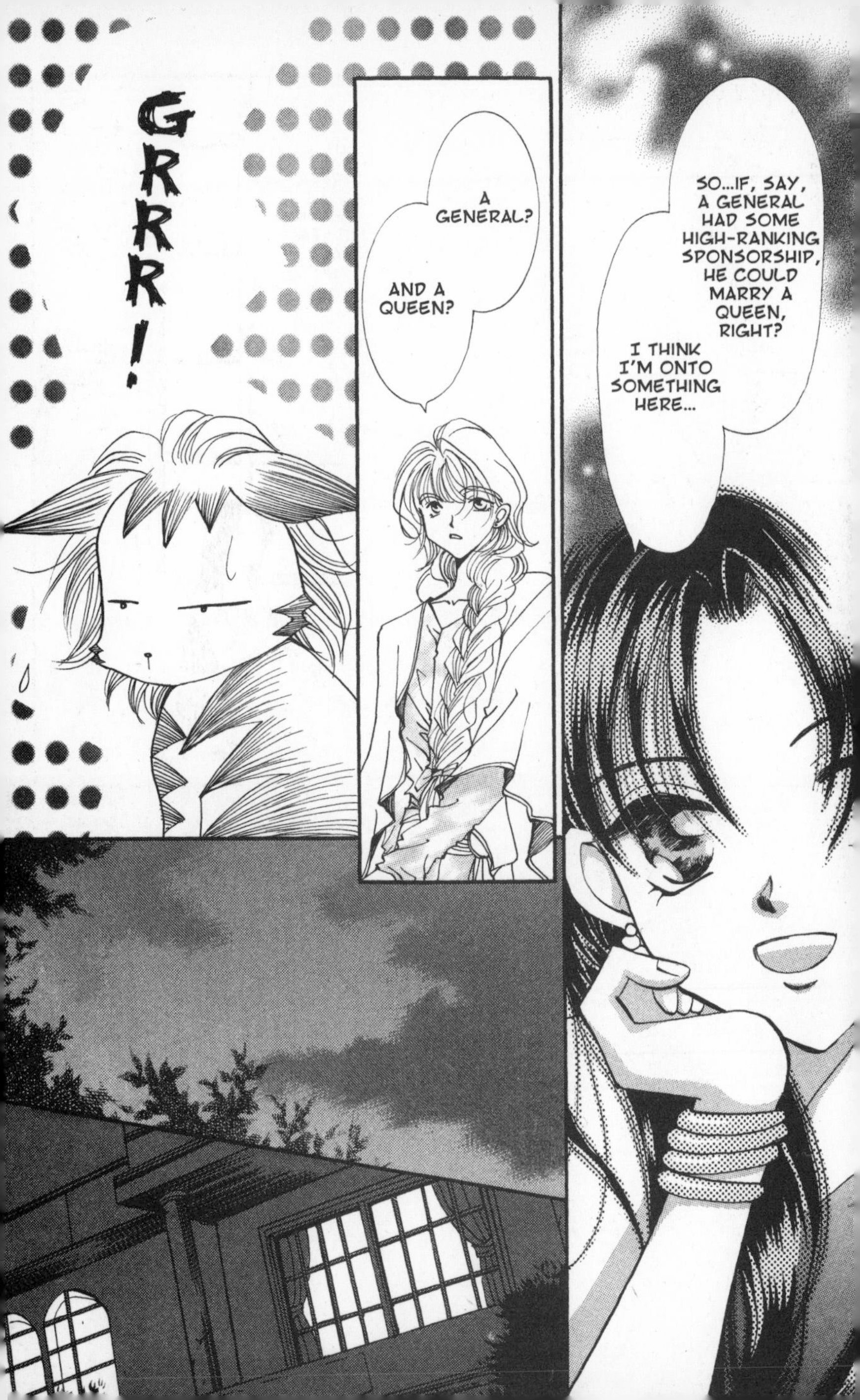
SO...IF, SAY, A GENERAL HAD SOME HIGH-RANKING SPONSORSHIP, HE COULD MARRY A QUEEN, RIGHT?
I THINK I'M ONTO SOMETHING HERE...
A GENERAL?
AND A QUEEN?
GRRR!

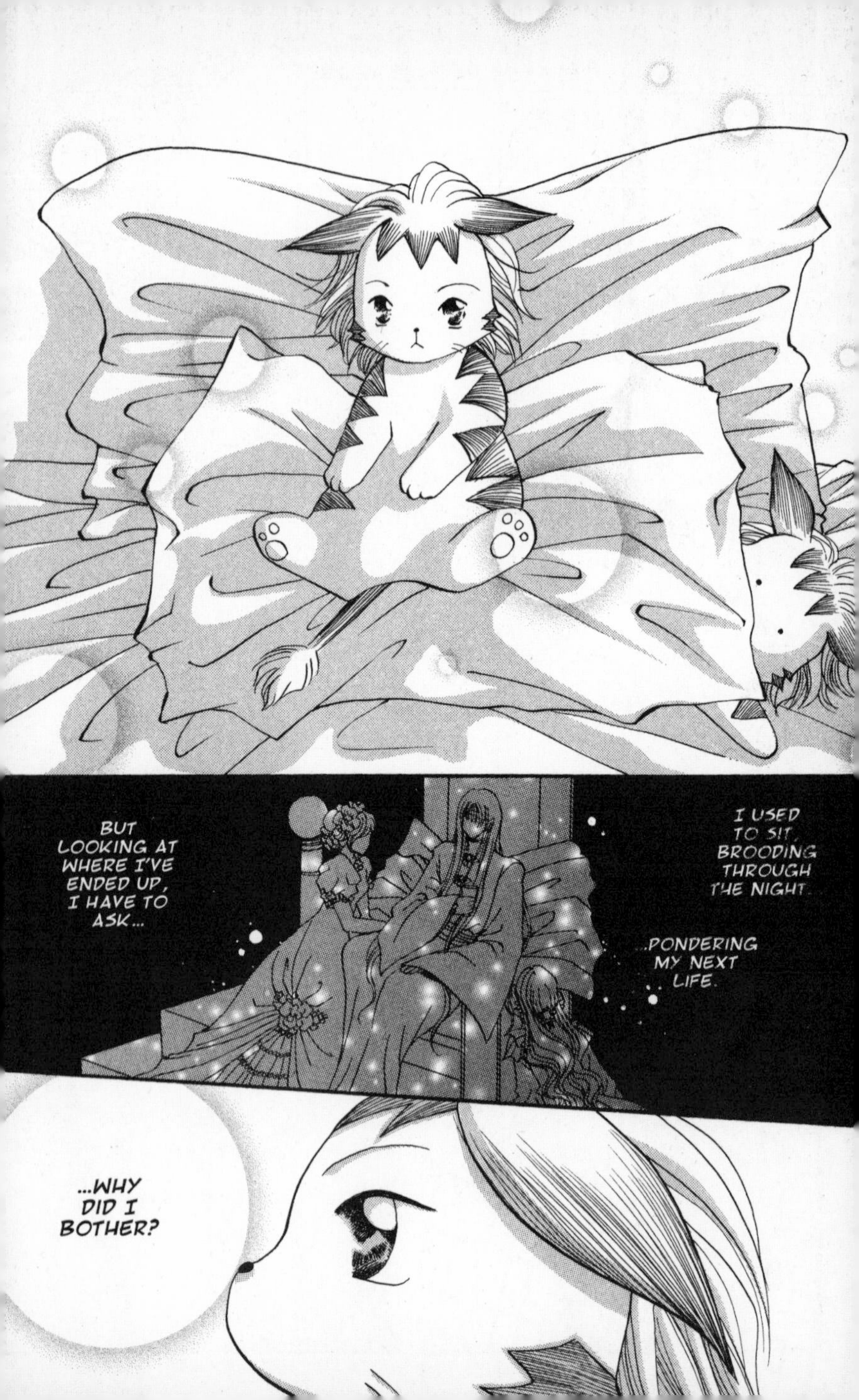
I USED TO SIT, BROODING THROUGH THE NIGHT...
...PONDERING MY NEXT LIFE.
BUT LOOKING AT WHERE I'VE ENDED UP, I HAVE TO ASK...
...WHY DID I BOTHER?

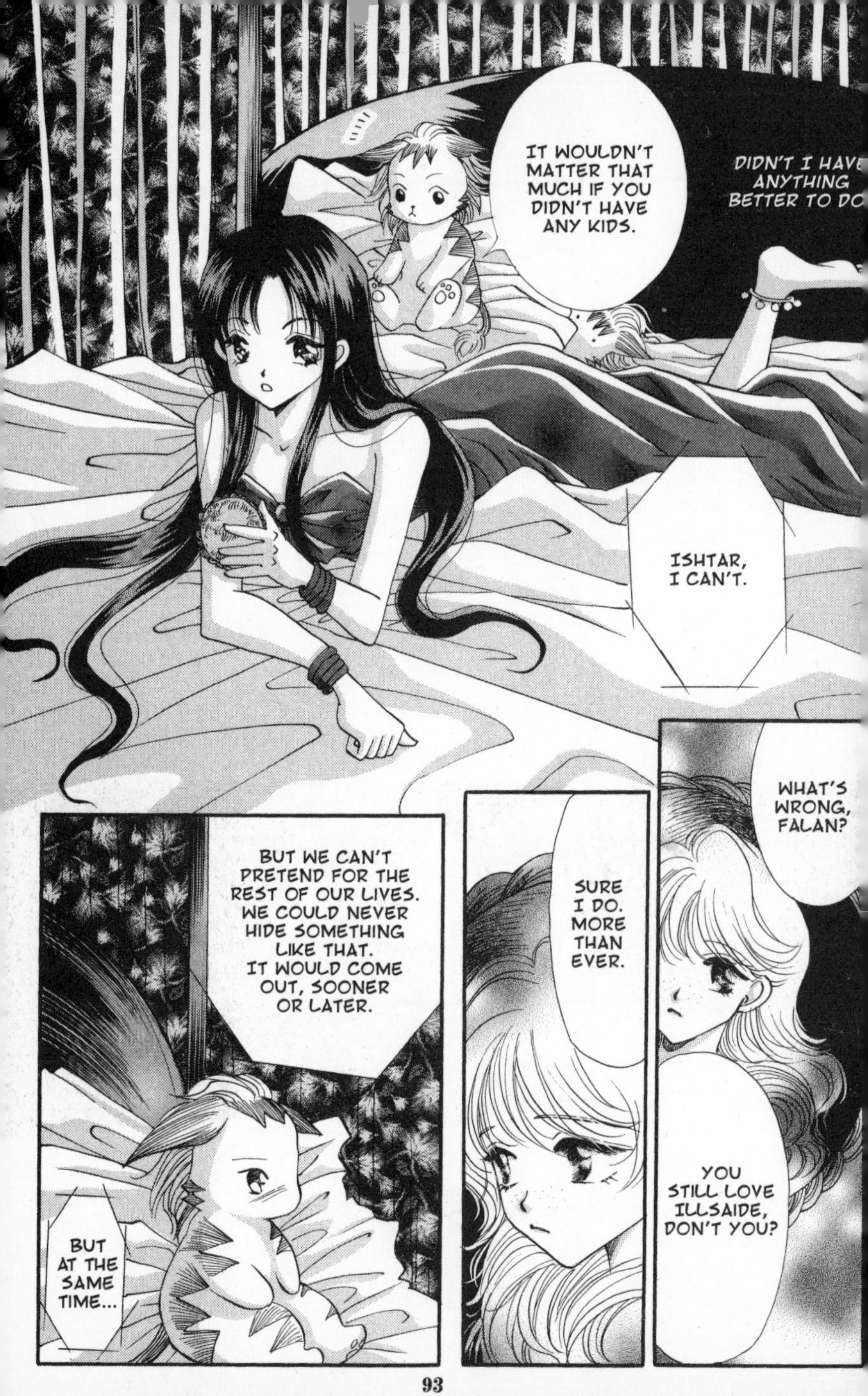

DIDN'T I HAVE ANYTHING BETTER TO DO
IT WOULDN'T MATTER THAT MUCH IF YOU DIDN'T HAVE ANY KIDS.
ISHTAR, I CAN'T.
WHAT'S WRONG, FALAN?
YOU STILL LOVE ILLSAIDE, DON'T YOU?
SURE I DO. MORE THAN EVER.
BUT WE CAN'T PRETEND FOR THE REST OF OUR LIVES. WE COULD NEVER HIDE SOMETHING LIKE THAT. IT WOULD COME OUT, SOONER OR LATER.
BUT AT THE SAME TIME...

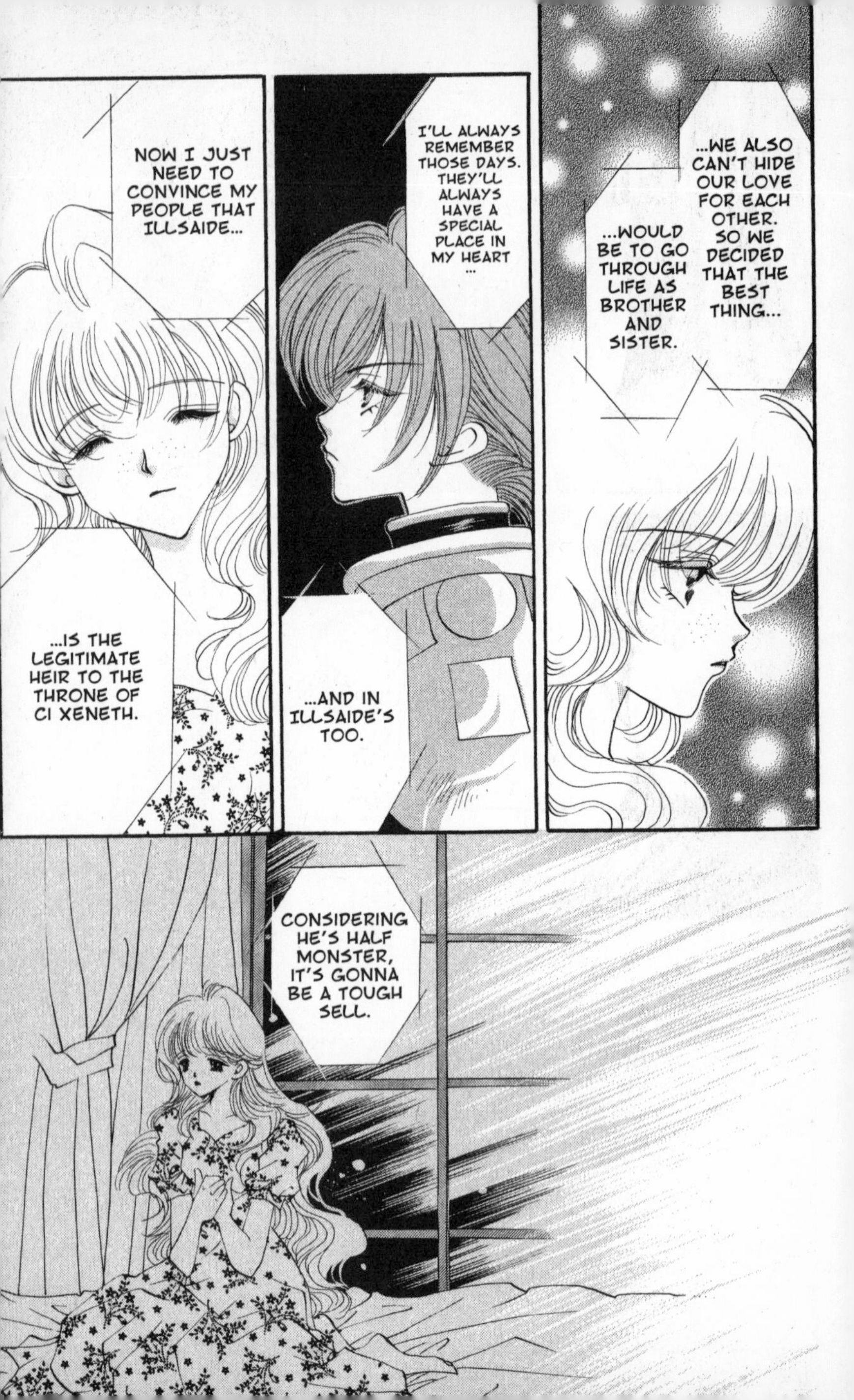
...WE ALSO CAN'T HIDE OUR LOVE FOR EACH OTHER. SO WE DECIDED THAT THE BEST THING...
...WOULD BE TO GO THROUGH LIFE AS BROTHER AND SISTER.
I'LL ALWAYS REMEMBER THOSE DAYS. THEY'LL ALWAYS HAVE A SPECIAL PLACE IN MY HEART ...
...AND IN ILLSAIDE'S TOO.
NOW I JUST NEED TO CONVINCE MY PEOPLE THAT ILLSAIDE...
...IS THE LEGITIMATE HEIR TO THE THRONE OF CI XENETH.
CONSIDERING HE'S HALF MONSTER, IT'S GONNA BE A TOUGH SELL.

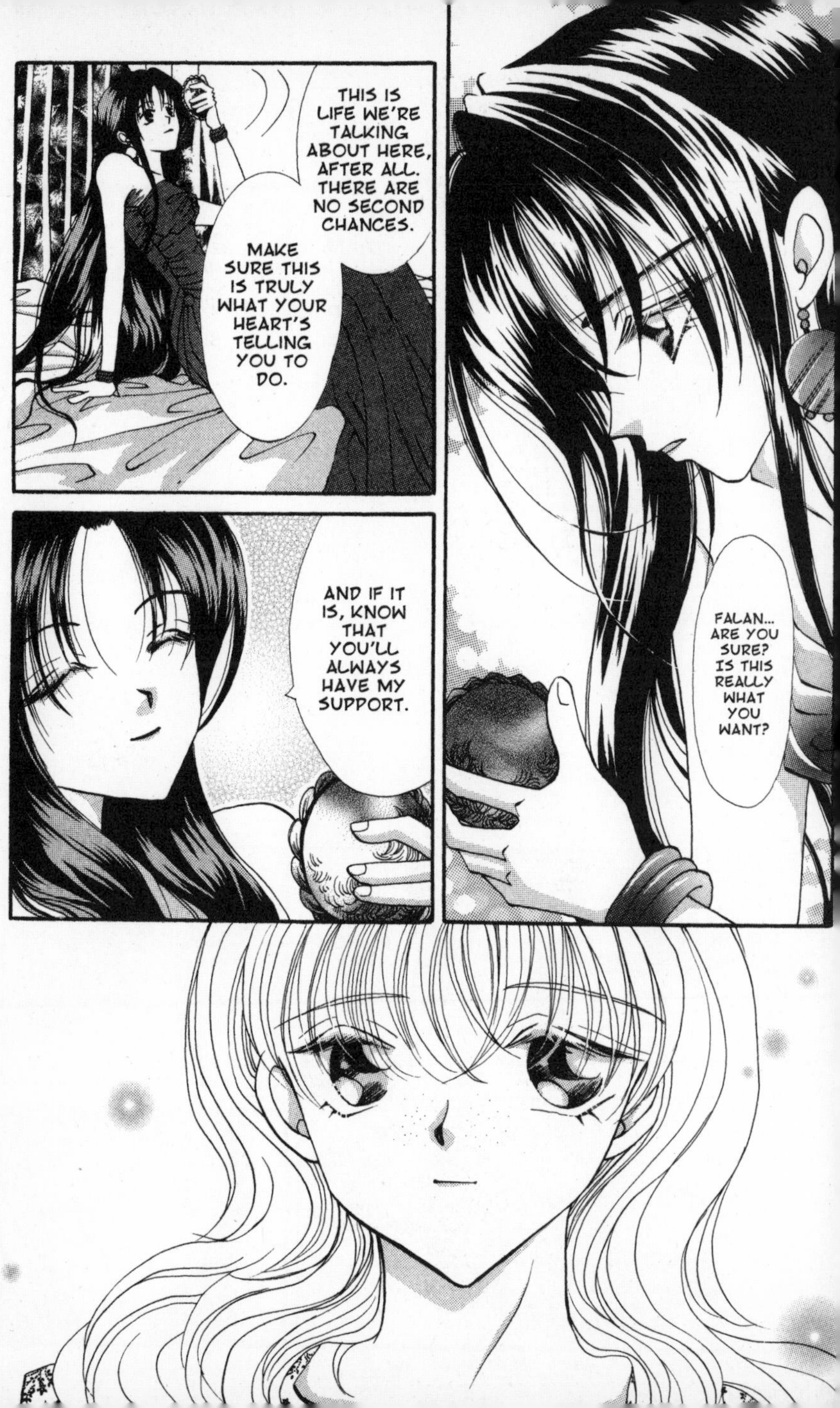
FALAN... ARE YOU SURE? IS THIS REALLY WHAT YOU WANT?
THIS IS LIFE WE'RE TALKING ABOUT HERE, AFTER ALL. THERE ARE NO SECOND CHANCES.
MAKE SURE THIS IS TRULY WHAT YOUR HEART'S TELLING YOU TO DO.
AND IF IT IS, KNOW THAT YOU'LL ALWAYS HAVE MY SUPPORT.

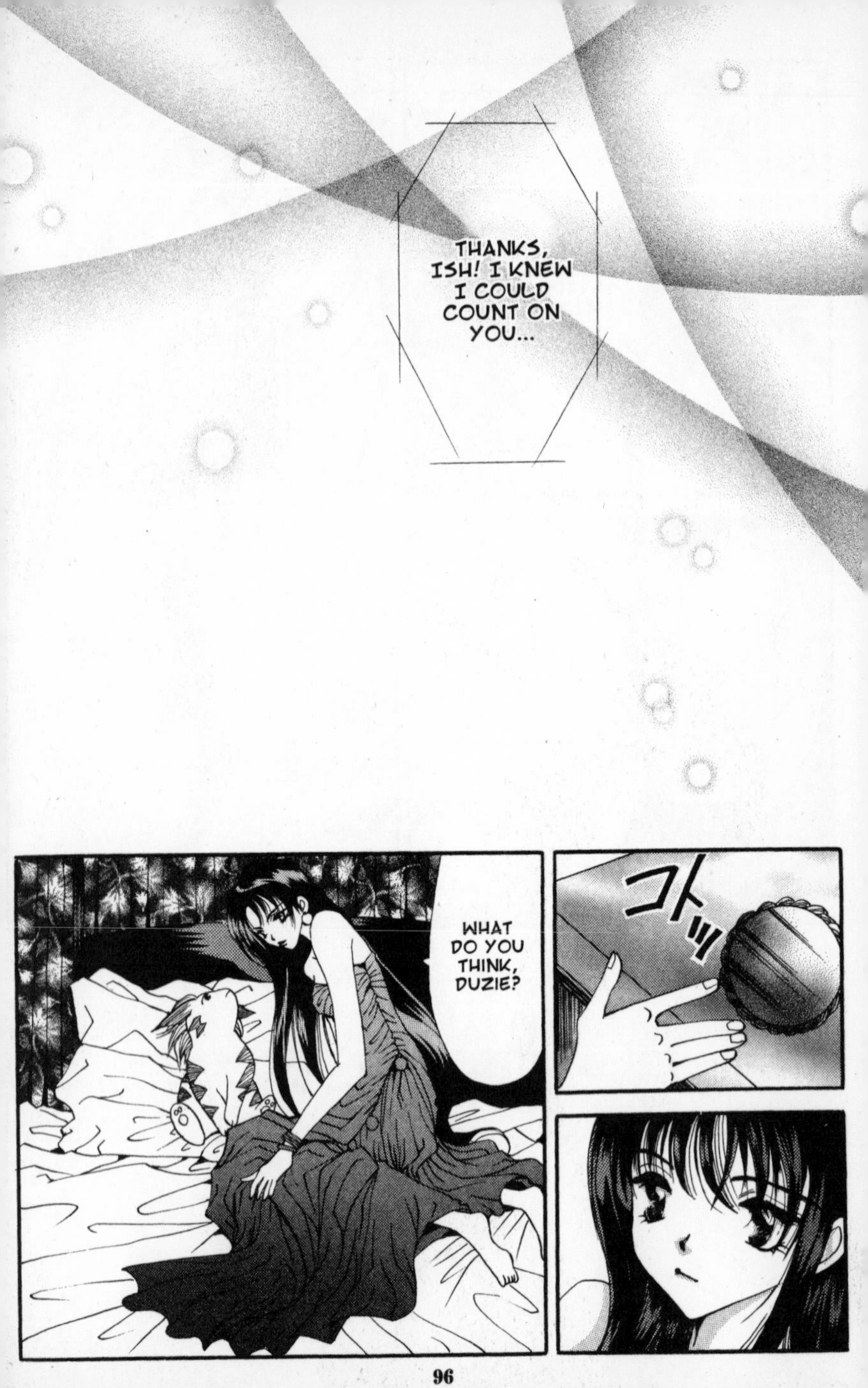
THANKS, ISH! I KNEW I COULD COUNT ON YOU...
コトッ
WHAT DO YOU THINK, DUZIE?

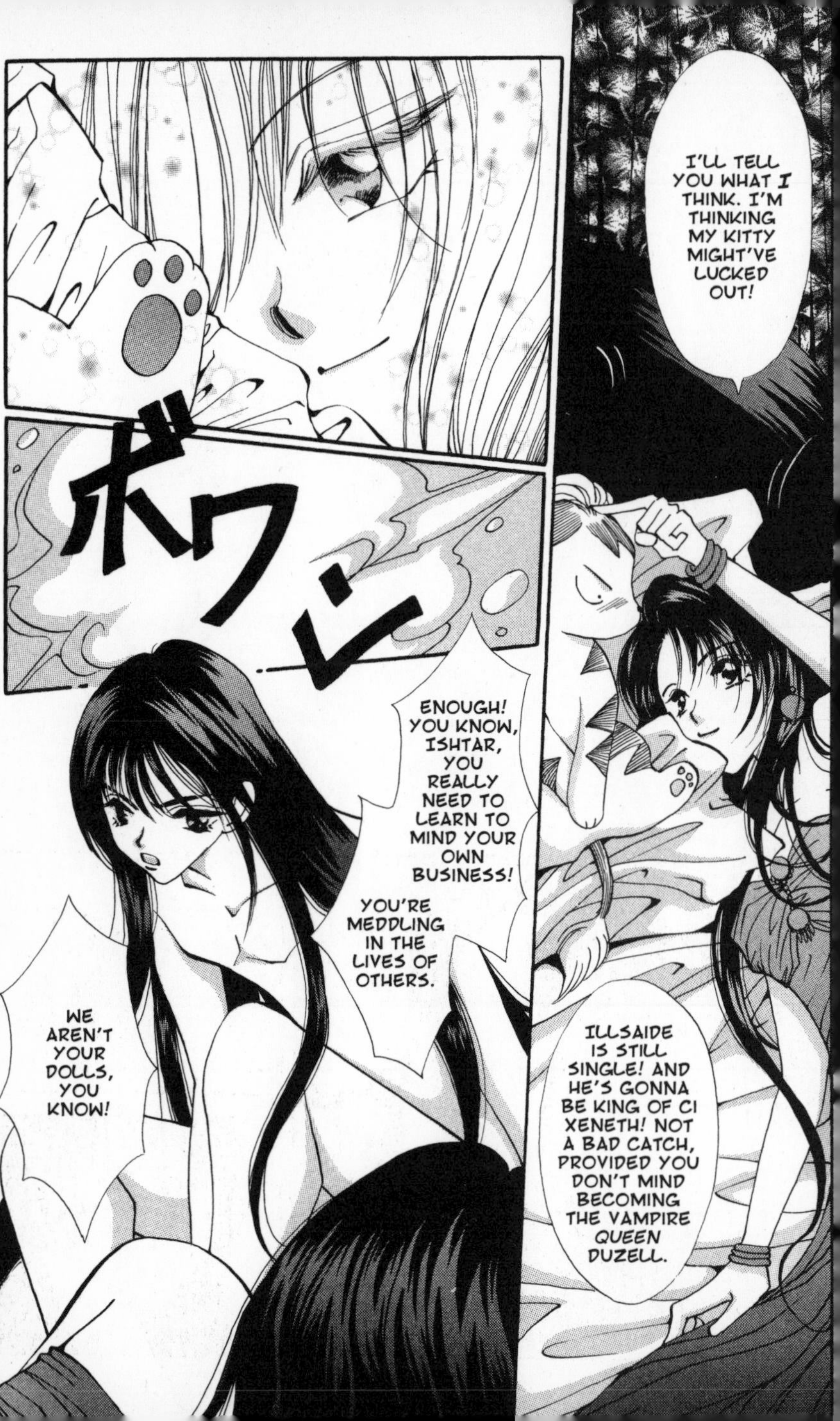
I'LL TELL YOU WHAT I THINK. I'M THINKING MY KITTY MIGHT'VE LUCKED OUT!
ILLSAIDE IS STILL SINGLE! AND HE'S GONNA BE KING OF CI XENETH! NOT A BAD CATCH, PROVIDED YOU DON'T MIND BECOMING THE VAMPIRE QUEEN DUZELL.
ボワン
ENOUGH! YOU KNOW, ISHTAR, YOU REALLY NEED TO LEARN TO MIND YOUR OWN BUSINESS!
YOU'RE MEDDLING IN THE LIVES OF OTHERS.
WE AREN'T YOUR DOLLS, YOU KNOW!

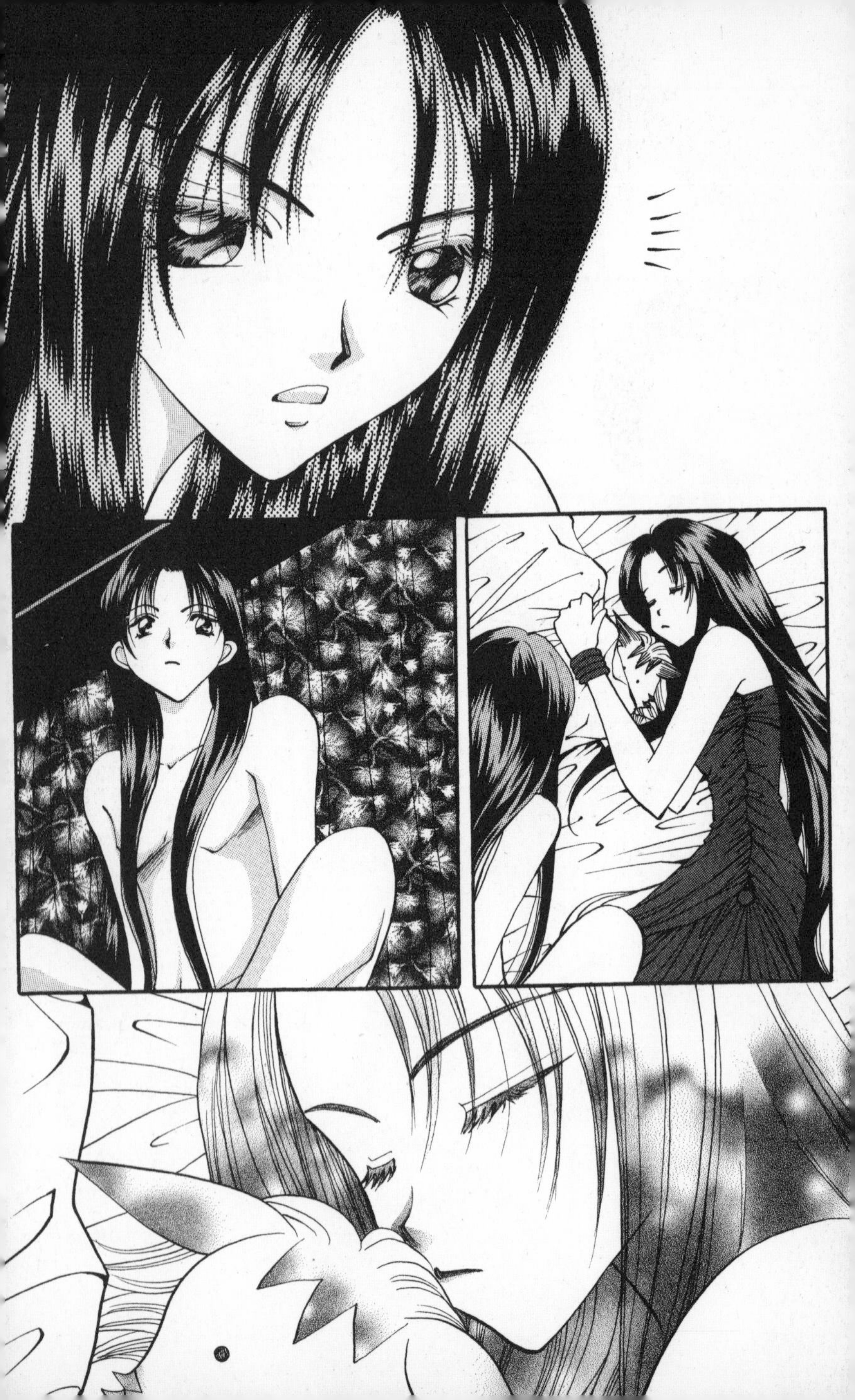

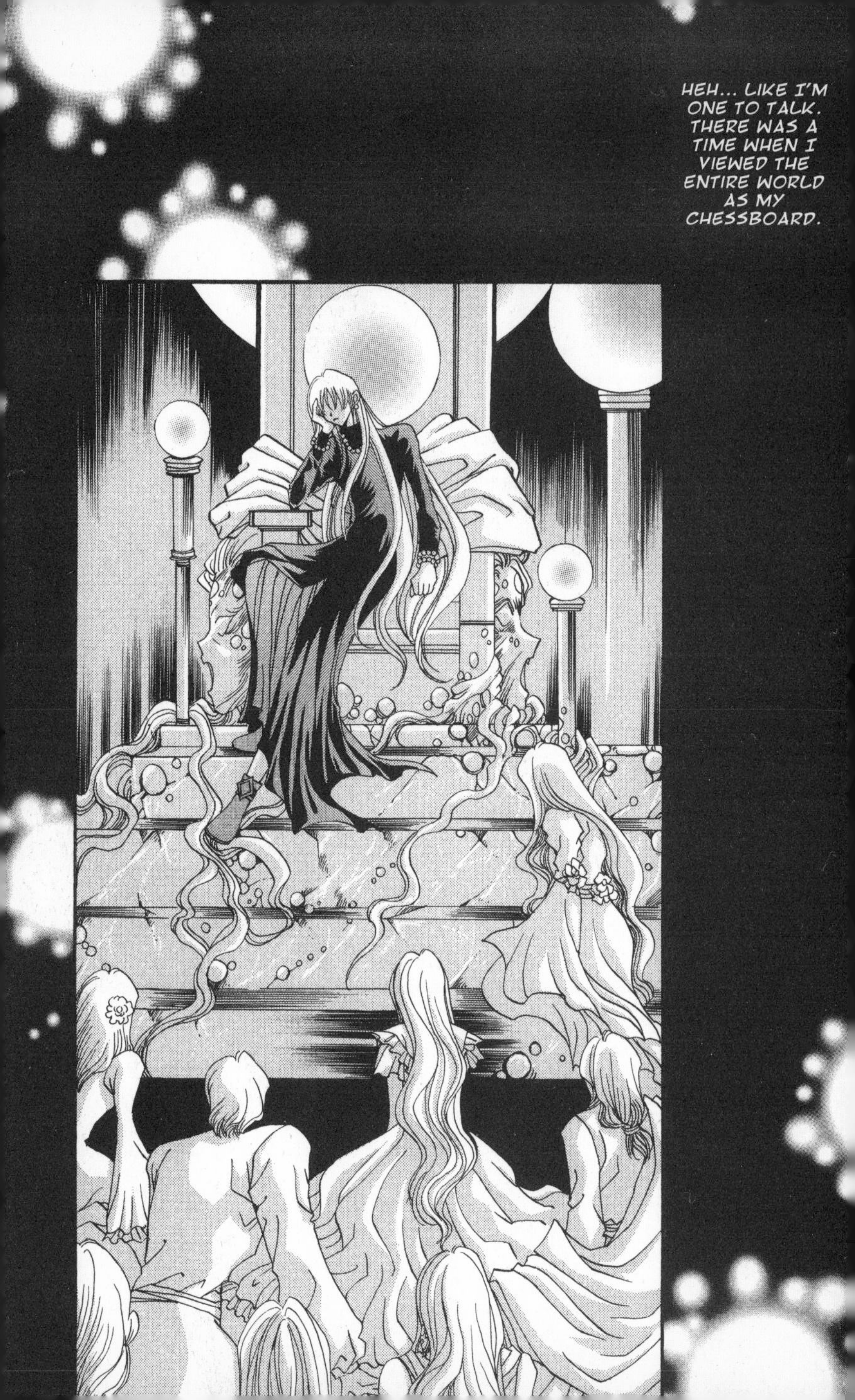
HEH... LIKE I'M ONE TO TALK. THERE WAS A TIME WHEN I VIEWED THE ENTIRE WORLD AS MY CHESSBOARD.

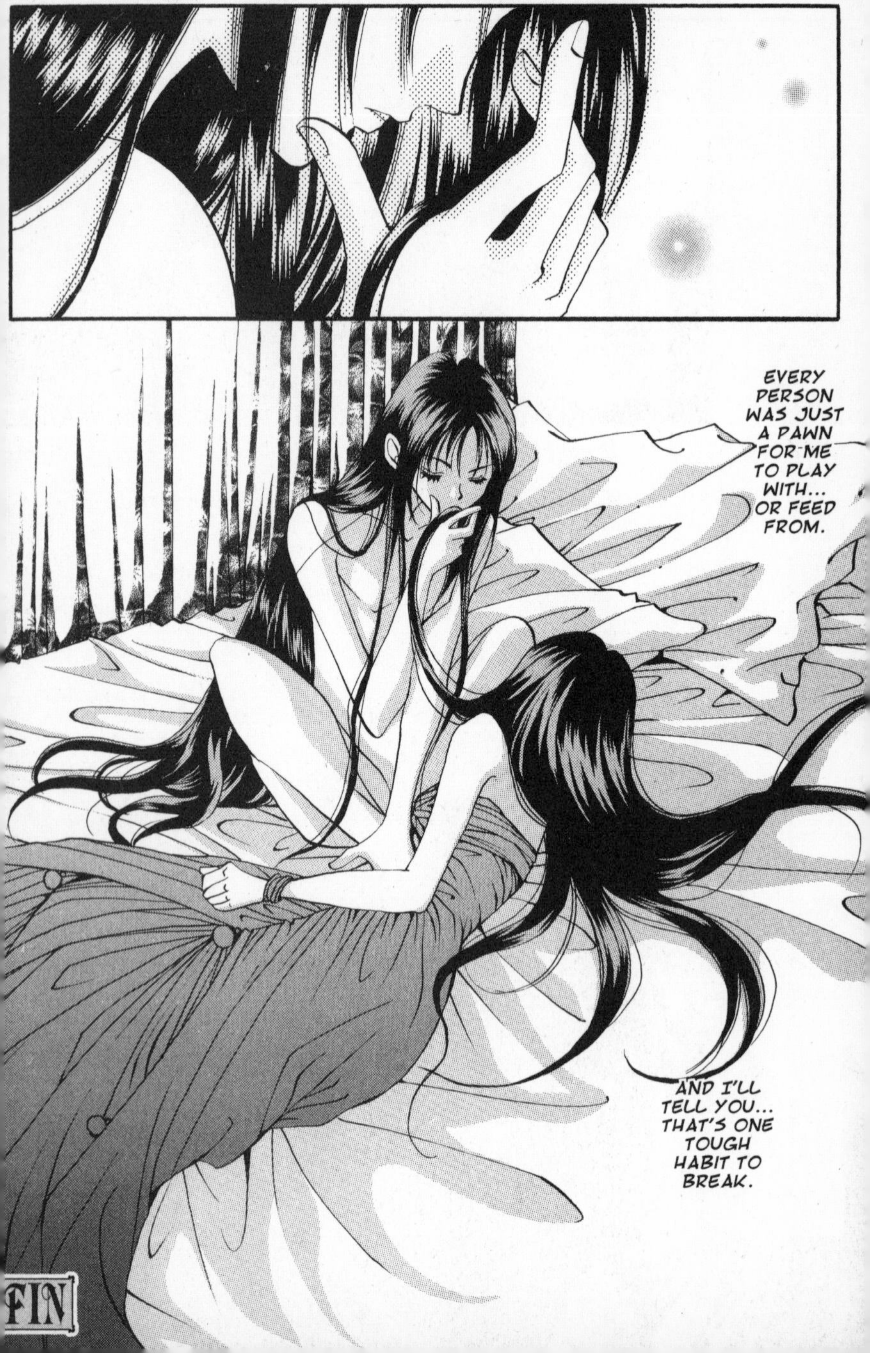
EVERY PERSON WAS JUST A PAWN FOR ME TO PLAY WITH... OR FEED FROM.
AND I'LL TELL YOU... THAT'S ONE TOUGH HABIT TO BREAK.
FIN

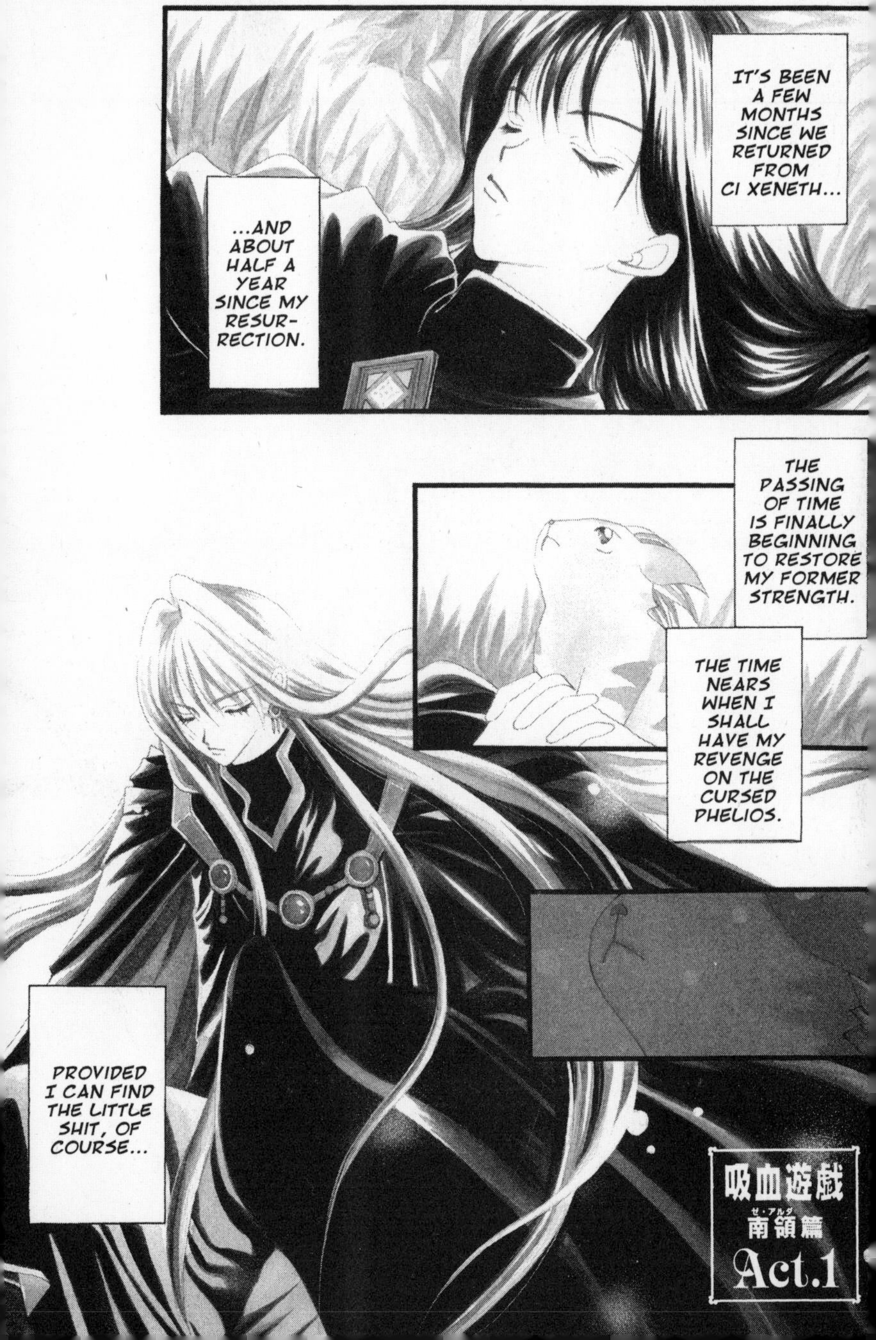
IT'S BEEN A FEW MONTHS SINCE WE RETURNED FROM CI XENETH...
...AND ABOUT HALF A YEAR SINCE MY RESUR-RECTION.
THE PASSING OF TIME IS FINALLY BEGINNING TO RESTORE MY FORMER STRENGTH.
THE TIME NEARS WHEN I SHALL HAVE MY REVENGE ON THE CURSED PHELIOS.
PROVIDED I CAN FIND THE LITTLE SHIT, OF COURSE...
吸血遊戯
ゼ・アルダ
南領篇
Act.1

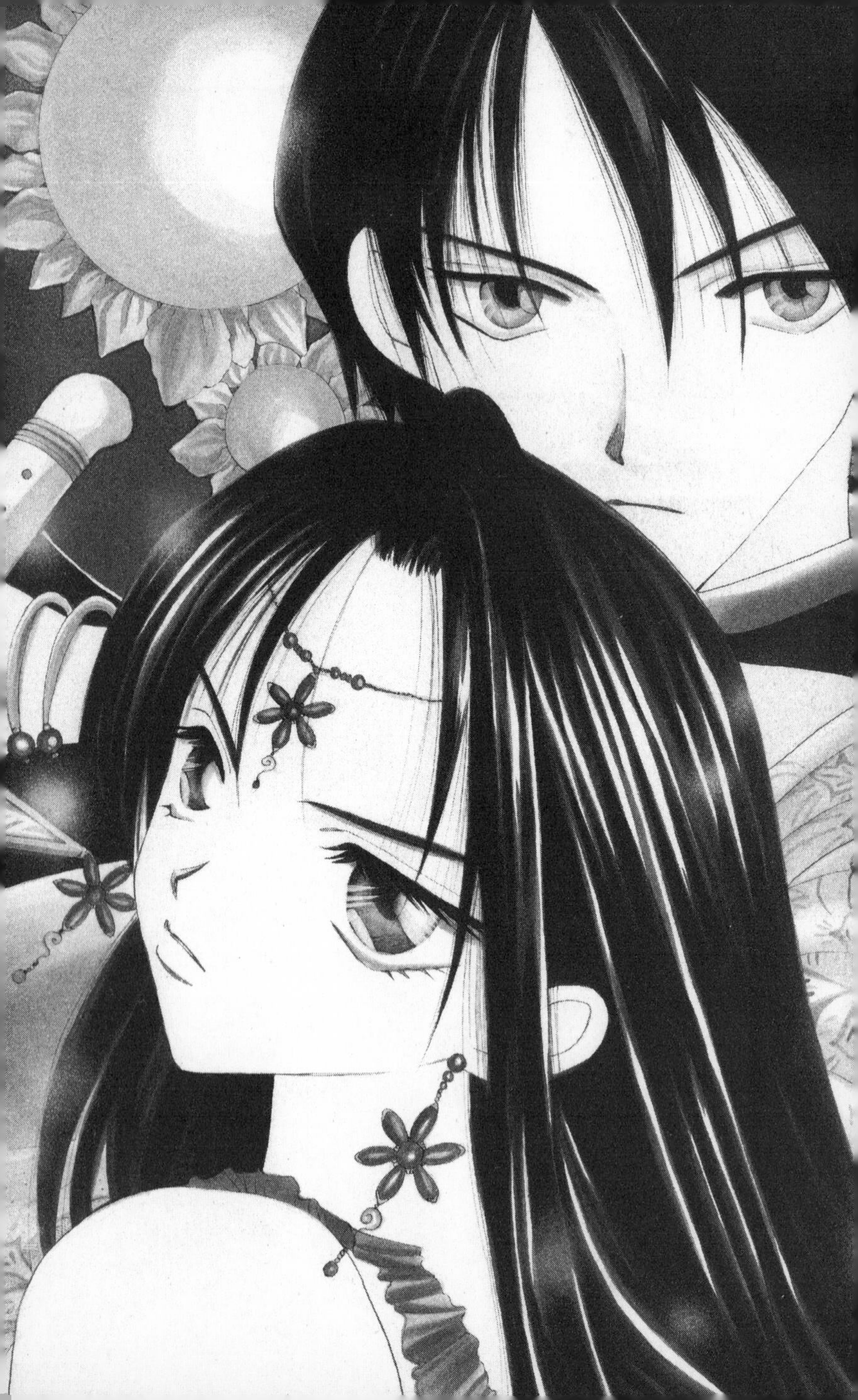

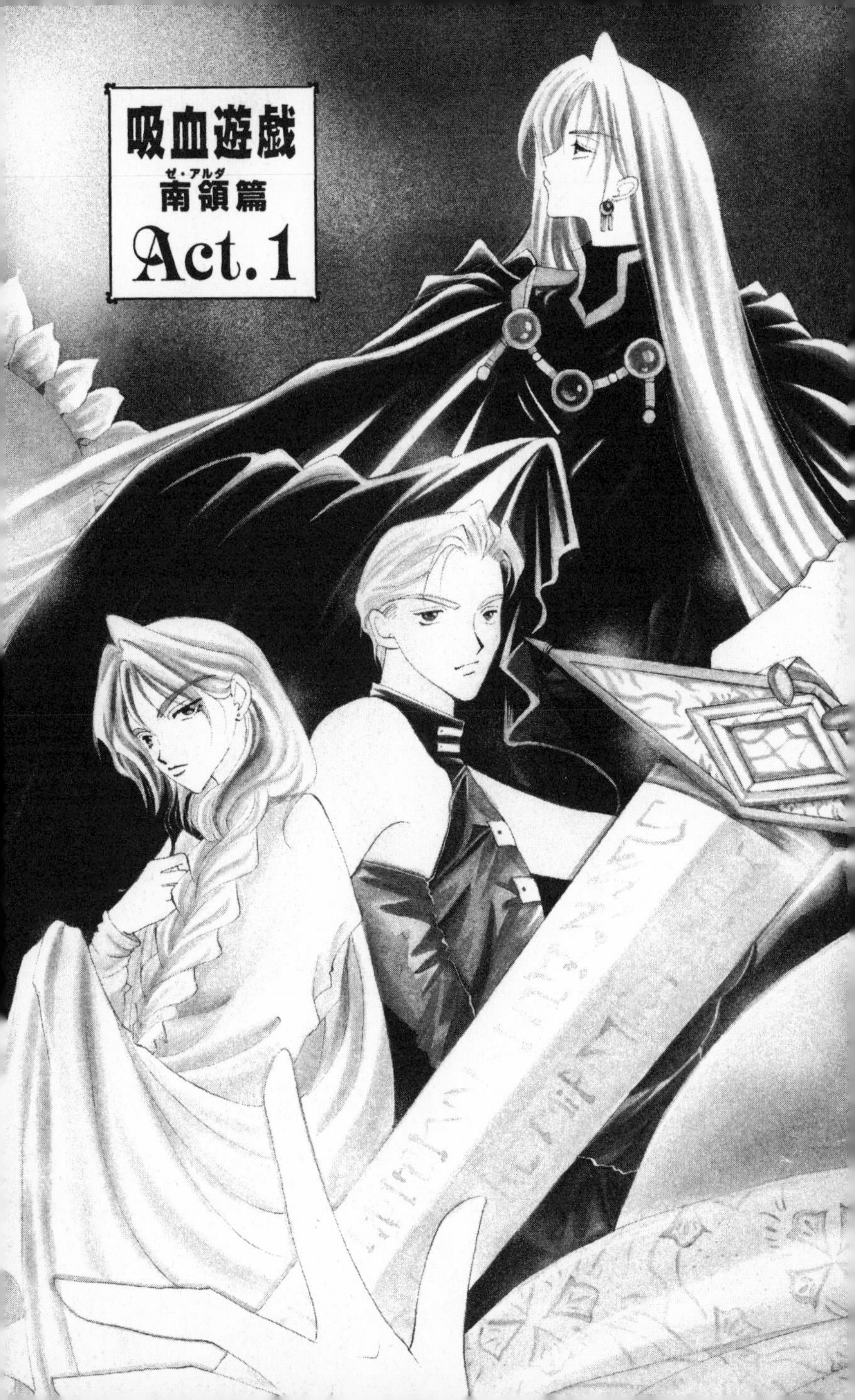
吸血遊戯
南領(ゼ・アルダ)篇
Act.1

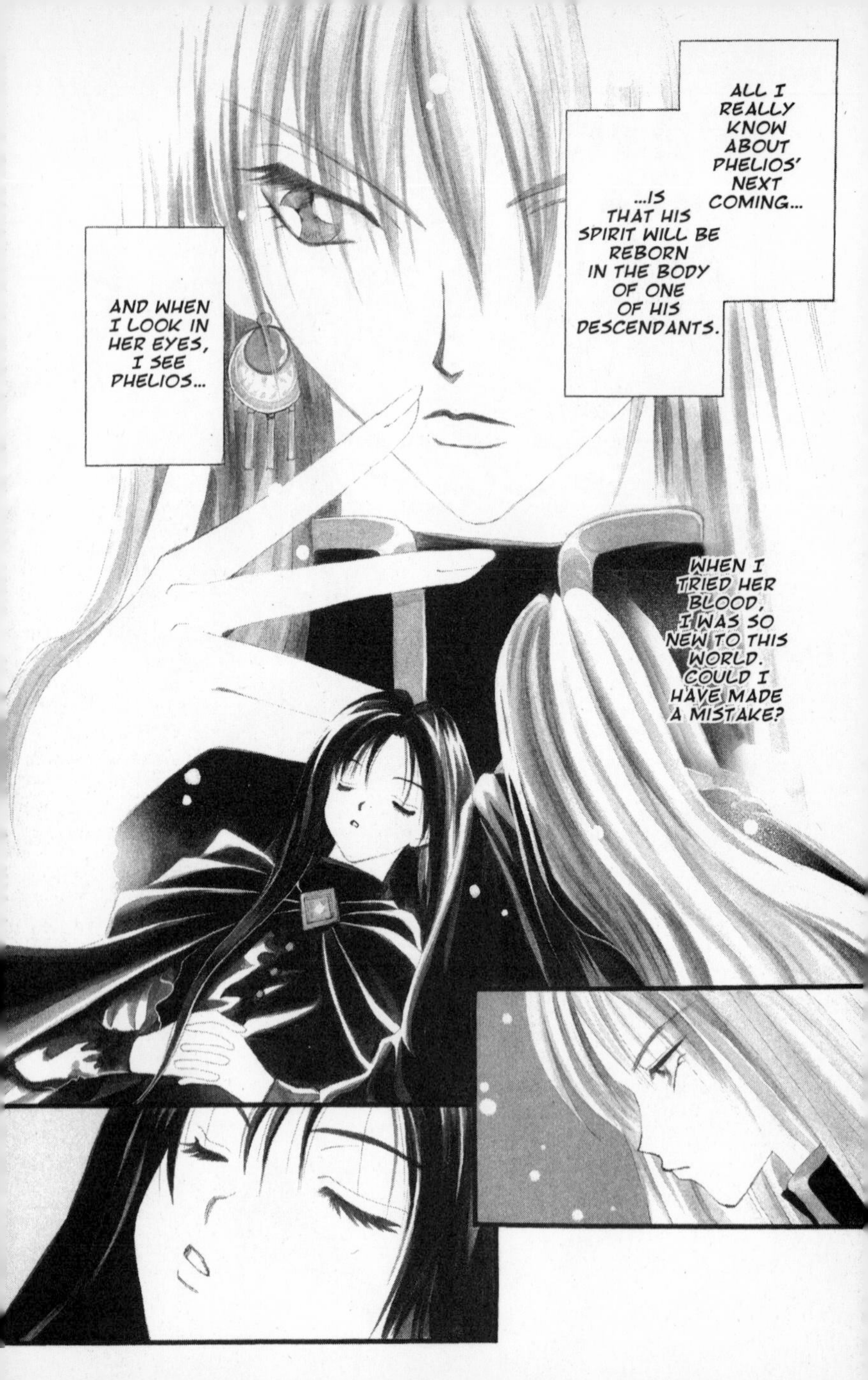
ALL I REALLY KNOW ABOUT PHELIOS' NEXT COMING...
...IS THAT HIS SPIRIT WILL BE REBORN IN THE BODY OF ONE OF HIS DESCENDANTS.
AND WHEN I LOOK IN HER EYES, I SEE PHELIOS...
WHEN I TRIED HER BLOOD, I WAS SO NEW TO THIS WORLD. COULD I HAVE MADE A MISTAKE?

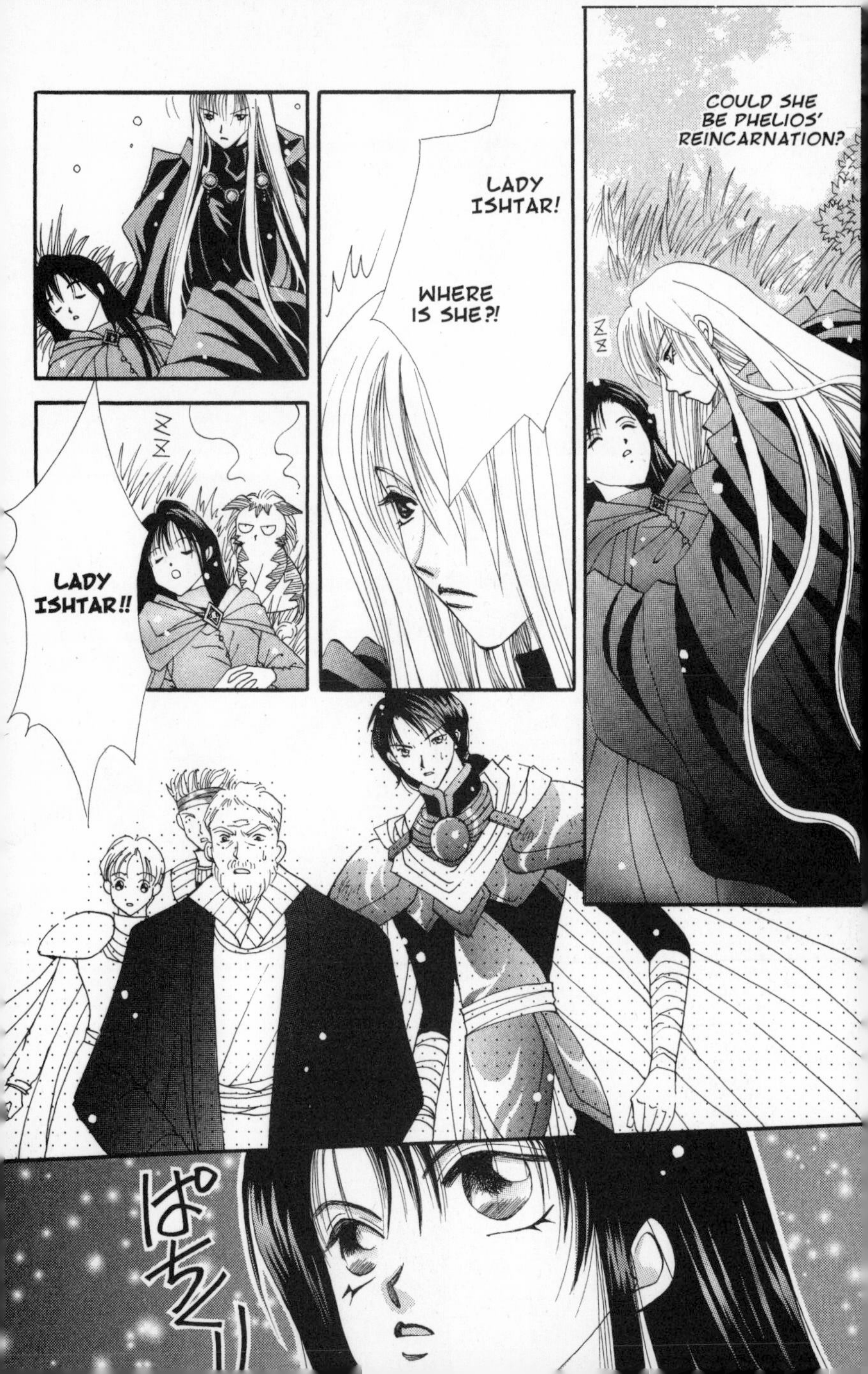
COULD SHE BE PHELIOS' REINCARNATION?
LADY ISHTAR!
WHERE IS SHE?!
LADY ISHTAR!!
ぱちく

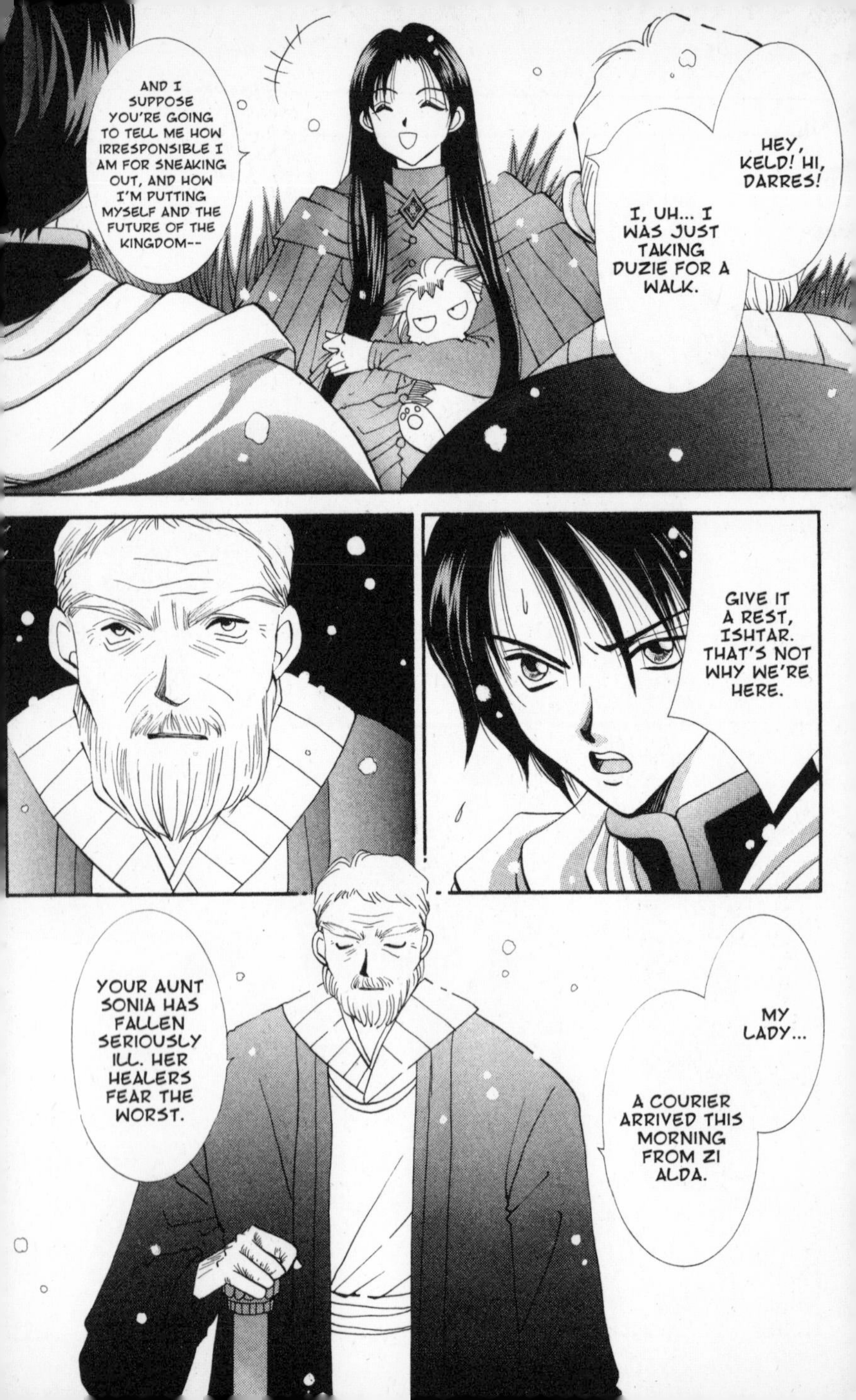
HEY, KELD! HI, DARRES!
I, UH... I WAS JUST TAKING DUZIE FOR A WALK.
AND I SUPPOSE YOU'RE GOING TO TELL ME HOW IRRESPONSIBLE I AM FOR SNEAKING OUT, AND HOW I'M PUTTING MYSELF AND THE FUTURE OF THE KINGDOM--
GIVE IT A REST, ISHTAR. THAT'S NOT WHY WE'RE HERE.
MY LADY...
A COURIER ARRIVED THIS MORNING FROM ZI ALDA.
YOUR AUNT SONIA HAS FALLEN SERIOUSLY ILL. HER HEALERS FEAR THE WORST.

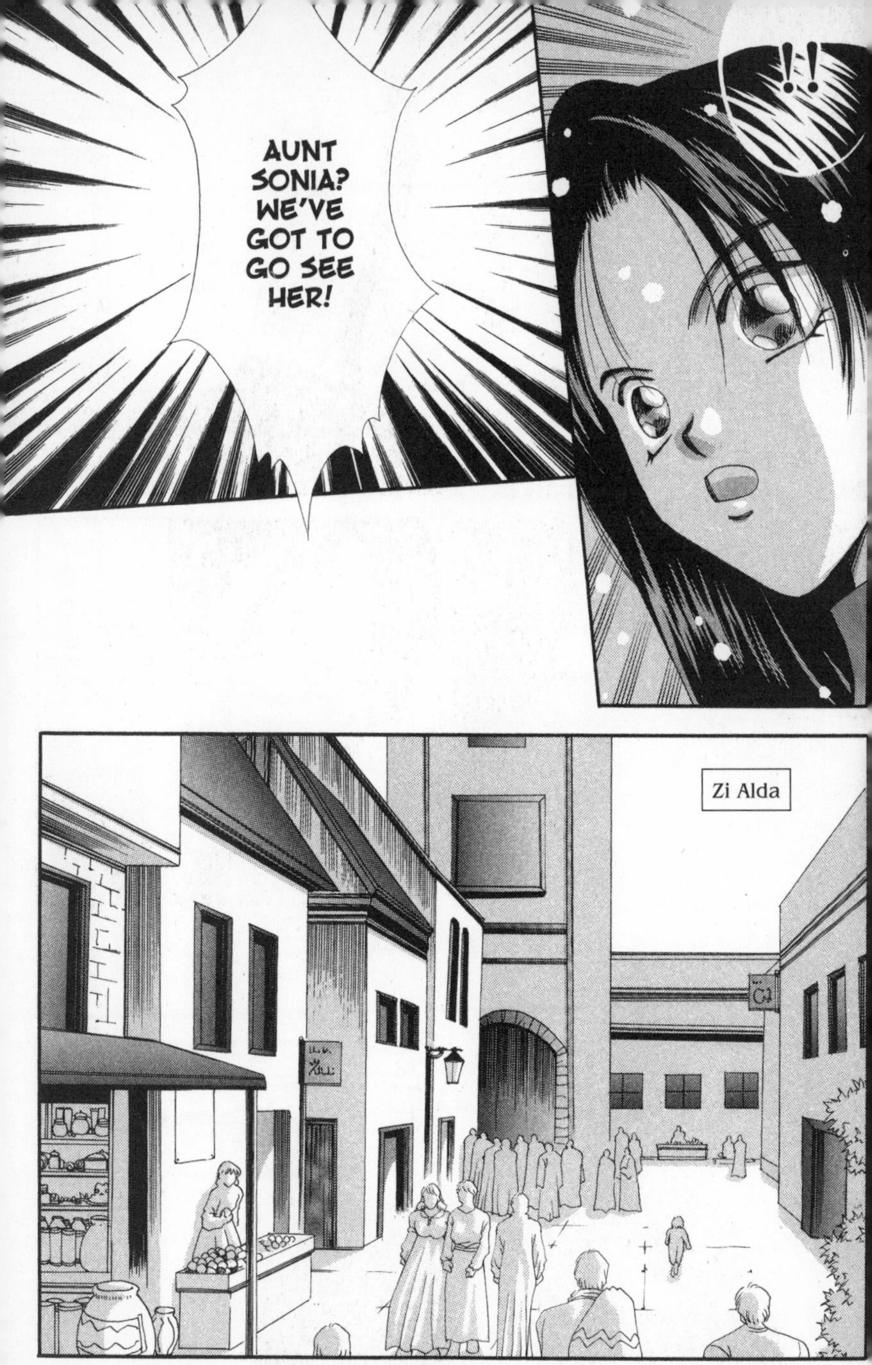
!!
AUNT SONIA? WE'VE GOT TO GO SEE HER!
Zi Alda

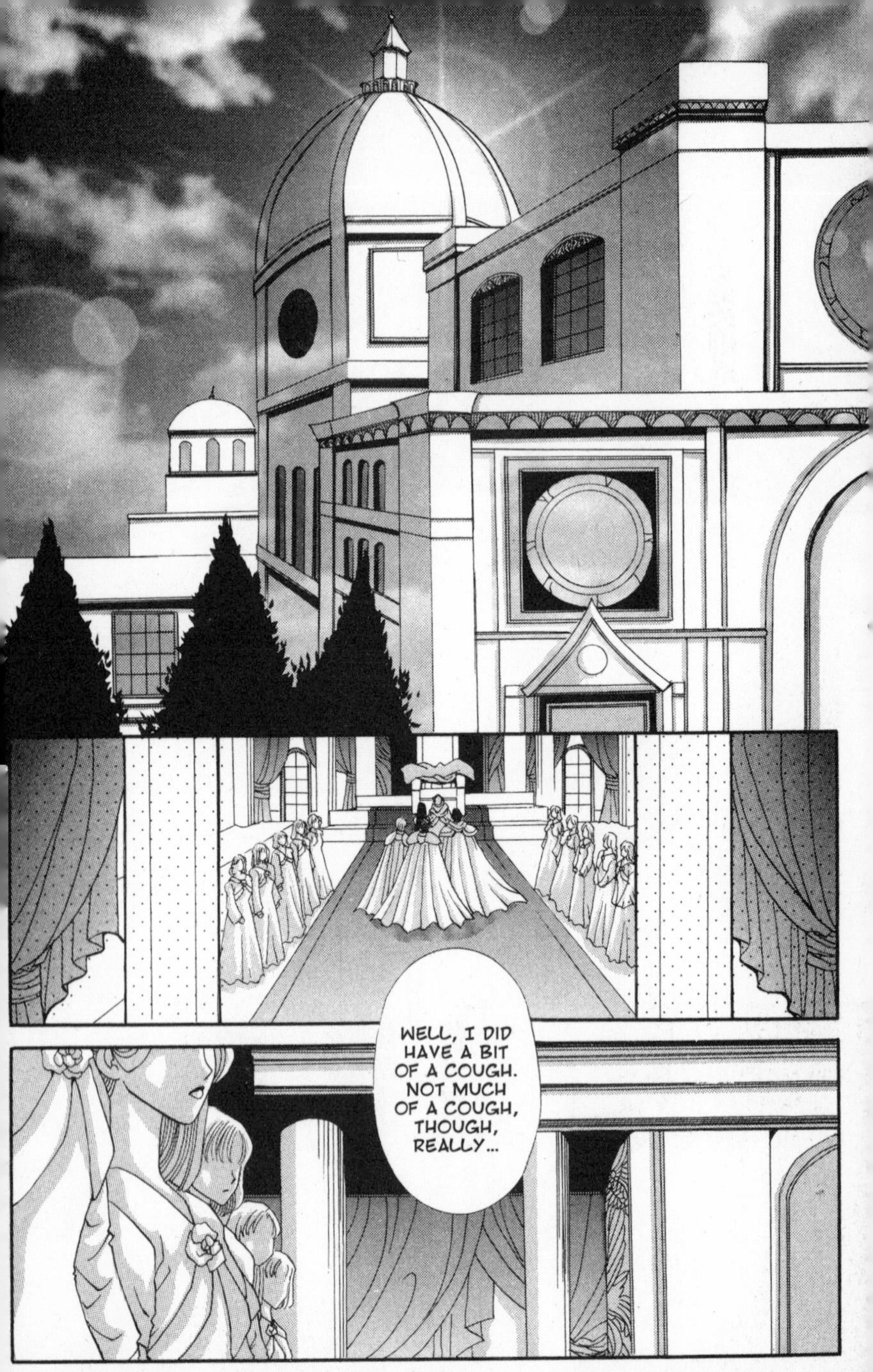
WELL, I DID HAVE A BIT OF A COUGH. NOT MUCH OF A COUGH, THOUGH, REALLY...

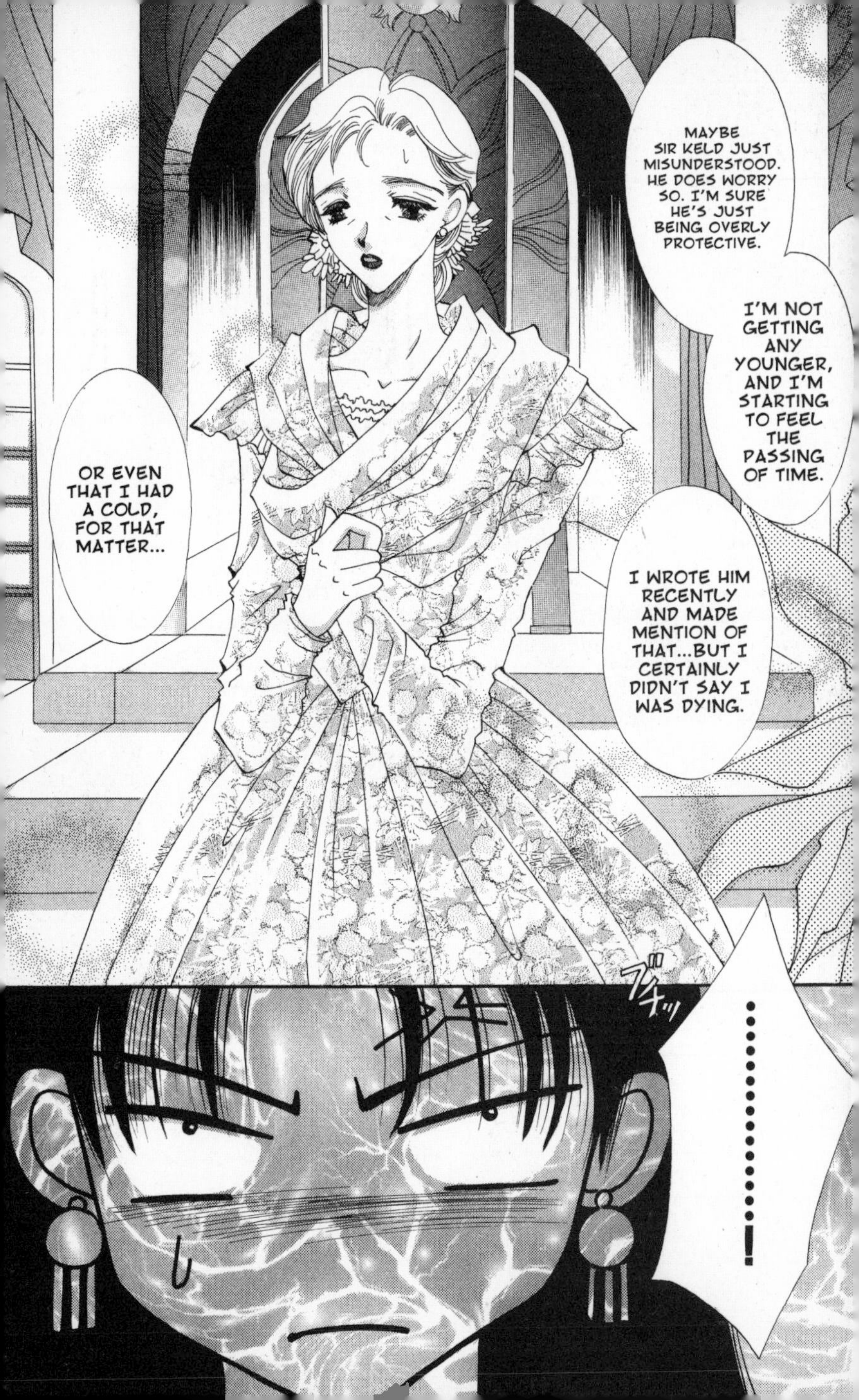
MAYBE SIR KELD JUST MISUNDERSTOOD. HE DOES WORRY SO. I'M SURE HE'S JUST BEING OVERLY PROTECTIVE.
I'M NOT GETTING ANY YOUNGER, AND I'M STARTING TO FEEL THE PASSING OF TIME.
I WROTE HIM RECENTLY AND MADE MENTION OF THAT...BUT I CERTAINLY DIDN'T SAY I WAS DYING.
OR EVEN THAT I HAD A COLD, FOR THAT MATTER...
ブチッ
..........!

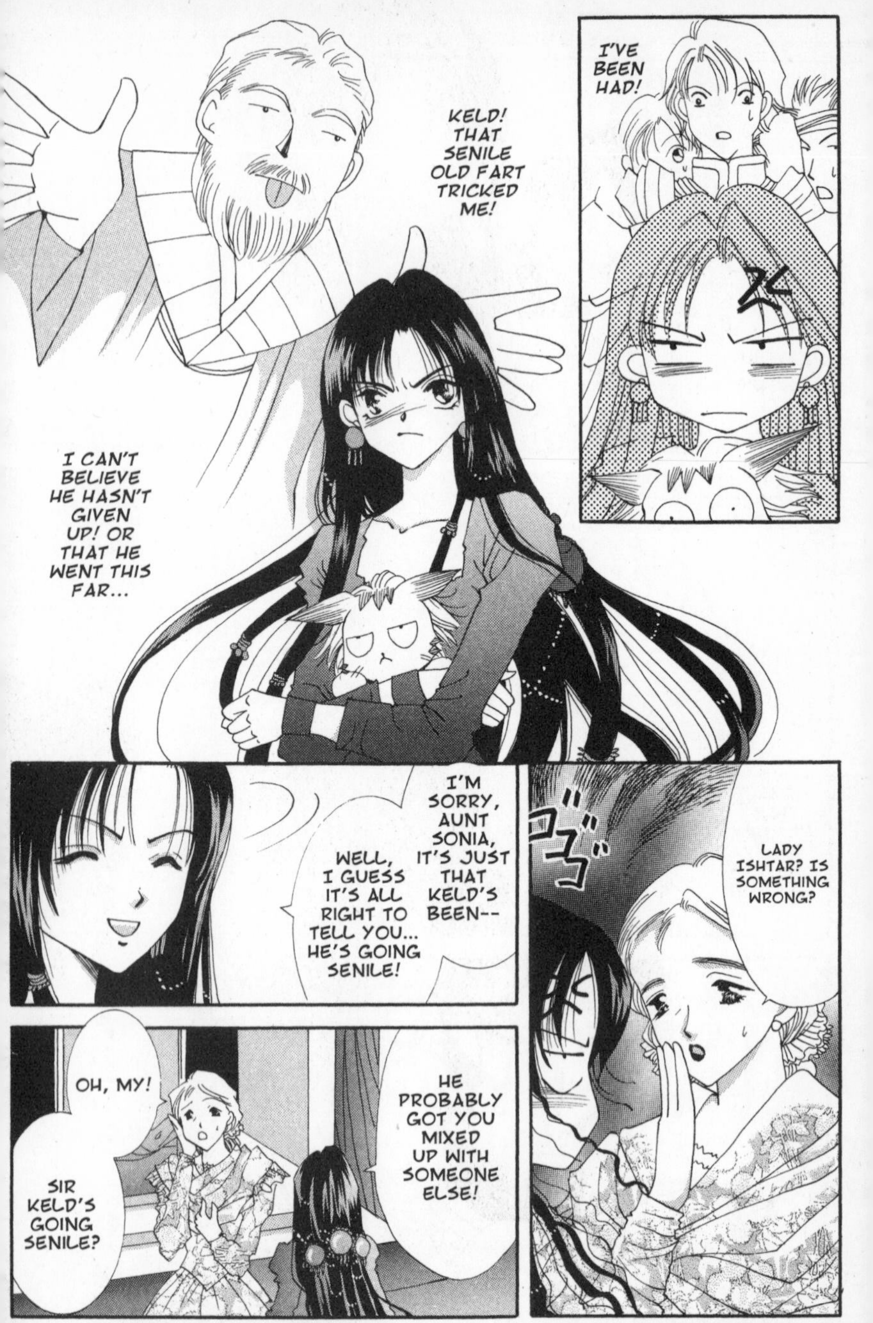
I'VE BEEN HAD!
KELD! THAT SENILE OLD FART TRICKED ME!
I CAN'T BELIEVE HE HASN'T GIVEN UP! OR THAT HE WENT THIS FAR...
ゴゴ
LADY ISHTAR? IS SOMETHING WRONG?
I'M SORRY, AUNT SONIA, IT'S JUST THAT KELD'S BEEN--
WELL, I GUESS IT'S ALL RIGHT TO TELL YOU... HE'S GOING SENILE!
HE PROBABLY GOT YOU MIXED UP WITH SOMEONE ELSE!
OH, MY!
SIR KELD'S GOING SENILE?

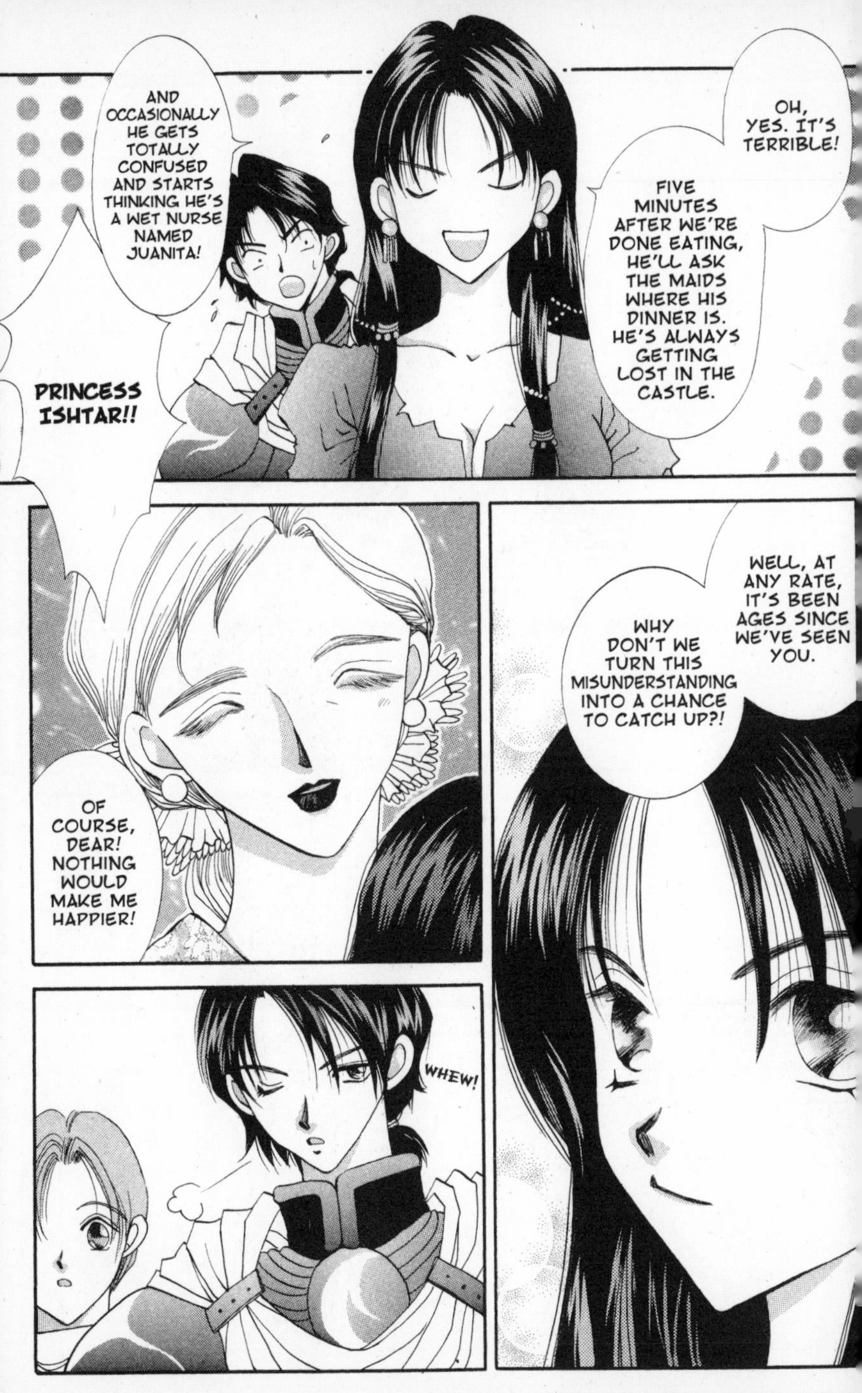
OH, YES. IT'S TERRIBLE!
FIVE MINUTES AFTER WE'RE DONE EATING, HE'LL ASK THE MAIDS WHERE HIS DINNER IS. HE'S ALWAYS GETTING LOST IN THE CASTLE.
AND OCCASIONALLY HE GETS TOTALLY CONFUSED AND STARTS THINKING HE'S A WET NURSE NAMED JUANITA!
PRINCESS ISHTAR!!
WELL, AT ANY RATE, IT'S BEEN AGES SINCE WE'VE SEEN YOU.
WHY DON'T WE TURN THIS MISUNDERSTANDING INTO A CHANCE TO CATCH UP?!
OF COURSE, DEAR! NOTHING WOULD MAKE ME HAPPIER!
WHEW!

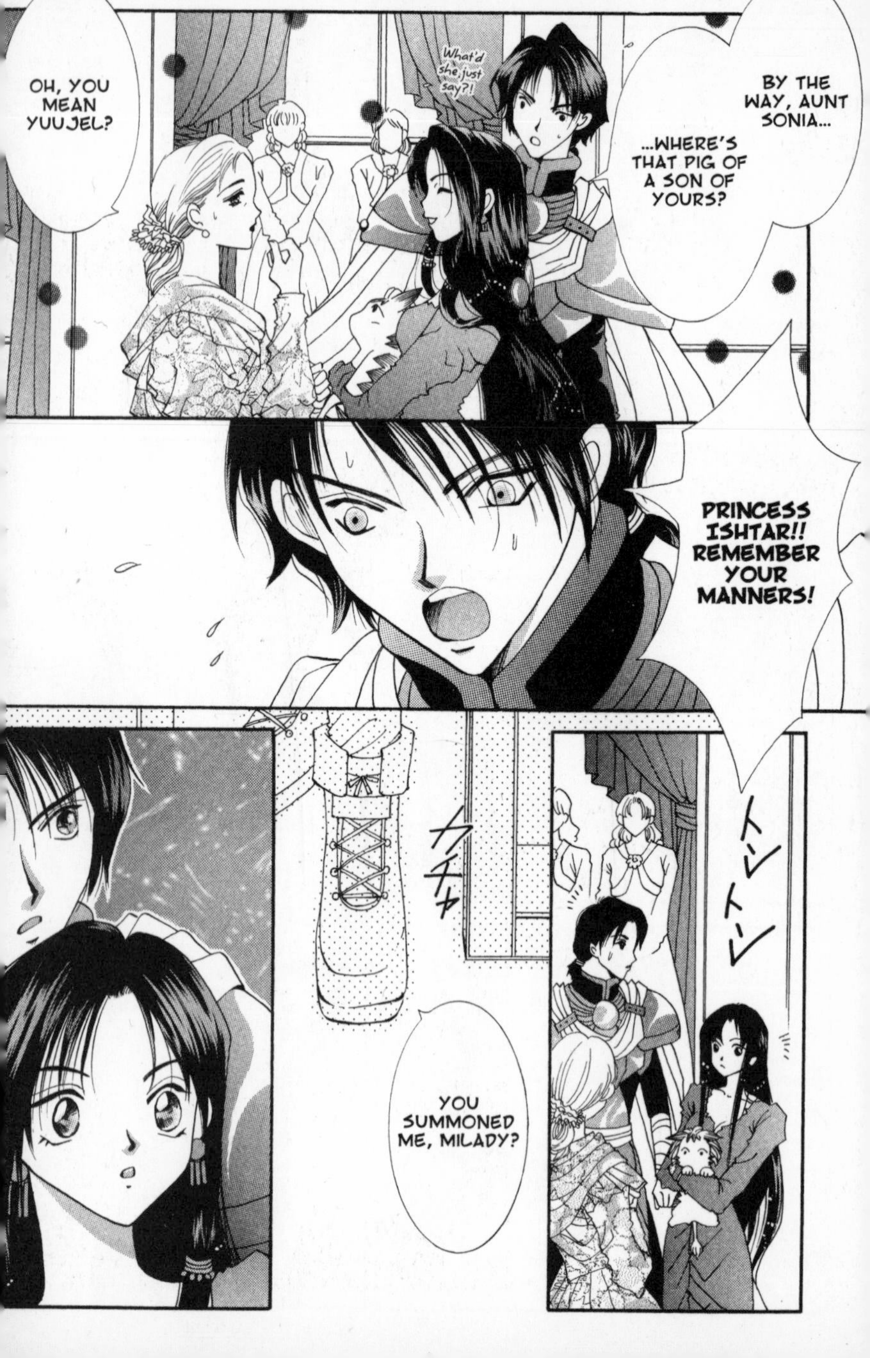
BY THE WAY, AUNT SONIA...
...WHERE'S THAT PIG OF A SON OF YOURS?
What'd she just say?!
OH, YOU MEAN YUUJEL?
PRINCESS ISHTAR!! REMEMBER YOUR MANNERS!
トントン
ガチャ
YOU SUMMONED ME, MILADY?

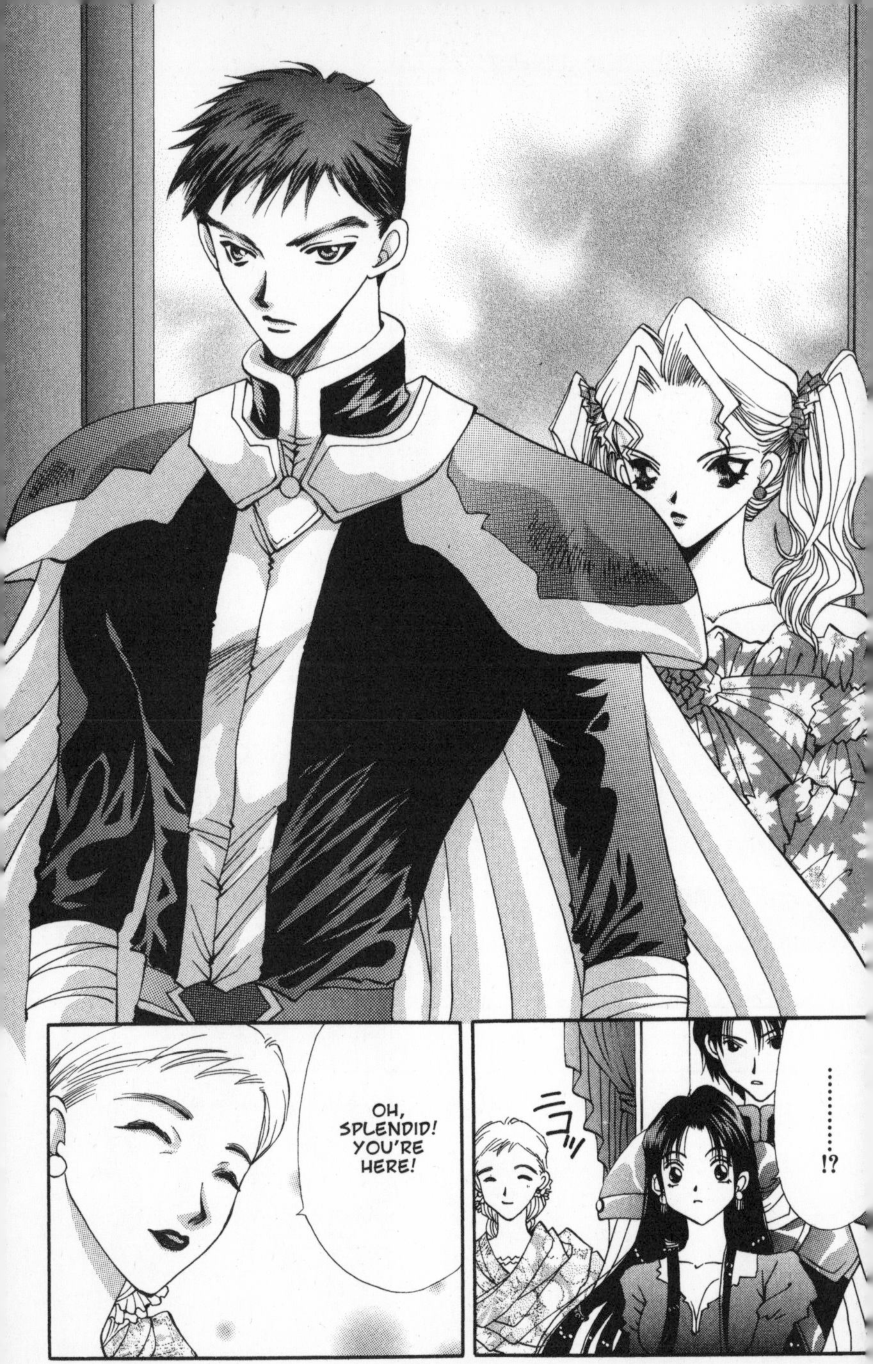
ニコッ
……!?
OH, SPLENDID! YOU'RE HERE!

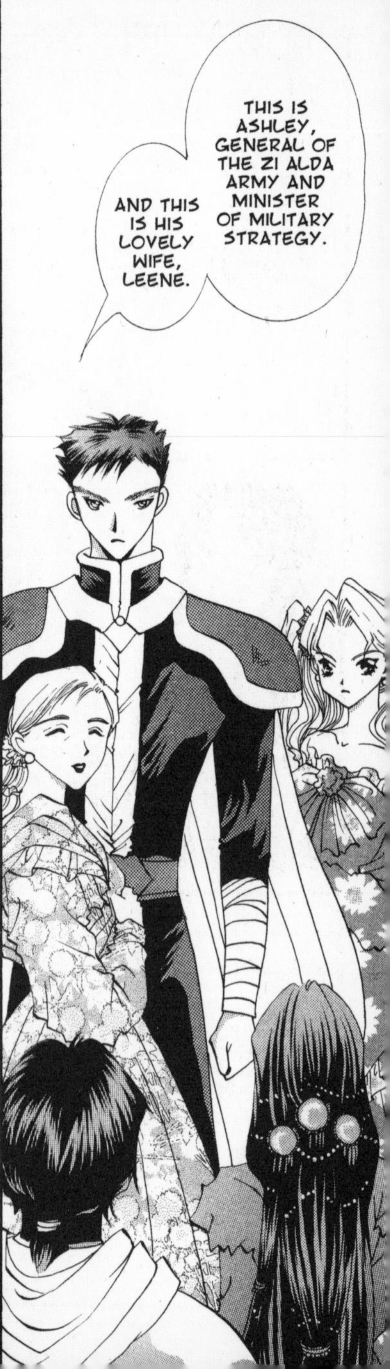
THIS IS ASHLEY, GENERAL OF THE ZI ALDA ARMY AND MINISTER OF MILITARY STRATEGY.
AND THIS IS HIS LOVELY WIFE, LEENE.

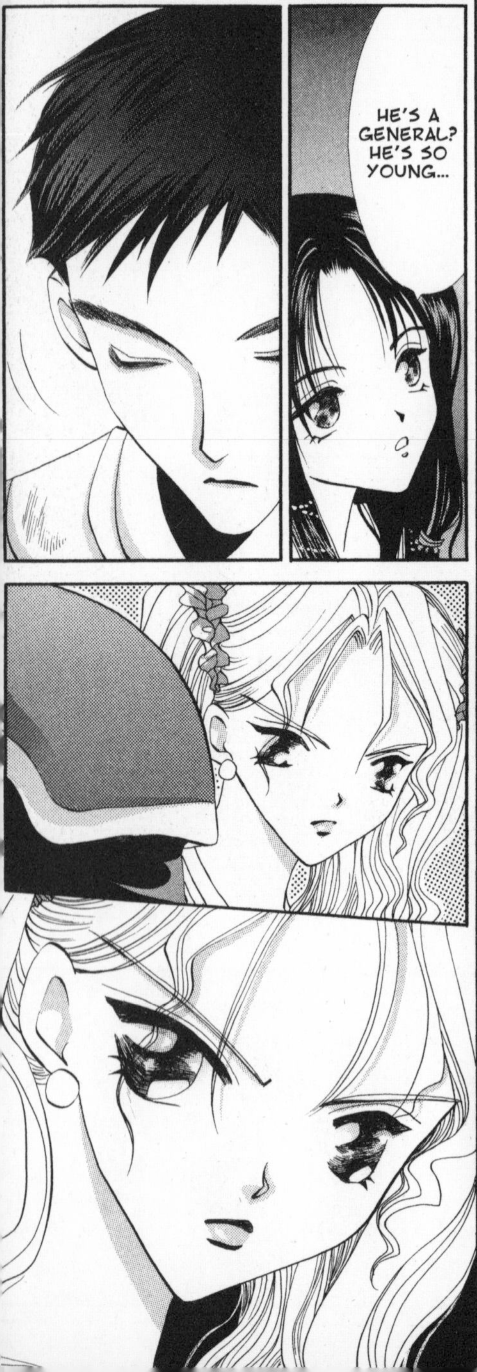
HE'S A GENERAL? HE'S SO YOUNG...

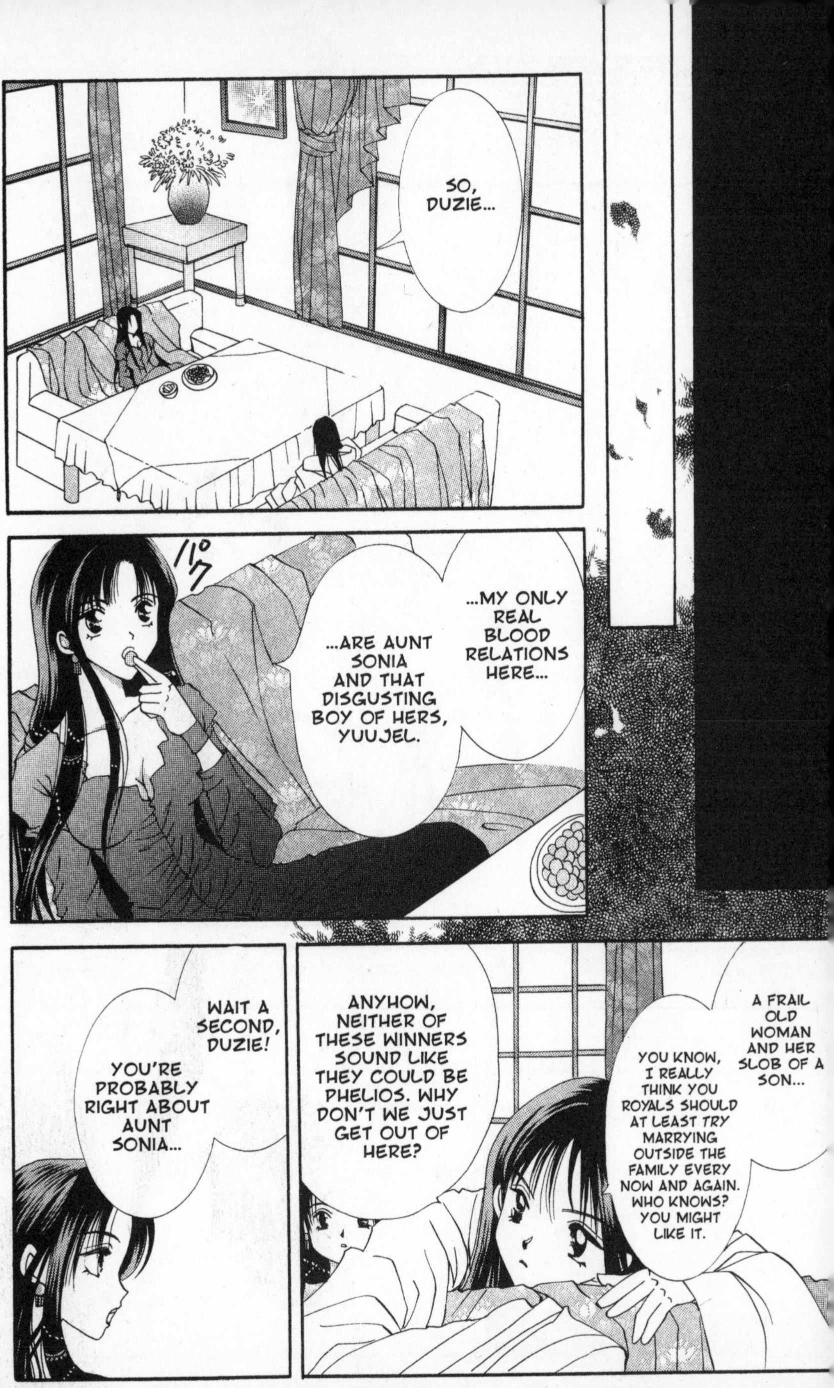
SO, DUZIE...
...MY ONLY REAL BLOOD RELATIONS HERE...
パク
...ARE AUNT SONIA AND THAT DISGUSTING BOY OF HERS, YUUJEL.
A FRAIL OLD WOMAN AND HER SLOB OF A SON...
YOU KNOW, I REALLY THINK YOU ROYALS SHOULD AT LEAST *TRY* MARRYING OUTSIDE THE FAMILY EVERY NOW AND AGAIN. WHO KNOWS? YOU MIGHT LIKE IT.
ANYHOW, NEITHER OF THESE WINNERS SOUND LIKE THEY COULD BE PHELIOS. WHY DON'T WE JUST GET OUT OF HERE?
WAIT A SECOND, DUZIE!
YOU'RE PROBABLY RIGHT ABOUT AUNT SONIA...

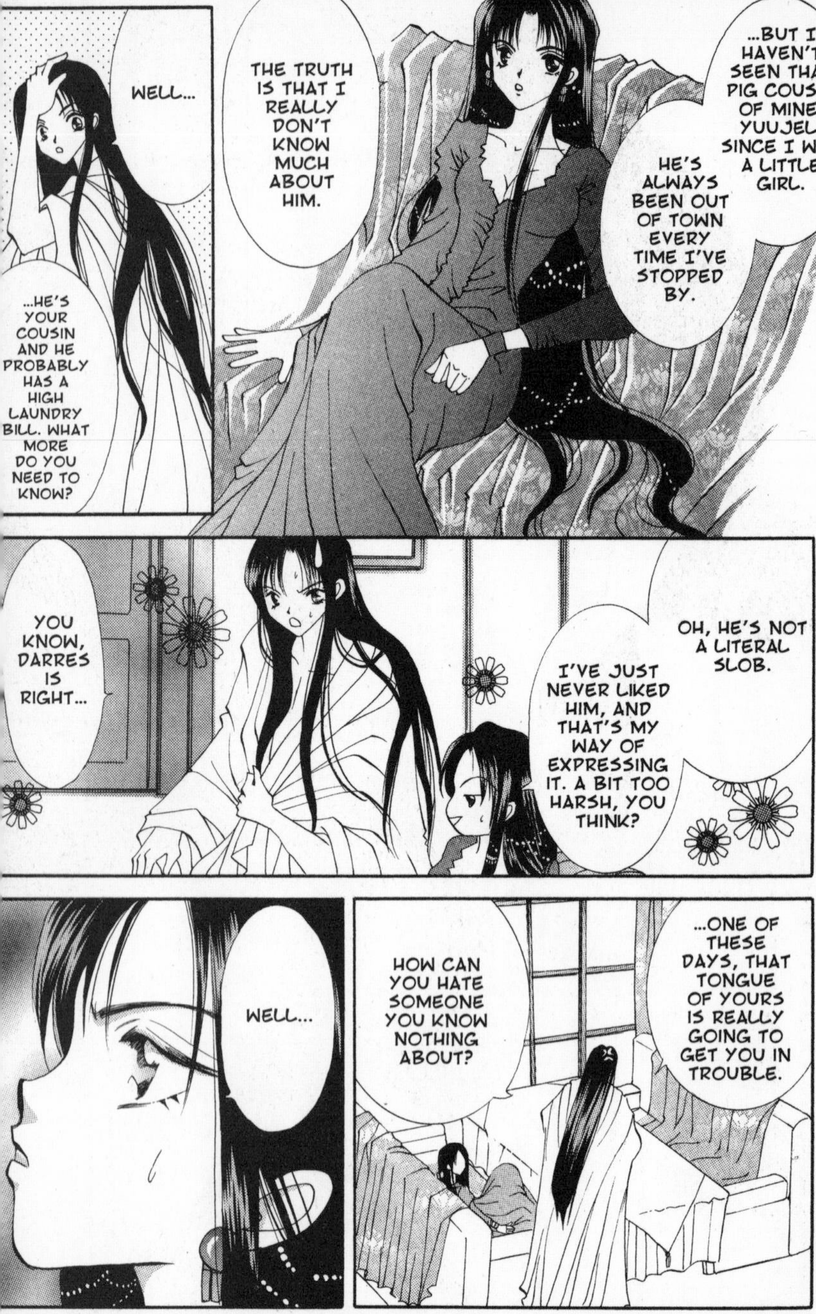
...BUT I HAVEN'T SEEN THAT PIG COUSIN OF MINE, YUUJEL, SINCE I WAS A LITTLE GIRL.
HE'S ALWAYS BEEN OUT OF TOWN EVERY TIME I'VE STOPPED BY.
THE TRUTH IS THAT I REALLY DON'T KNOW MUCH ABOUT HIM.
WELL...
...HE'S YOUR COUSIN AND HE PROBABLY HAS A HIGH LAUNDRY BILL. WHAT MORE DO YOU NEED TO KNOW?
OH, HE'S NOT A LITERAL SLOB.
I'VE JUST NEVER LIKED HIM, AND THAT'S MY WAY OF EXPRESSING IT. A BIT TOO HARSH, YOU THINK?
YOU KNOW, DARRES IS RIGHT...
...ONE OF THESE DAYS, THAT TONGUE OF YOURS IS REALLY GOING TO GET YOU IN TROUBLE.
HOW CAN YOU HATE SOMEONE YOU KNOW NOTHING ABOUT?
WELL...

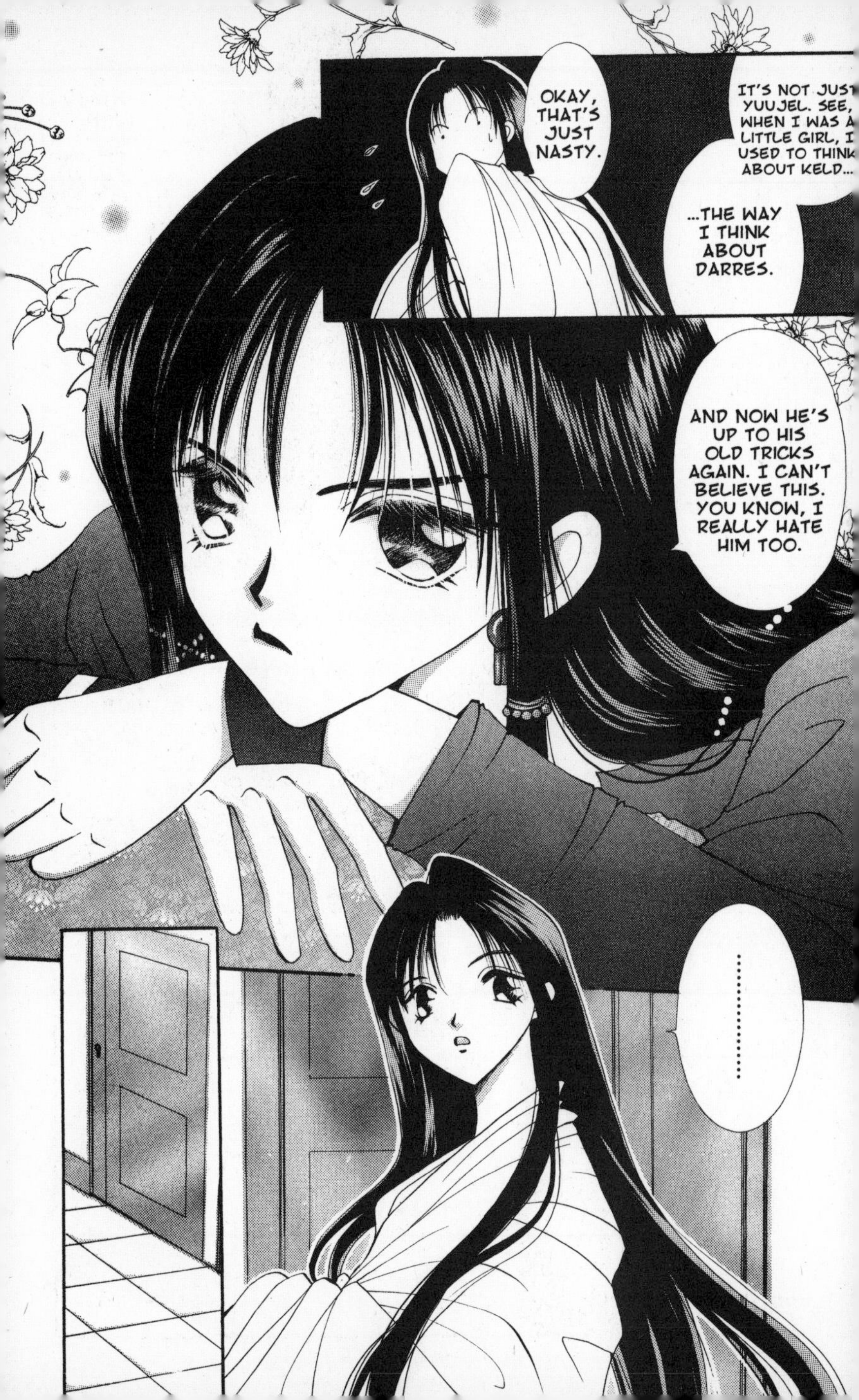
IT'S NOT JUST YUUJEL. SEE, WHEN I WAS A LITTLE GIRL, I USED TO THINK ABOUT KELD...
...THE WAY I THINK ABOUT DARRES.
OKAY, THAT'S JUST NASTY.
AND NOW HE'S UP TO HIS OLD TRICKS AGAIN. I CAN'T BELIEVE THIS. YOU KNOW, I REALLY HATE HIM TOO.
......

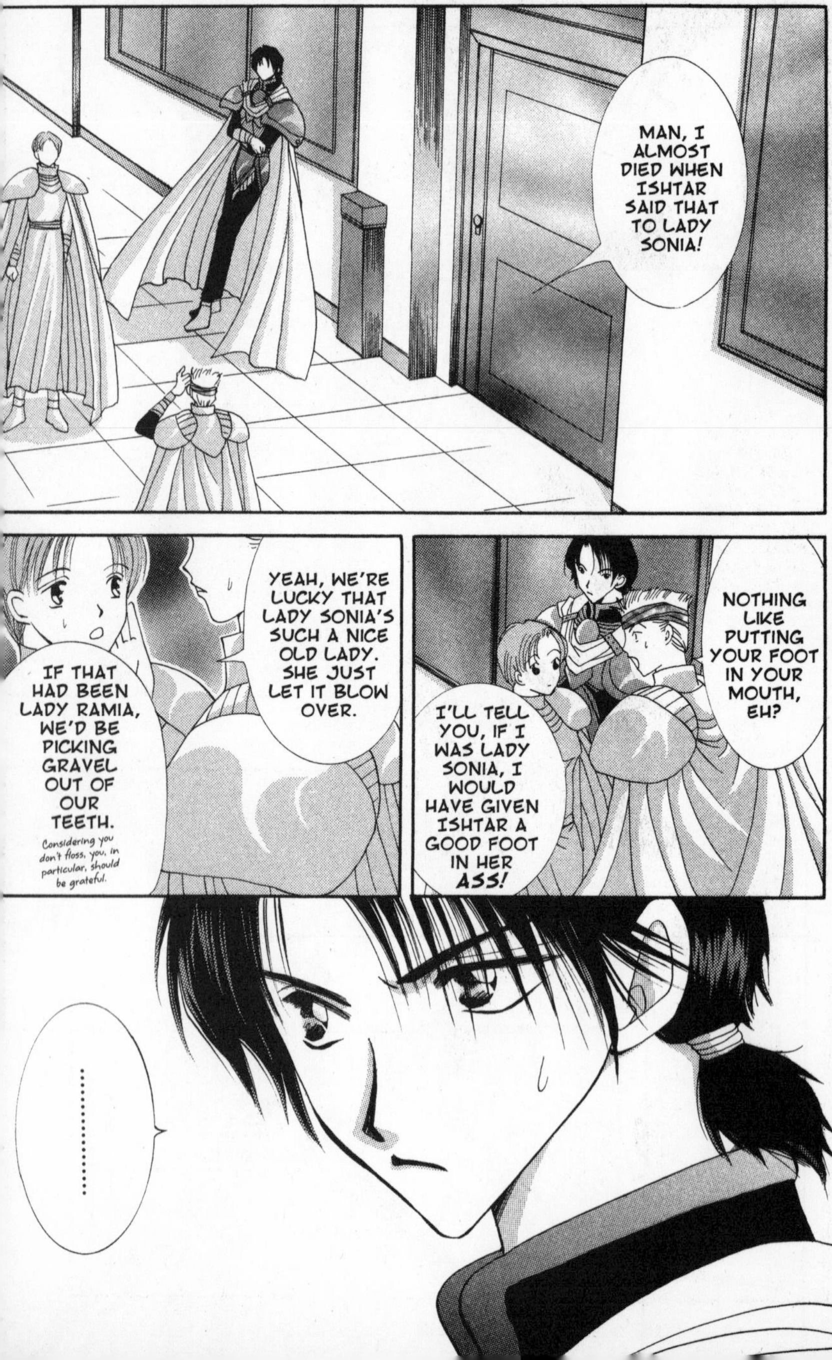
MAN, I ALMOST DIED WHEN ISHTAR SAID THAT TO LADY SONIA!
NOTHING LIKE PUTTING YOUR FOOT IN YOUR MOUTH, EH?
I'LL TELL YOU, IF I WAS LADY SONIA, I WOULD HAVE GIVEN ISHTAR A GOOD FOOT IN HER ASS!
YEAH, WE'RE LUCKY THAT LADY SONIA'S SUCH A NICE OLD LADY. SHE JUST LET IT BLOW OVER.
IF THAT HAD BEEN LADY RAMIA, WE'D BE PICKING GRAVEL OUT OF OUR TEETH.
Considering you don't floss, you, in particular, should be grateful.
……

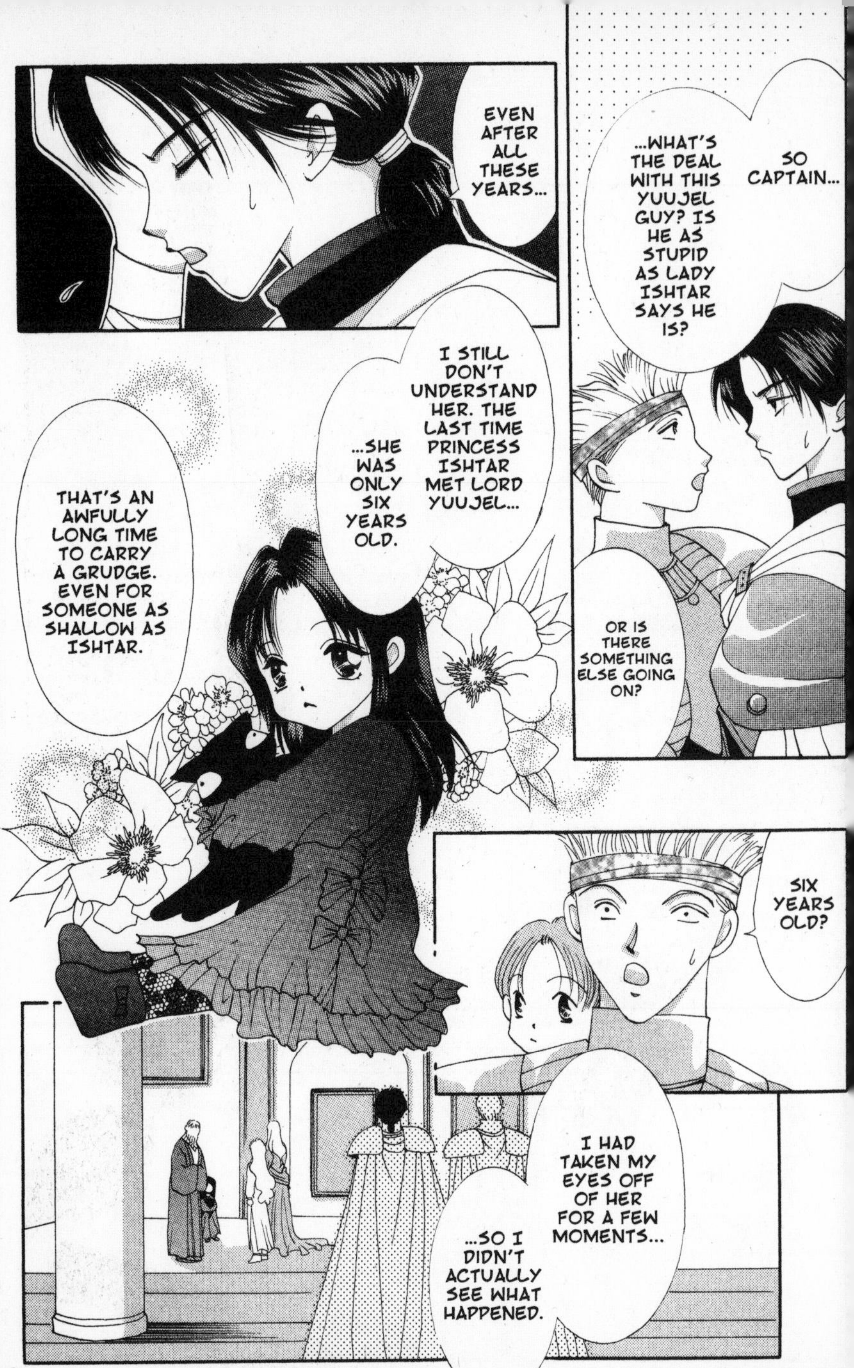
SO CAPTAIN...
...WHAT'S THE DEAL WITH THIS YUUJEL GUY? IS HE AS STUPID AS LADY ISHTAR SAYS HE IS?
OR IS THERE SOMETHING ELSE GOING ON?
EVEN AFTER ALL THESE YEARS...
I STILL DON'T UNDERSTAND HER. THE LAST TIME PRINCESS ISHTAR MET LORD YUUJEL...
...SHE WAS ONLY SIX YEARS OLD.
THAT'S AN AWFULLY LONG TIME TO CARRY A GRUDGE. EVEN FOR SOMEONE AS SHALLOW AS ISHTAR.
SIX YEARS OLD?
I HAD TAKEN MY EYES OFF OF HER FOR A FEW MOMENTS...
...SO I DIDN'T ACTUALLY SEE WHAT HAPPENED.

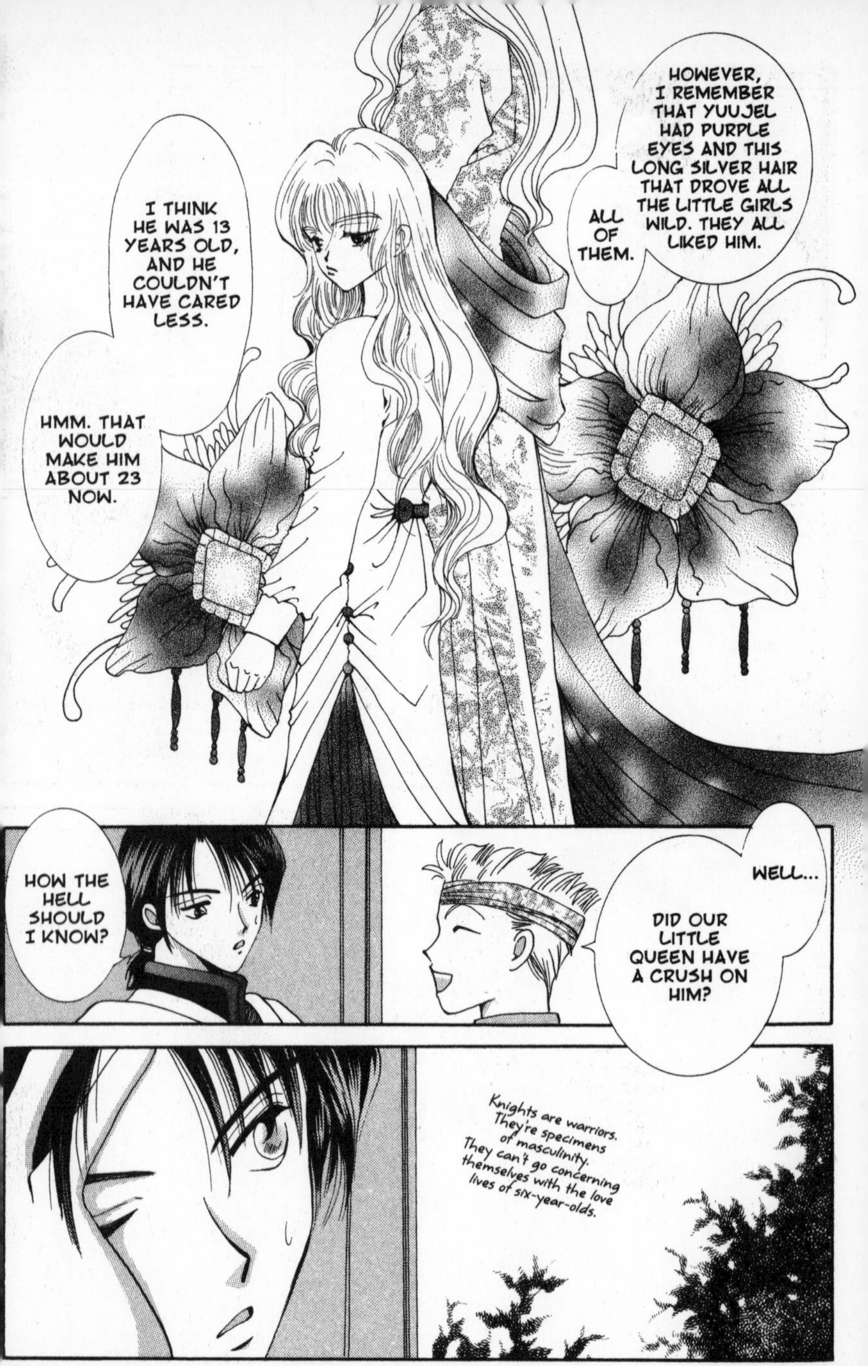
HOWEVER, I REMEMBER THAT YUUJEL HAD PURPLE EYES AND THIS LONG SILVER HAIR THAT DROVE ALL THE LITTLE GIRLS WILD. THEY ALL LIKED HIM.
ALL OF THEM.
I THINK HE WAS 13 YEARS OLD, AND HE COULDN'T HAVE CARED LESS.
HMM. THAT WOULD MAKE HIM ABOUT 23 NOW.
WELL...
DID OUR LITTLE QUEEN HAVE A CRUSH ON HIM?
HOW THE HELL SHOULD I KNOW?
Knights are warriors. They're specimens of masculinity. They can't go concerning themselves with the love lives of six-year-olds.

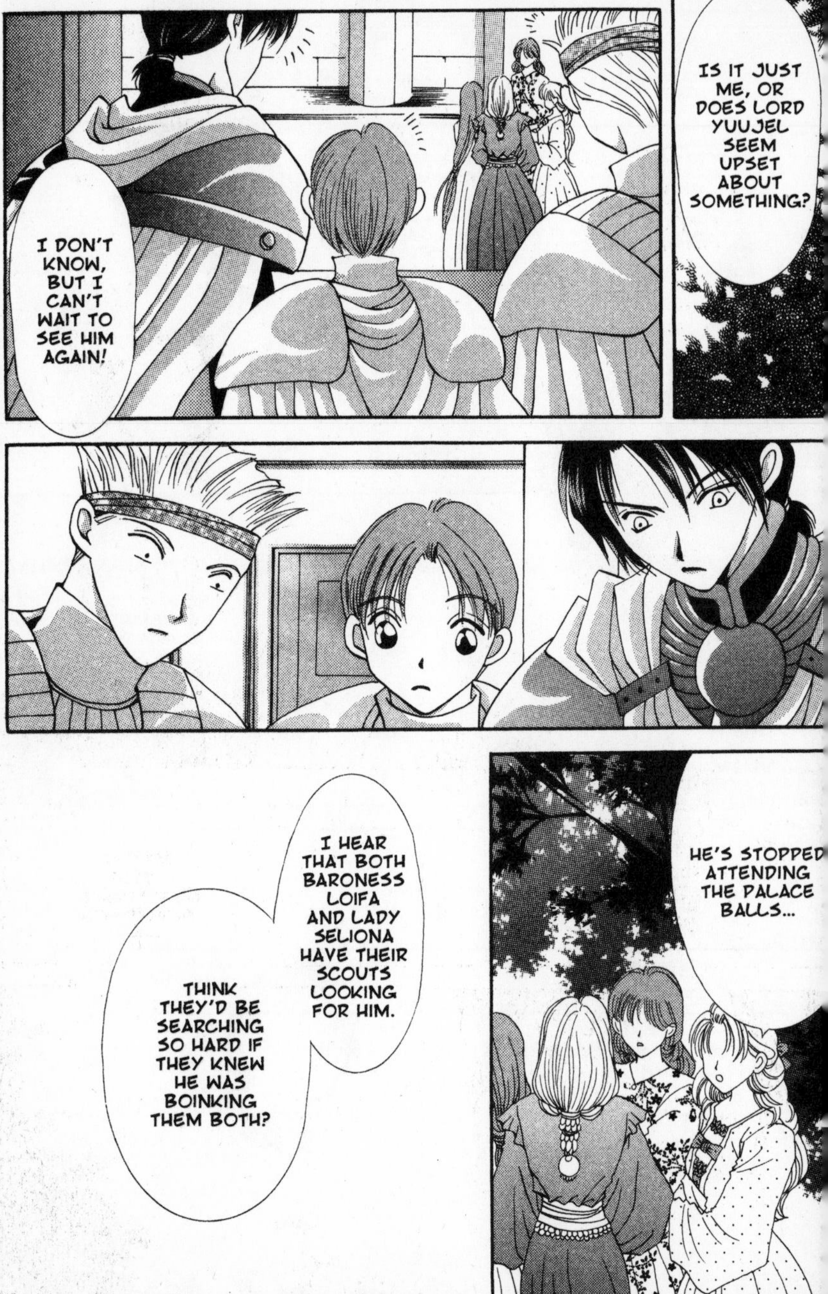
IS IT JUST ME, OR DOES LORD YUUJEL SEEM UPSET ABOUT SOMETHING?
I DON'T KNOW, BUT I CAN'T WAIT TO SEE HIM AGAIN!
HE'S STOPPED ATTENDING THE PALACE BALLS...
I HEAR THAT BOTH BARONESS LOIFA AND LADY SELIONA HAVE THEIR SCOUTS LOOKING FOR HIM.
THINK THEY'D BE SEARCHING SO HARD IF THEY KNEW HE WAS BOINKING THEM BOTH?

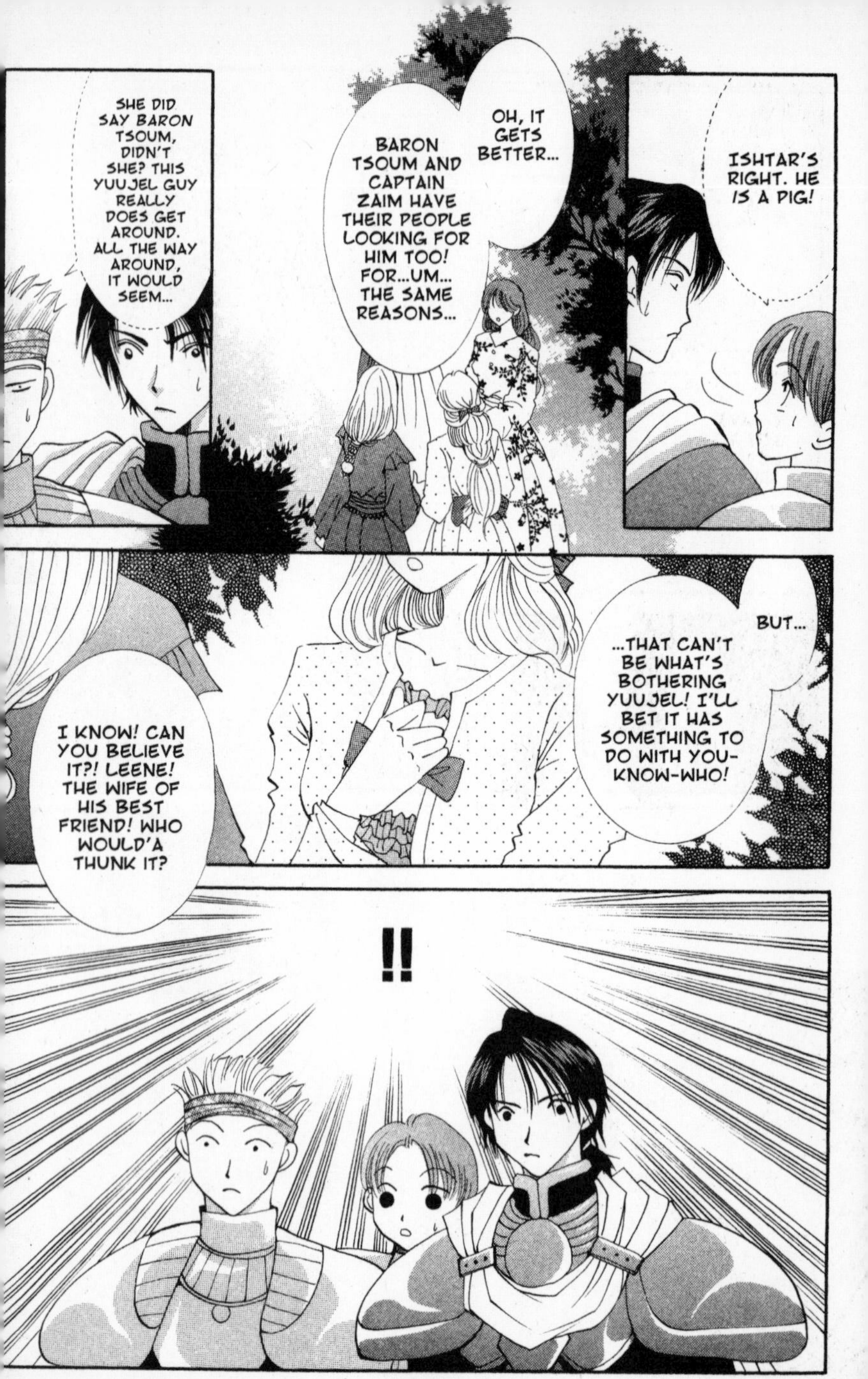

ISHTAR'S RIGHT. HE IS A PIG!
OH, IT GETS BETTER...
BARON TSOUM AND CAPTAIN ZAIM HAVE THEIR PEOPLE LOOKING FOR HIM TOO! FOR...UM... THE SAME REASONS...
SHE DID SAY BARON TSOUM, DIDN'T SHE? THIS YUUJEL GUY REALLY DOES GET AROUND. ALL THE WAY AROUND, IT WOULD SEEM...
BUT...
...THAT CAN'T BE WHAT'S BOTHERING YUUJEL! I'LL BET IT HAS SOMETHING TO DO WITH YOU-KNOW-WHO!
I KNOW! CAN YOU BELIEVE IT?! LEENE! THE WIFE OF HIS BEST FRIEND! WHO WOULD'A THUNK IT?
!!

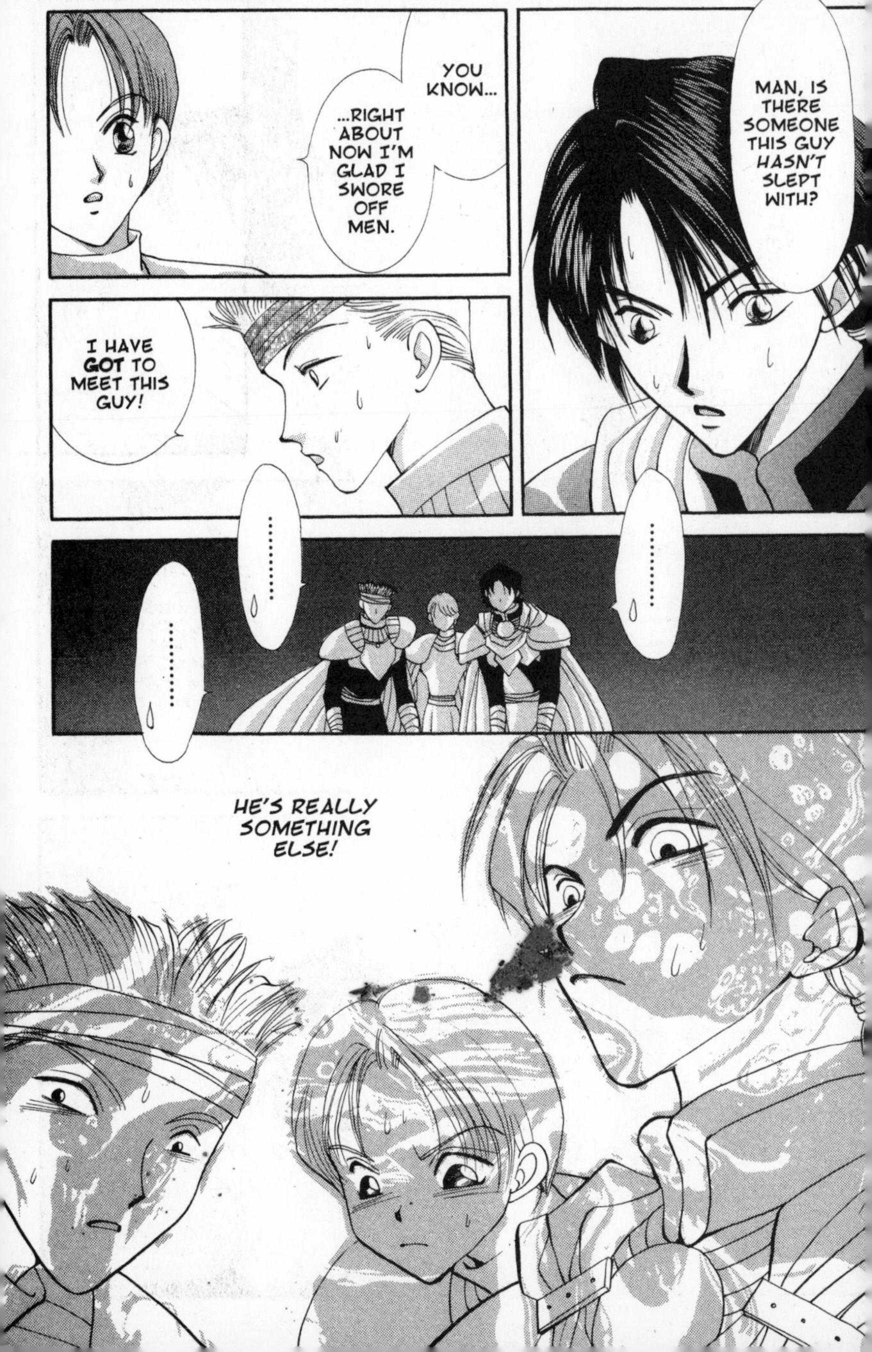

MAN, IS THERE SOMEONE THIS GUY HASN'T SLEPT WITH?
YOU KNOW...
...RIGHT ABOUT NOW I'M GLAD I SWORE OFF MEN.
I HAVE **GOT** TO MEET THIS GUY!
......
......
......
HE'S REALLY SOMETHING ELSE!

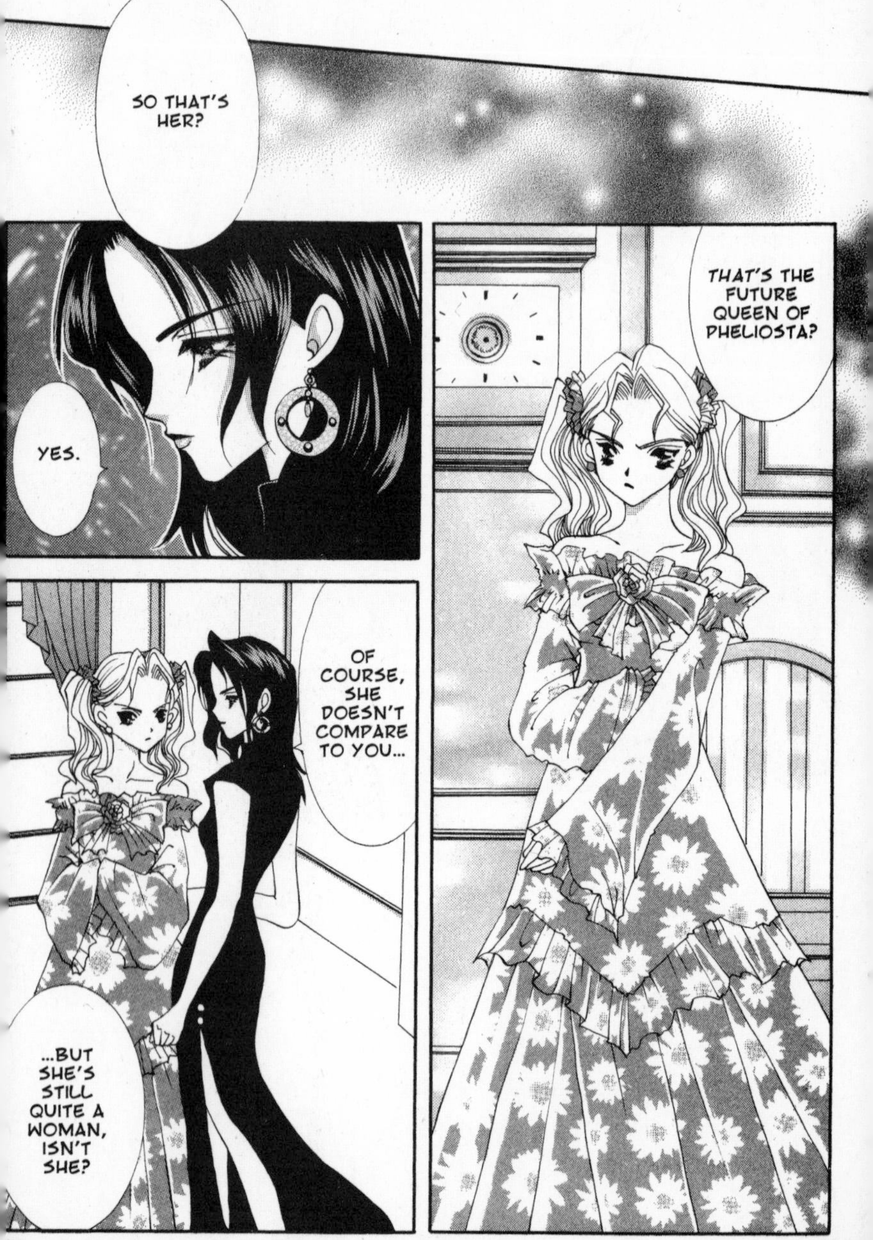
SO THAT'S HER?
THAT'S THE FUTURE QUEEN OF PHELIOSTA?
YES.
OF COURSE, SHE DOESN'T COMPARE TO YOU...
...BUT SHE'S STILL QUITE A WOMAN, ISN'T SHE?

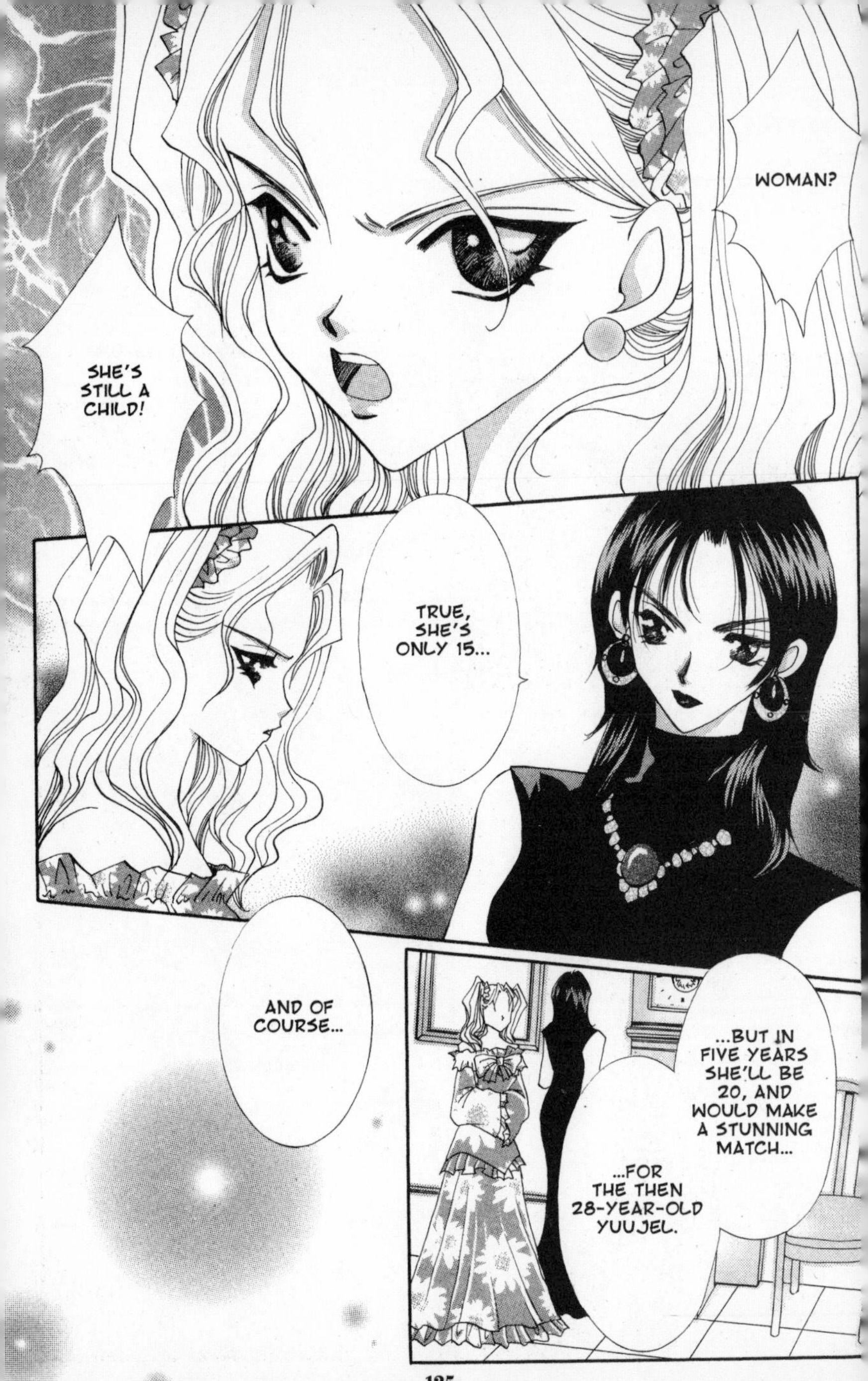
WOMAN?
SHE'S STILL A CHILD!
TRUE, SHE'S ONLY 15...
...BUT IN FIVE YEARS SHE'LL BE 20, AND WOULD MAKE A STUNNING MATCH...
...FOR THE THEN 28-YEAR-OLD YUUJEL.
AND OF COURSE...

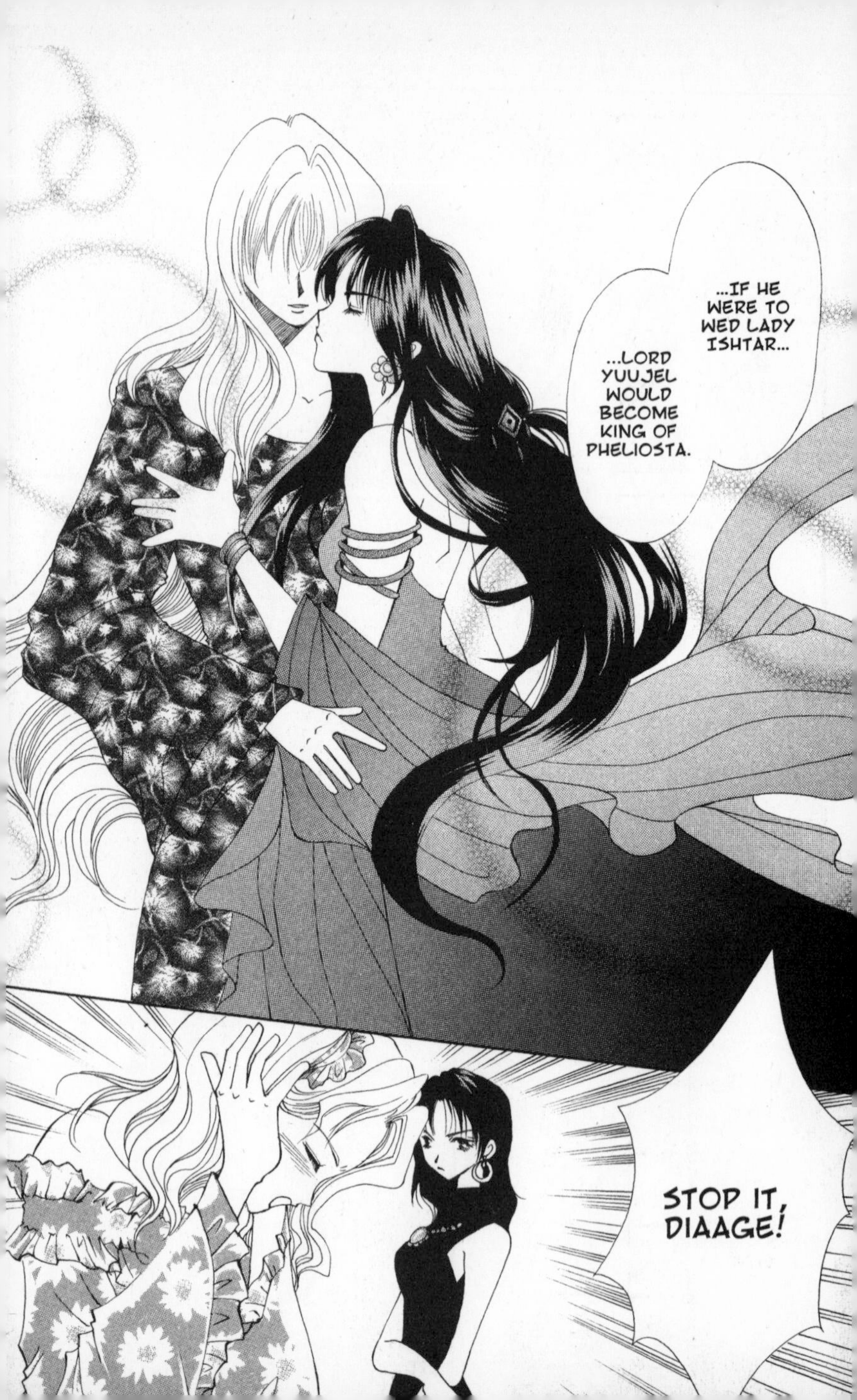
...IF HE WERE TO WED LADY ISHTAR...
...LORD YUUJEL WOULD BECOME KING OF PHELIOSTA.
STOP IT, DIAAGE!

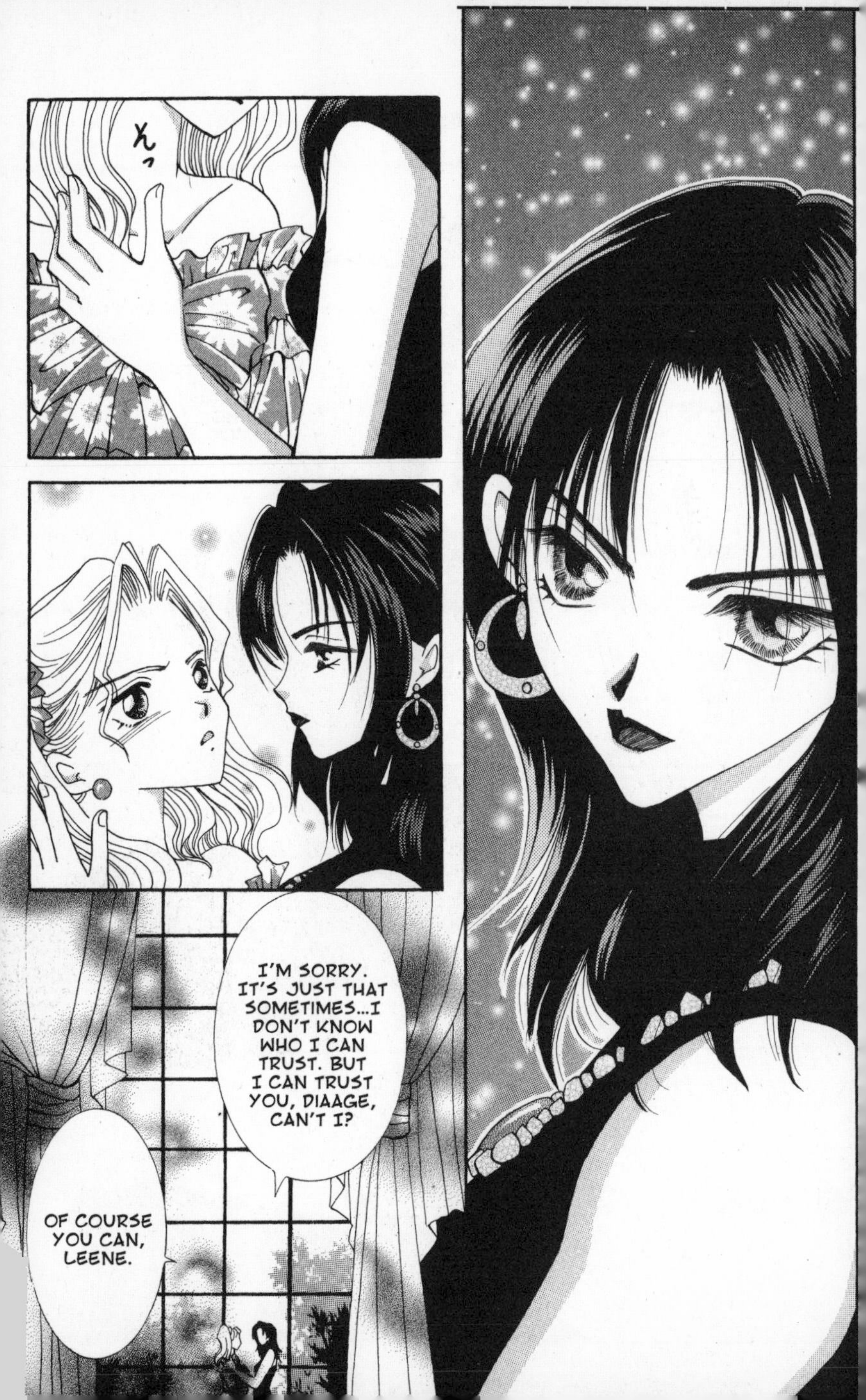
えっ
I'M SORRY. IT'S JUST THAT SOMETIMES...I DON'T KNOW WHO I CAN TRUST. BUT I CAN TRUST YOU, DIAAGE, CAN'T I?
OF COURSE YOU CAN, LEENE.

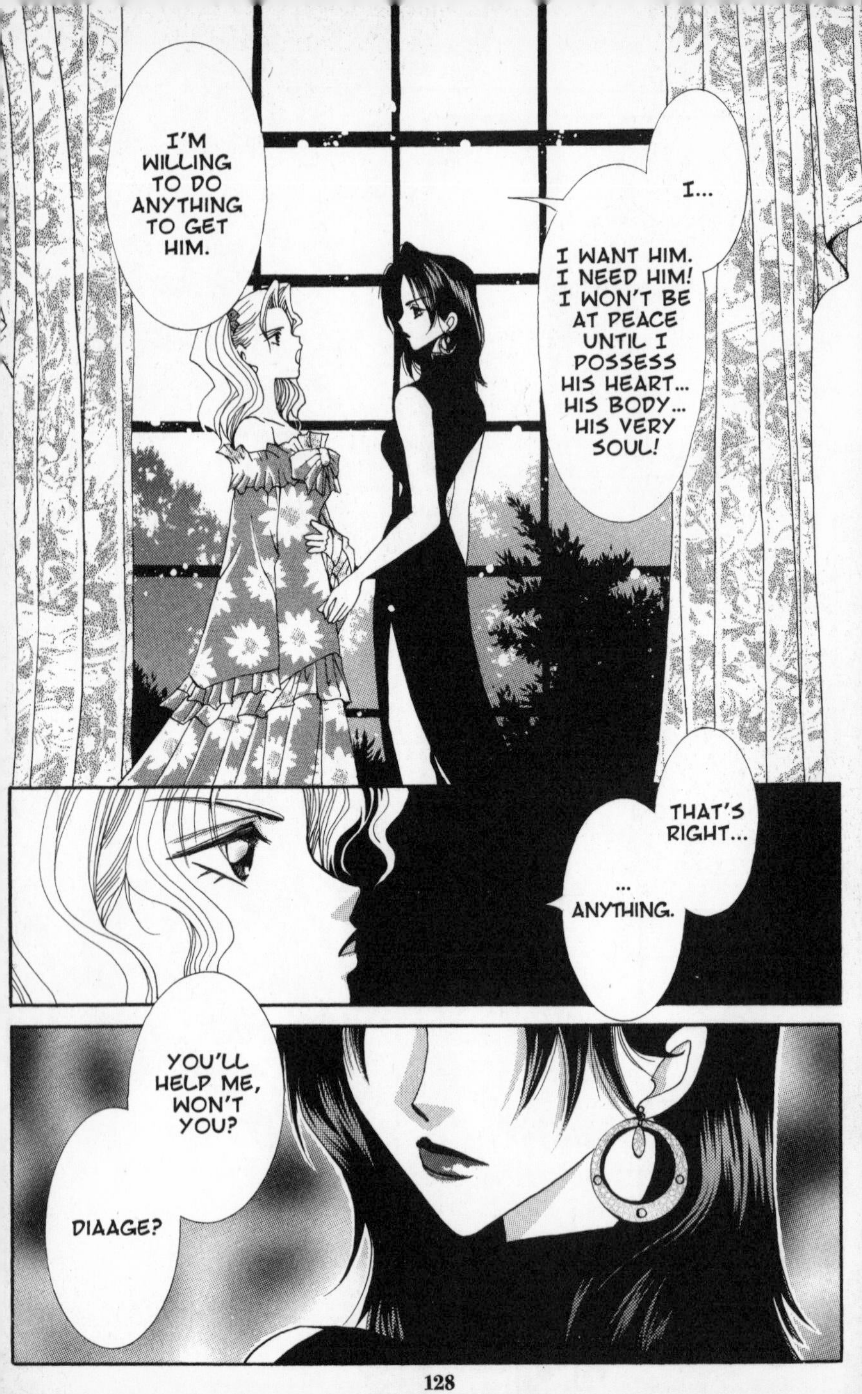
I...
I WANT HIM. I NEED HIM! I WON'T BE AT PEACE UNTIL I POSSESS HIS HEART... HIS BODY... HIS VERY SOUL!
I'M WILLING TO DO ANYTHING TO GET HIM.
THAT'S RIGHT...
... ANYTHING.
YOU'LL HELP ME, WON'T YOU?
DIAAGE?

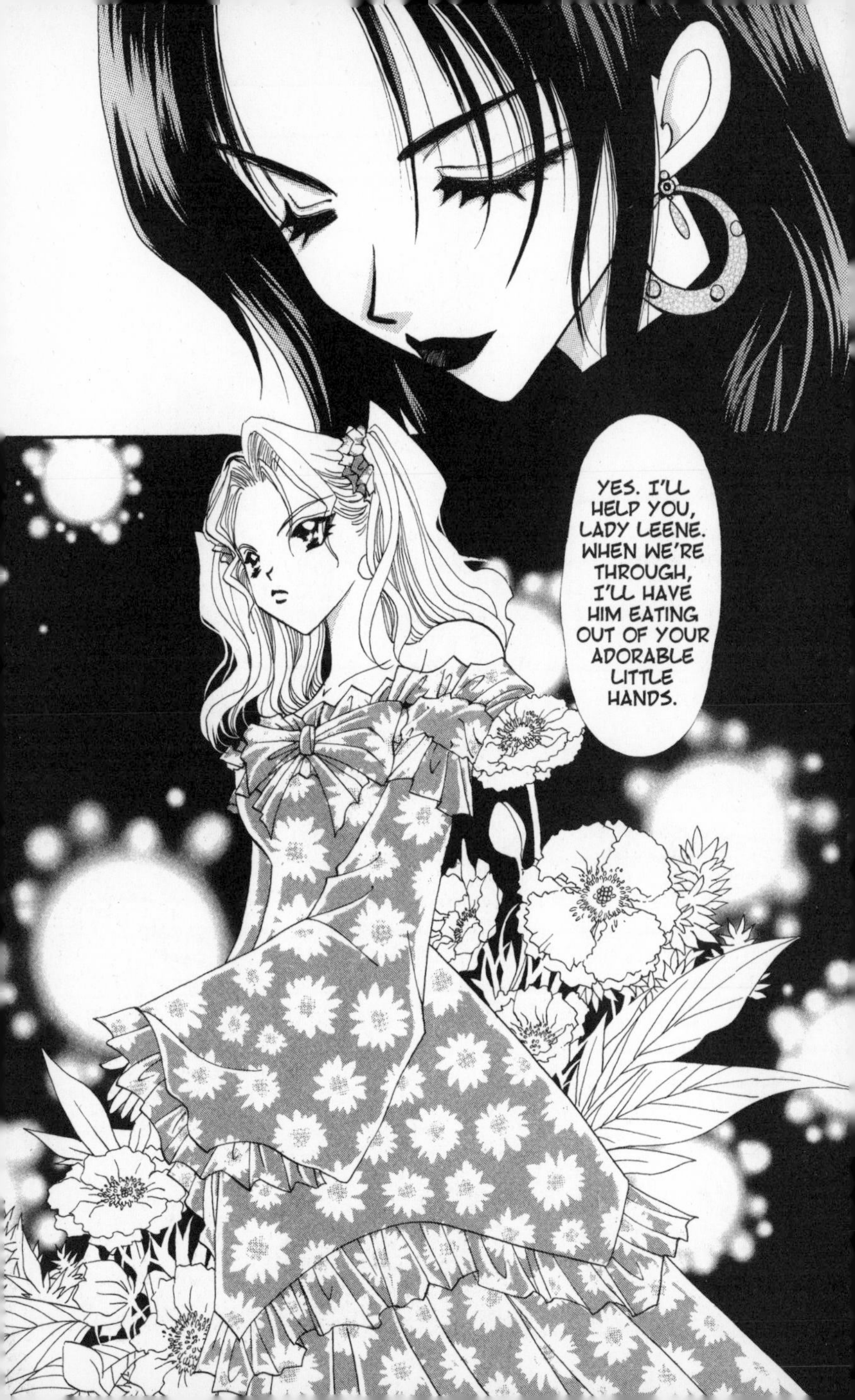
YES. I'LL HELP YOU, LADY LEENE. WHEN WE'RE THROUGH, I'LL HAVE HIM EATING OUT OF YOUR ADORABLE LITTLE HANDS.

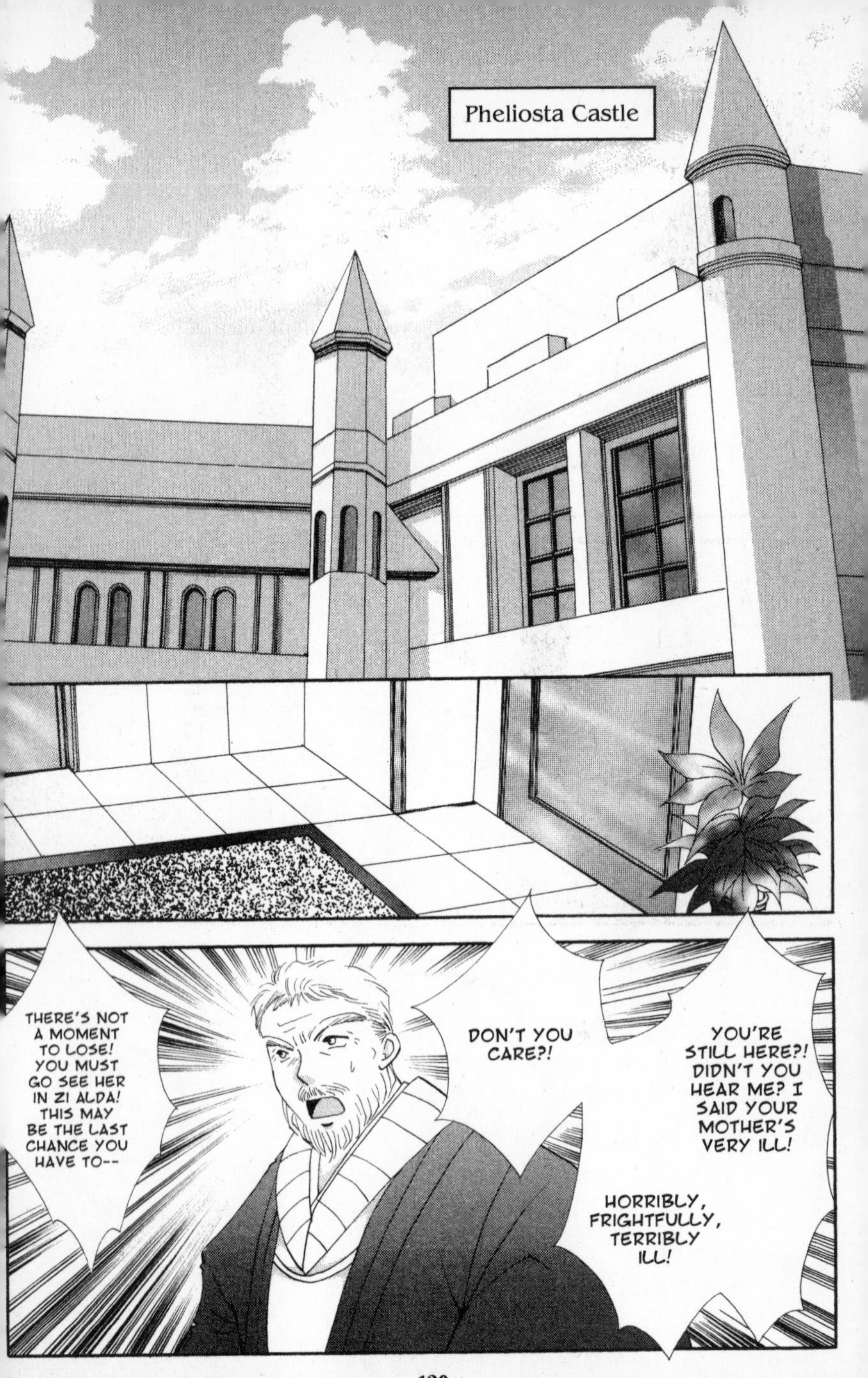
Pheliosta Castle
YOU'RE STILL HERE?! DIDN'T YOU HEAR ME? I SAID YOUR MOTHER'S VERY ILL!
HORRIBLY, FRIGHTFULLY, TERRIBLY ILL!
DON'T YOU CARE?!
THERE'S NOT A MOMENT TO LOSE! YOU MUST GO SEE HER IN ZI ALDA! THIS MAY BE THE LAST CHANCE YOU HAVE TO--

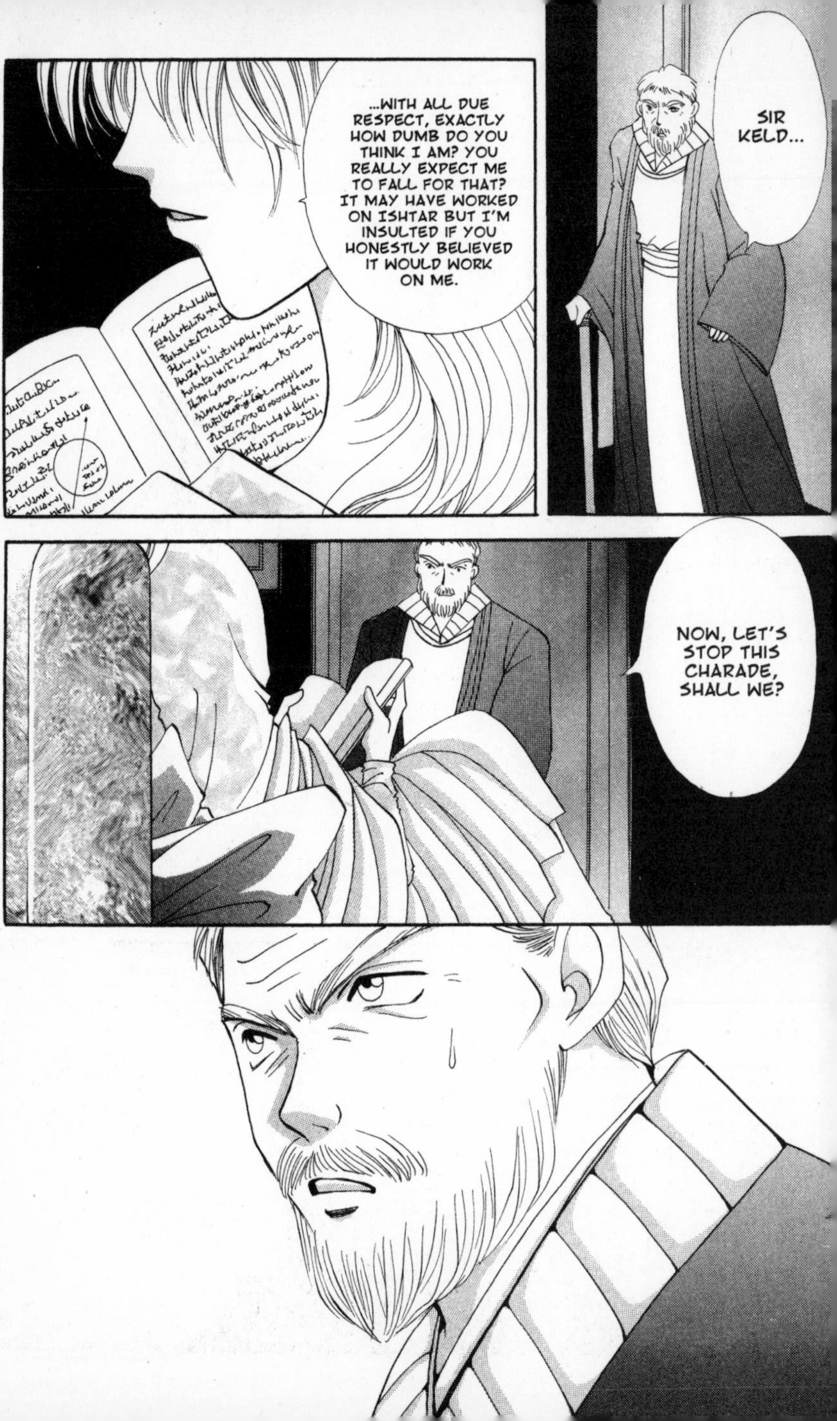
SIR KELD...
...WITH ALL DUE RESPECT, EXACTLY HOW DUMB DO YOU THINK I AM? YOU REALLY EXPECT ME TO FALL FOR THAT? IT MAY HAVE WORKED ON ISHTAR BUT I'M INSULTED IF YOU HONESTLY BELIEVED IT WOULD WORK ON ME.
NOW, LET'S STOP THIS CHARADE, SHALL WE?

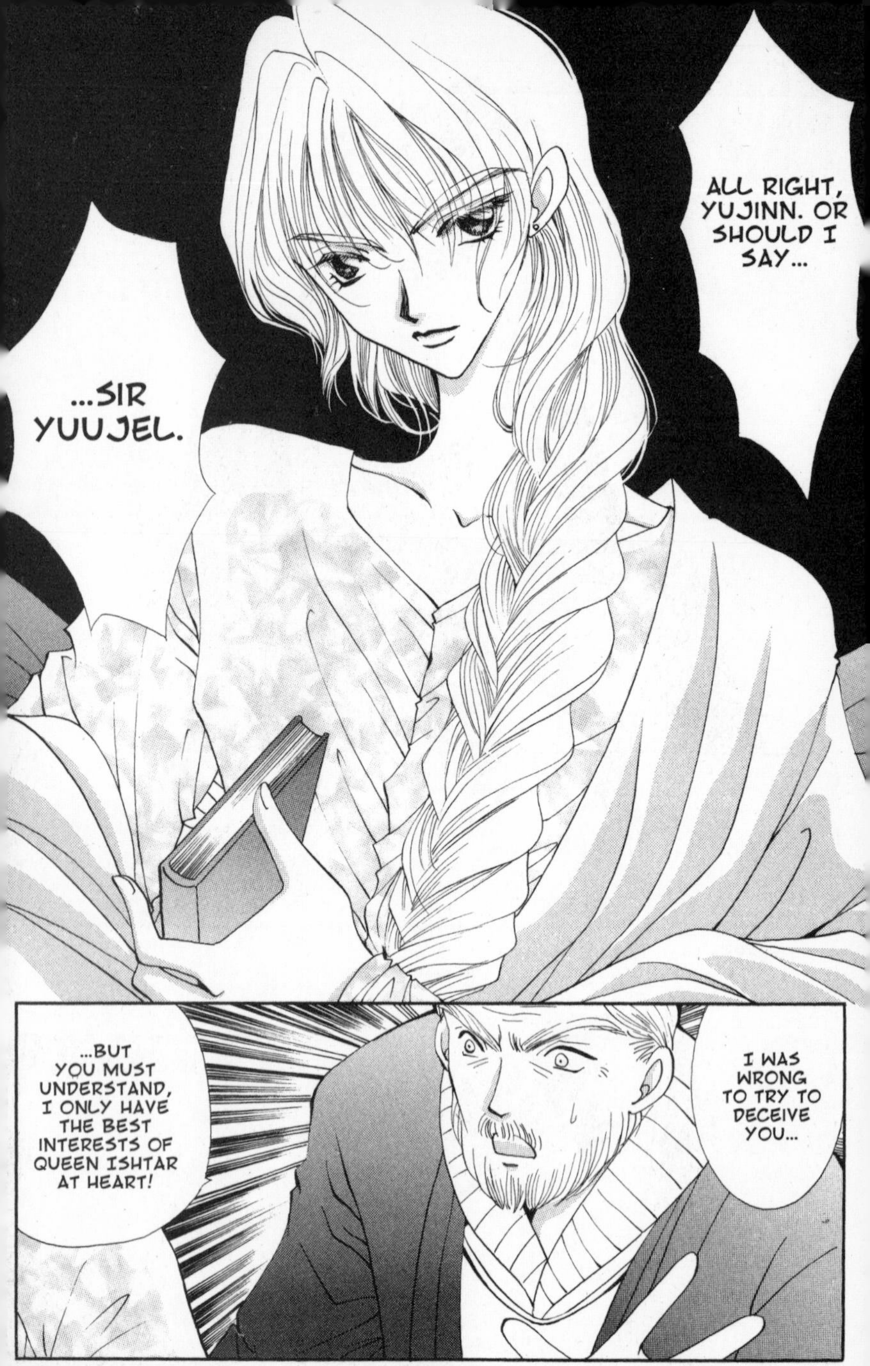
ALL RIGHT, YUJINN. OR SHOULD I SAY...
...SIR YUUJEL.
I WAS WRONG TO TRY TO DECEIVE YOU...
...BUT YOU MUST UNDERSTAND, I ONLY HAVE THE BEST INTERESTS OF QUEEN ISHTAR AT HEART!

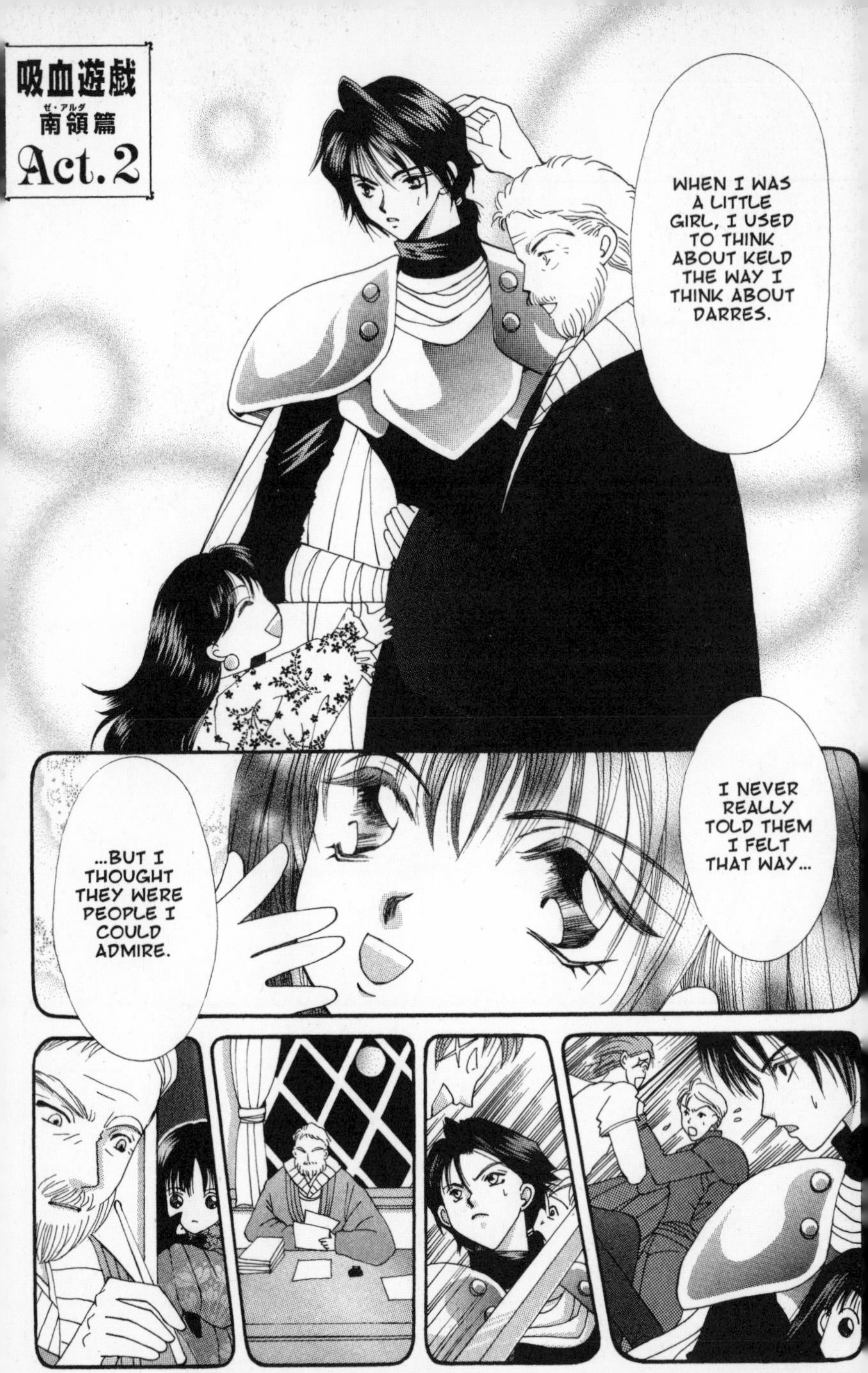
吸血遊戯
ゼ・アルダ
南領篇
Act.2
WHEN I WAS A LITTLE GIRL, I USED TO THINK ABOUT KELD THE WAY I THINK ABOUT DARRES.
I NEVER REALLY TOLD THEM I FELT THAT WAY...
...BUT I THOUGHT THEY WERE PEOPLE I COULD ADMIRE.

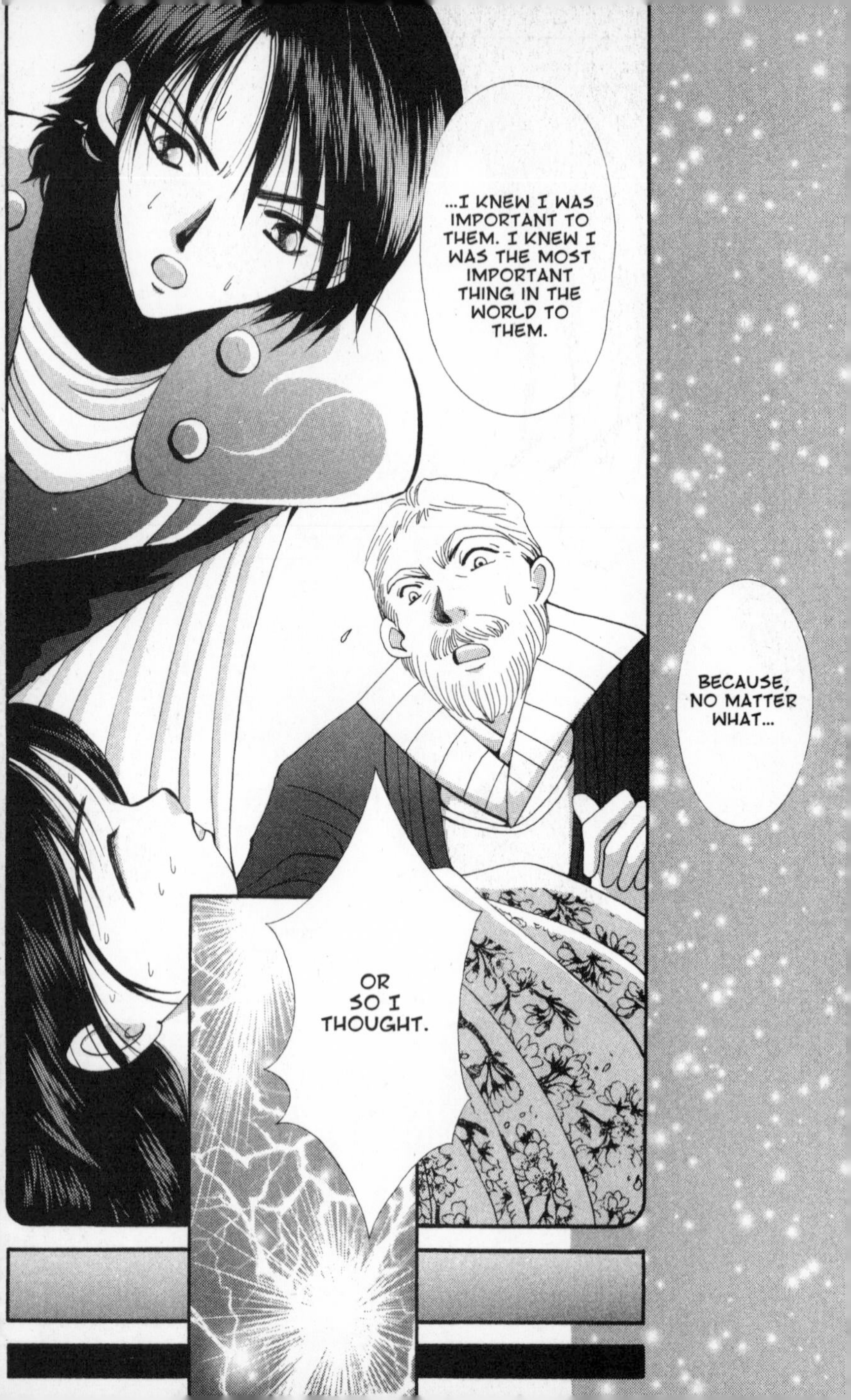
BECAUSE, NO MATTER WHAT...
...I KNEW I WAS IMPORTANT TO THEM. I KNEW I WAS THE MOST IMPORTANT THING IN THE WORLD TO THEM.
OR SO I THOUGHT.

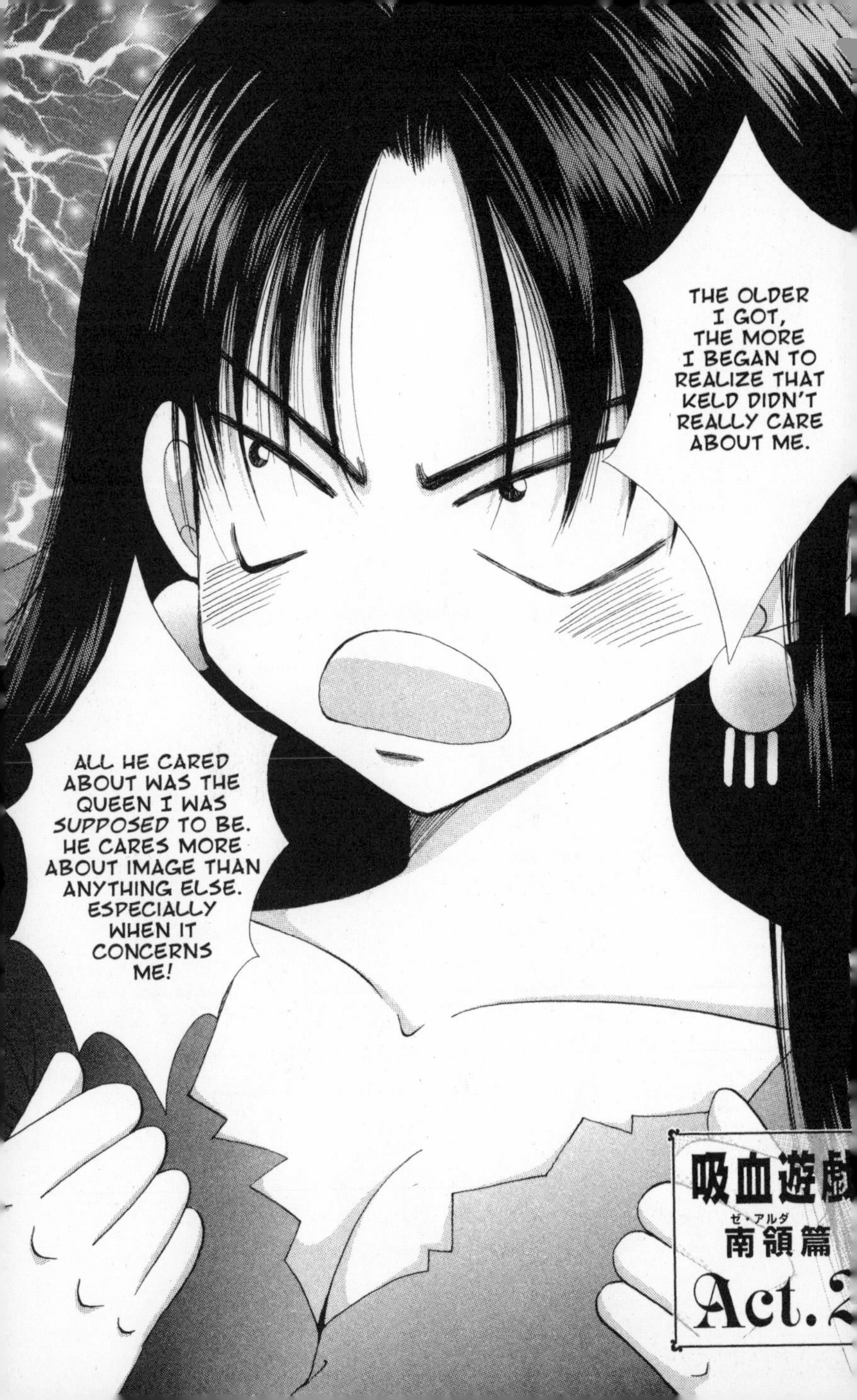
THE OLDER I GOT, THE MORE I BEGAN TO REALIZE THAT KELD DIDN'T REALLY CARE ABOUT ME.
ALL HE CARED ABOUT WAS THE QUEEN I WAS *SUPPOSED* TO BE. HE CARES MORE ABOUT IMAGE THAN ANYTHING ELSE. ESPECIALLY WHEN IT CONCERNS ME!
吸血遊戯
ゼ・アルダ
南領篇
Act.2

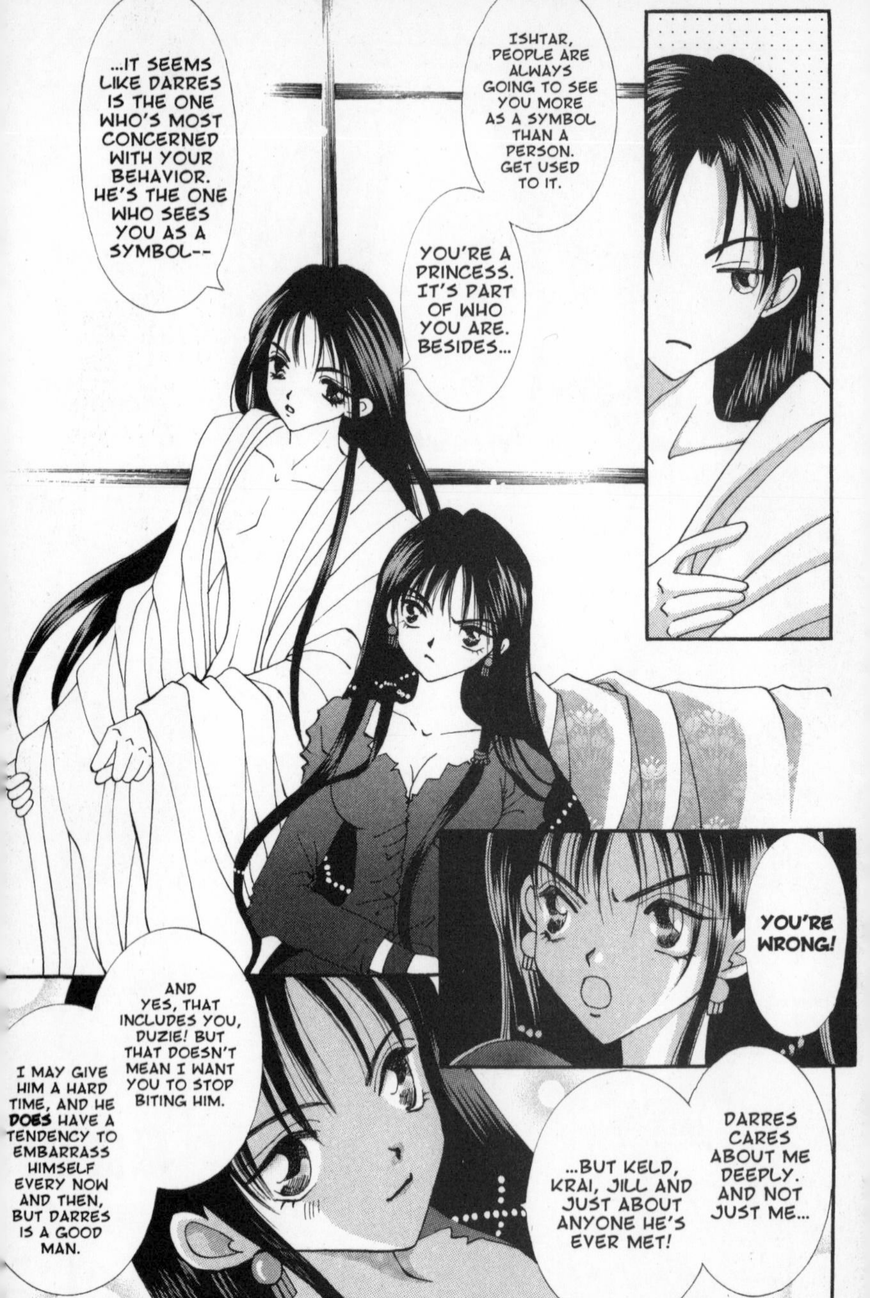
ISHTAR, PEOPLE ARE ALWAYS GOING TO SEE YOU MORE AS A SYMBOL THAN A PERSON. GET USED TO IT.
YOU'RE A PRINCESS. IT'S PART OF WHO YOU ARE. BESIDES...
...IT SEEMS LIKE DARRES IS THE ONE WHO'S MOST CONCERNED WITH YOUR BEHAVIOR. HE'S THE ONE WHO SEES YOU AS A SYMBOL--
YOU'RE WRONG!
DARRES CARES ABOUT ME DEEPLY. AND NOT JUST ME...
...BUT KELD, KRAI, JILL AND JUST ABOUT ANYONE HE'S EVER MET!
AND YES, THAT INCLUDES YOU, DUZIE! BUT THAT DOESN'T MEAN I WANT YOU TO STOP BITING HIM.
I MAY GIVE HIM A HARD TIME, AND HE **DOES** HAVE A TENDENCY TO EMBARRASS HIMSELF EVERY NOW AND THEN, BUT DARRES IS A GOOD MAN.

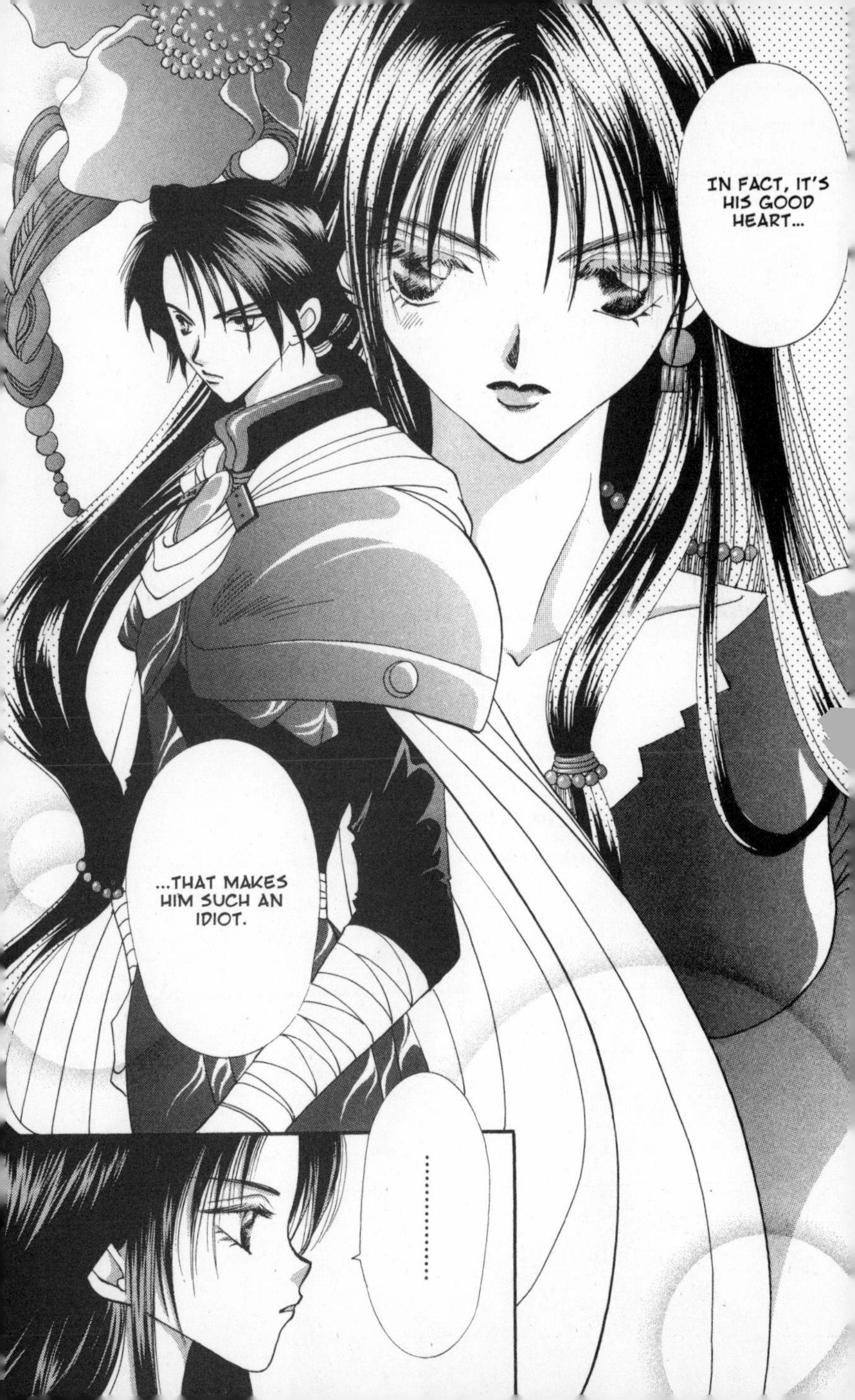
IN FACT, IT'S HIS GOOD HEART...
...THAT MAKES HIM SUCH AN IDIOT.
....

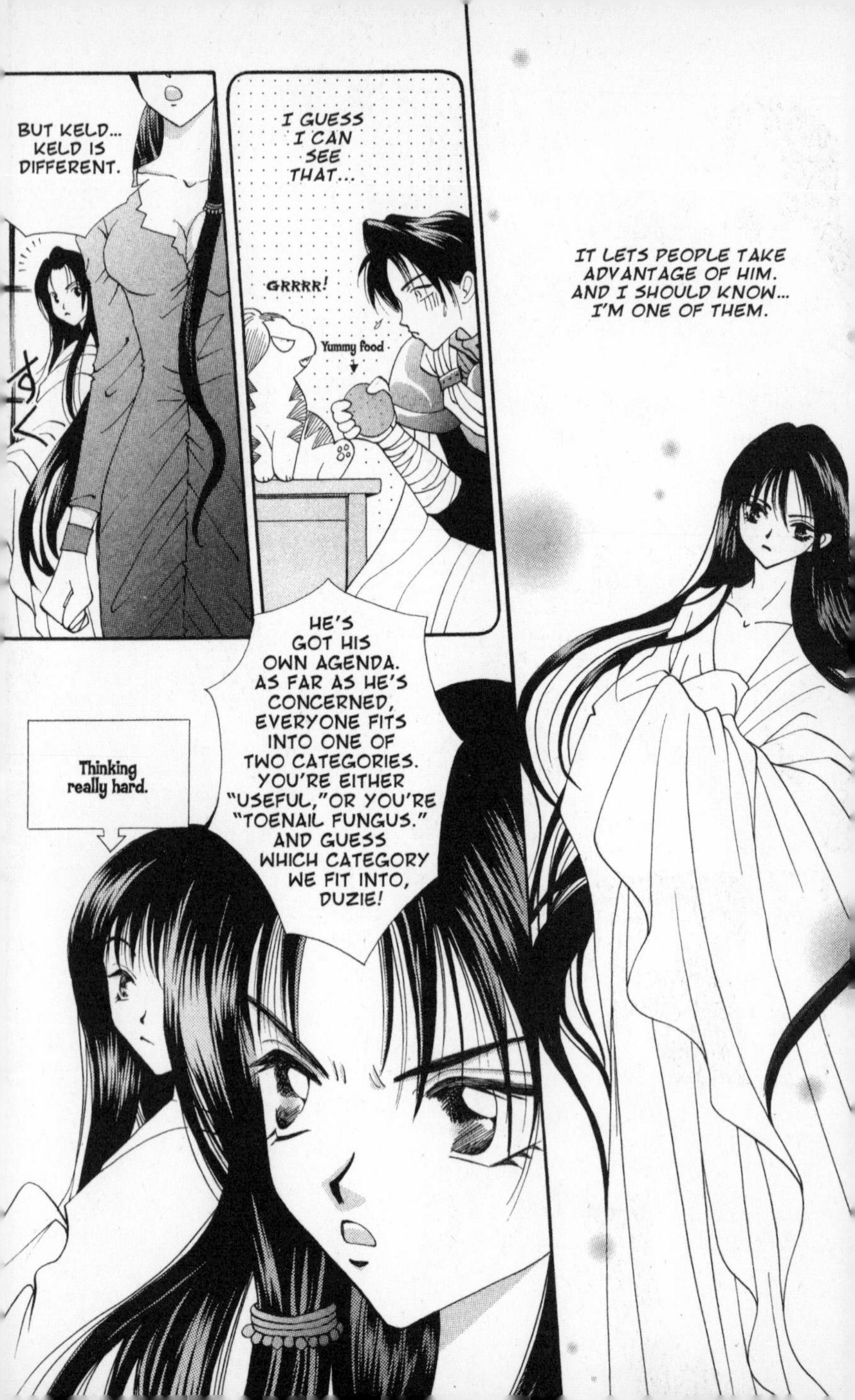
IT LETS PEOPLE TAKE ADVANTAGE OF HIM. AND I SHOULD KNOW... I'M ONE OF THEM.
I GUESS I CAN SEE THAT...
GRRRR!
Yummy food
BUT KELD... KELD IS DIFFERENT.
すく
HE'S GOT HIS OWN AGENDA. AS FAR AS HE'S CONCERNED, EVERYONE FITS INTO ONE OF TWO CATEGORIES. YOU'RE EITHER "USEFUL," OR YOU'RE "TOENAIL FUNGUS." AND GUESS WHICH CATEGORY WE FIT INTO, DUZIE!
Thinking really hard.

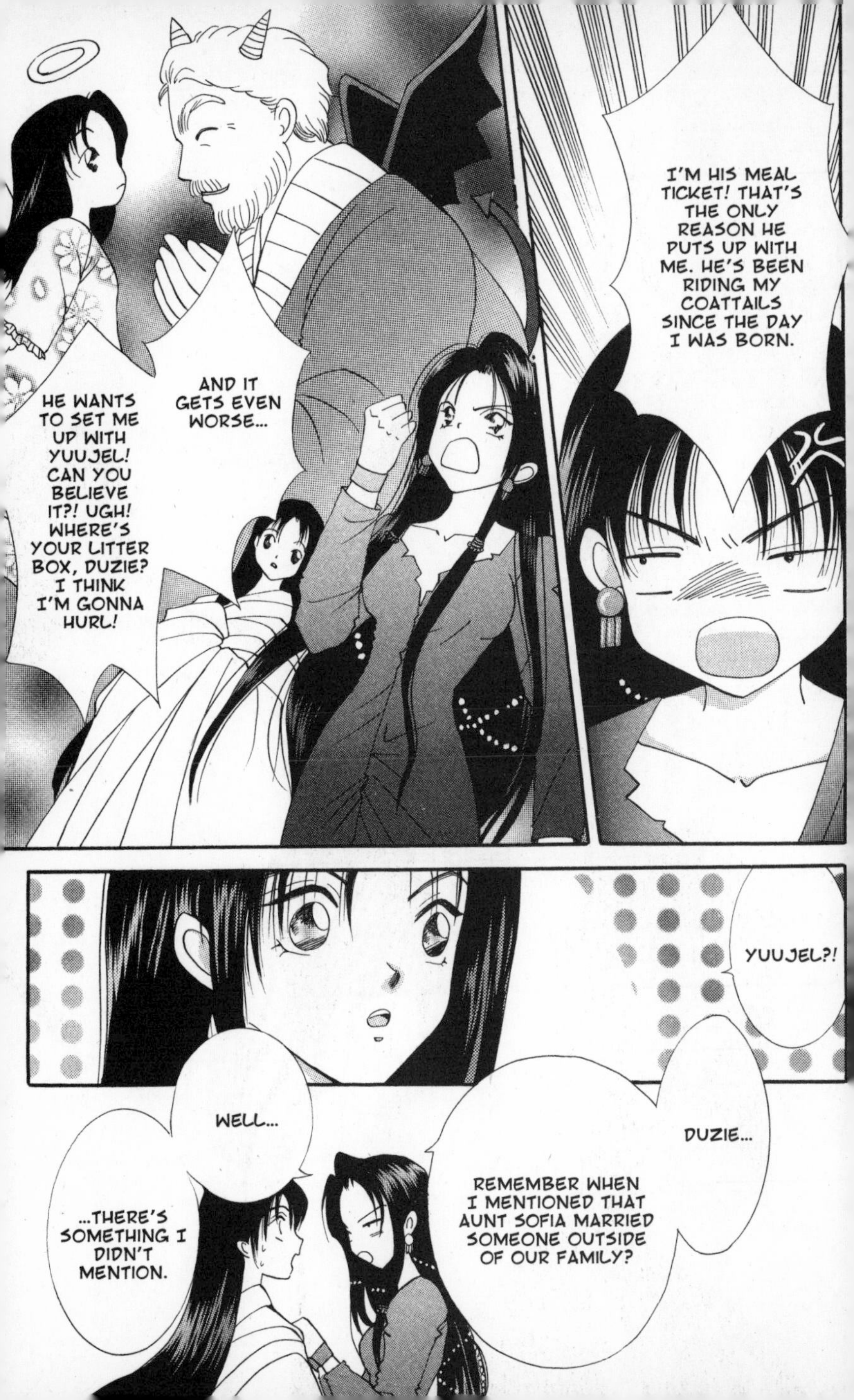
I'M HIS MEAL TICKET! THAT'S THE ONLY REASON HE PUTS UP WITH ME. HE'S BEEN RIDING MY COATTAILS SINCE THE DAY I WAS BORN.
AND IT GETS EVEN WORSE...
HE WANTS TO SET ME UP WITH YUUJEL! CAN YOU BELIEVE IT?! UGH! WHERE'S YOUR LITTER BOX, DUZIE? I THINK I'M GONNA HURL!
YUUJEL?!
DUZIE...
REMEMBER WHEN I MENTIONED THAT AUNT SOFIA MARRIED SOMEONE OUTSIDE OF OUR FAMILY?
WELL...
...THERE'S SOMETHING I DIDN'T MENTION.

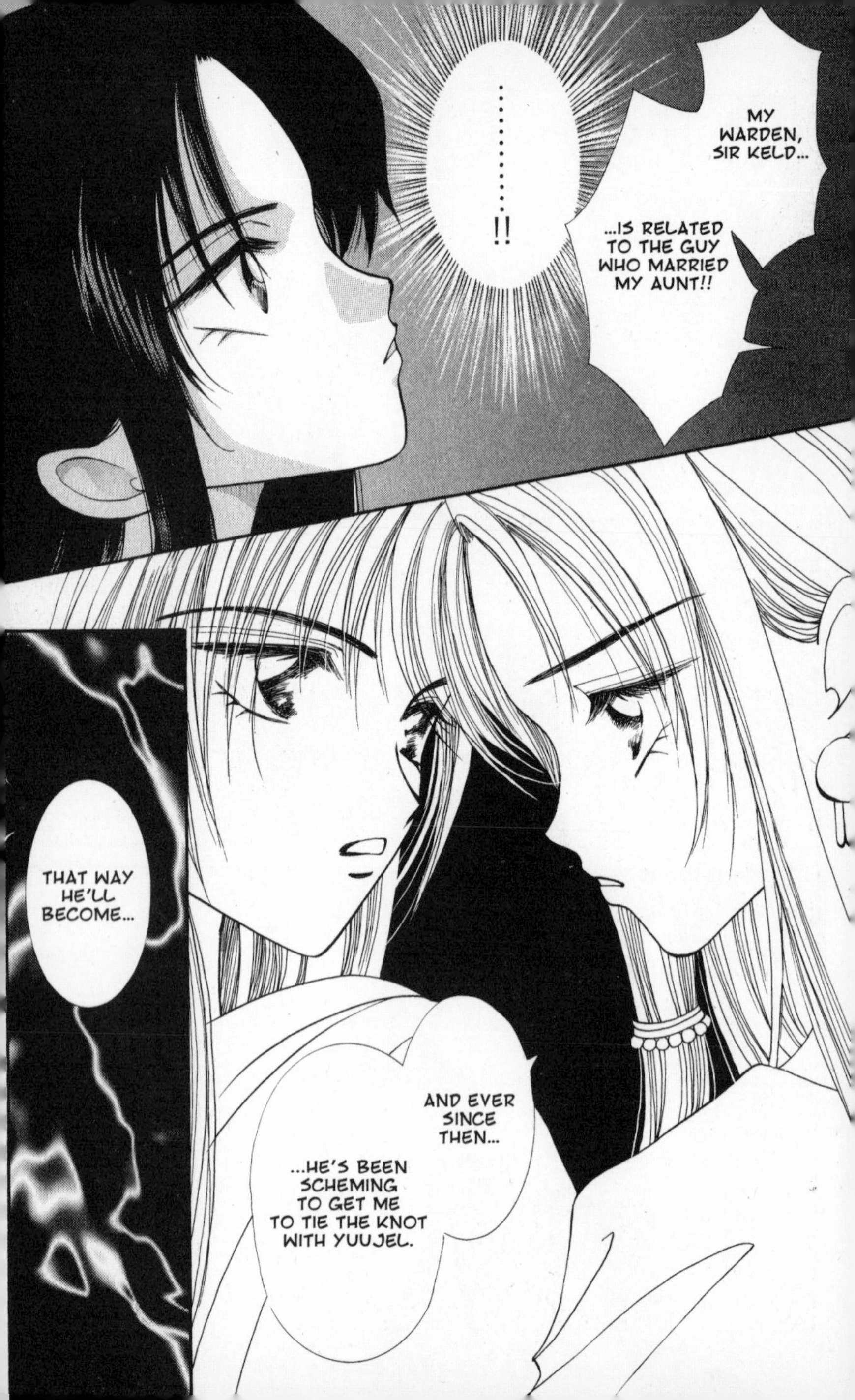
MY WARDEN, SIR KELD...
...IS RELATED TO THE GUY WHO MARRIED MY AUNT!!
......!!
AND EVER SINCE THEN...
...HE'S BEEN SCHEMING TO GET ME TO TIE THE KNOT WITH YUUJEL.
THAT WAY HE'LL BECOME...

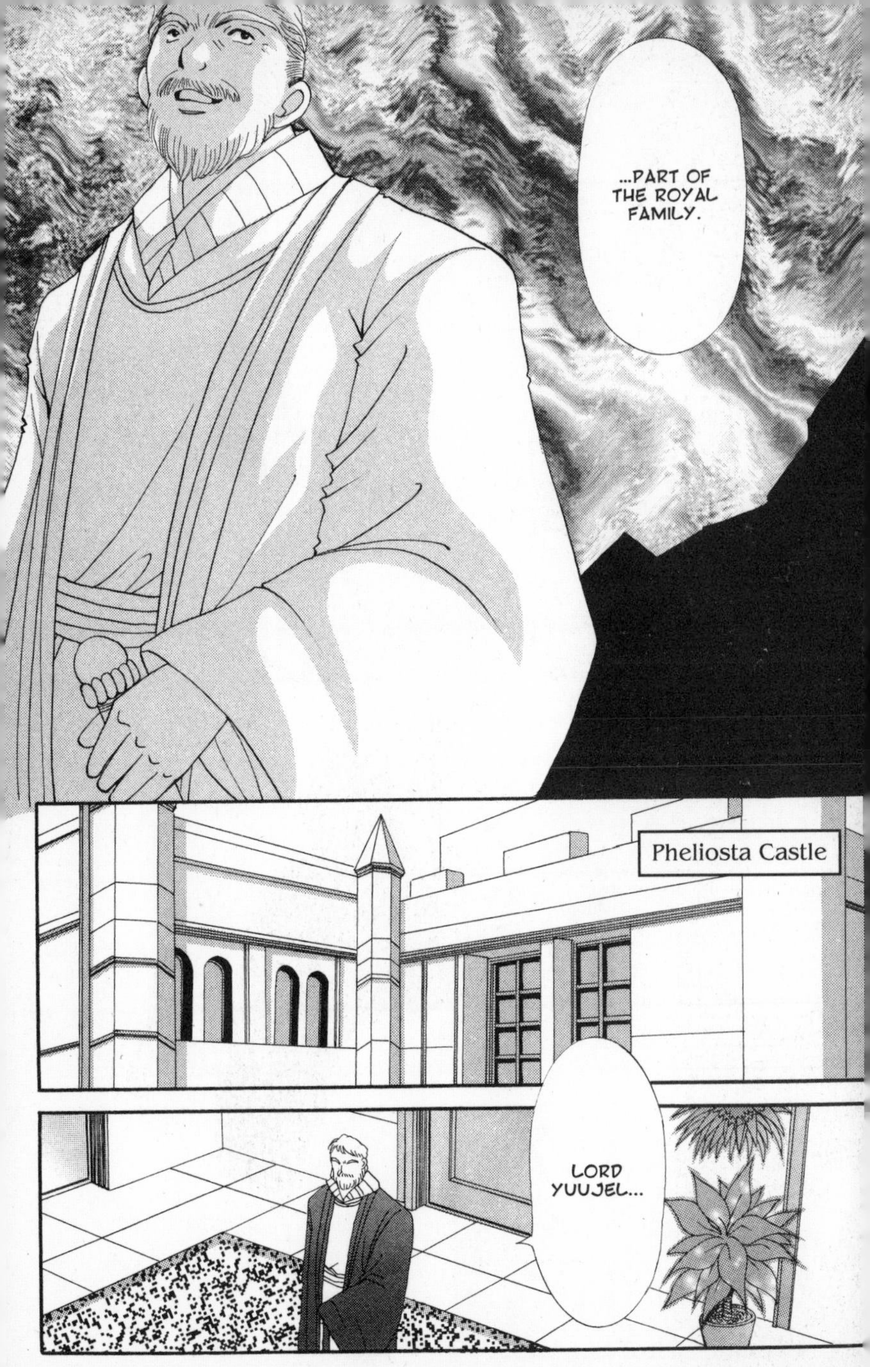
...PART OF THE ROYAL FAMILY.
Pheliosta Castle
LORD YUUJEL...

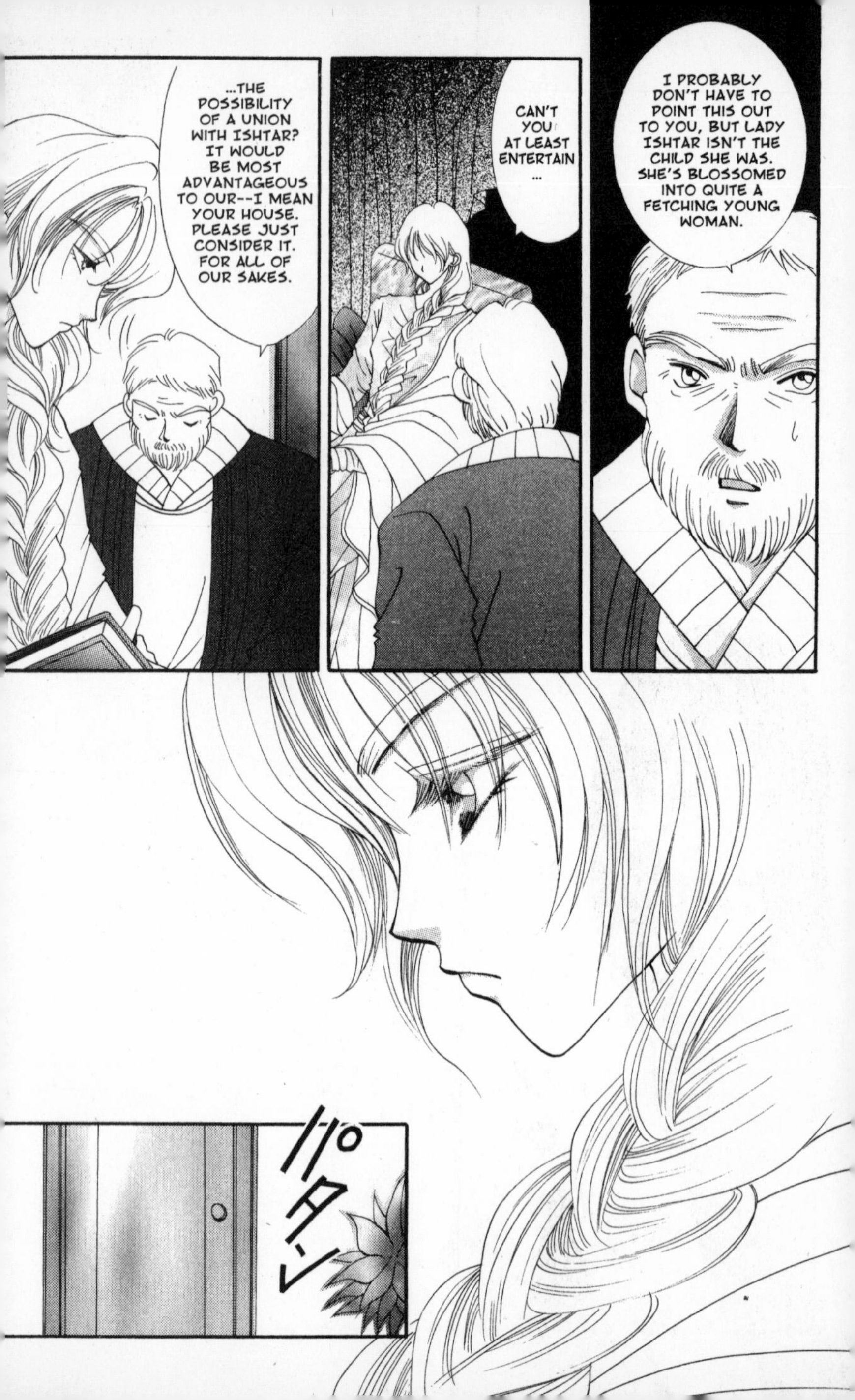
I PROBABLY DON'T HAVE TO POINT THIS OUT TO YOU, BUT LADY ISHTAR ISN'T THE CHILD SHE WAS. SHE'S BLOSSOMED INTO QUITE A FETCHING YOUNG WOMAN.
CAN'T YOU AT LEAST ENTERTAIN ...
...THE POSSIBILITY OF A UNION WITH ISHTAR? IT WOULD BE MOST ADVANTAGEOUS TO OUR--I MEAN YOUR HOUSE. PLEASE JUST CONSIDER IT. FOR ALL OF OUR SAKES.
パターン

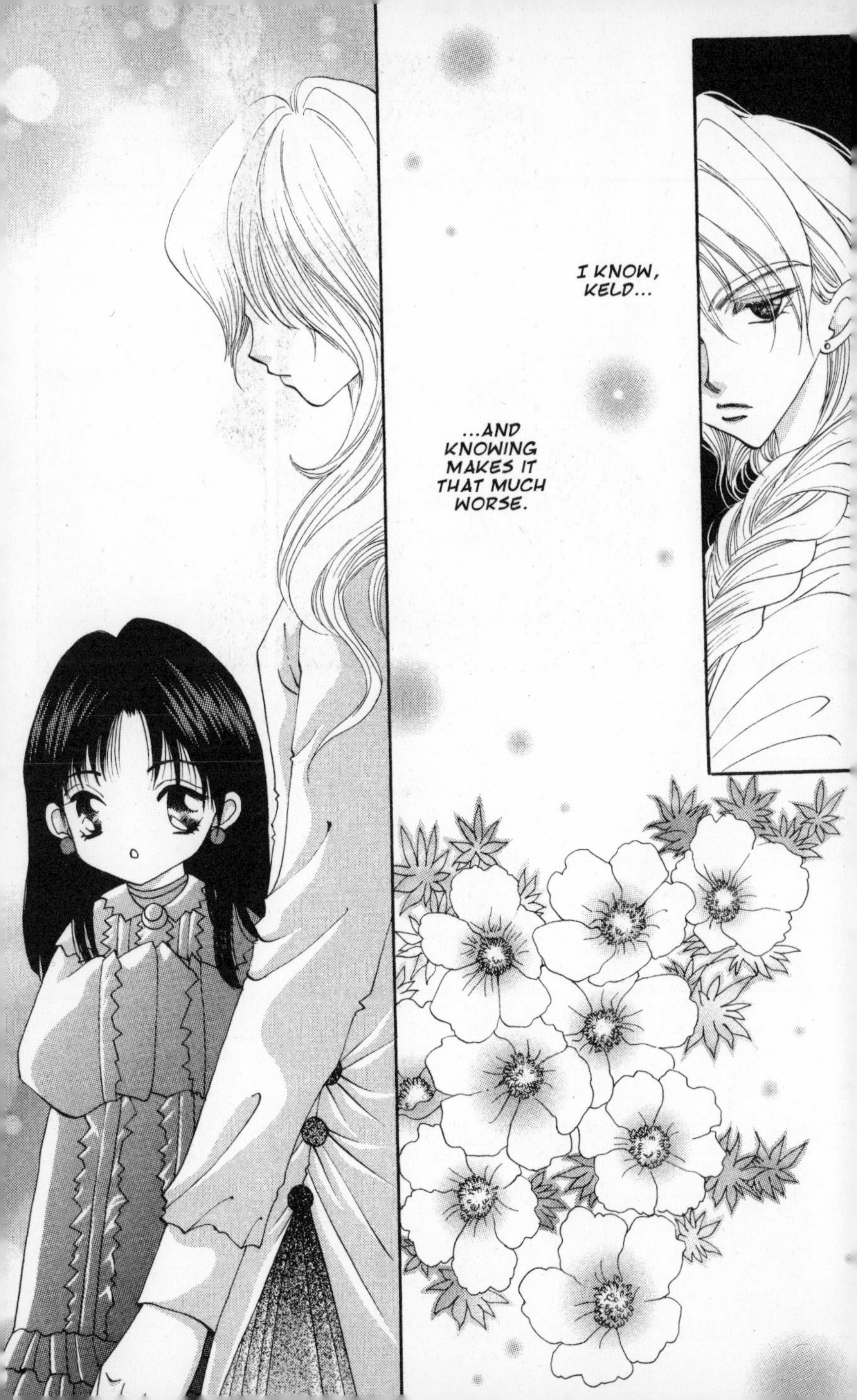
I KNOW, KELD...
...AND KNOWING MAKES IT THAT MUCH WORSE.

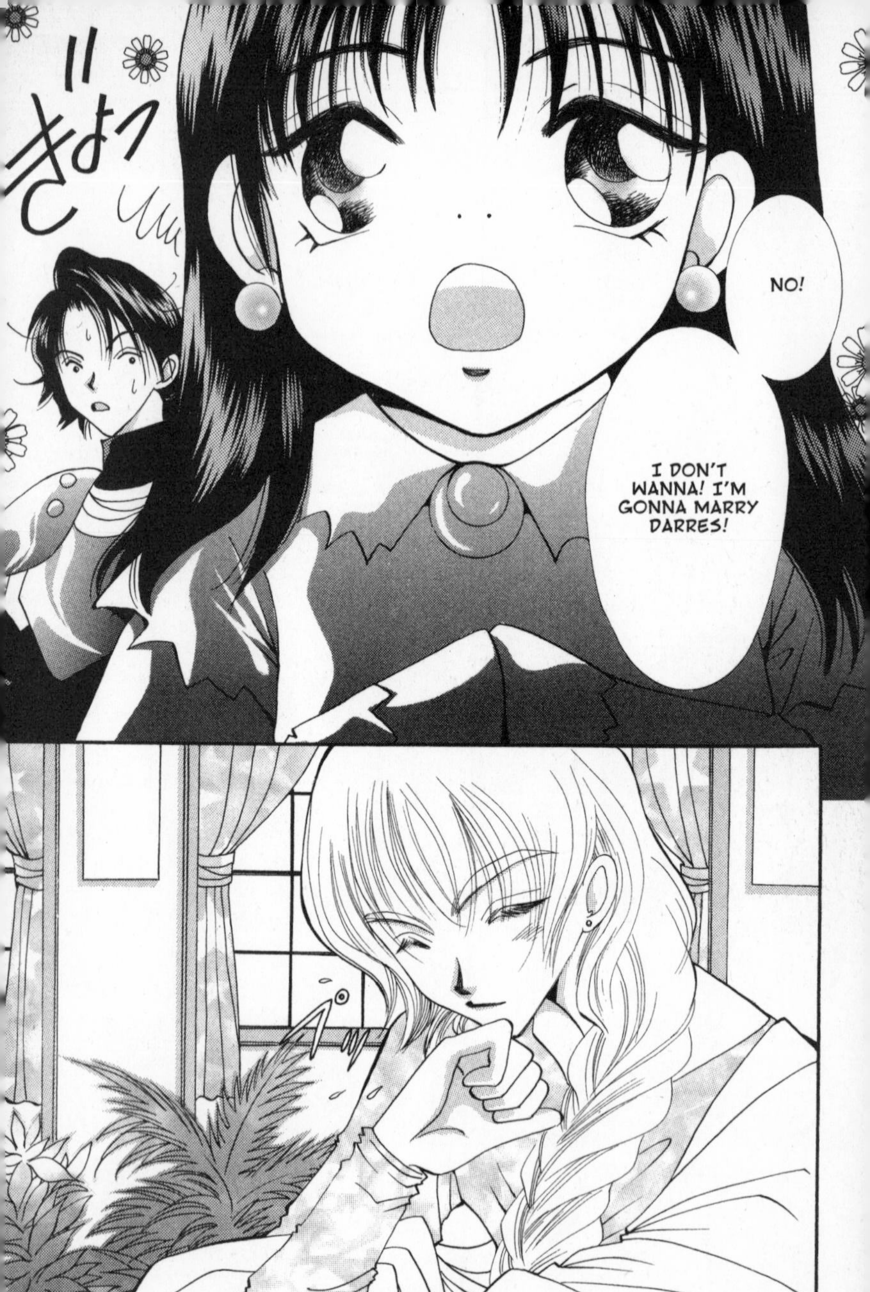
NO!
I DON'T WANNA! I'M GONNA MARRY DARRES!
ぎょっ

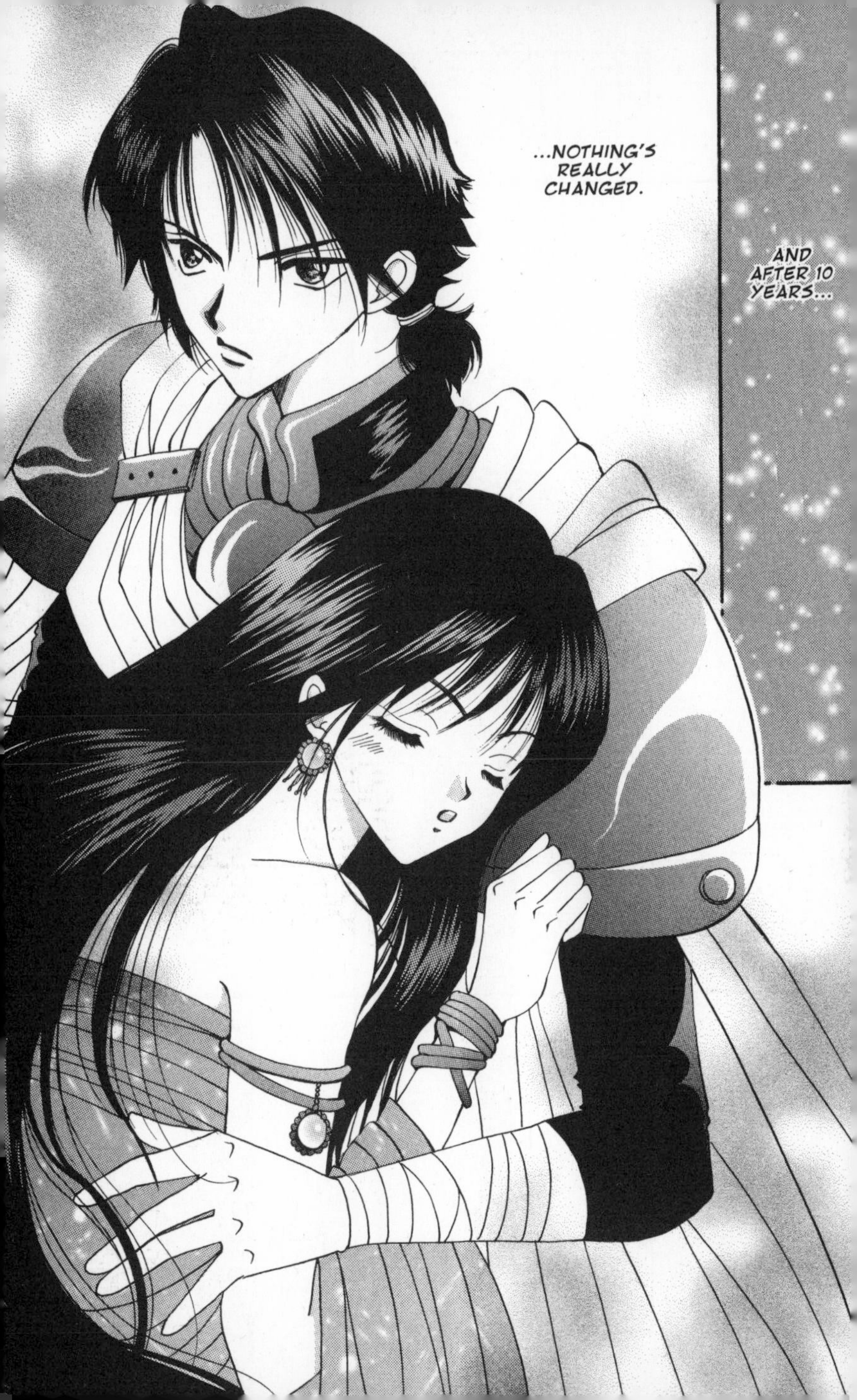
AND AFTER 10 YEARS...
...NOTHING'S REALLY CHANGED.

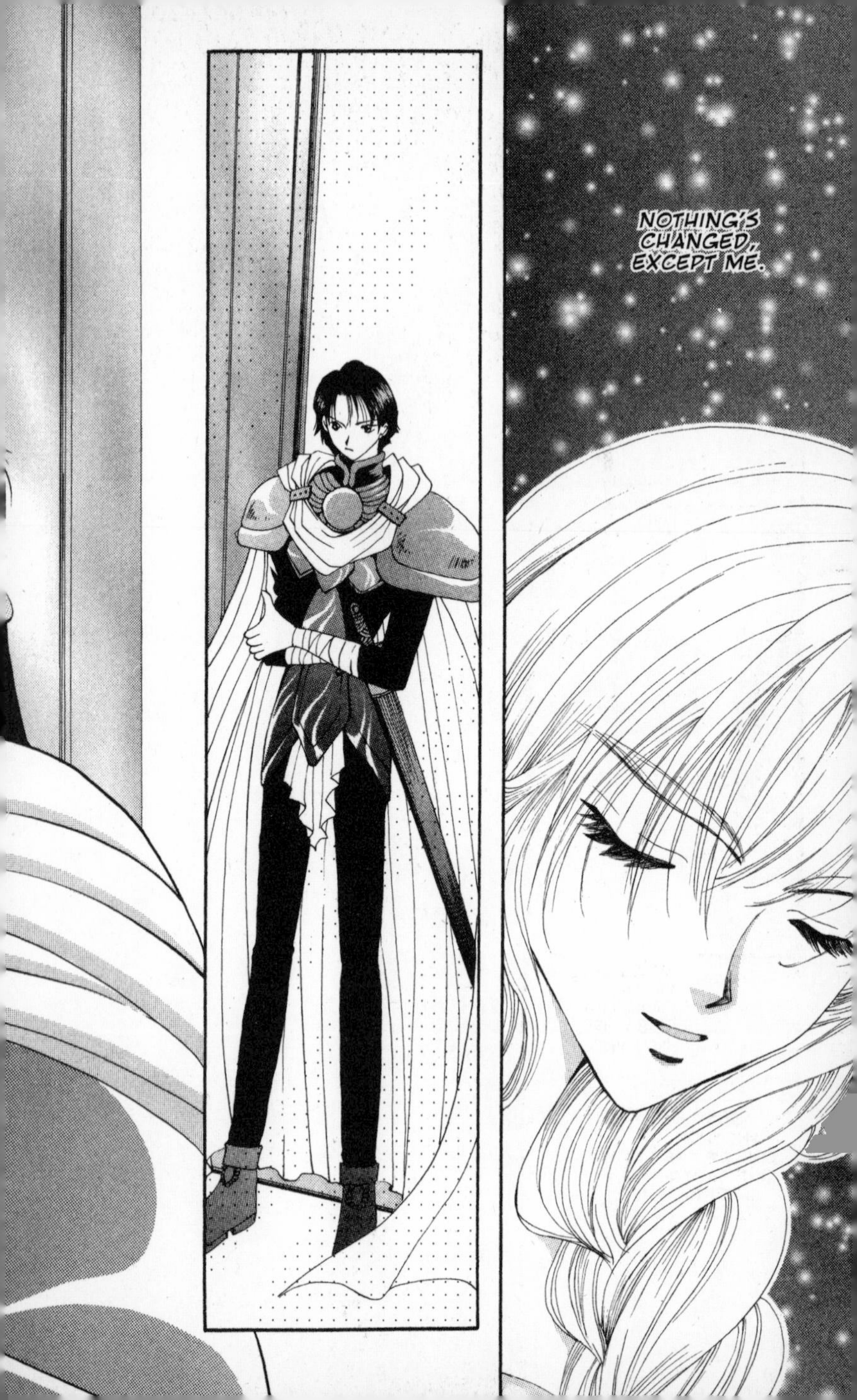
NOTHING'S CHANGED, EXCEPT ME.

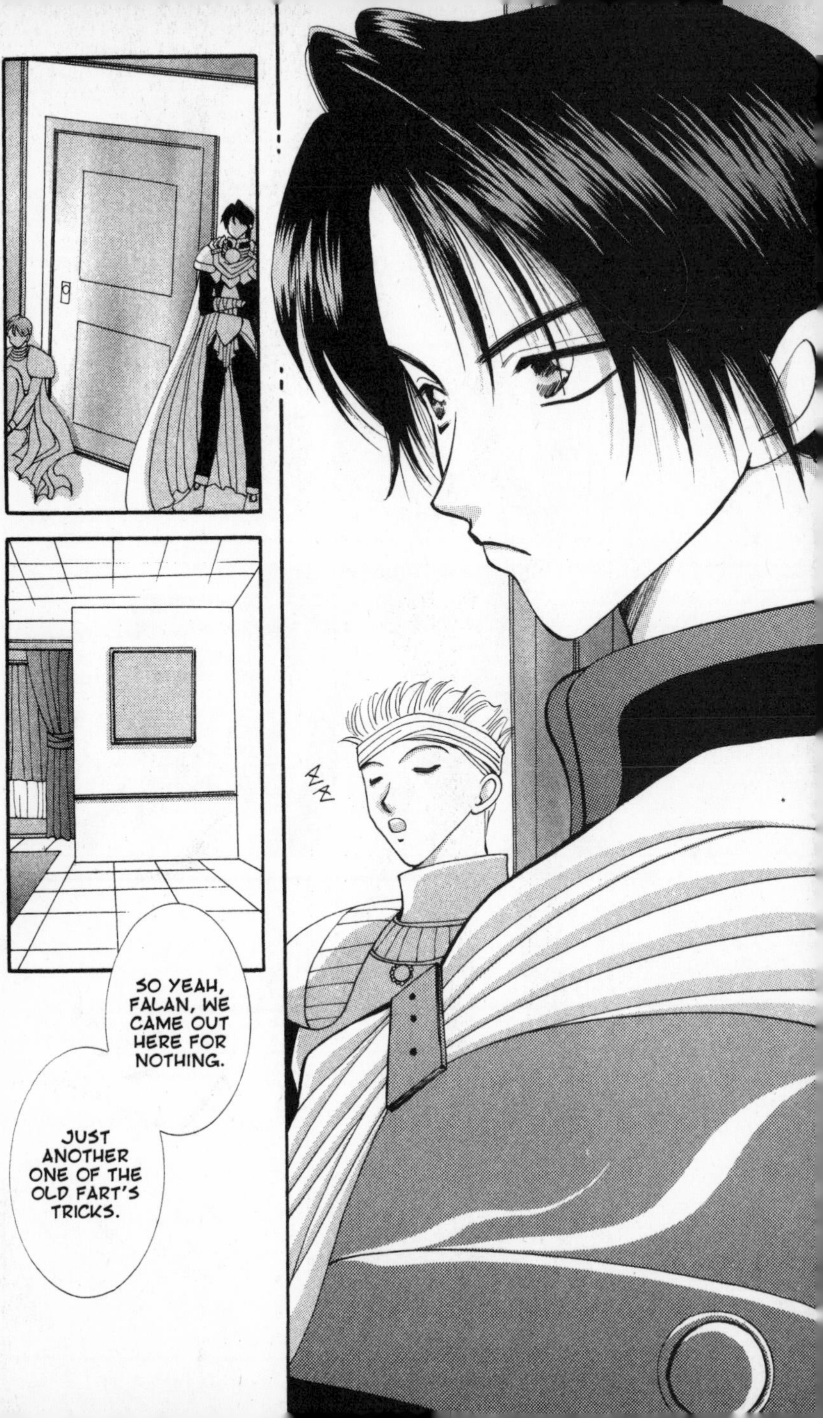
SO YEAH, FALAN, WE CAME OUT HERE FOR NOTHING.
JUST ANOTHER ONE OF THE OLD FART'S TRICKS.

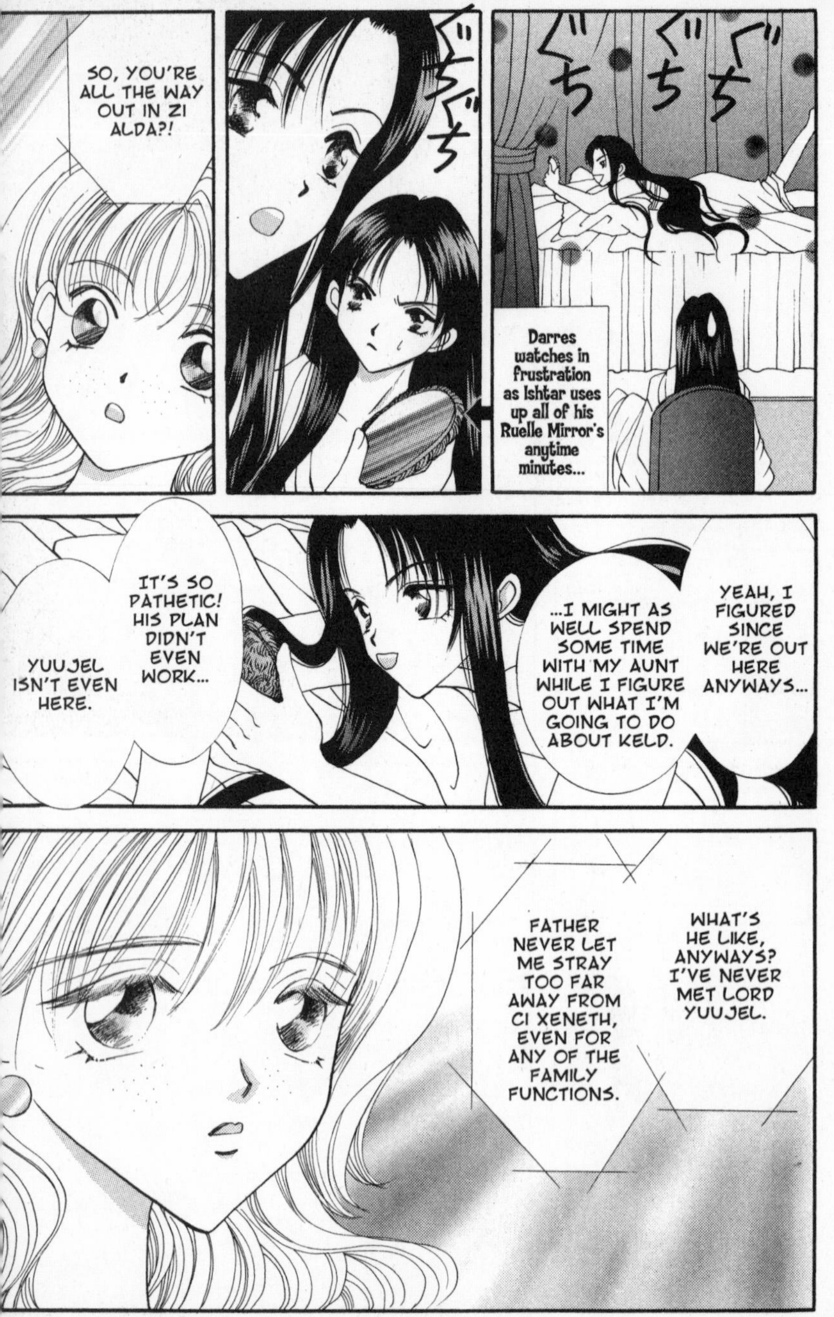

ぐち ぐち ぐち
Darres watches in frustration as Ishtar uses up all of his Ruelle Mirror's anytime minutes...
ぐちぐち
SO, YOU'RE ALL THE WAY OUT IN ZI ALDA?!
YEAH, I FIGURED SINCE WE'RE OUT HERE ANYWAYS...
...I MIGHT AS WELL SPEND SOME TIME WITH MY AUNT WHILE I FIGURE OUT WHAT I'M GOING TO DO ABOUT KELD.
IT'S SO PATHETIC! HIS PLAN DIDN'T EVEN WORK...
YUUJEL ISN'T EVEN HERE.
WHAT'S HE LIKE, ANYWAYS? I'VE NEVER MET LORD YUUJEL.
FATHER NEVER LET ME STRAY TOO FAR AWAY FROM CI XENETH, EVEN FOR ANY OF THE FAMILY FUNCTIONS.

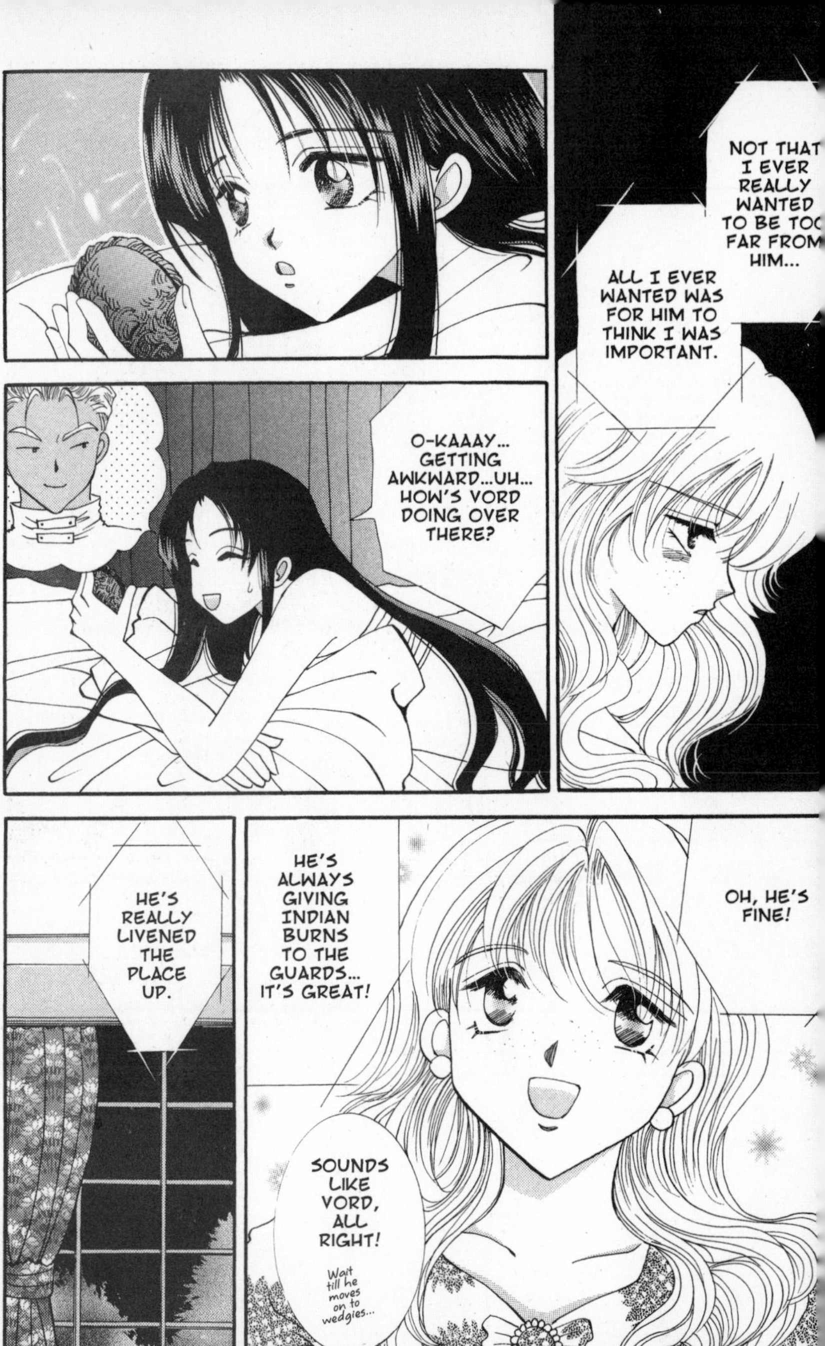
NOT THAT I EVER REALLY WANTED TO BE TOO FAR FROM HIM...
ALL I EVER WANTED WAS FOR HIM TO THINK I WAS IMPORTANT.
O-KAAAY... GETTING AWKWARD...UH... HOW'S VORD DOING OVER THERE?
OH, HE'S FINE!
HE'S ALWAYS GIVING INDIAN BURNS TO THE GUARDS... IT'S GREAT!
SOUNDS LIKE VORD, ALL RIGHT!
Wait till he moves on to wedgies...
HE'S REALLY LIVENED THE PLACE UP.

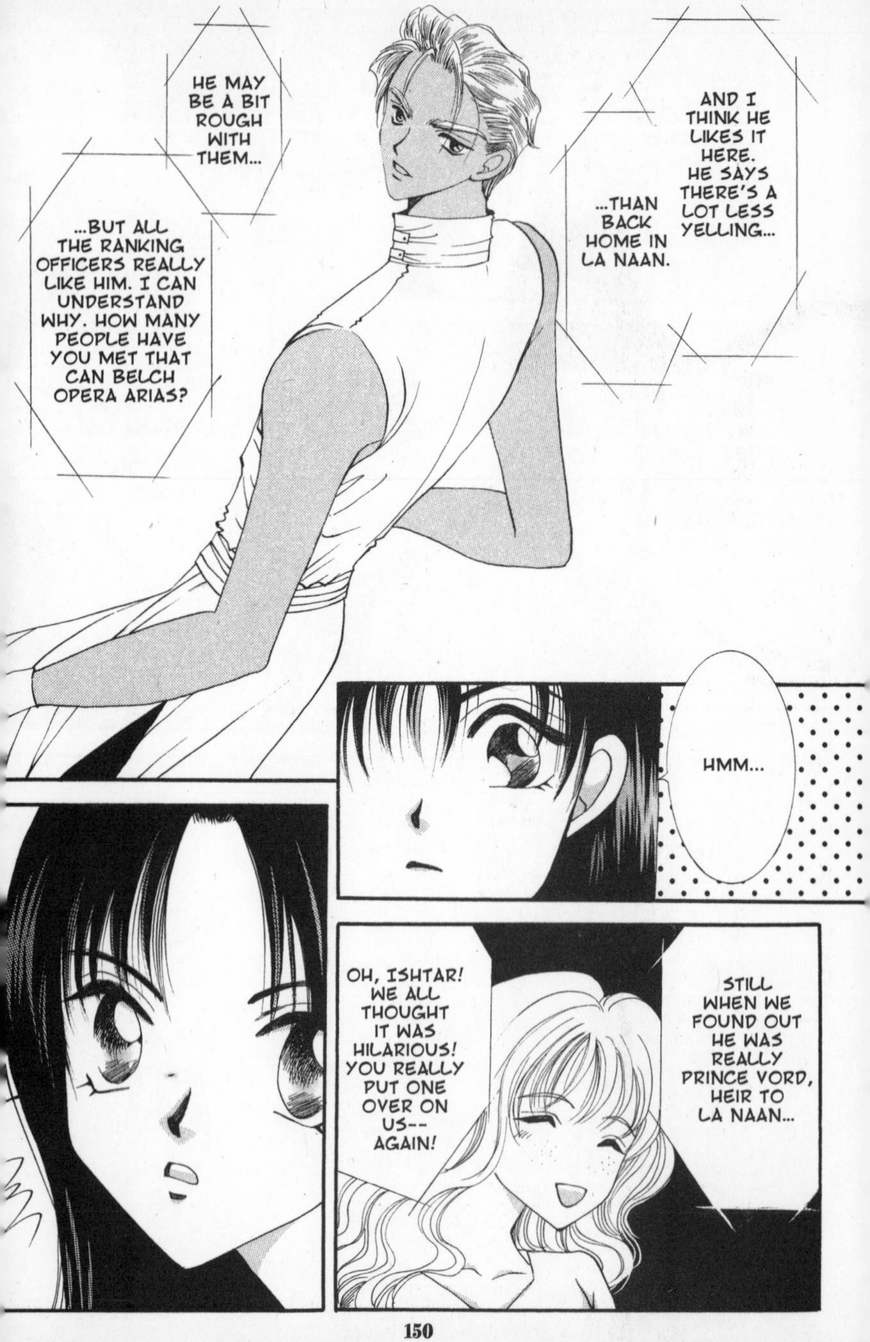
AND I THINK HE LIKES IT HERE. HE SAYS THERE'S A LOT LESS YELLING...
...THAN BACK HOME IN LA NAAN.
HE MAY BE A BIT ROUGH WITH THEM...
...BUT ALL THE RANKING OFFICERS REALLY LIKE HIM. I CAN UNDERSTAND WHY. HOW MANY PEOPLE HAVE YOU MET THAT CAN BELCH OPERA ARIAS?
HMM...
STILL WHEN WE FOUND OUT HE WAS REALLY PRINCE VORD, HEIR TO LA NAAN...
OH, ISHTAR! WE ALL THOUGHT IT WAS HILARIOUS! YOU REALLY PUT ONE OVER ON US-- AGAIN!

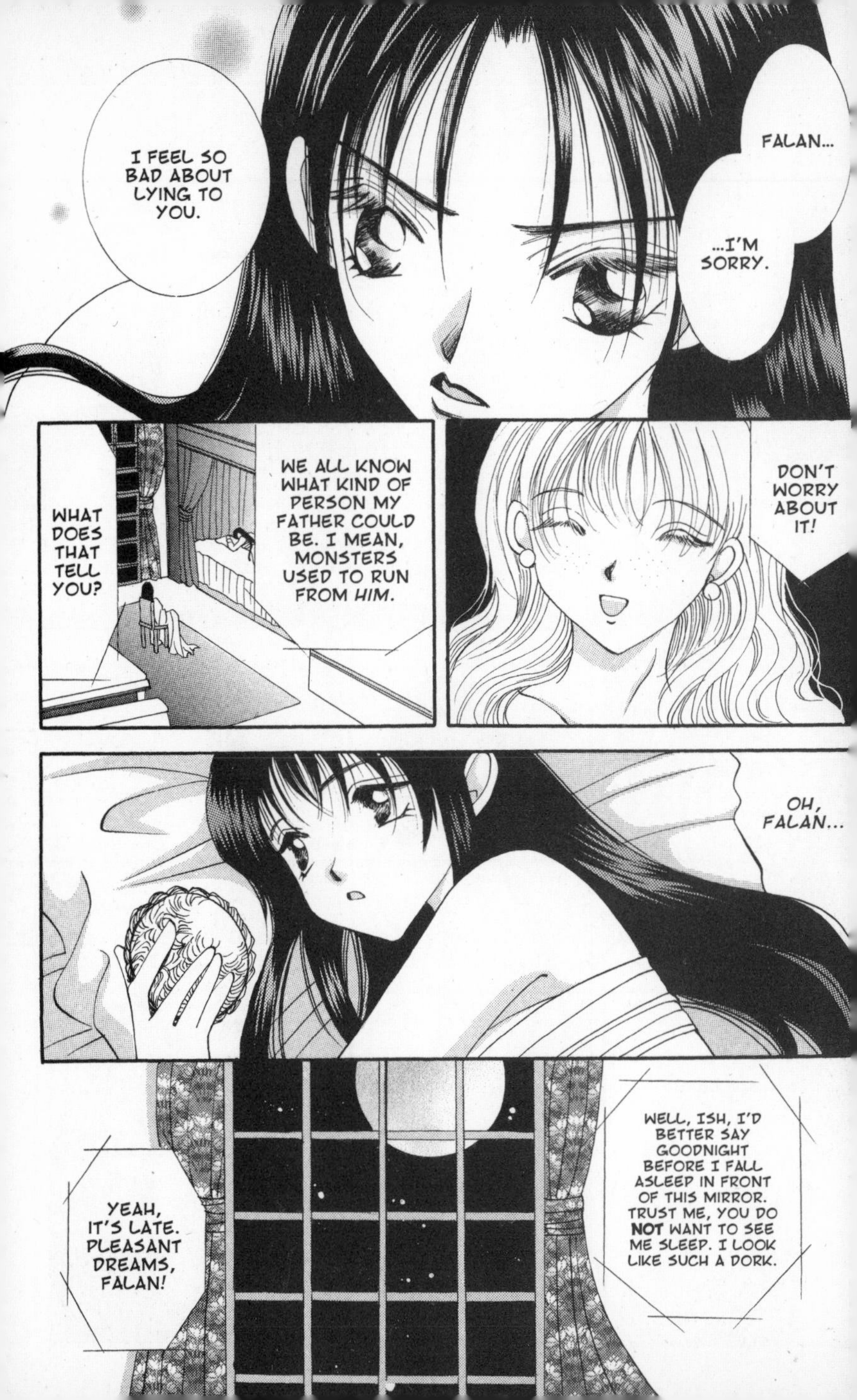
FALAN...
...I'M SORRY.
I FEEL SO BAD ABOUT LYING TO YOU.
DON'T WORRY ABOUT IT!
WE ALL KNOW WHAT KIND OF PERSON MY FATHER COULD BE. I MEAN, MONSTERS USED TO RUN FROM *HIM*.
WHAT DOES THAT TELL YOU?
OH, FALAN...
WELL, ISH, I'D BETTER SAY GOODNIGHT BEFORE I FALL ASLEEP IN FRONT OF THIS MIRROR. TRUST ME, YOU DO **NOT** WANT TO SEE ME SLEEP. I LOOK LIKE SUCH A DORK.
YEAH, IT'S LATE. PLEASANT DREAMS, FALAN!

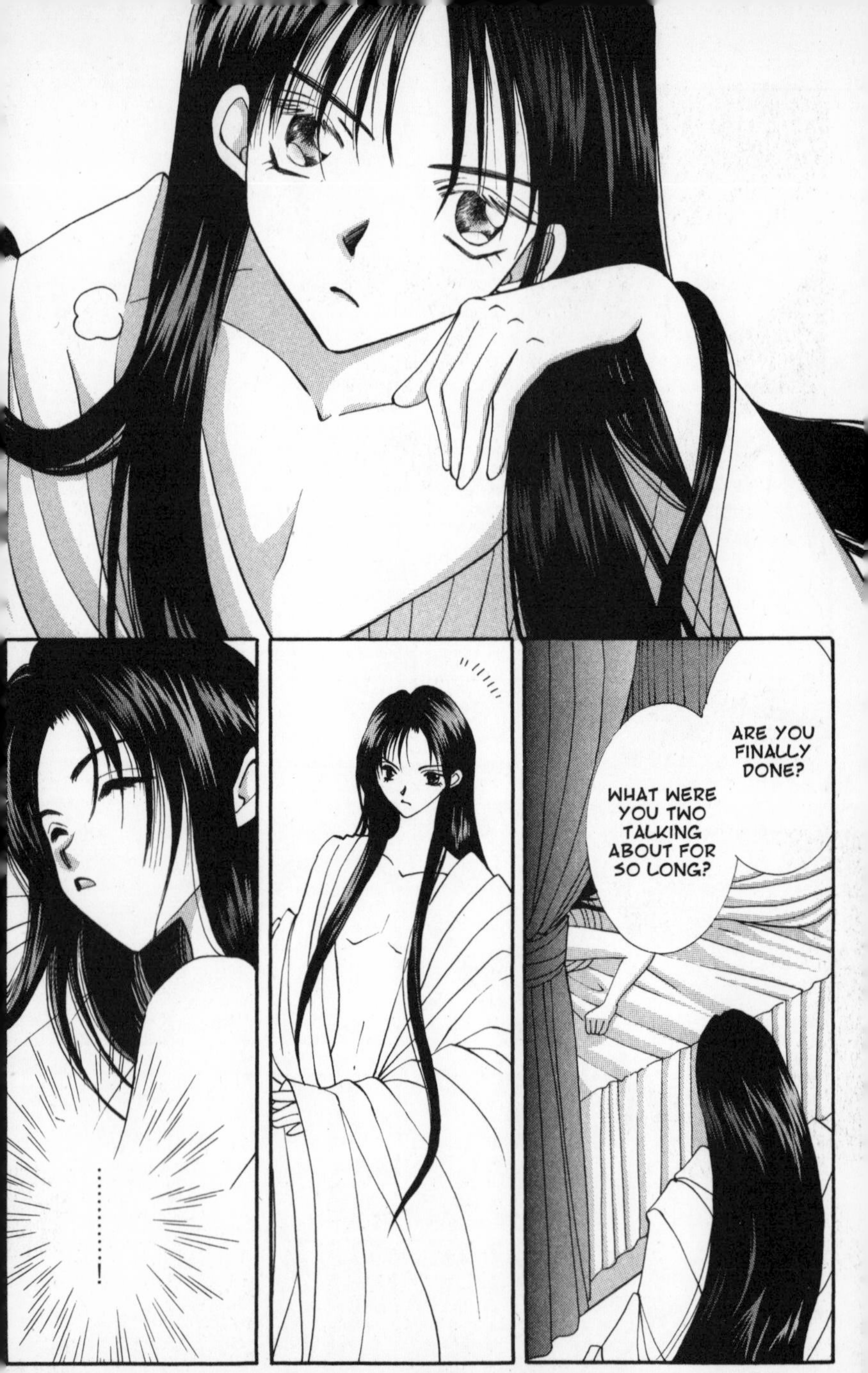
ARE YOU FINALLY DONE?
WHAT WERE YOU TWO TALKING ABOUT FOR SO LONG?
......!

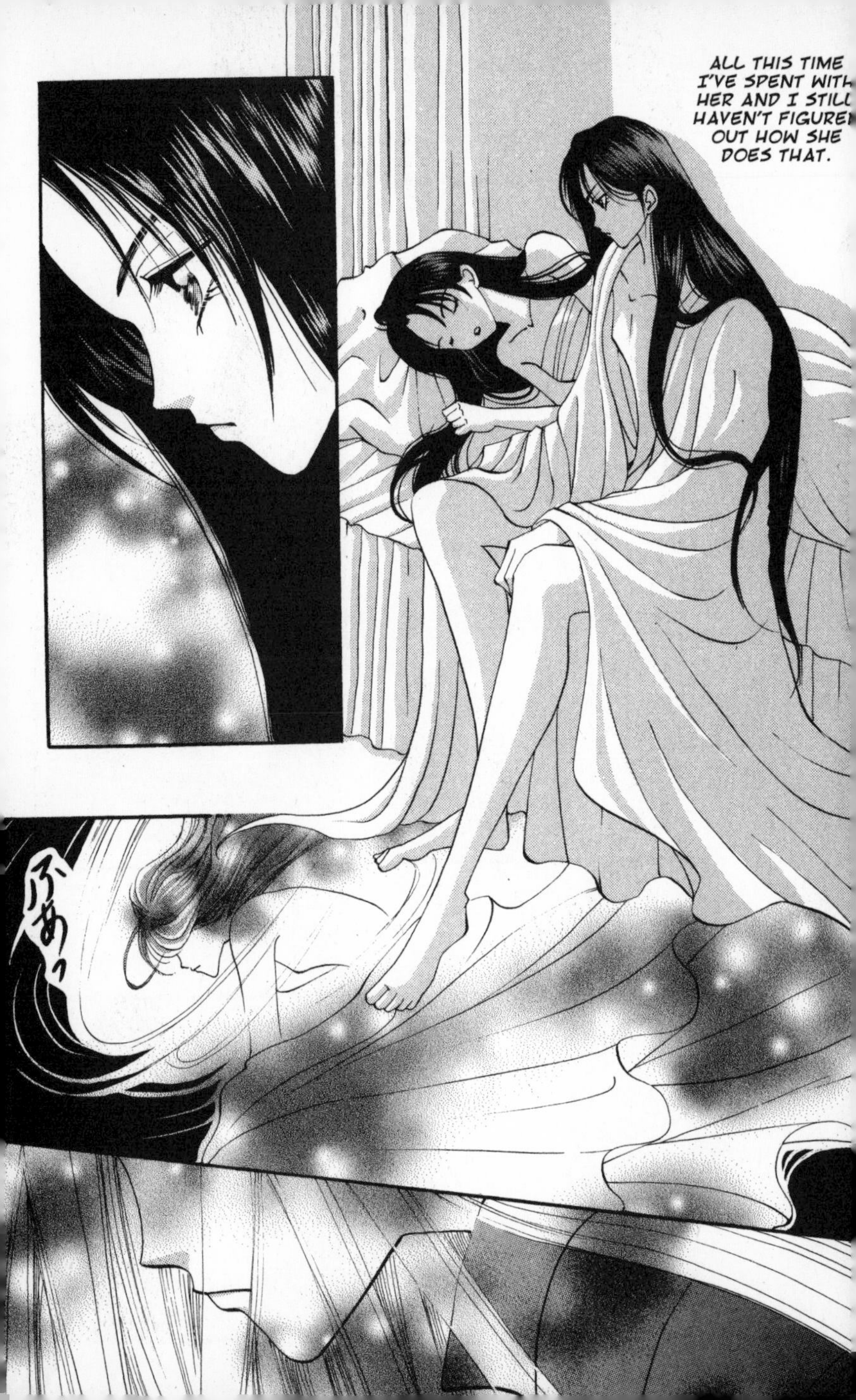
ALL THIS TIME I'VE SPENT WITH HER AND I STILL HAVEN'T FIGURED OUT HOW SHE DOES THAT.
ふあっ

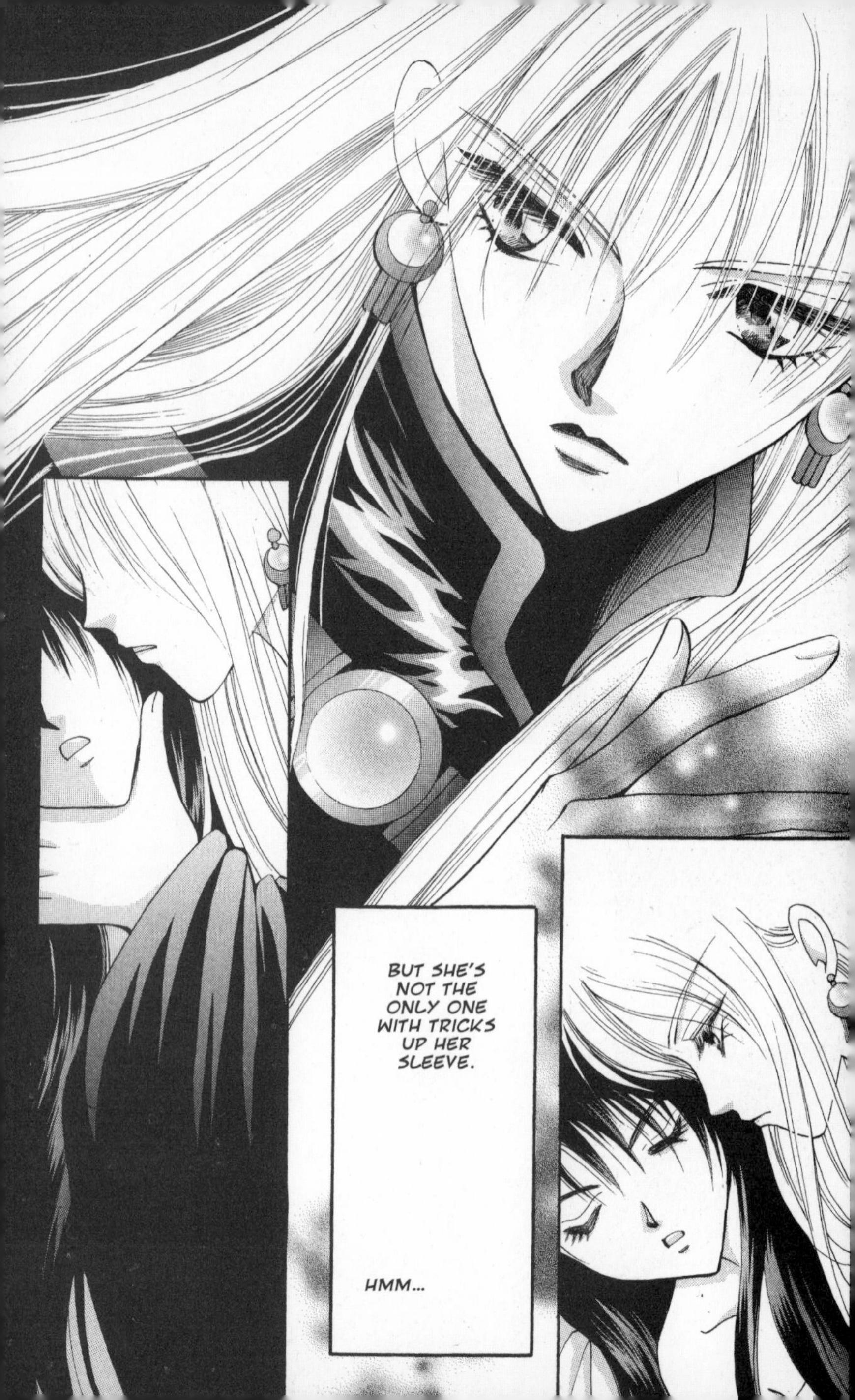
BUT SHE'S NOT THE ONLY ONE WITH TRICKS UP HER SLEEVE.
HMM...

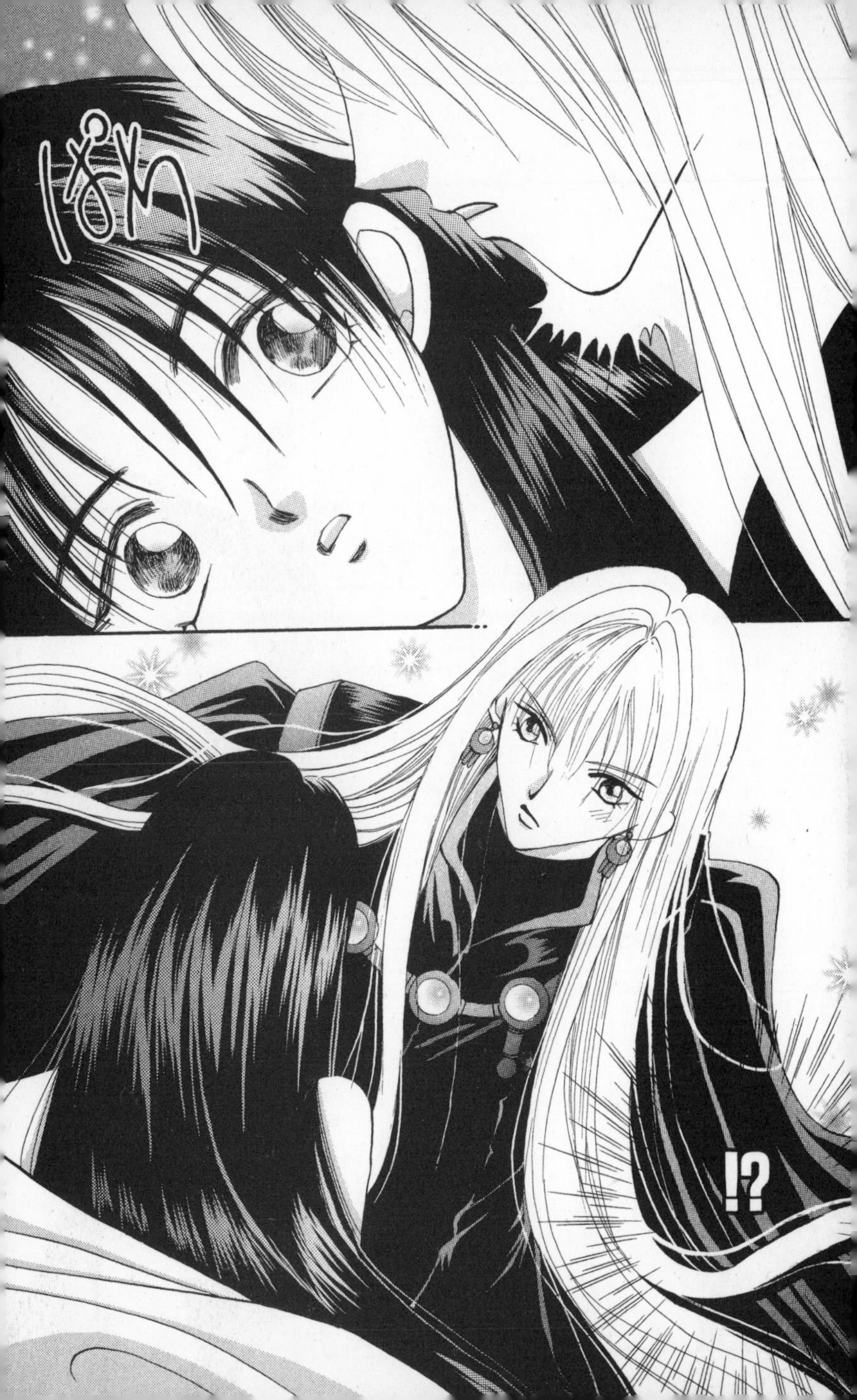
!?

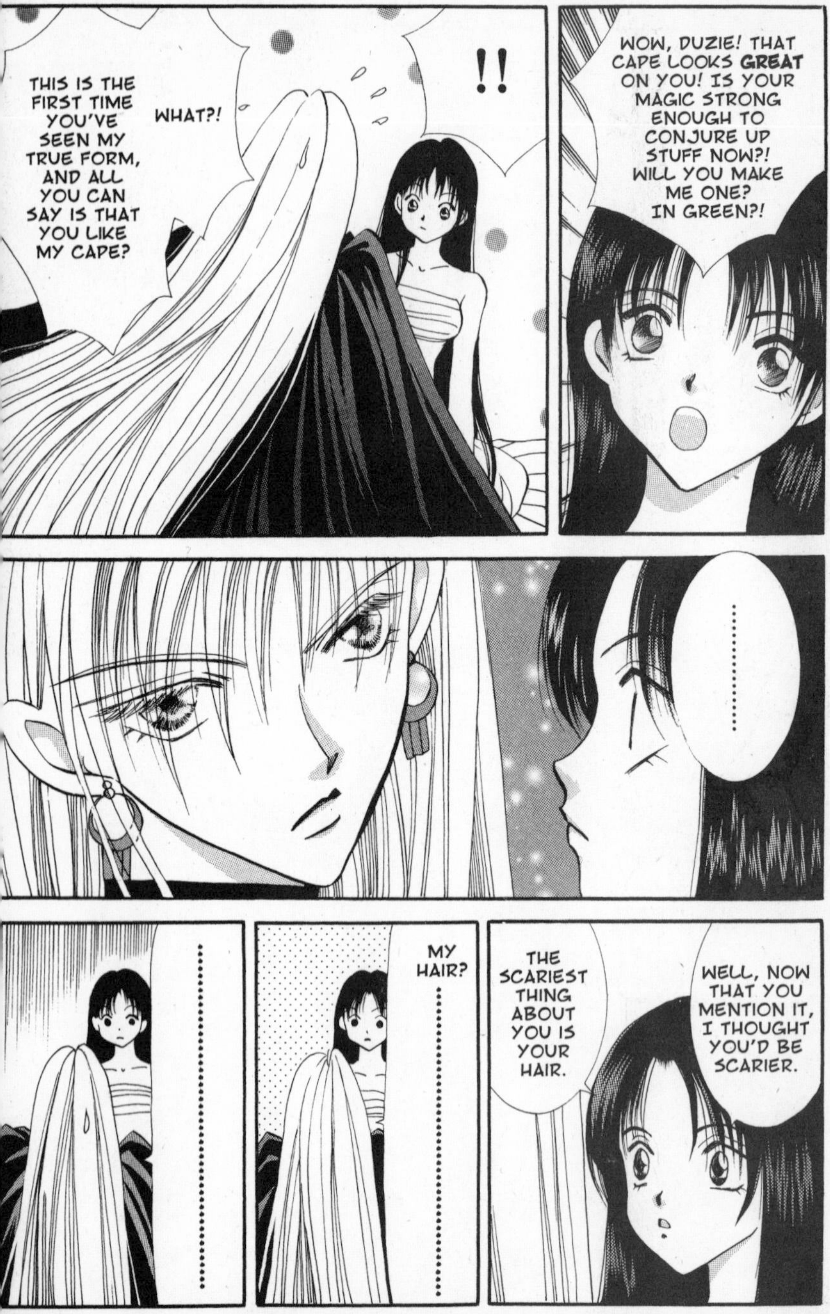
WOW, DUZIE! THAT CAPE LOOKS **GREAT** ON YOU! IS YOUR MAGIC STRONG ENOUGH TO CONJURE UP STUFF NOW?! WILL YOU MAKE ME ONE? IN GREEN?!
!!
WHAT?!
THIS IS THE FIRST TIME YOU'VE SEEN MY TRUE FORM, AND ALL YOU CAN SAY IS THAT YOU LIKE MY CAPE?
......
WELL, NOW THAT YOU MENTION IT, I THOUGHT YOU'D BE SCARIER.
THE SCARIEST THING ABOUT YOU IS YOUR HAIR.
MY HAIR?
......
......

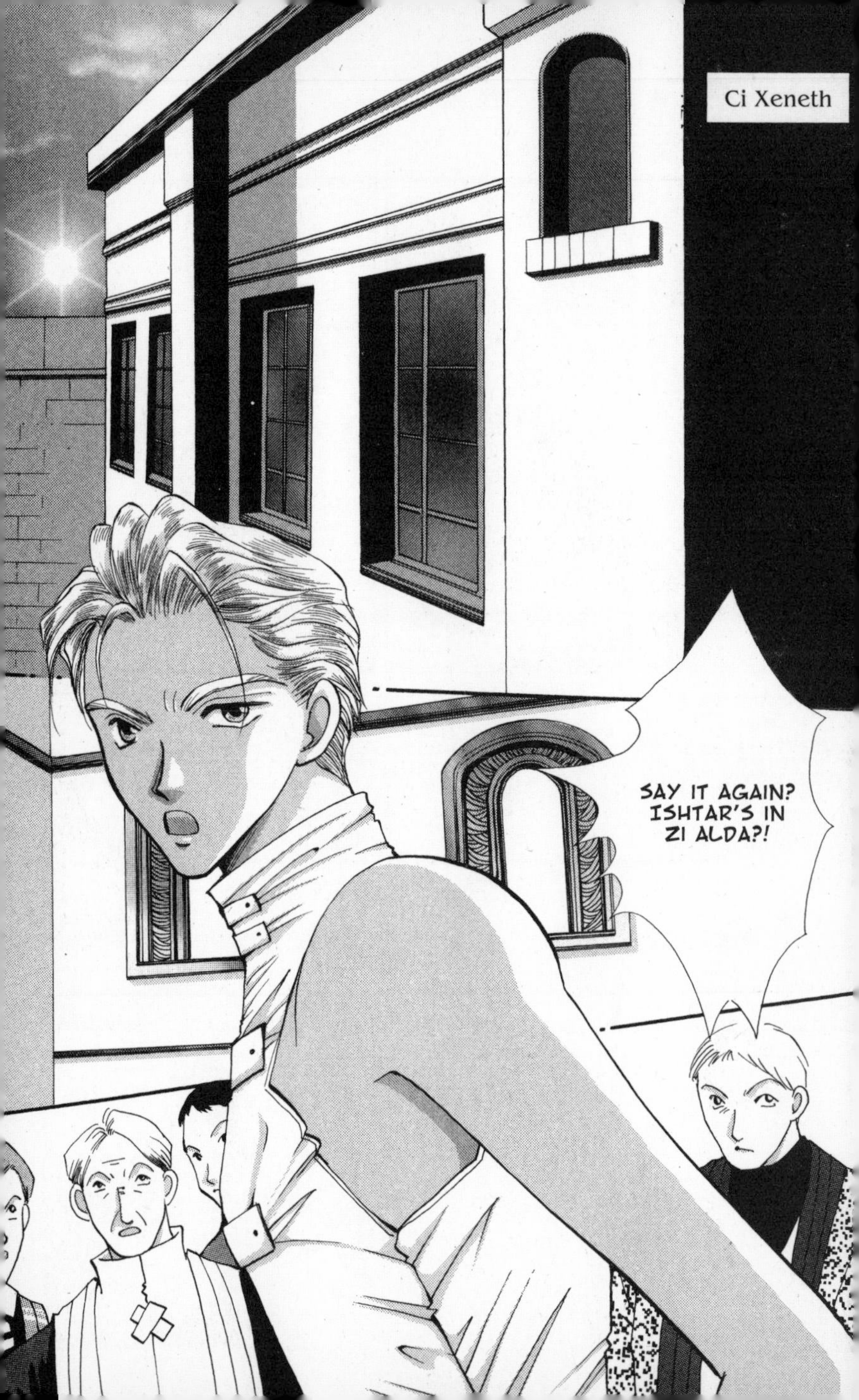
Ci Xeneth
SAY IT AGAIN? ISHTAR'S IN ZI ALDA?!

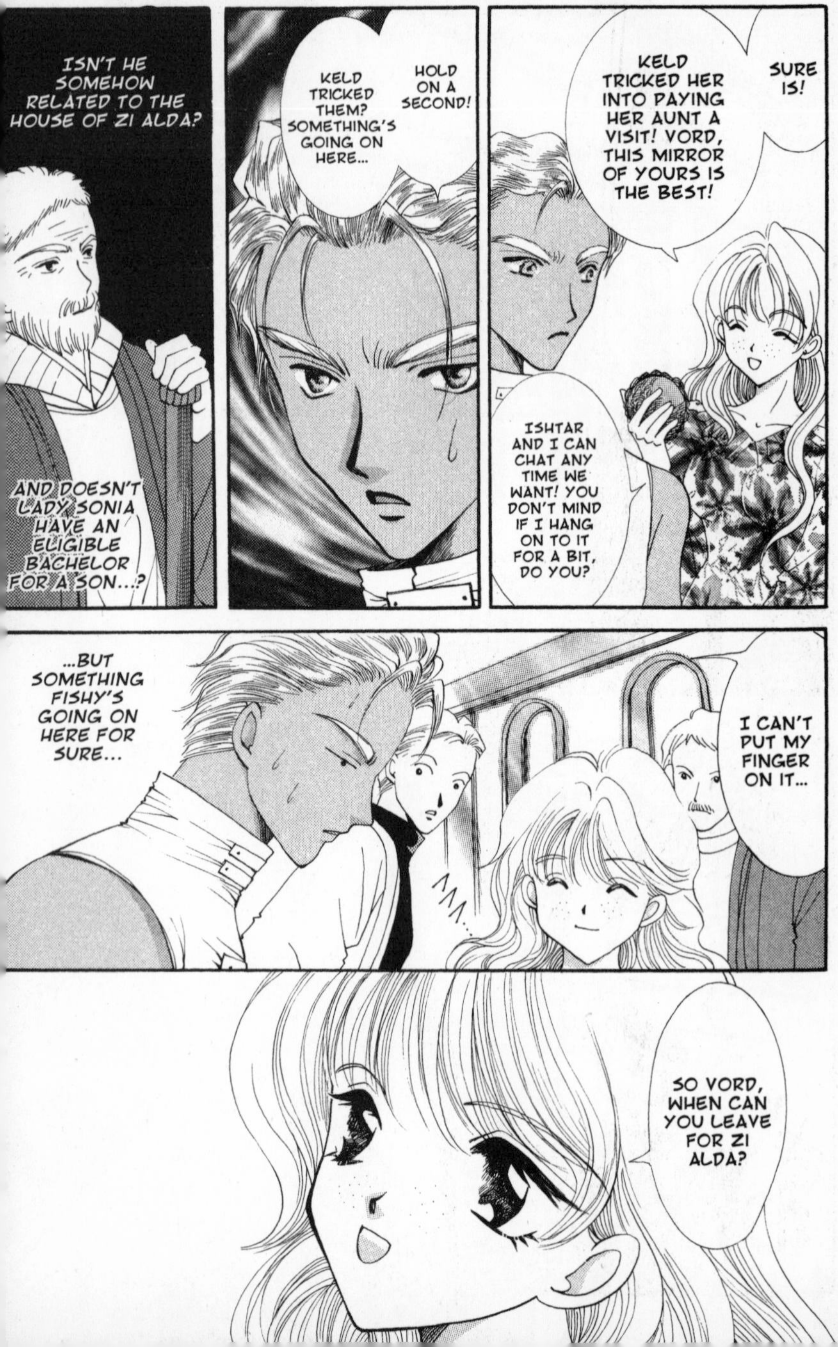
SURE IS!
KELD TRICKED HER INTO PAYING HER AUNT A VISIT! VORD, THIS MIRROR OF YOURS IS THE BEST!
ISHTAR AND I CAN CHAT ANY TIME WE WANT! YOU DON'T MIND IF I HANG ON TO IT FOR A BIT, DO YOU?
HOLD ON A SECOND!
KELD TRICKED THEM? SOMETHING'S GOING ON HERE...
ISN'T HE SOMEHOW RELATED TO THE HOUSE OF ZI ALDA?
AND DOESN'T LADY SONIA HAVE AN ELIGIBLE BACHELOR FOR A SON...?
I CAN'T PUT MY FINGER ON IT...
...BUT SOMETHING FISHY'S GOING ON HERE FOR SURE...
SO VORD, WHEN CAN YOU LEAVE FOR ZI ALDA?

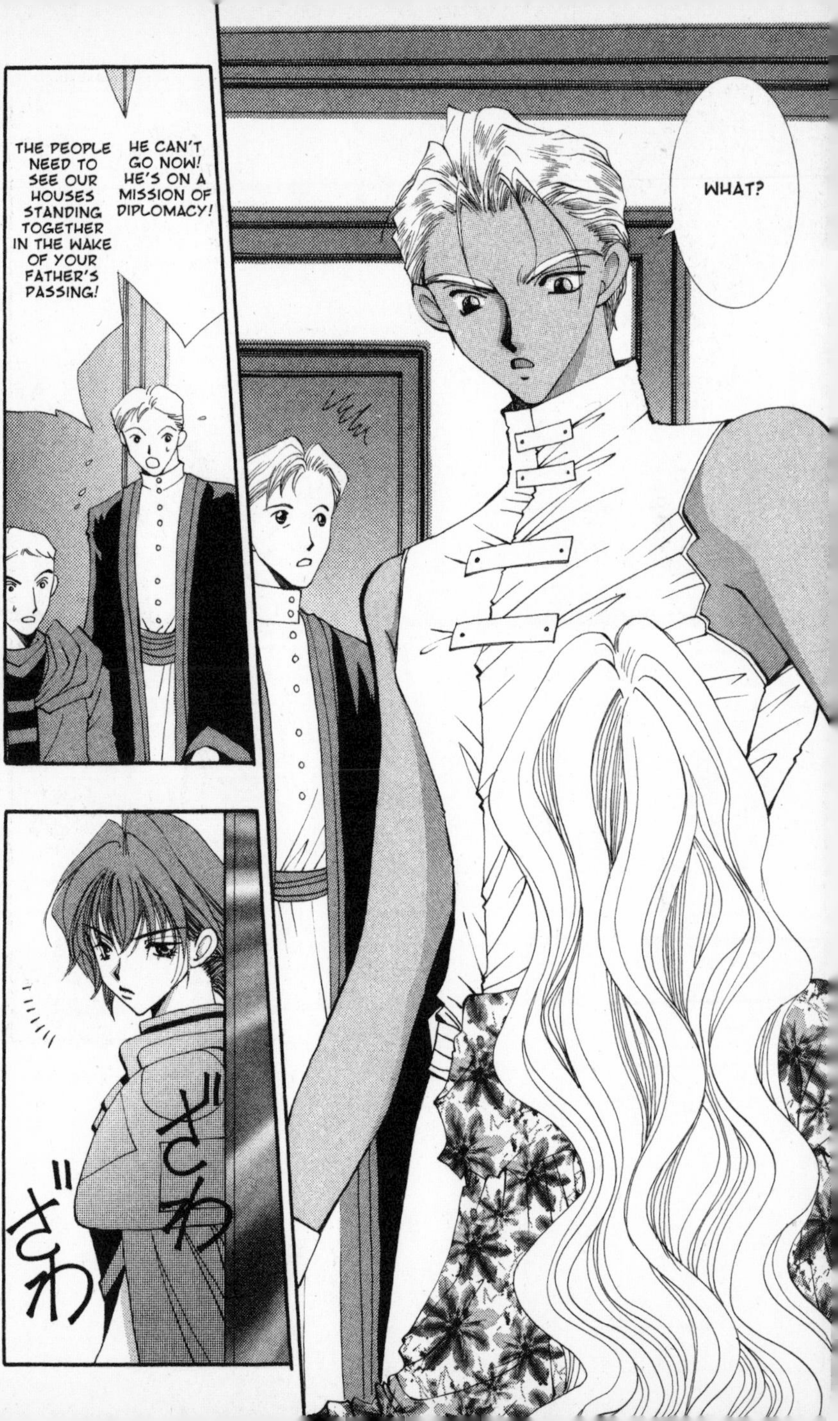
WHAT?
HE CAN'T GO NOW! HE'S ON A MISSION OF DIPLOMACY!
THE PEOPLE NEED TO SEE OUR HOUSES STANDING TOGETHER IN THE WAKE OF YOUR FATHER'S PASSING!
ざわ
ざわ

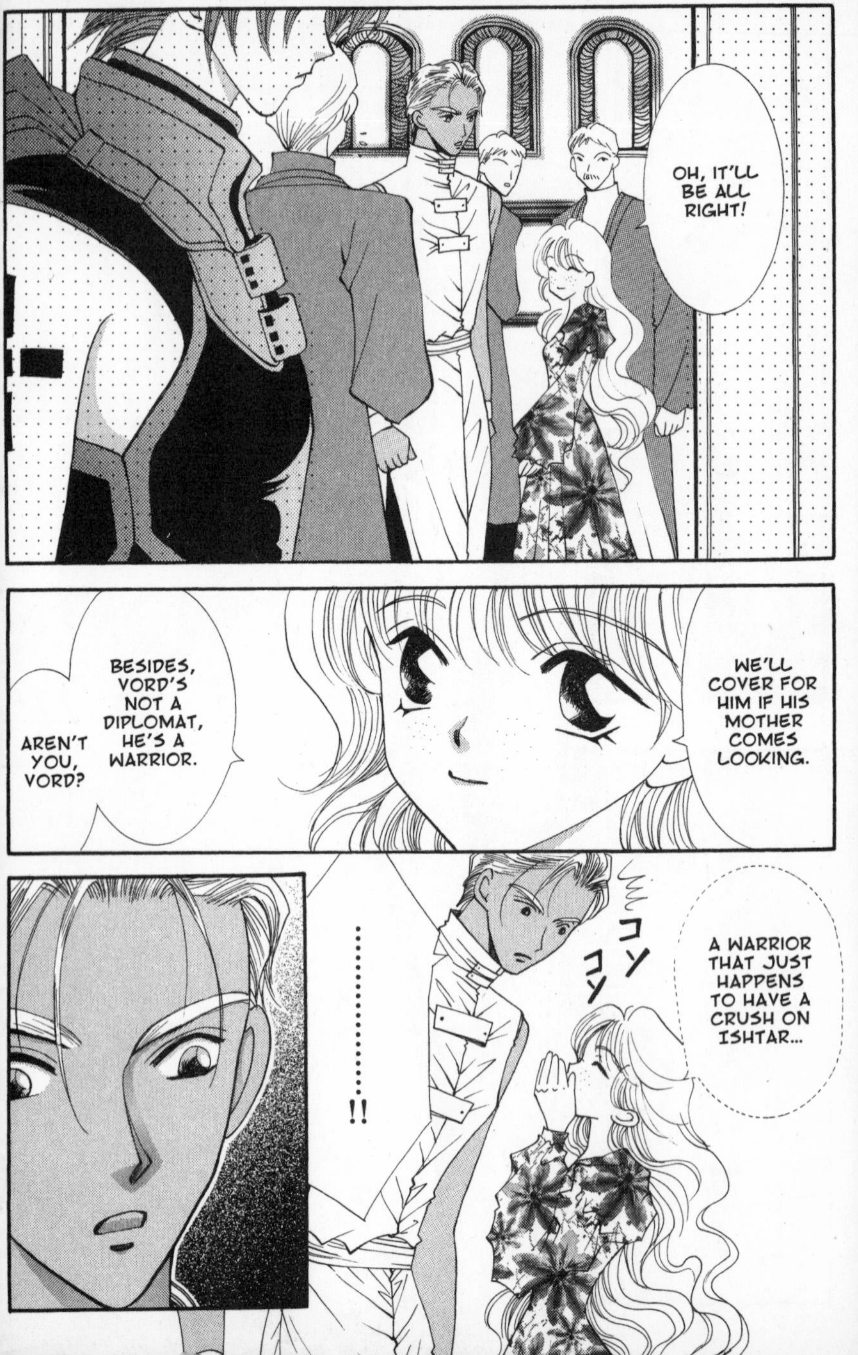
OH, IT'LL BE ALL RIGHT!
WE'LL COVER FOR HIM IF HIS MOTHER COMES LOOKING.
BESIDES, VORD'S NOT A DIPLOMAT, HE'S A WARRIOR.
AREN'T YOU, VORD?
A WARRIOR THAT JUST HAPPENS TO HAVE A CRUSH ON ISHTAR...
コソ
コソ
........!!

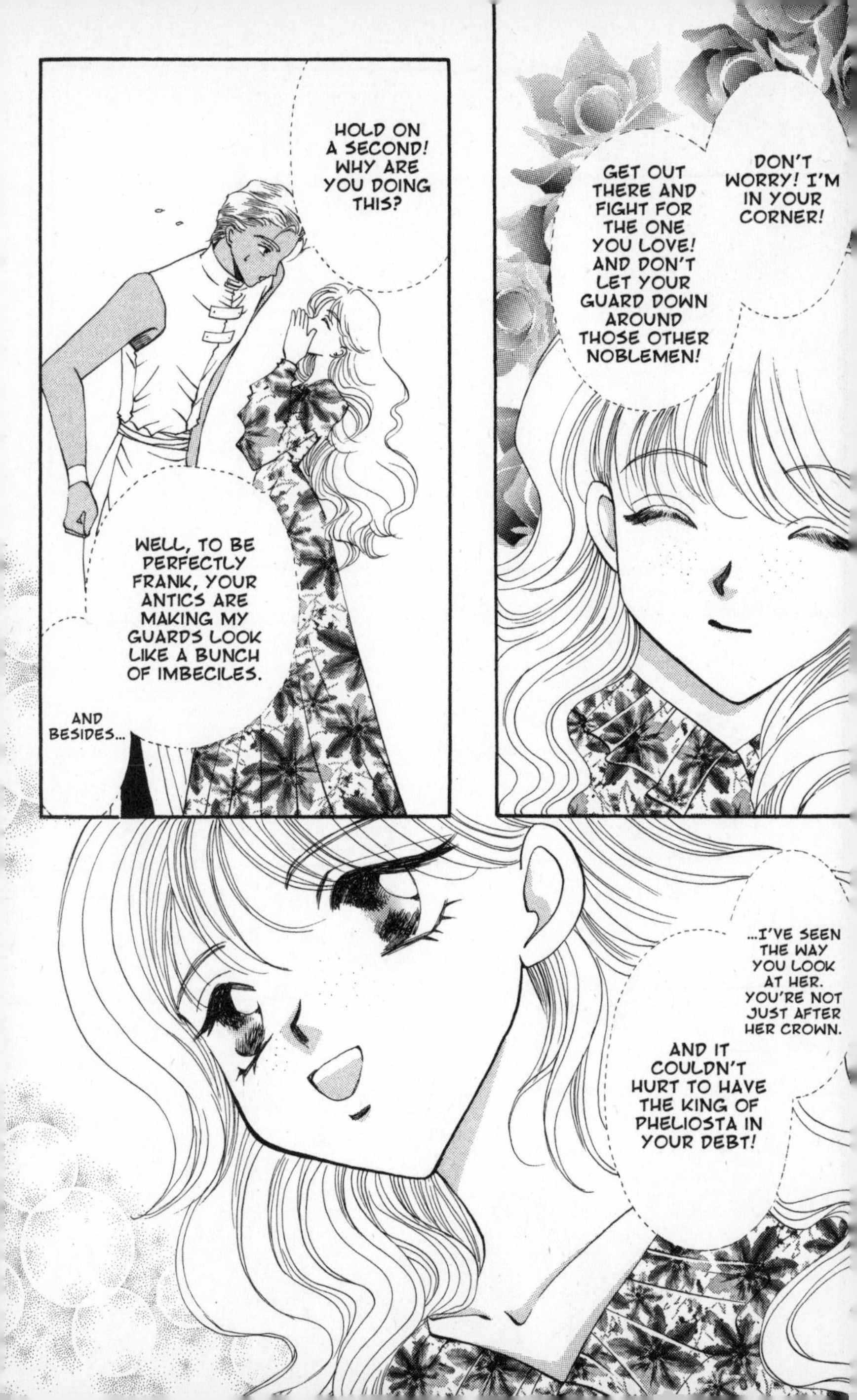
DON'T WORRY! I'M IN YOUR CORNER!
GET OUT THERE AND FIGHT FOR THE ONE YOU LOVE! AND DON'T LET YOUR GUARD DOWN AROUND THOSE OTHER NOBLEMEN!
HOLD ON A SECOND! WHY ARE YOU DOING THIS?
WELL, TO BE PERFECTLY FRANK, YOUR ANTICS ARE MAKING MY GUARDS LOOK LIKE A BUNCH OF IMBECILES.
AND BESIDES...
...I'VE SEEN THE WAY YOU LOOK AT HER. YOU'RE NOT JUST AFTER HER CROWN.
AND IT COULDN'T HURT TO HAVE THE KING OF PHELIOSTA IN YOUR DEBT!

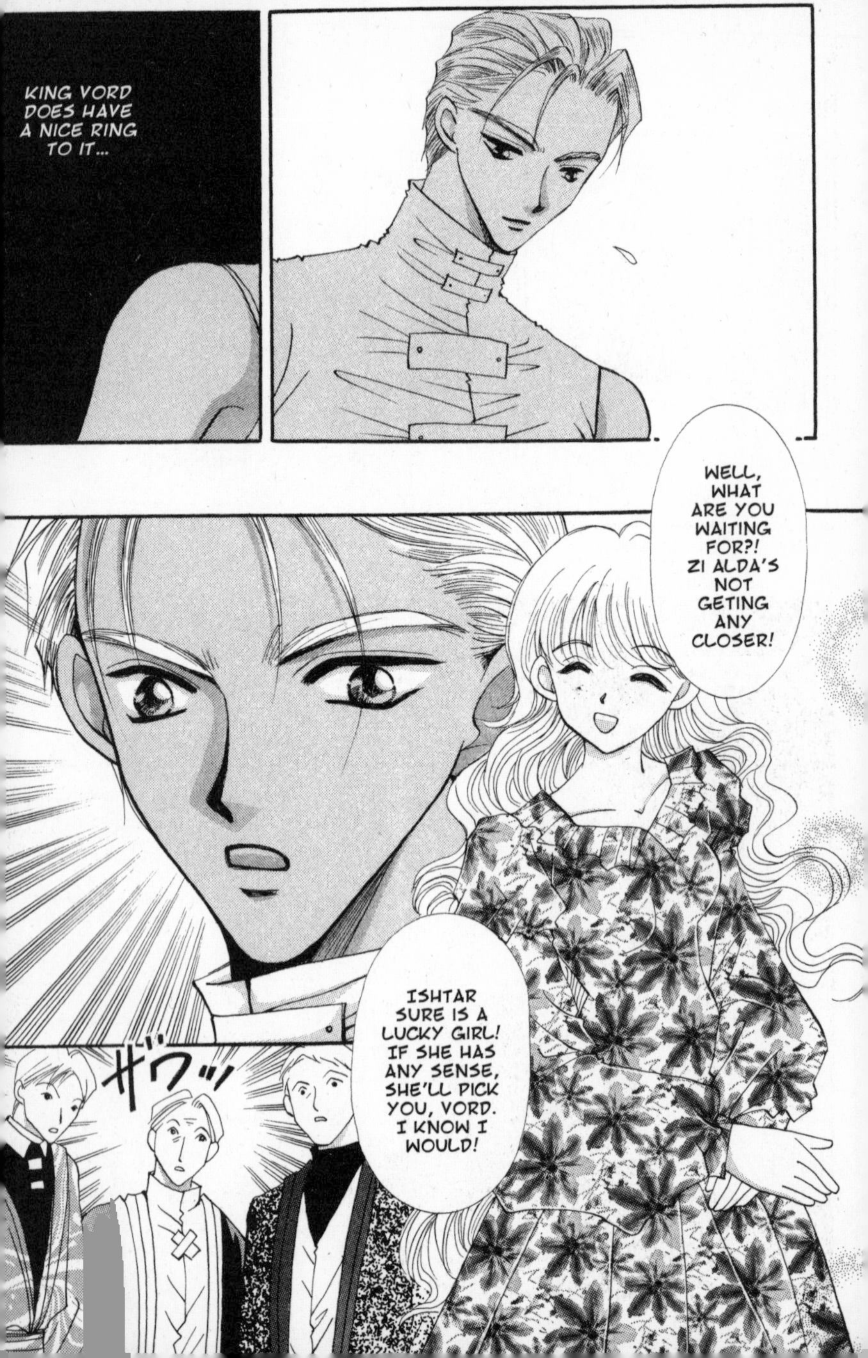
KING VORD DOES HAVE A NICE RING TO IT...
WELL, WHAT ARE YOU WAITING FOR?! ZI ALDA'S NOT GETING ANY CLOSER!
ISHTAR SURE IS A LUCKY GIRL! IF SHE HAS ANY SENSE, SHE'LL PICK YOU, VORD. I KNOW I WOULD!
ザワッ

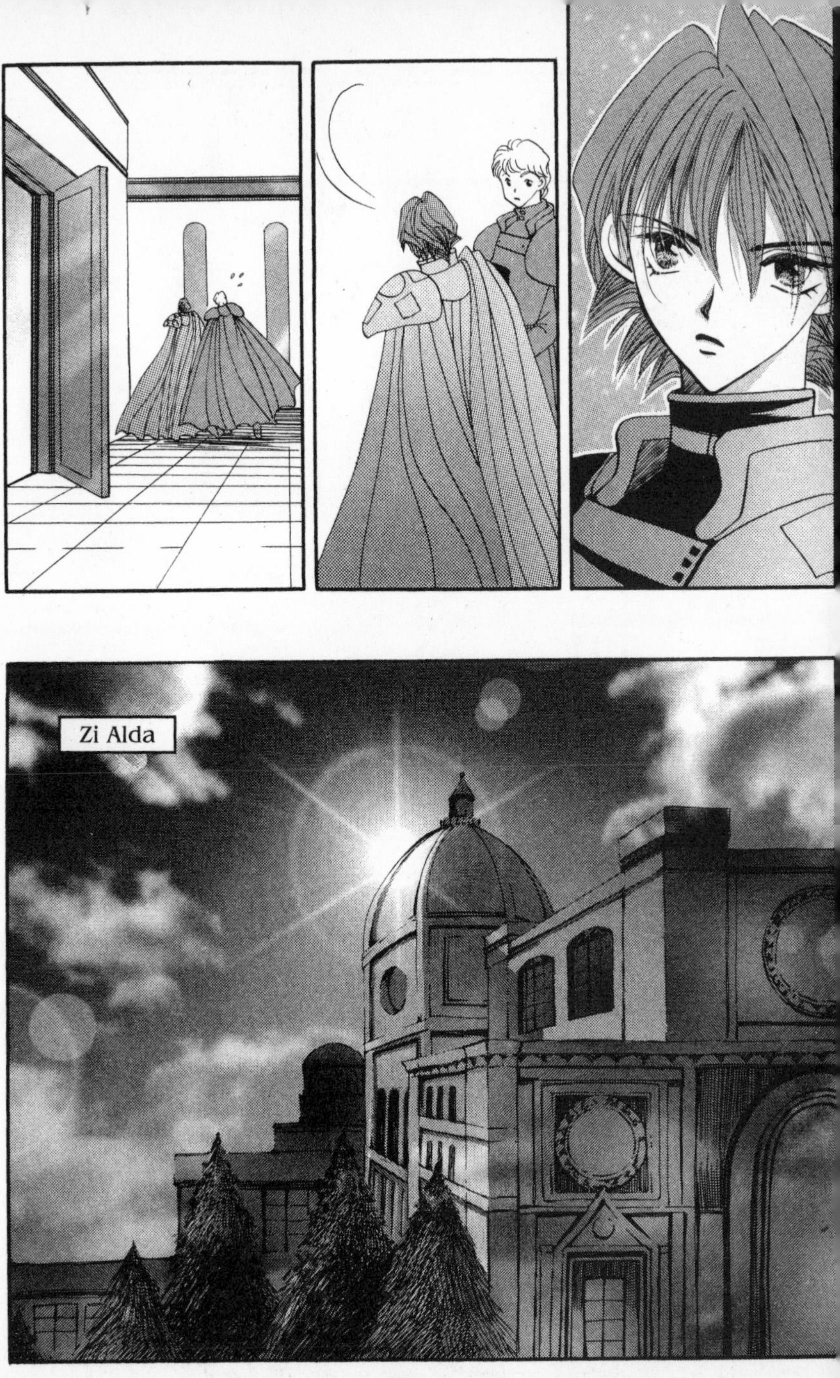
Zi Alda

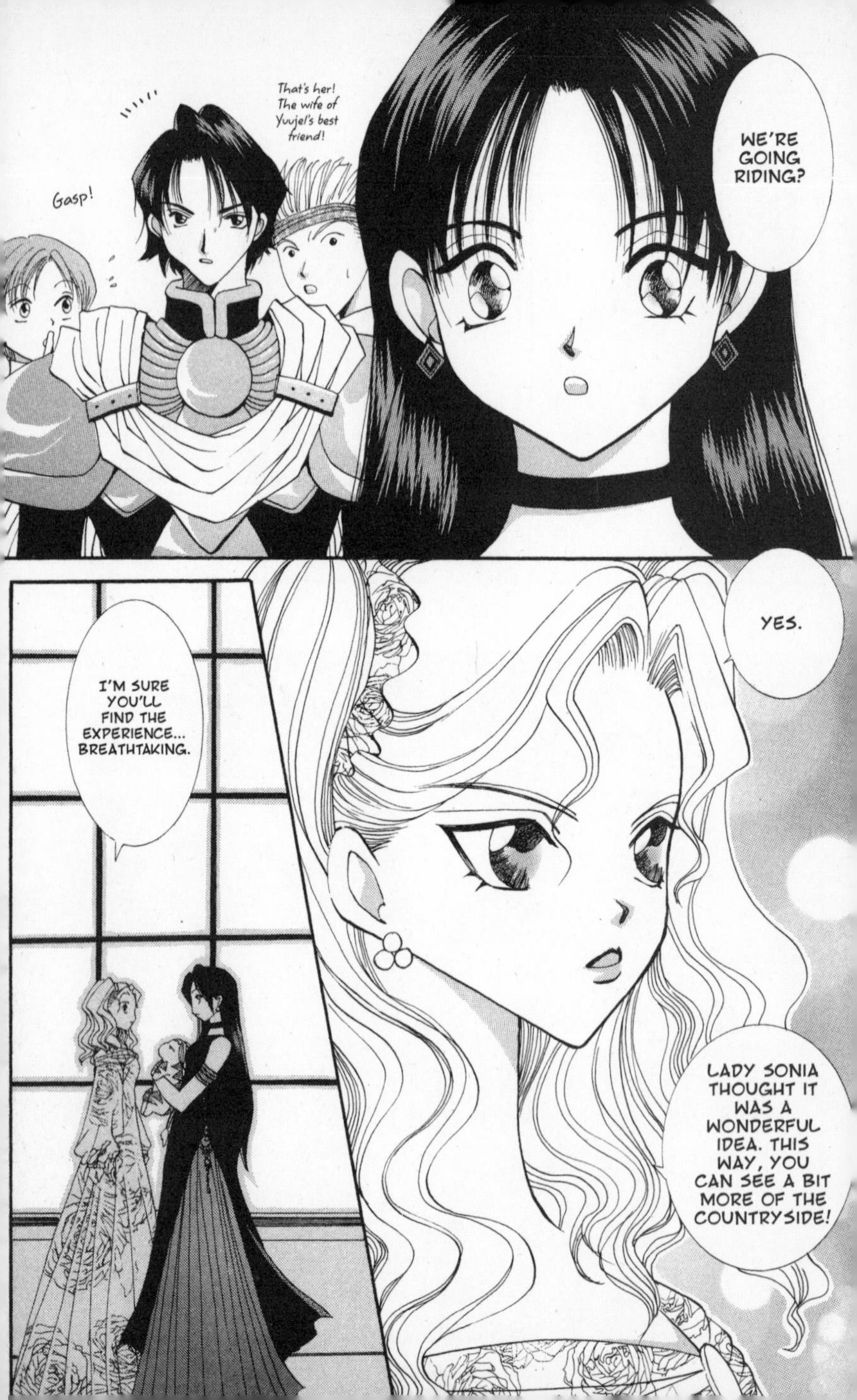
WE'RE GOING RIDING?
That's her! The wife of Yuujel's best friend!
Gasp!
YES.
I'M SURE YOU'LL FIND THE EXPERIENCE... BREATHTAKING.
LADY SONIA THOUGHT IT WAS A WONDERFUL IDEA. THIS WAY, YOU CAN SEE A BIT MORE OF THE COUNTRYSIDE!

吸血遊戯

南領篇(ゼ・アルダ)

Act.3

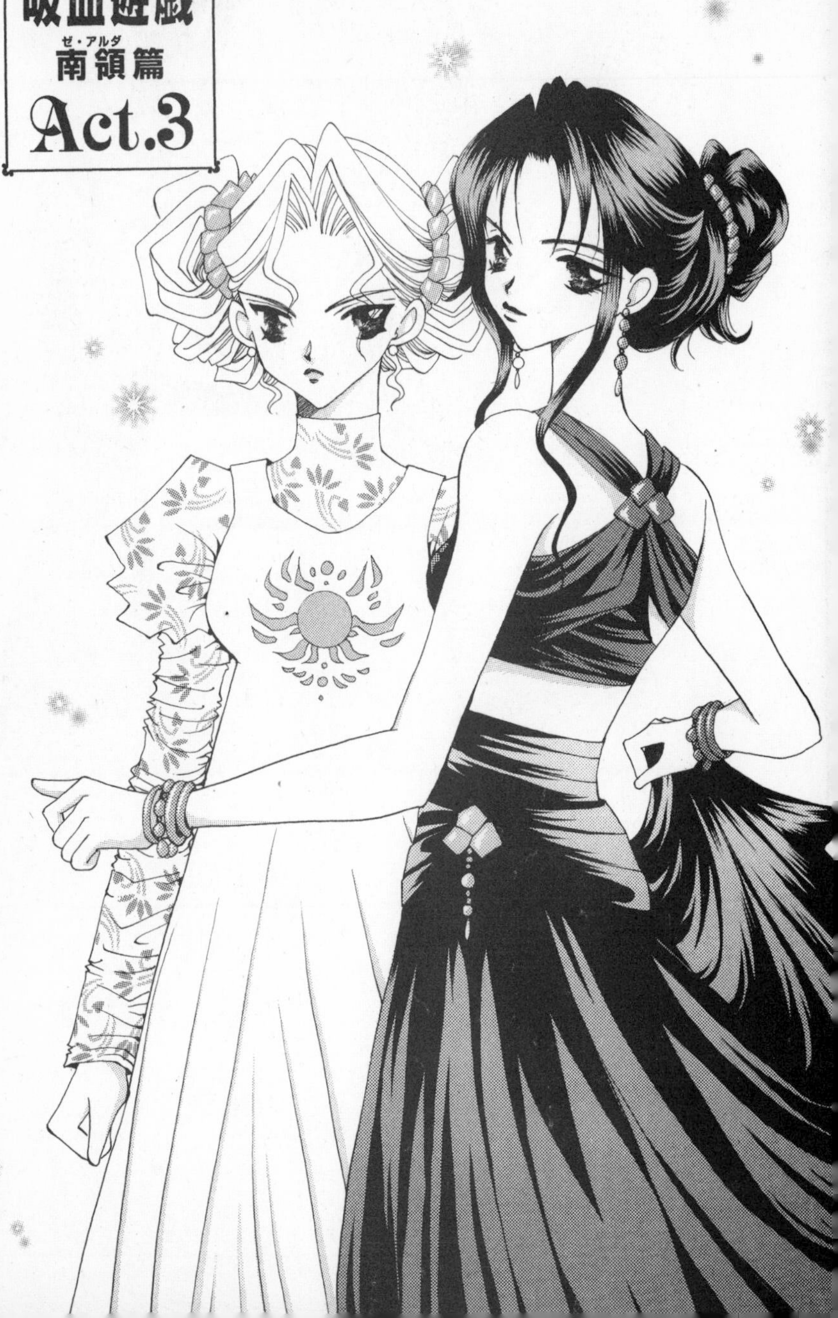

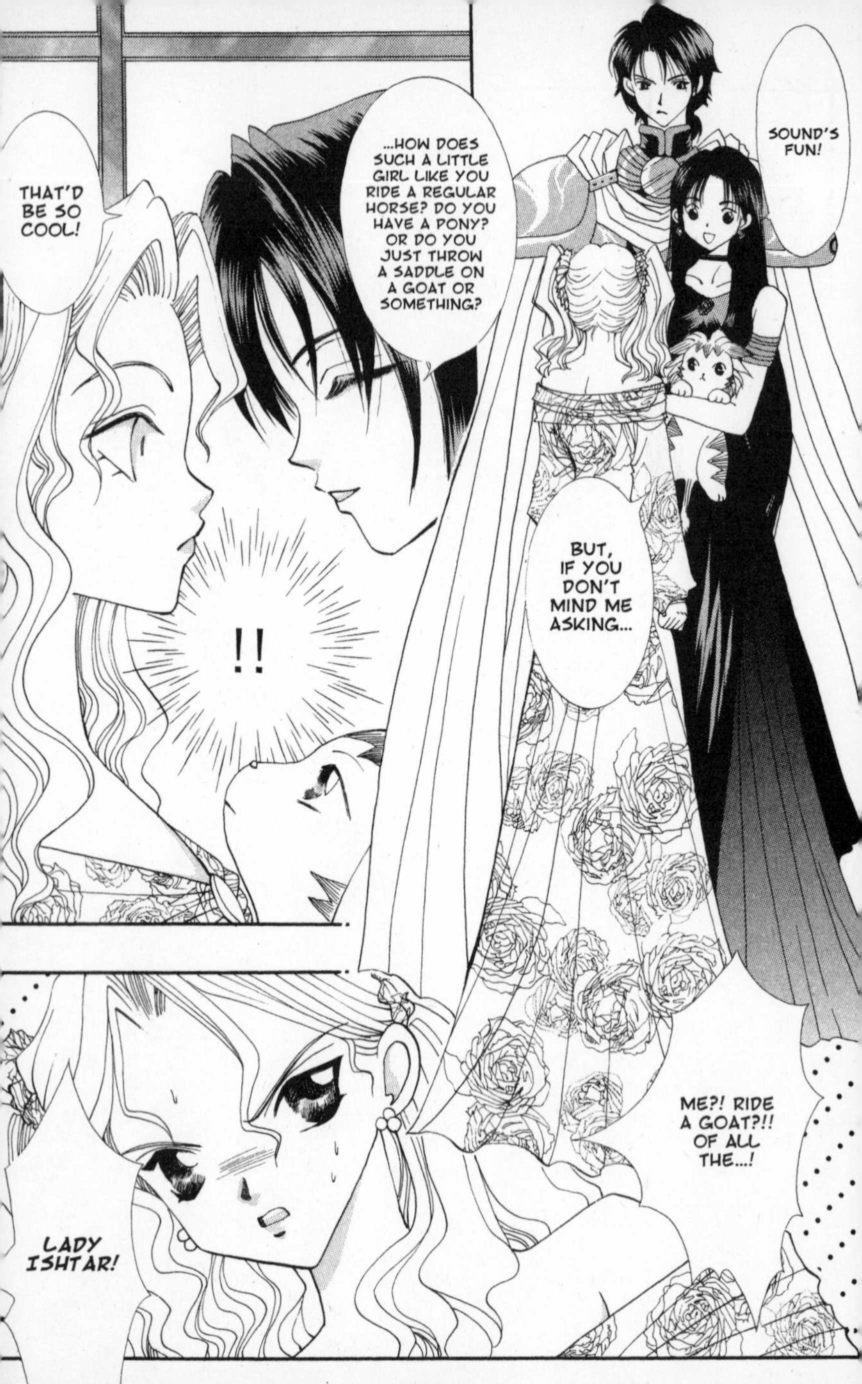
SOUND'S FUN!
BUT, IF YOU DON'T MIND ME ASKING...
...HOW DOES SUCH A LITTLE GIRL LIKE YOU RIDE A REGULAR HORSE? DO YOU HAVE A PONY? OR DO YOU JUST THROW A SADDLE ON A GOAT OR SOMETHING?
THAT'D BE SO COOL!
!!
ME?! RIDE A GOAT?!! OF ALL THE...!
LADY ISHTAR!

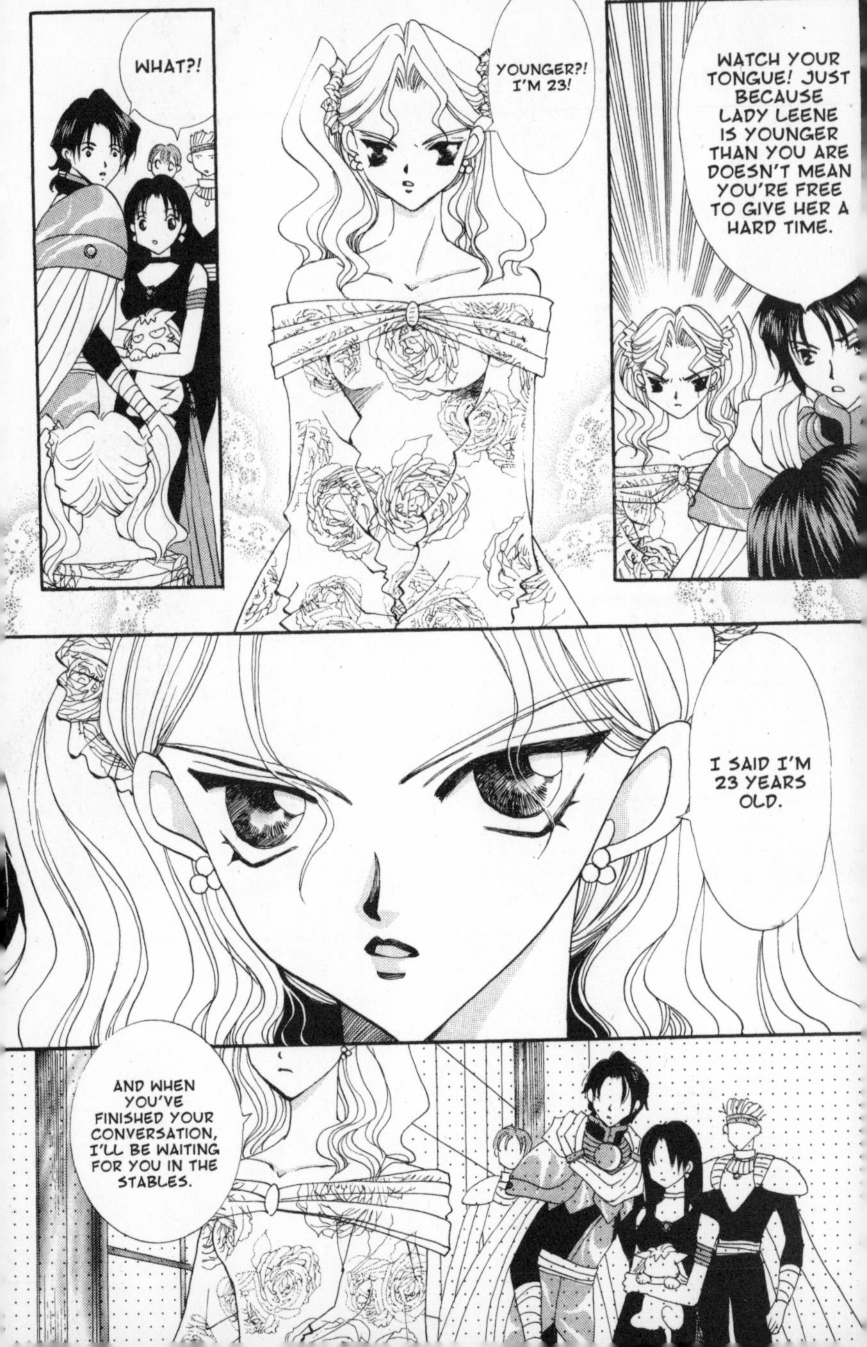
WATCH YOUR TONGUE! JUST BECAUSE LADY LEENE IS YOUNGER THAN YOU ARE DOESN'T MEAN YOU'RE FREE TO GIVE HER A HARD TIME.
YOUNGER?! I'M 23!
WHAT?!
I SAID I'M 23 YEARS OLD.
AND WHEN YOU'VE FINISHED YOUR CONVERSATION, I'LL BE WAITING FOR YOU IN THE STABLES.

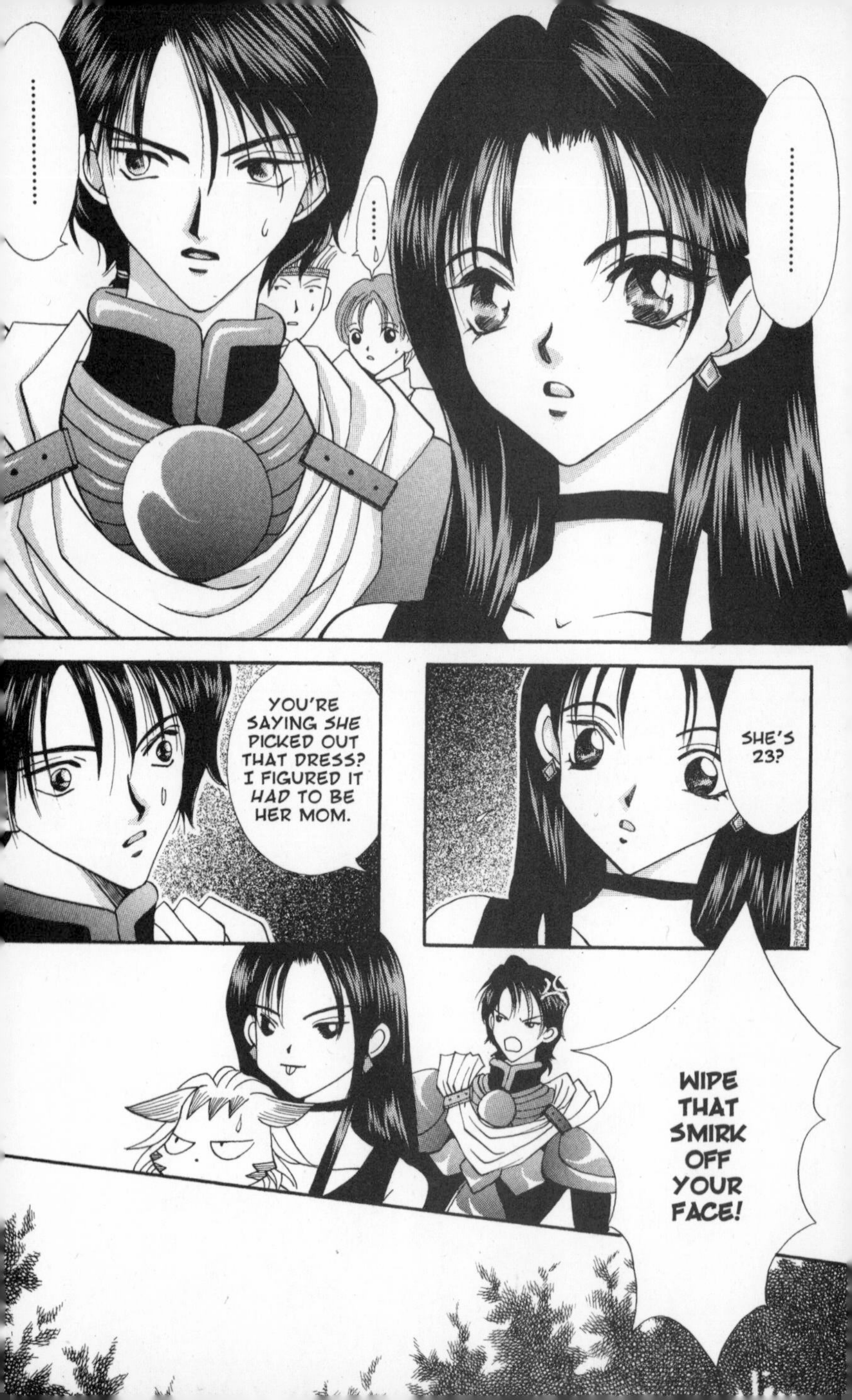
......
......
......
SHE'S 23?
YOU'RE SAYING SHE PICKED OUT THAT DRESS? I FIGURED IT HAD TO BE HER MOM.
WIPE THAT SMIRK OFF YOUR FACE!

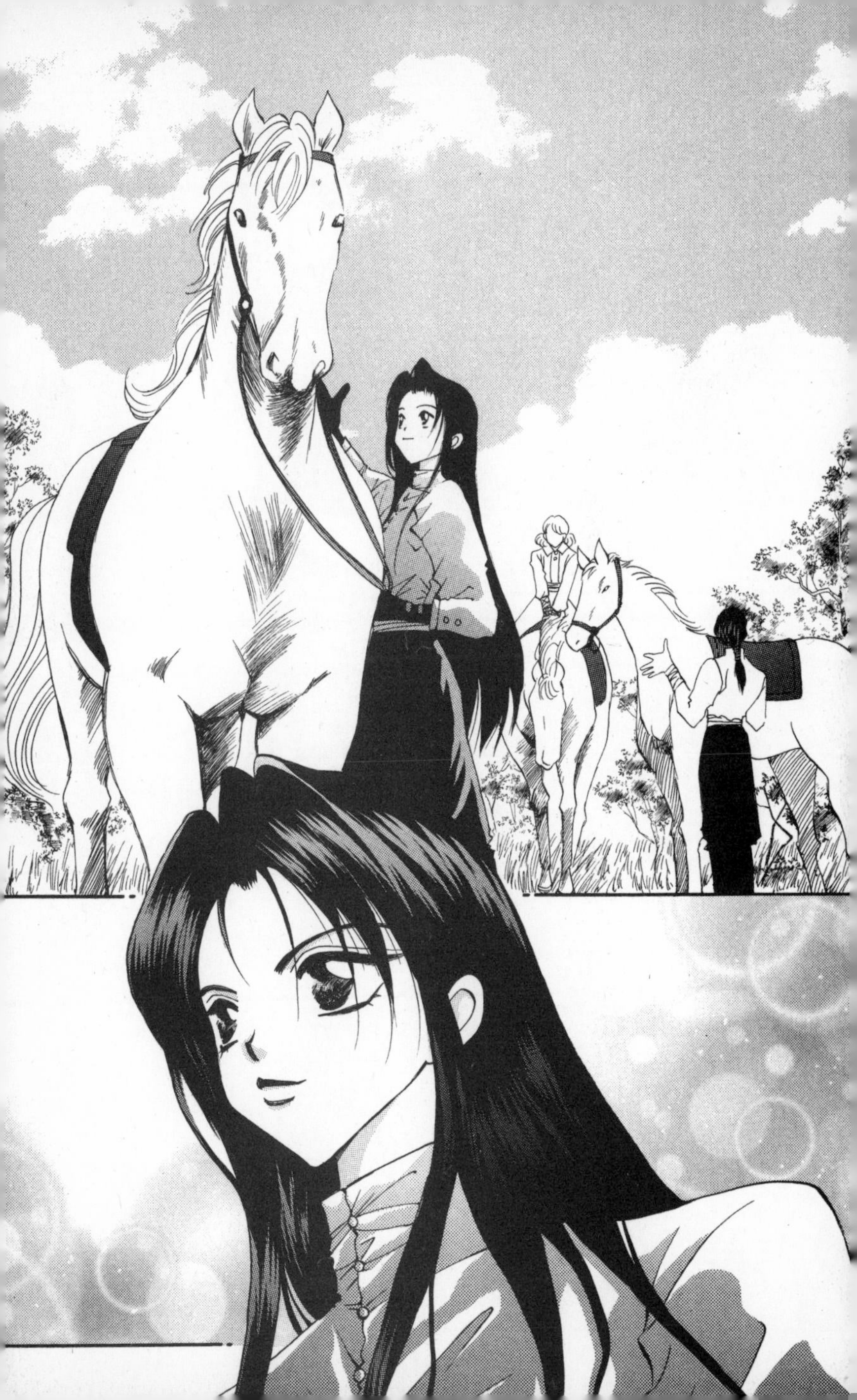

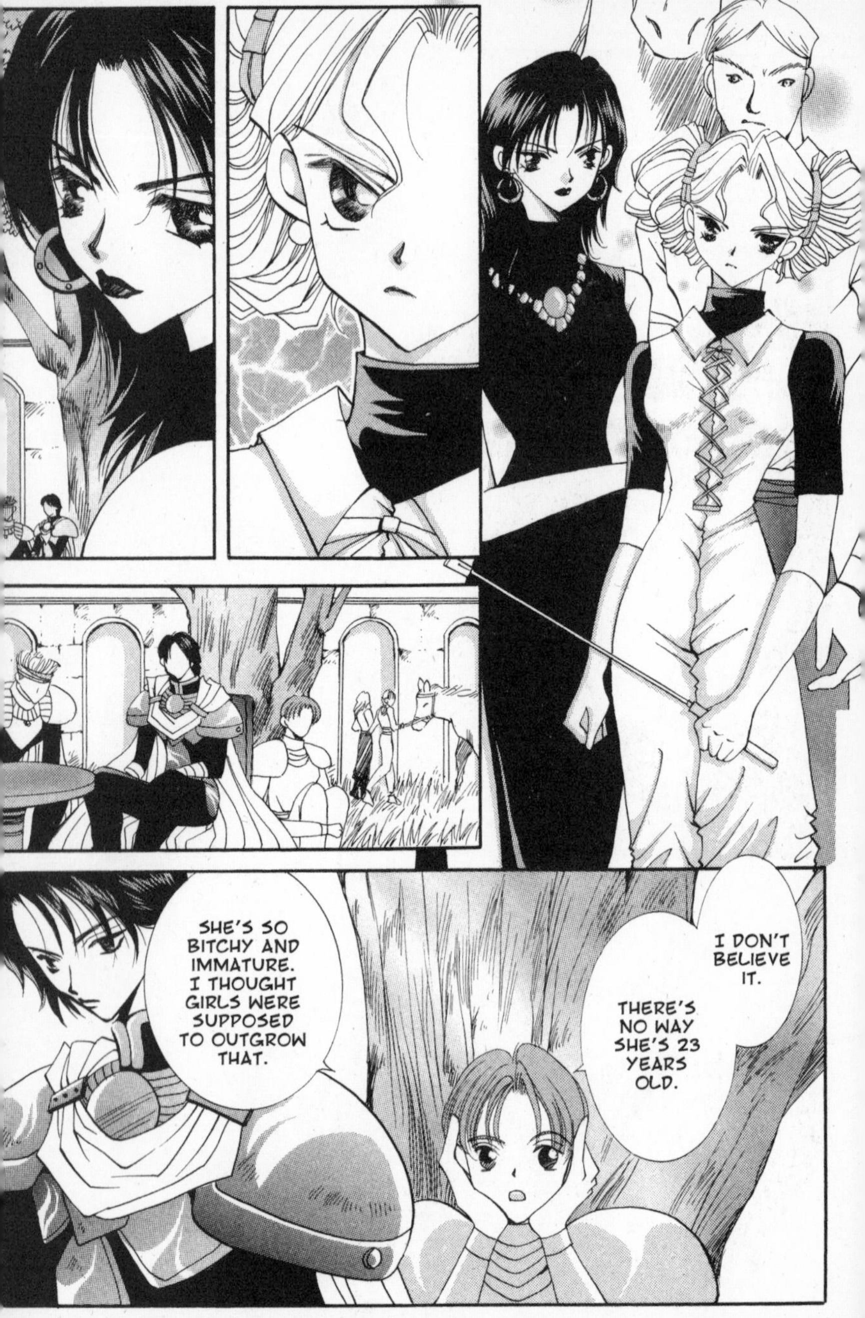
I DON'T BELIEVE IT.
THERE'S NO WAY SHE'S 23 YEARS OLD.
SHE'S SO BITCHY AND IMMATURE. I THOUGHT GIRLS WERE SUPPOSED TO OUTGROW THAT.

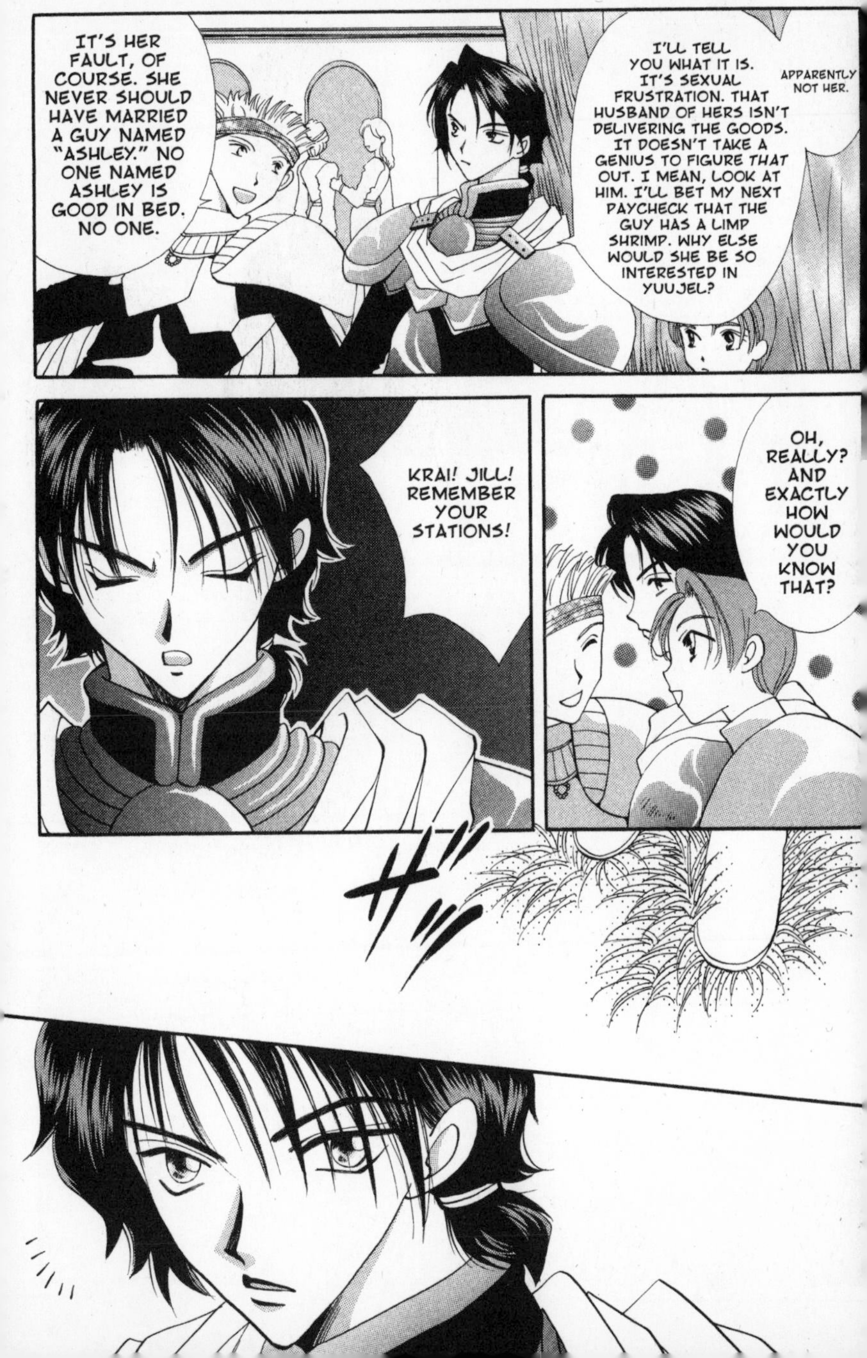

APPARENTLY NOT HER.
I'LL TELL YOU WHAT IT IS. IT'S SEXUAL FRUSTRATION. THAT HUSBAND OF HERS ISN'T DELIVERING THE GOODS. IT DOESN'T TAKE A GENIUS TO FIGURE *THAT* OUT. I MEAN, LOOK AT HIM. I'LL BET MY NEXT PAYCHECK THAT THE GUY HAS A LIMP SHRIMP. WHY ELSE WOULD SHE BE SO INTERESTED IN YUUJEL?
IT'S HER FAULT, OF COURSE. SHE NEVER SHOULD HAVE MARRIED A GUY NAMED "ASHLEY." NO ONE NAMED ASHLEY IS GOOD IN BED. NO ONE.
OH, REALLY? AND EXACTLY HOW WOULD YOU KNOW THAT?
KRAI! JILL! REMEMBER YOUR STATIONS!

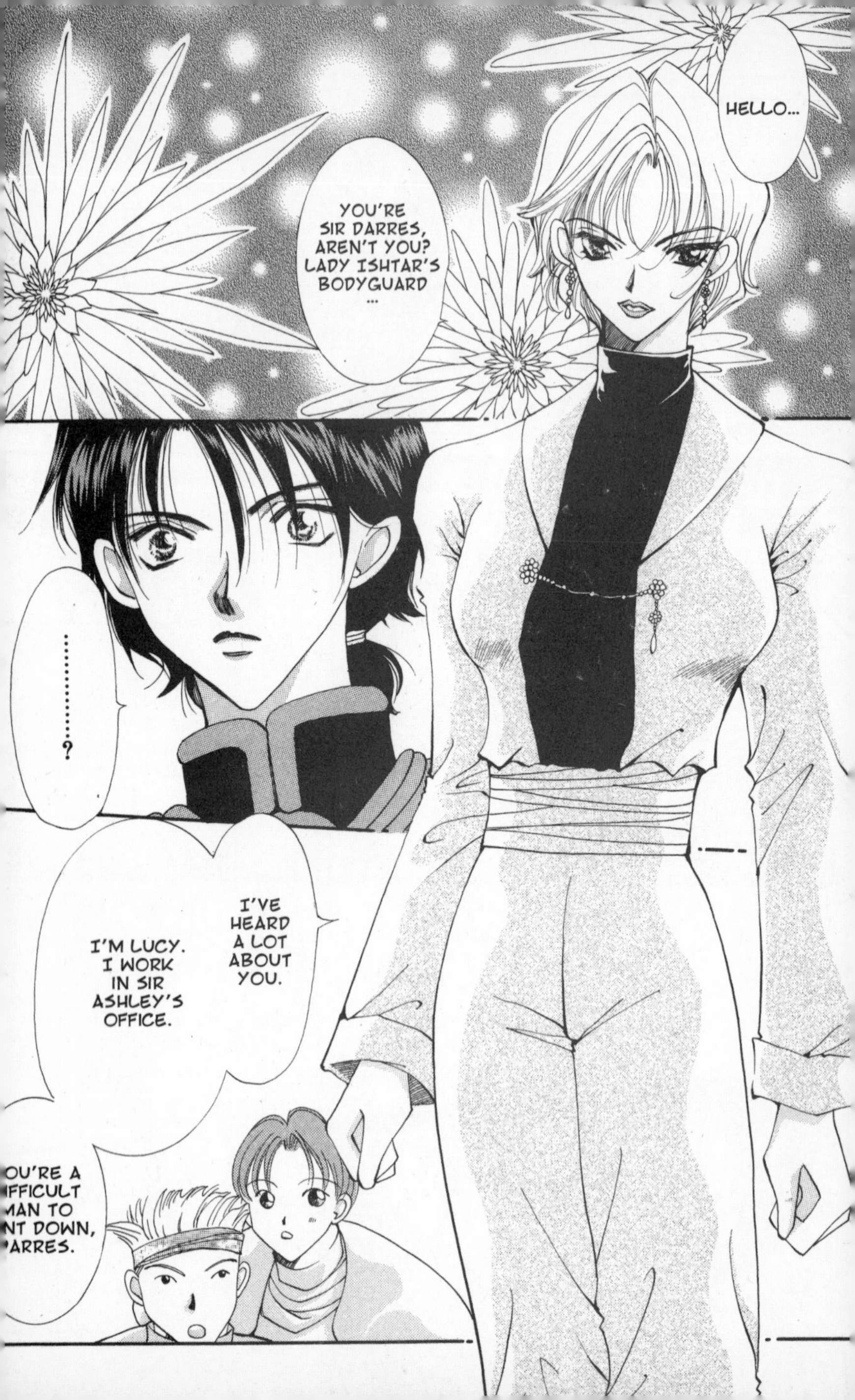
HELLO...
YOU'RE SIR DARRES, AREN'T YOU? LADY ISHTAR'S BODYGUARD ...
.........?
I'VE HEARD A LOT ABOUT YOU.
I'M LUCY. I WORK IN SIR ASHLEY'S OFFICE.
OU'RE A FFICULT MAN TO NT DOWN, ARRES.

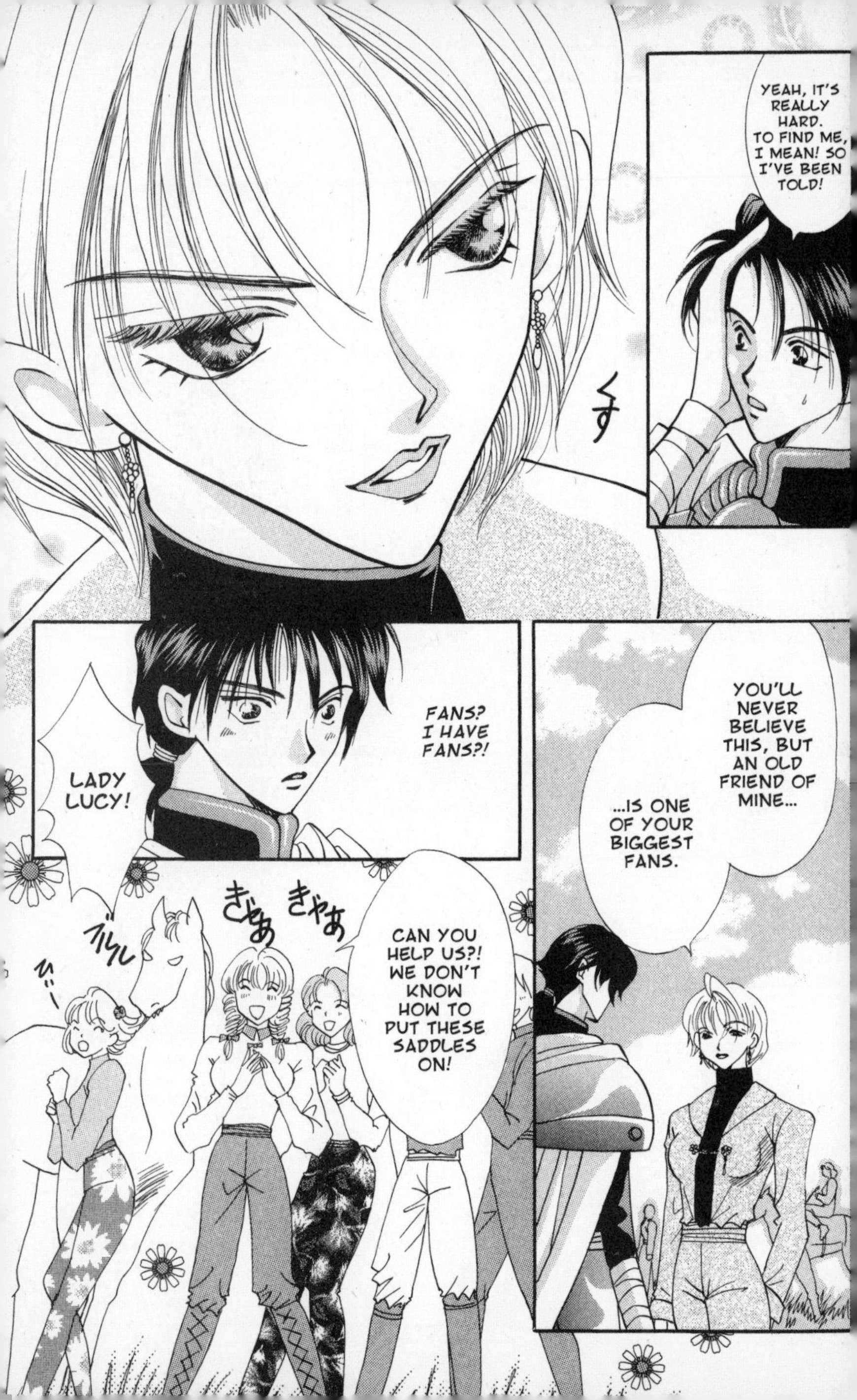

YEAH, IT'S REALLY HARD. TO FIND ME, I MEAN! SO I'VE BEEN TOLD!
くす
YOU'LL NEVER BELIEVE THIS, BUT AN OLD FRIEND OF MINE...
...IS ONE OF YOUR BIGGEST FANS.
FANS? I HAVE FANS?!
LADY LUCY!
CAN YOU HELP US?! WE DON'T KNOW HOW TO PUT THESE SADDLES ON!
きゃあ
きゃあ
ブルル
ひー

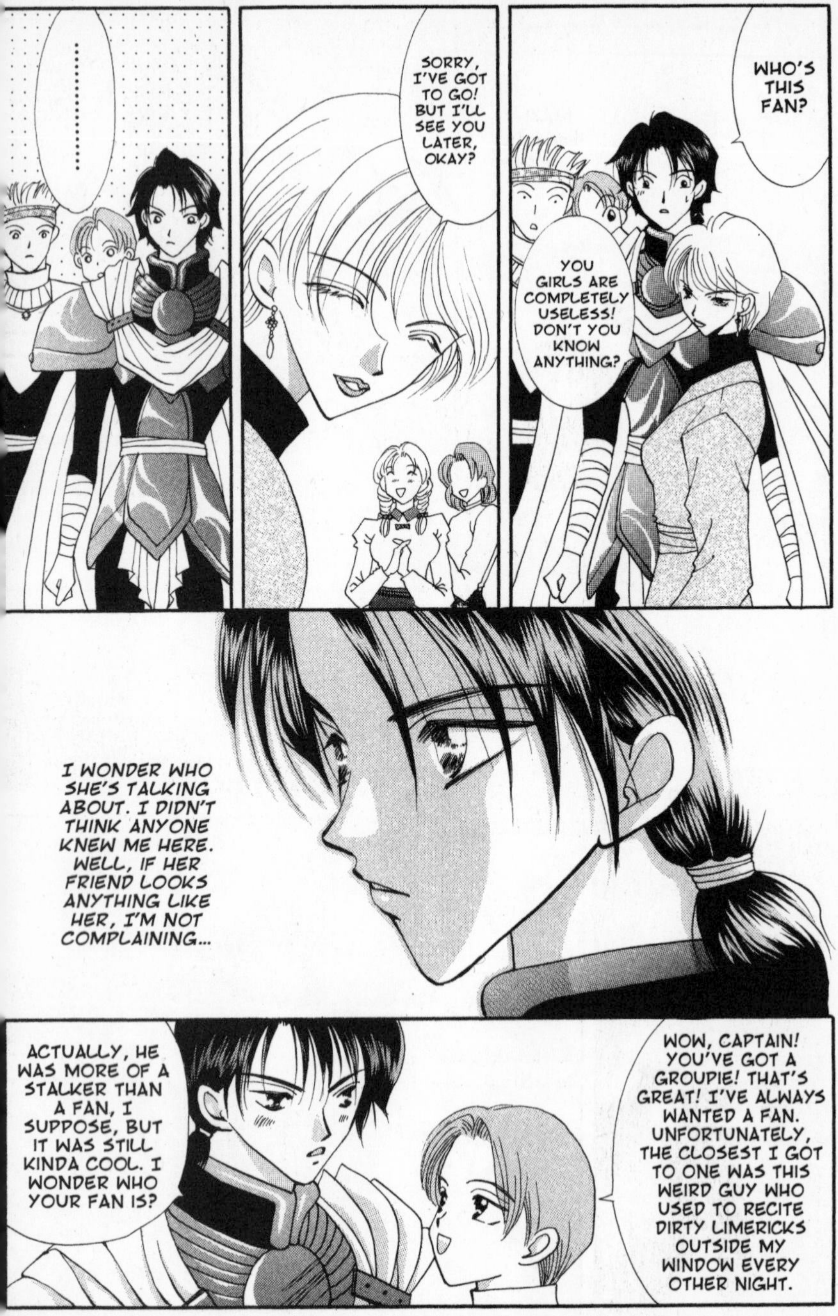
WHO'S THIS FAN?
YOU GIRLS ARE COMPLETELY USELESS! DON'T YOU KNOW ANYTHING?
SORRY, I'VE GOT TO GO! BUT I'LL SEE YOU LATER, OKAY?
......
I WONDER WHO SHE'S TALKING ABOUT. I DIDN'T THINK ANYONE KNEW ME HERE. WELL, IF HER FRIEND LOOKS ANYTHING LIKE HER, I'M NOT COMPLAINING...
WOW, CAPTAIN! YOU'VE GOT A GROUPIE! THAT'S GREAT! I'VE ALWAYS WANTED A FAN. UNFORTUNATELY, THE CLOSEST I GOT TO ONE WAS THIS WEIRD GUY WHO USED TO RECITE DIRTY LIMERICKS OUTSIDE MY WINDOW EVERY OTHER NIGHT.
ACTUALLY, HE WAS MORE OF A STALKER THAN A FAN, I SUPPOSE, BUT IT WAS STILL KINDA COOL. I WONDER WHO YOUR FAN IS?

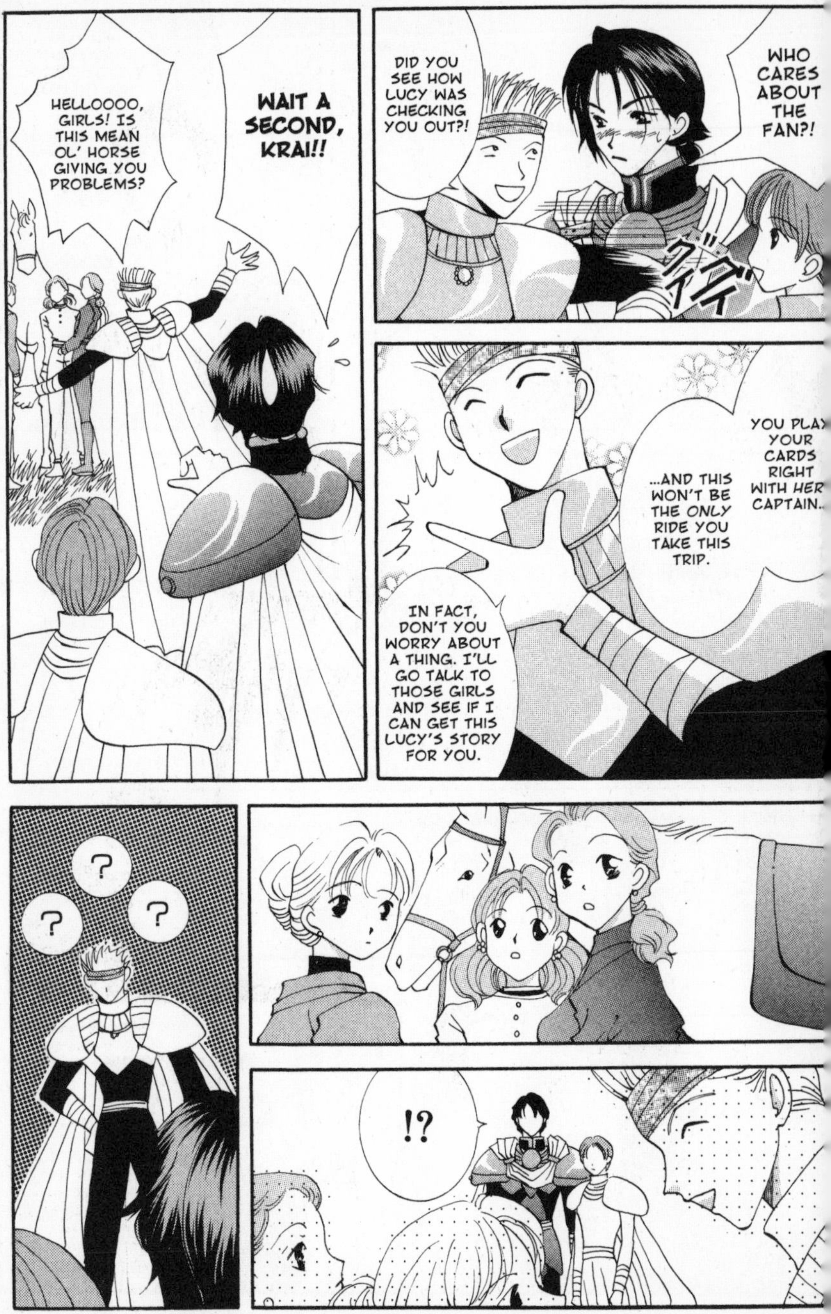
WHO CARES ABOUT THE FAN?!
DID YOU SEE HOW LUCY WAS CHECKING YOU OUT?!
YOU PLAY YOUR CARDS RIGHT WITH HER CAPTAIN..
...AND THIS WON'T BE THE ONLY RIDE YOU TAKE THIS TRIP.
IN FACT, DON'T YOU WORRY ABOUT A THING. I'LL GO TALK TO THOSE GIRLS AND SEE IF I CAN GET THIS LUCY'S STORY FOR YOU.
WAIT A SECOND, KRAI!!
HELLOOOO, GIRLS! IS THIS MEAN OL' HORSE GIVING YOU PROBLEMS?
!?
?
?
?

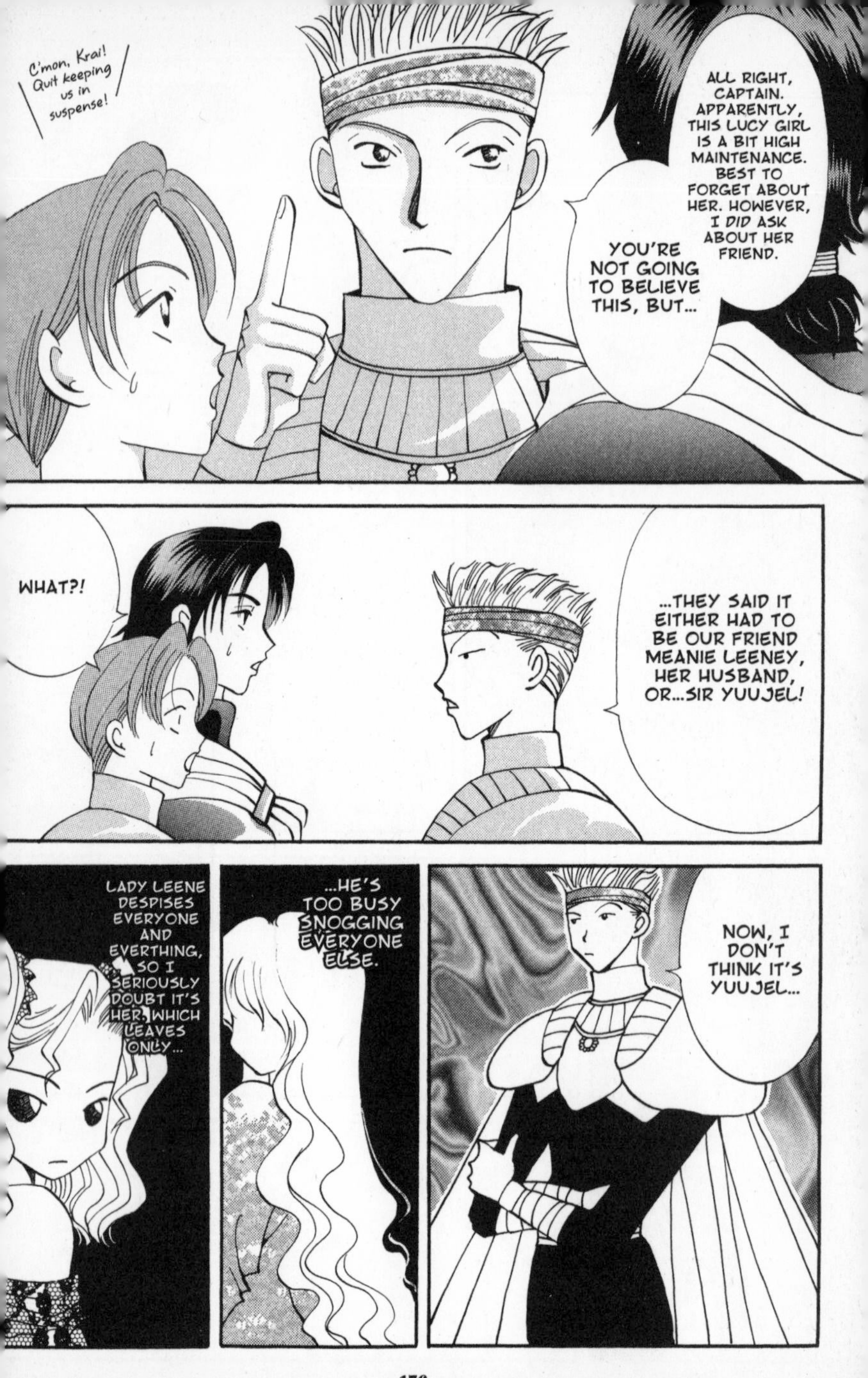
ALL RIGHT, CAPTAIN. APPARENTLY, THIS LUCY GIRL IS A BIT HIGH MAINTENANCE. BEST TO FORGET ABOUT HER. HOWEVER, I DID ASK ABOUT HER FRIEND.
YOU'RE NOT GOING TO BELIEVE THIS, BUT...
C'mon, Krai! Quit keeping us in suspense!
...THEY SAID IT EITHER HAD TO BE OUR FRIEND MEANIE LEENEY, HER HUSBAND, OR...SIR YUUJEL!
WHAT?!
NOW, I DON'T THINK IT'S YUUJEL...
...HE'S TOO BUSY SNOGGING EVERYONE ELSE.
LADY LEENE DESPISES EVERYONE AND EVERTHING, SO I SERIOUSLY DOUBT IT'S HER, WHICH LEAVES ONLY...

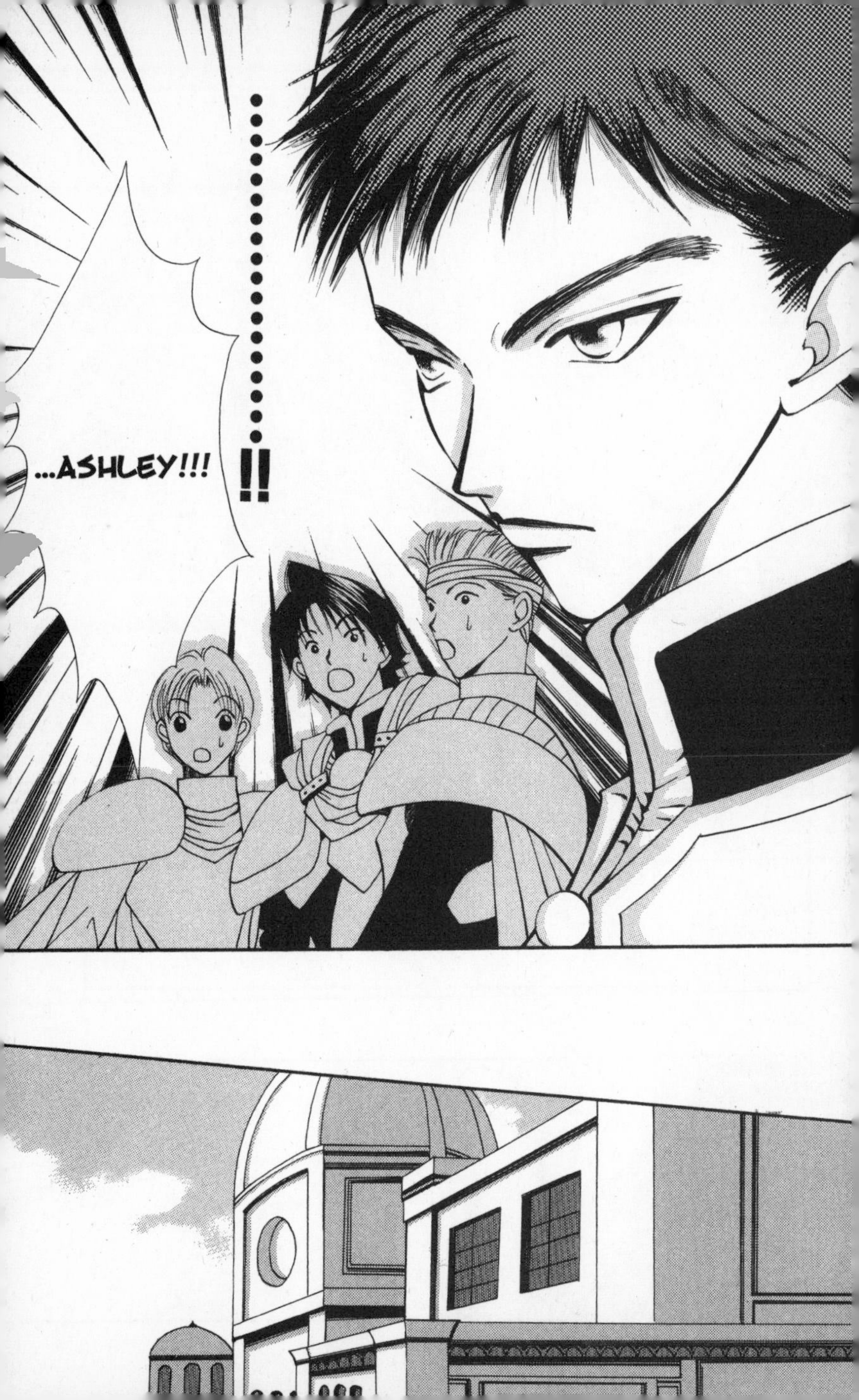

...
!!
...ASHLEY!!!

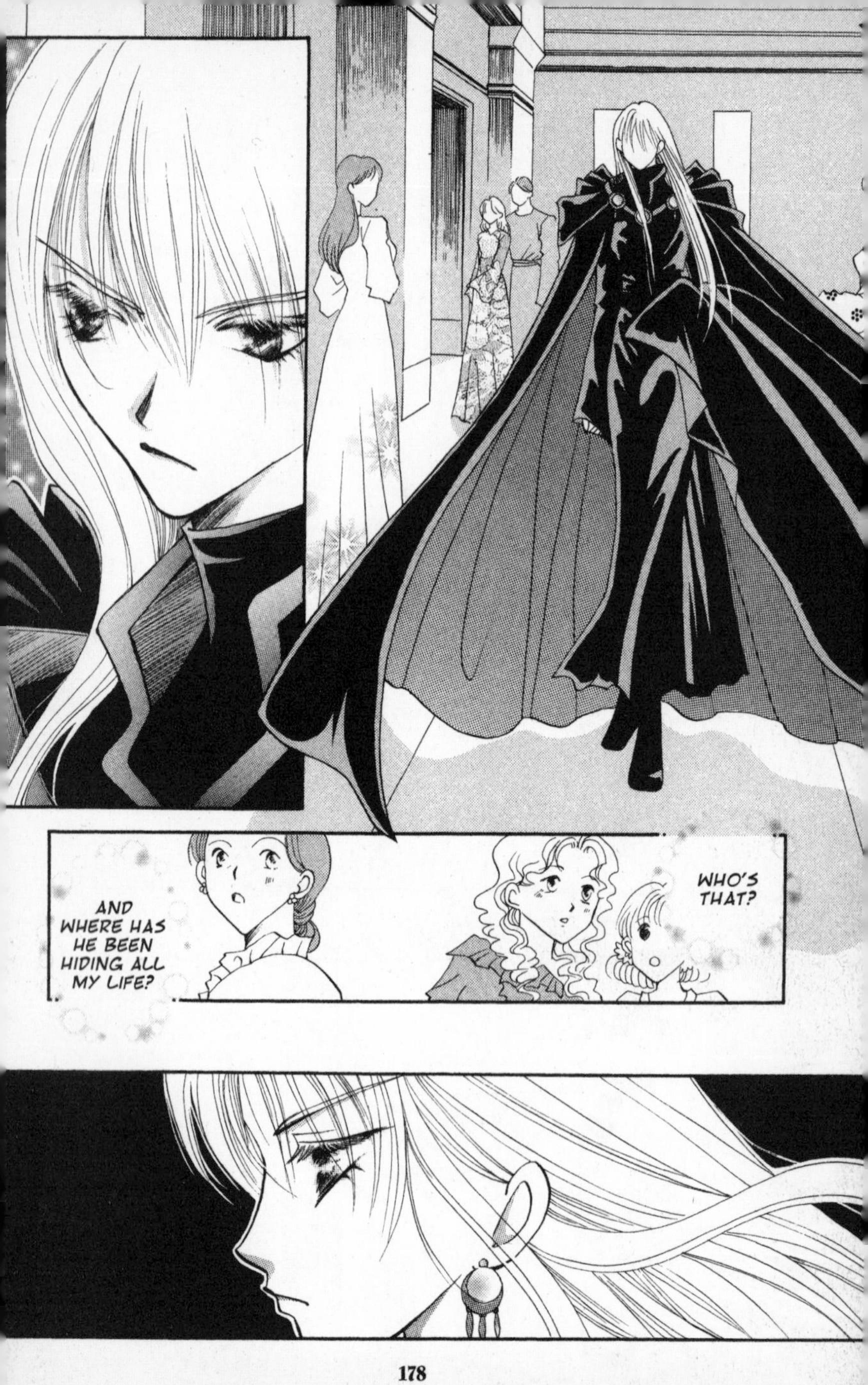
WHO'S THAT?
AND WHERE HAS HE BEEN HIDING ALL MY LIFE?

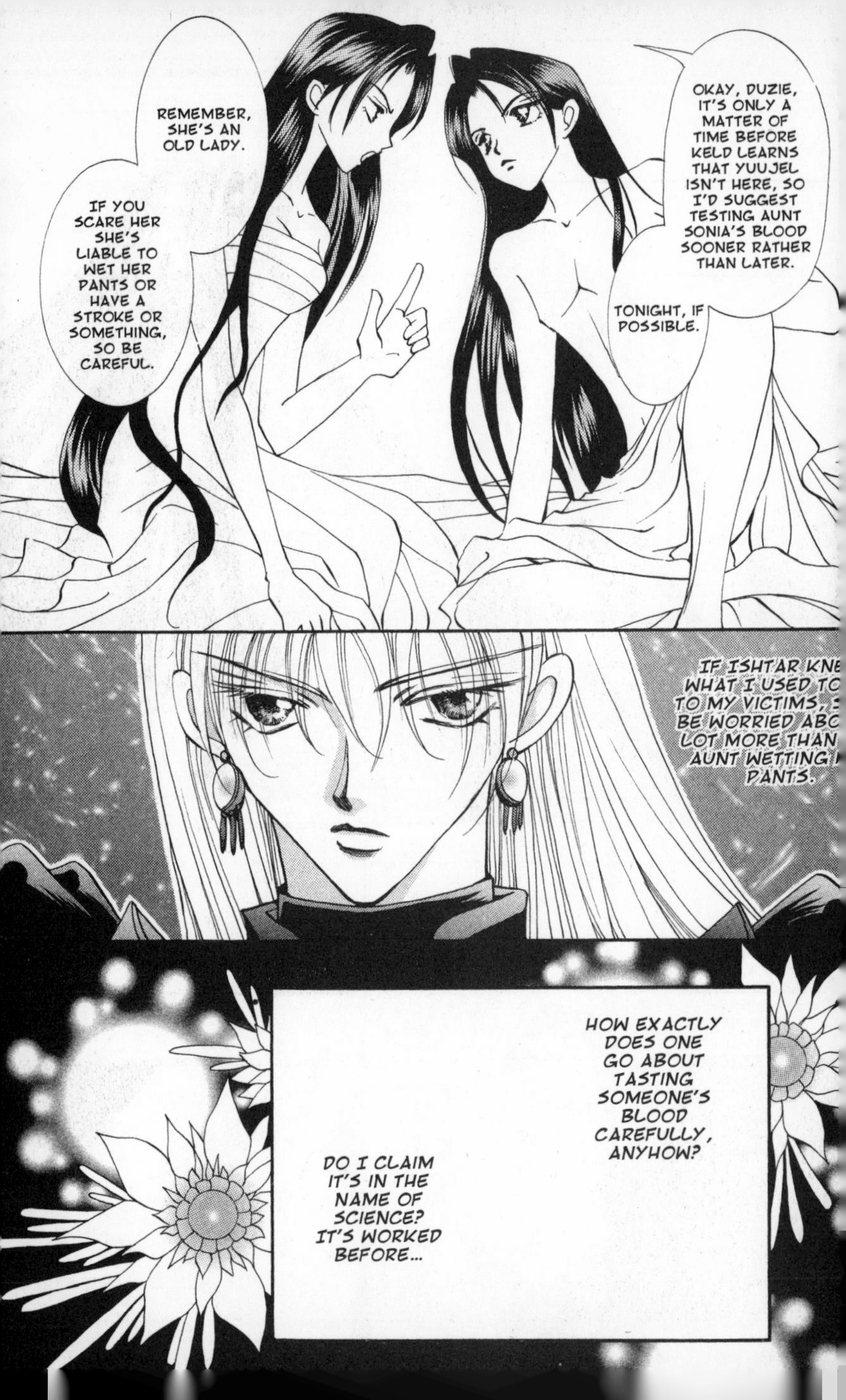
OKAY, DUZIE, IT'S ONLY A MATTER OF TIME BEFORE KELD LEARNS THAT YUUJEL ISN'T HERE, SO I'D SUGGEST TESTING AUNT SONIA'S BLOOD SOONER RATHER THAN LATER.
TONIGHT, IF POSSIBLE.
REMEMBER, SHE'S AN OLD LADY.
IF YOU SCARE HER SHE'S LIABLE TO WET HER PANTS OR HAVE A STROKE OR SOMETHING, SO BE CAREFUL.
IF ISHTAR KNE WHAT I USED TO TO MY VICTIMS, S BE WORRIED ABO LOT MORE THAN AUNT WETTING PANTS.
HOW EXACTLY DOES ONE GO ABOUT TASTING SOMEONE'S BLOOD CAREFULLY, ANYHOW?
DO I CLAIM IT'S IN THE NAME OF SCIENCE? IT'S WORKED BEFORE...

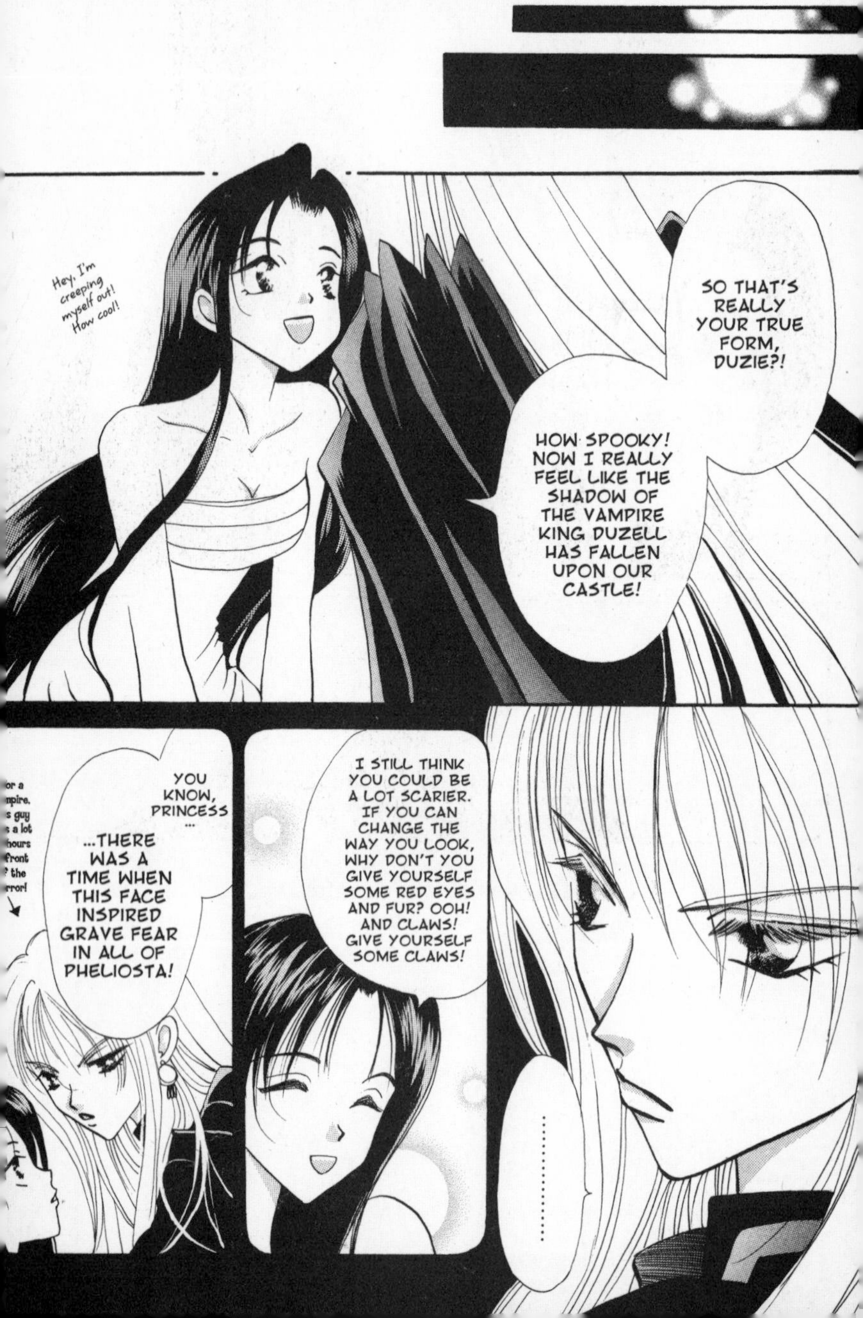

SO THAT'S REALLY YOUR TRUE FORM, DUZIE?!
HOW SPOOKY! NOW I REALLY FEEL LIKE THE SHADOW OF THE VAMPIRE KING DUZELL HAS FALLEN UPON OUR CASTLE!
Hey, I'm creeping myself out! How cool!
......
I STILL THINK YOU COULD BE A LOT SCARIER. IF YOU CAN CHANGE THE WAY YOU LOOK, WHY DON'T YOU GIVE YOURSELF SOME RED EYES AND FUR? OOH! AND CLAWS! GIVE YOURSELF SOME CLAWS!
YOU KNOW, PRINCESS...
...THERE WAS A TIME WHEN THIS FACE INSPIRED GRAVE FEAR IN ALL OF PHELIOSTA!

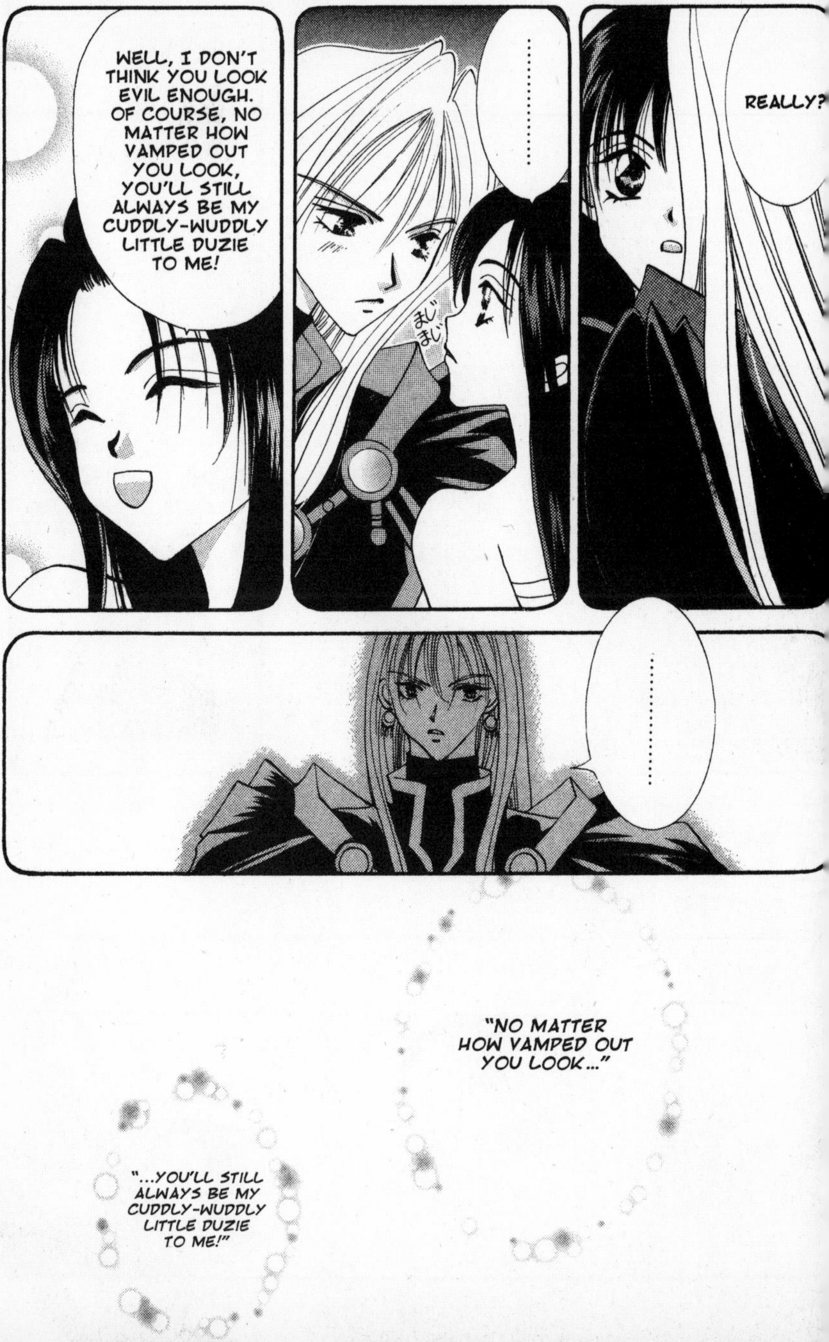
REALLY?
......
まじまじ
WELL, I DON'T THINK YOU LOOK EVIL ENOUGH. OF COURSE, NO MATTER HOW VAMPED OUT YOU LOOK, YOU'LL STILL ALWAYS BE MY CUDDLY-WUDDLY LITTLE DUZIE TO ME!
......
"NO MATTER HOW VAMPED OUT YOU LOOK..."
"...YOU'LL STILL ALWAYS BE MY CUDDLY-WUDDLY LITTLE DUZIE TO ME!"

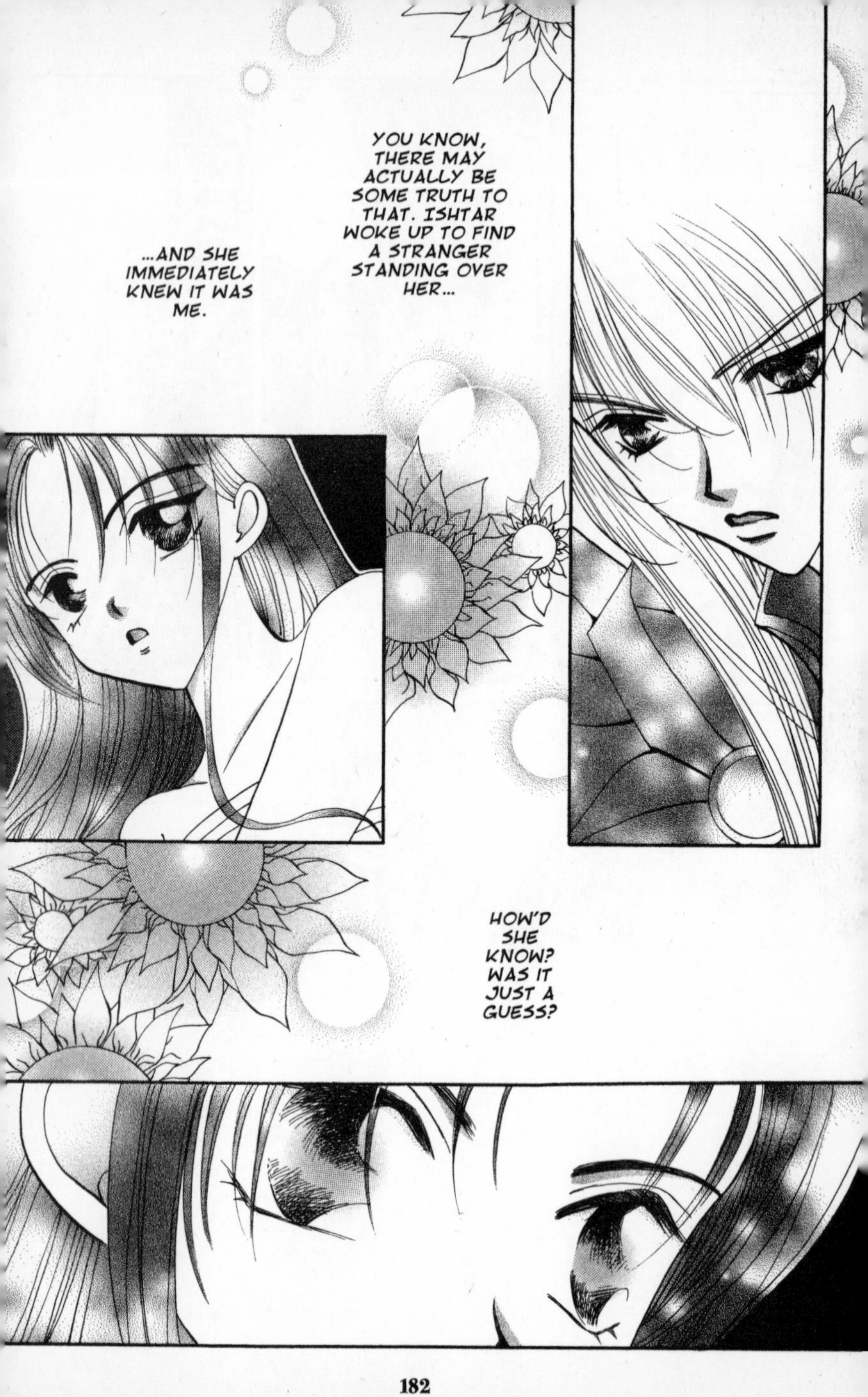
YOU KNOW, THERE MAY ACTUALLY BE SOME TRUTH TO THAT. ISHTAR WOKE UP TO FIND A STRANGER STANDING OVER HER...
...AND SHE IMMEDIATELY KNEW IT WAS ME.
HOW'D SHE KNOW? WAS IT JUST A GUESS?

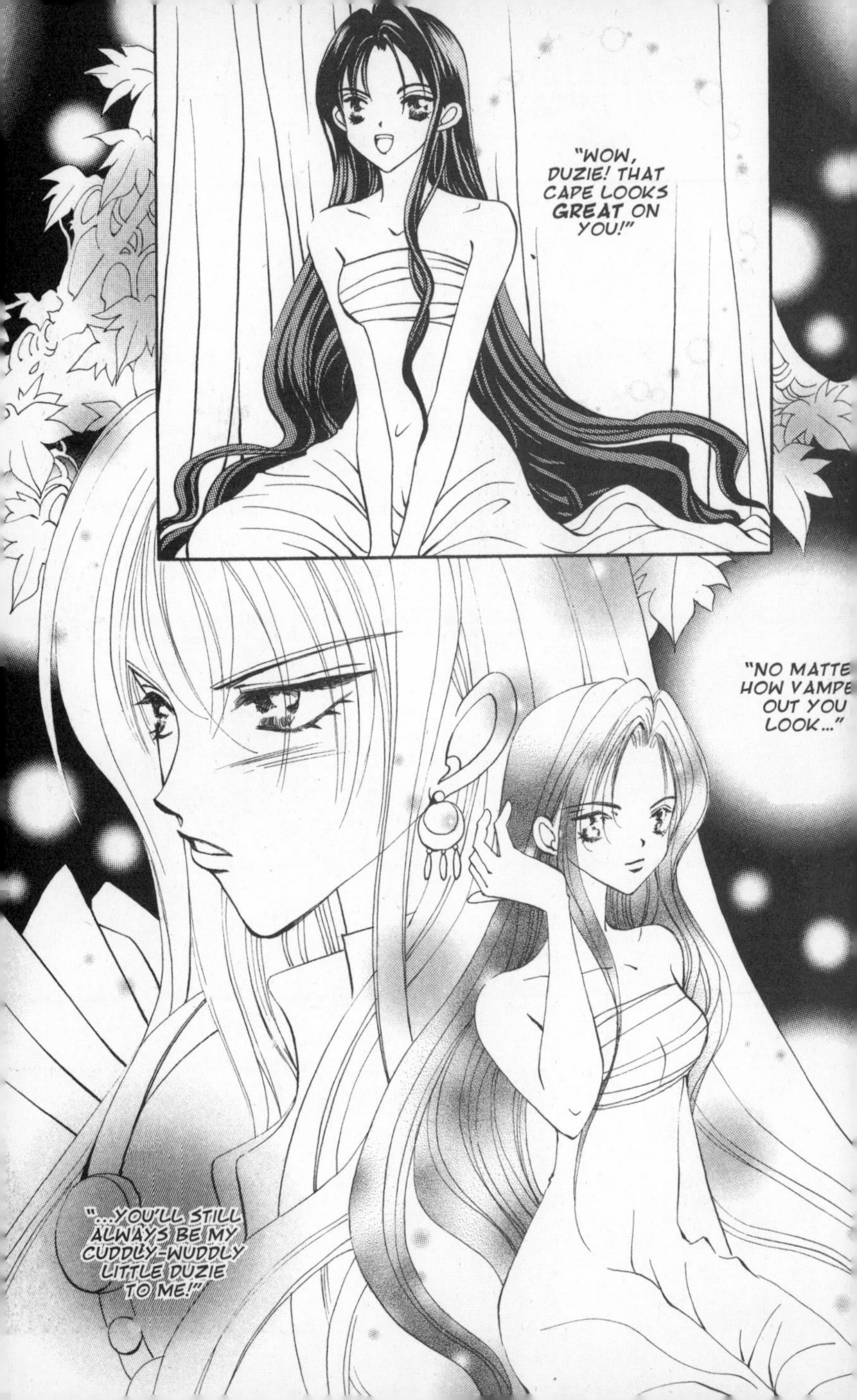
"WOW, DUZIE! THAT CAPE LOOKS GREAT ON YOU!"
"NO MATTE HOW VAMPE OUT YOU LOOK..."
"...YOU'LL STILL ALWAYS BE MY CUDDLY-WUDDLY LITTLE DUZIE TO ME!"

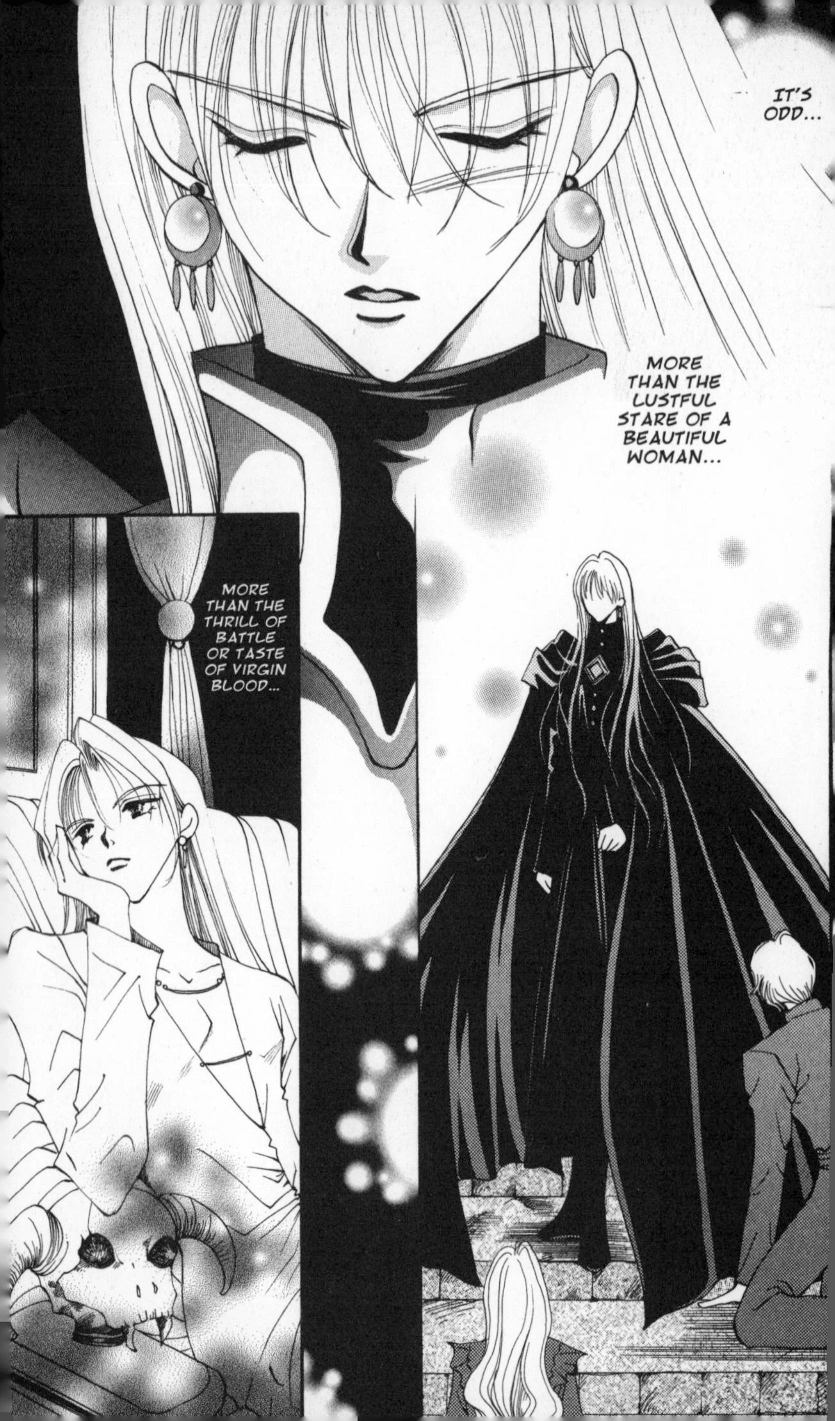
IT'S ODD...
MORE THAN THE LUSTFUL STARE OF A BEAUTIFUL WOMAN...
MORE THAN THE THRILL OF BATTLE OR TASTE OF VIRGIN BLOOD...

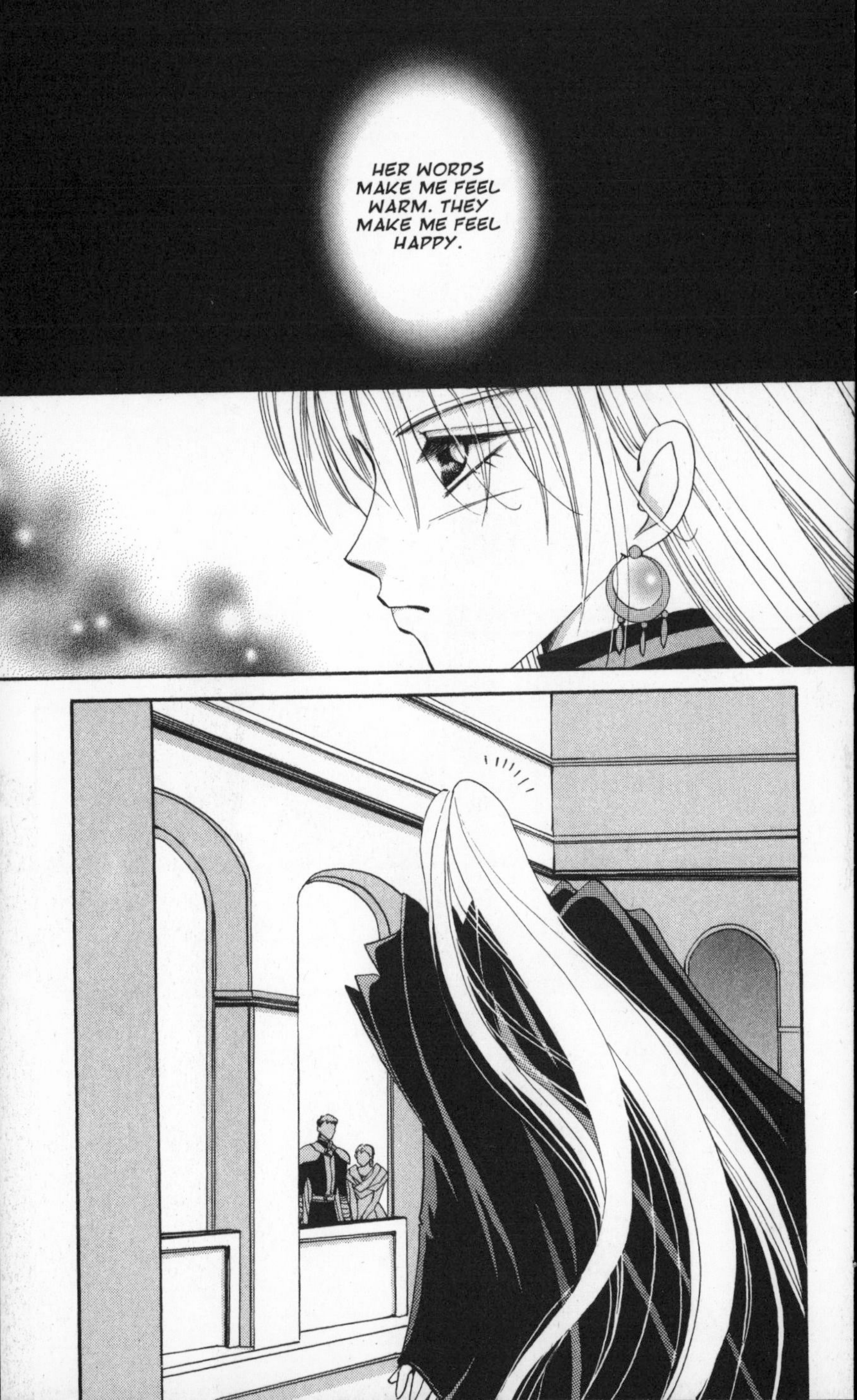
HER WORDS MAKE ME FEEL WARM. THEY MAKE ME FEEL HAPPY.

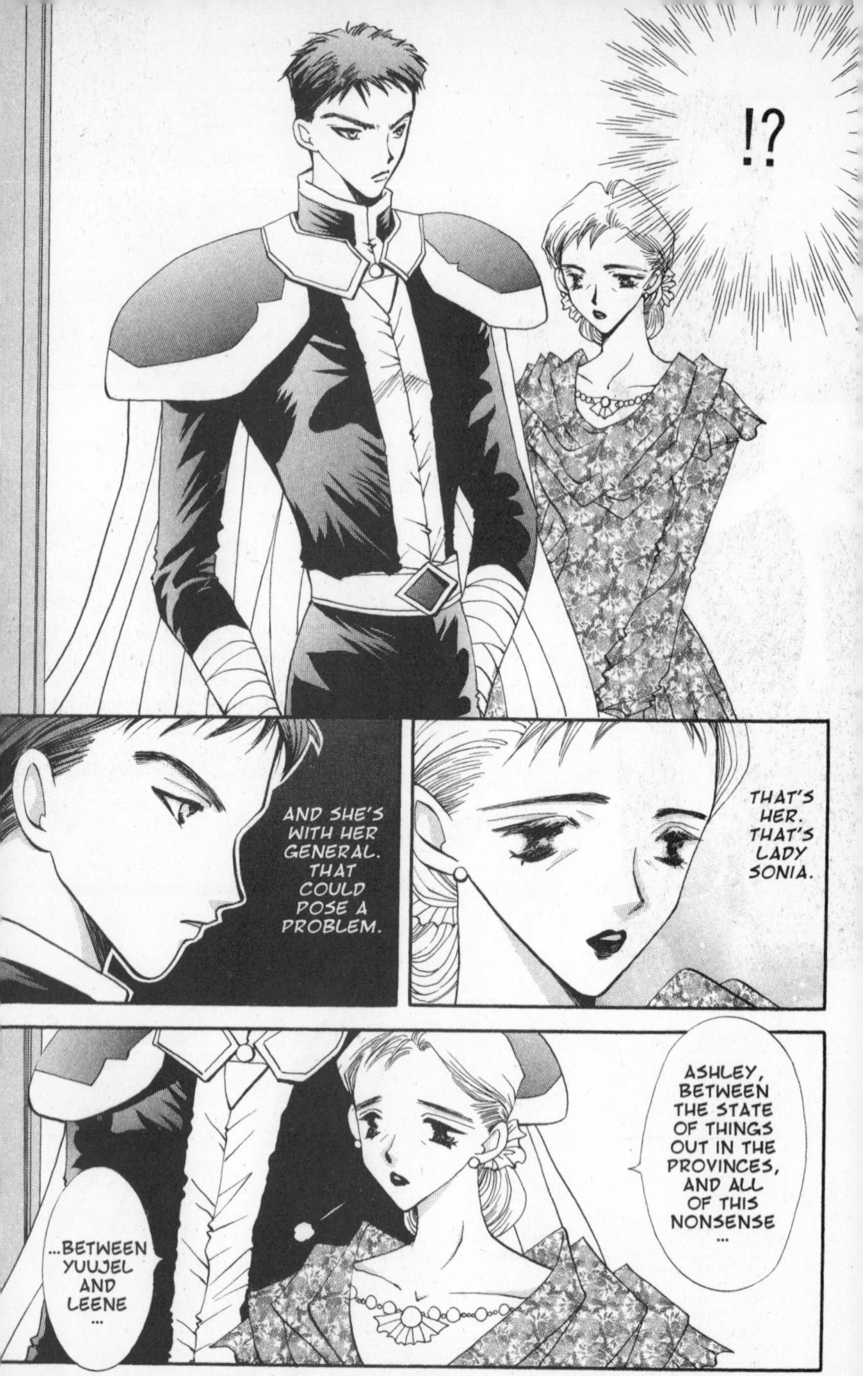
!?
THAT'S HER. THAT'S LADY SONIA.
AND SHE'S WITH HER GENERAL. THAT COULD POSE A PROBLEM.
ASHLEY, BETWEEN THE STATE OF THINGS OUT IN THE PROVINCES, AND ALL OF THIS NONSENSE ...
...BETWEEN YUUJEL AND LEENE ...

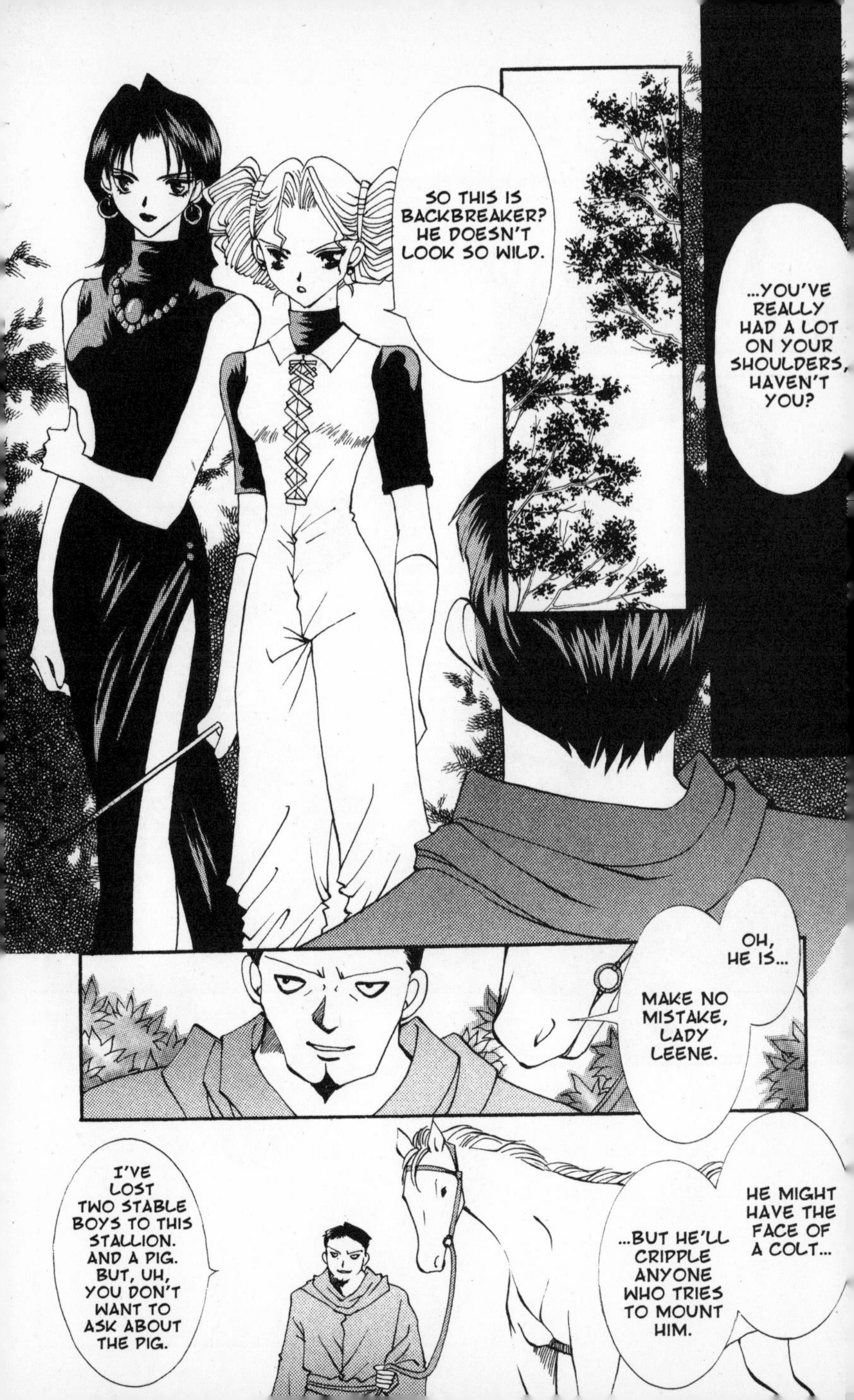
...YOU'VE REALLY HAD A LOT ON YOUR SHOULDERS, HAVEN'T YOU?
SO THIS IS BACKBREAKER? HE DOESN'T LOOK SO WILD.
OH, HE IS...
MAKE NO MISTAKE, LADY LEENE.
HE MIGHT HAVE THE FACE OF A COLT...
...BUT HE'LL CRIPPLE ANYONE WHO TRIES TO MOUNT HIM.
I'VE LOST TWO STABLE BOYS TO THIS STALLION. AND A PIG. BUT, UH, YOU DON'T WANT TO ASK ABOUT THE PIG.

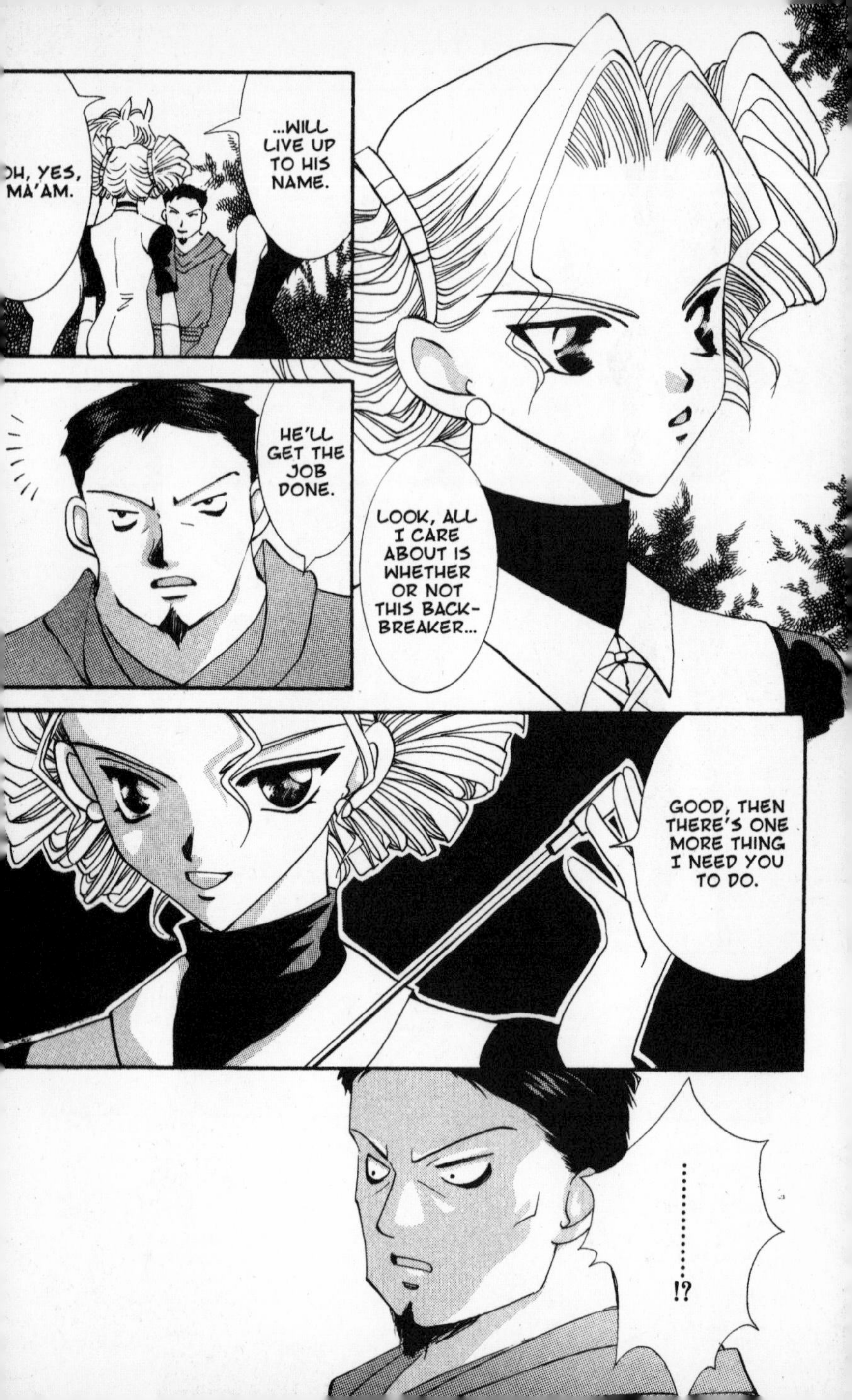
LOOK, ALL I CARE ABOUT IS WHETHER OR NOT THIS BACK-BREAKER...
...WILL LIVE UP TO HIS NAME.
OH, YES, MA'AM.
HE'LL GET THE JOB DONE.
GOOD, THEN THERE'S ONE MORE THING I NEED YOU TO DO.
........!?

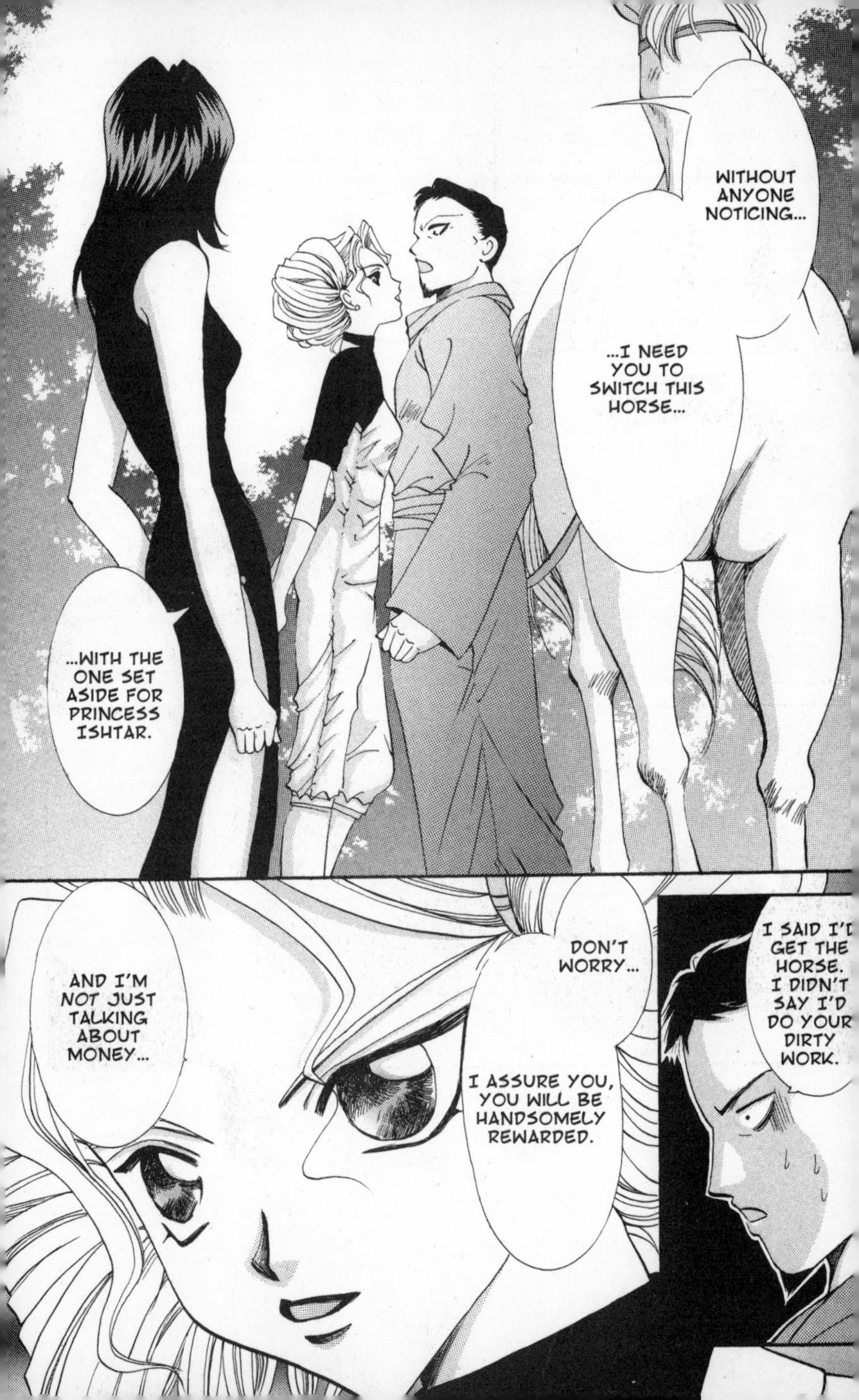
WITHOUT ANYONE NOTICING...
...I NEED YOU TO SWITCH THIS HORSE...
...WITH THE ONE SET ASIDE FOR PRINCESS ISHTAR.
I SAID I'D GET THE HORSE. I DIDN'T SAY I'D DO YOUR DIRTY WORK.
DON'T WORRY...
I ASSURE YOU, YOU WILL BE HANDSOMELY REWARDED.
AND I'M *NOT* JUST TALKING ABOUT MONEY...

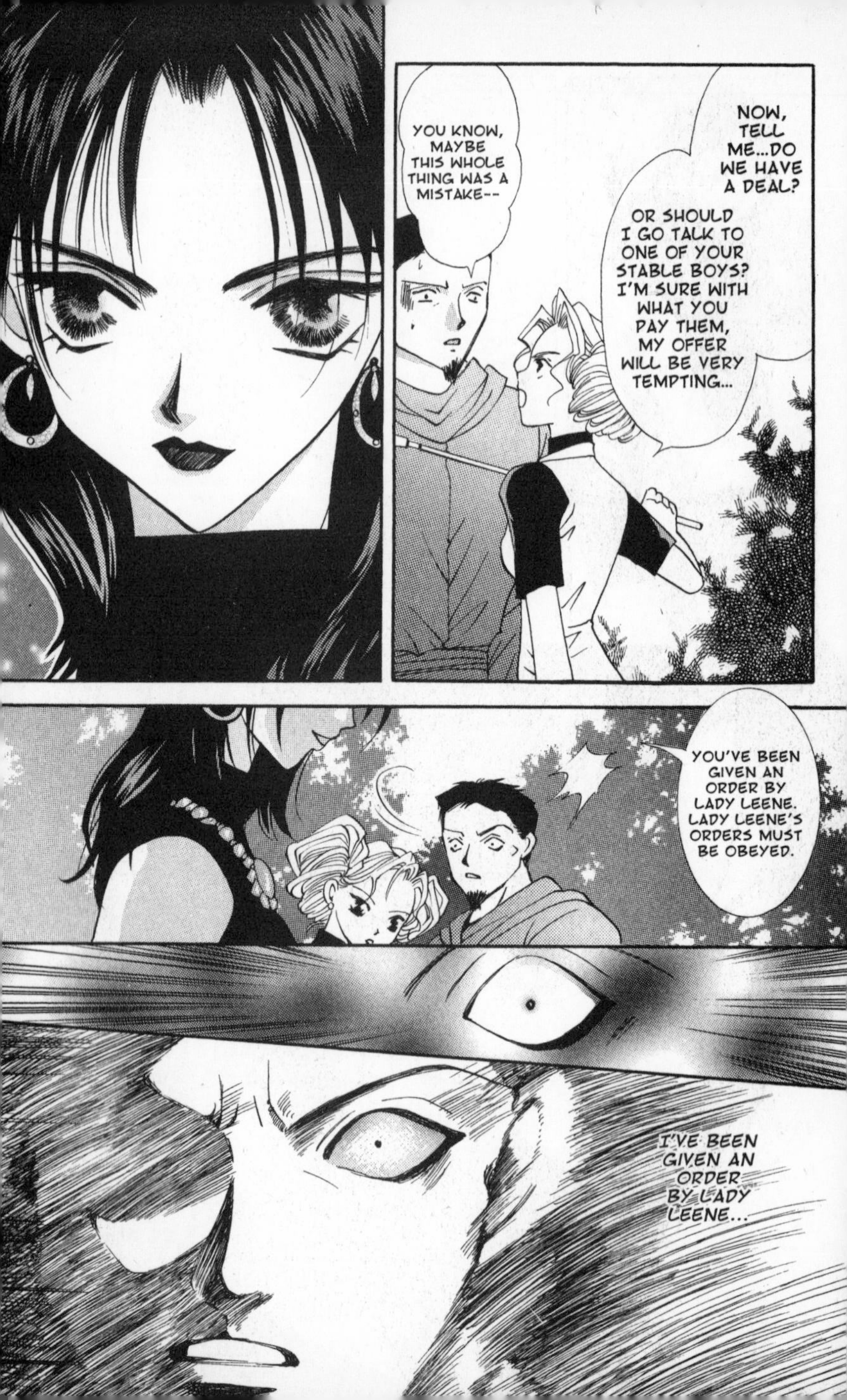
NOW, TELL ME...DO WE HAVE A DEAL?
OR SHOULD I GO TALK TO ONE OF YOUR STABLE BOYS? I'M SURE WITH WHAT YOU PAY THEM, MY OFFER WILL BE VERY TEMPTING...
YOU KNOW, MAYBE THIS WHOLE THING WAS A MISTAKE--
YOU'VE BEEN GIVEN AN ORDER BY LADY LEENE. LADY LEENE'S ORDERS MUST BE OBEYED.
I'VE BEEN GIVEN AN ORDER BY LADY LEENE...

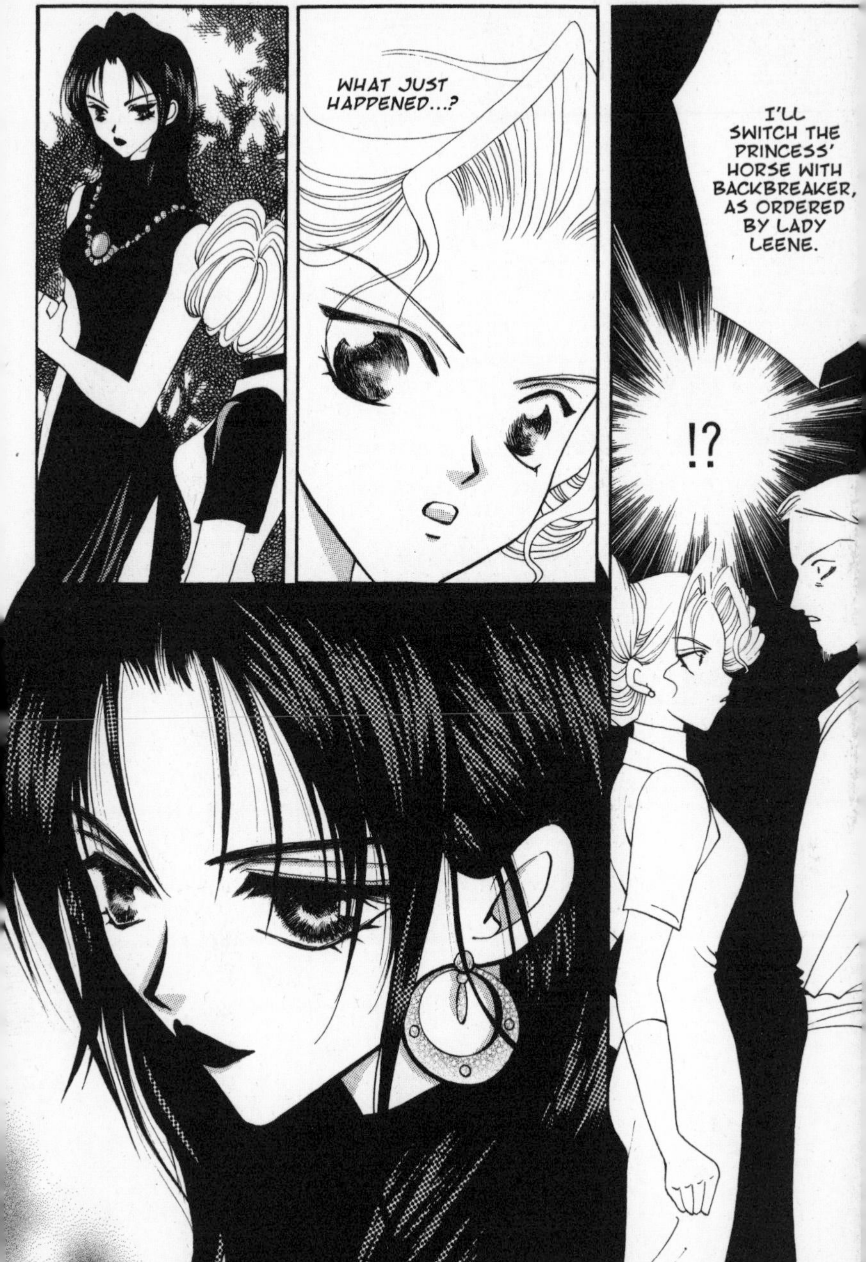

I'LL SWITCH THE PRINCESS' HORSE WITH BACKBREAKER, AS ORDERED BY LADY LEENE.
!?
WHAT JUST HAPPENED...?

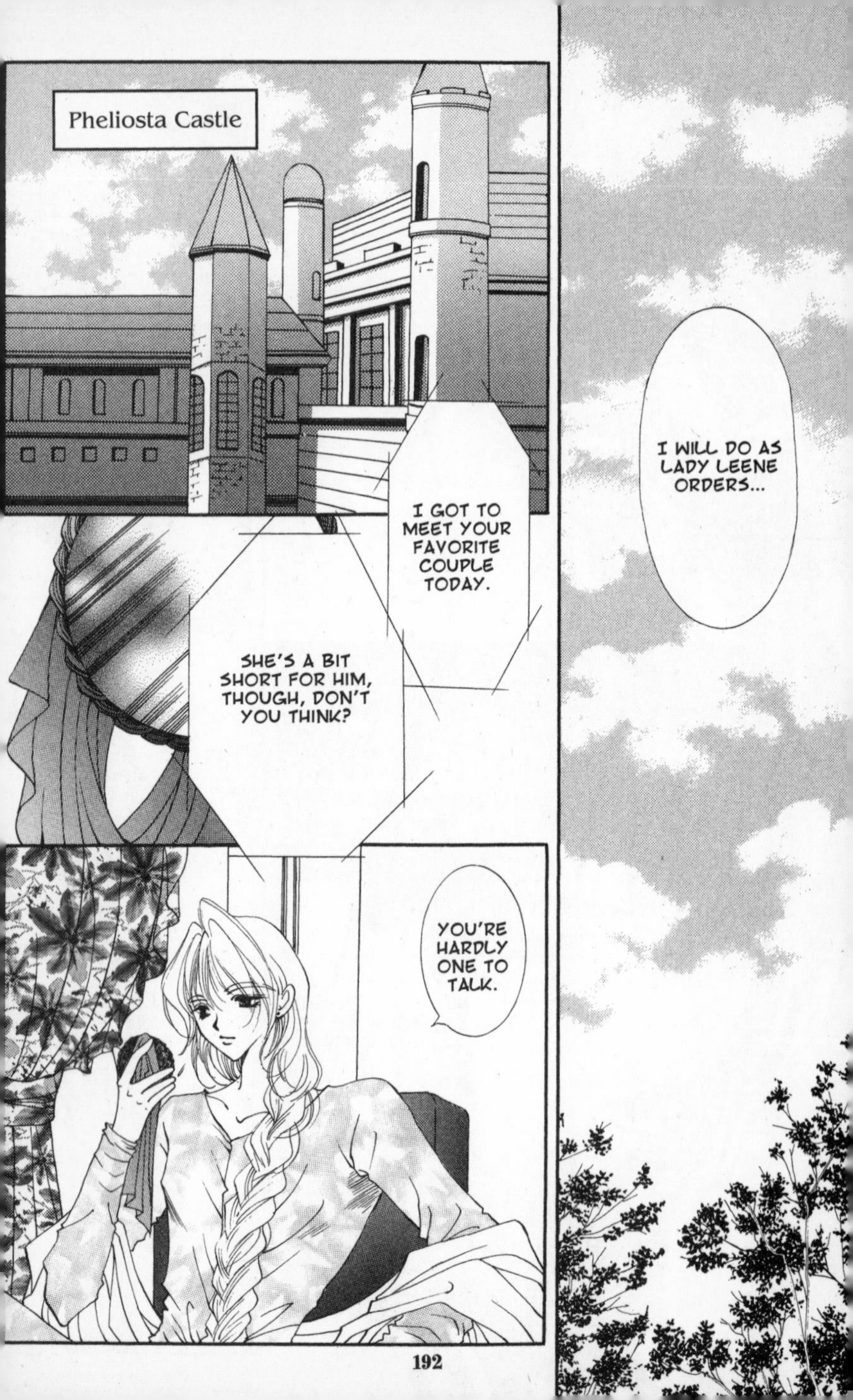
I WILL DO AS LADY LEENE ORDERS...
Pheliosta Castle
I GOT TO MEET YOUR FAVORITE COUPLE TODAY.
SHE'S A BIT SHORT FOR HIM, THOUGH, DON'T YOU THINK?
YOU'RE HARDLY ONE TO TALK.

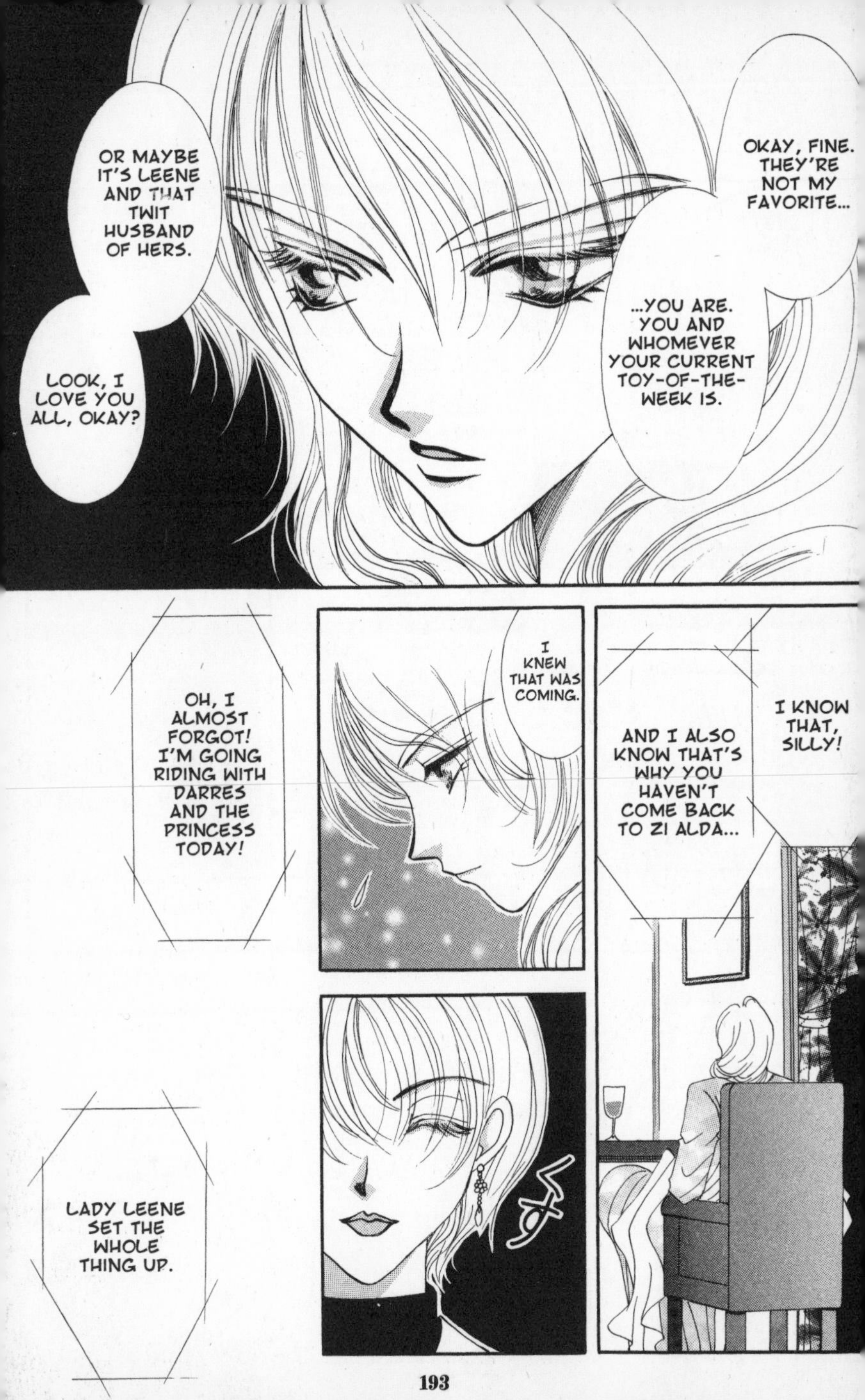
OKAY, FINE. THEY'RE NOT MY FAVORITE...
...YOU ARE. YOU AND WHOMEVER YOUR CURRENT TOY-OF-THE-WEEK IS.
OR MAYBE IT'S LEENE AND THAT TWIT HUSBAND OF HERS.
LOOK, I LOVE YOU ALL, OKAY?
I KNOW THAT, SILLY!
AND I ALSO KNOW THAT'S WHY YOU HAVEN'T COME BACK TO ZI ALDA...
I KNEW THAT WAS COMING.
OH, I ALMOST FORGOT! I'M GOING RIDING WITH DARRES AND THE PRINCESS TODAY!
LADY LEENE SET THE WHOLE THING UP.

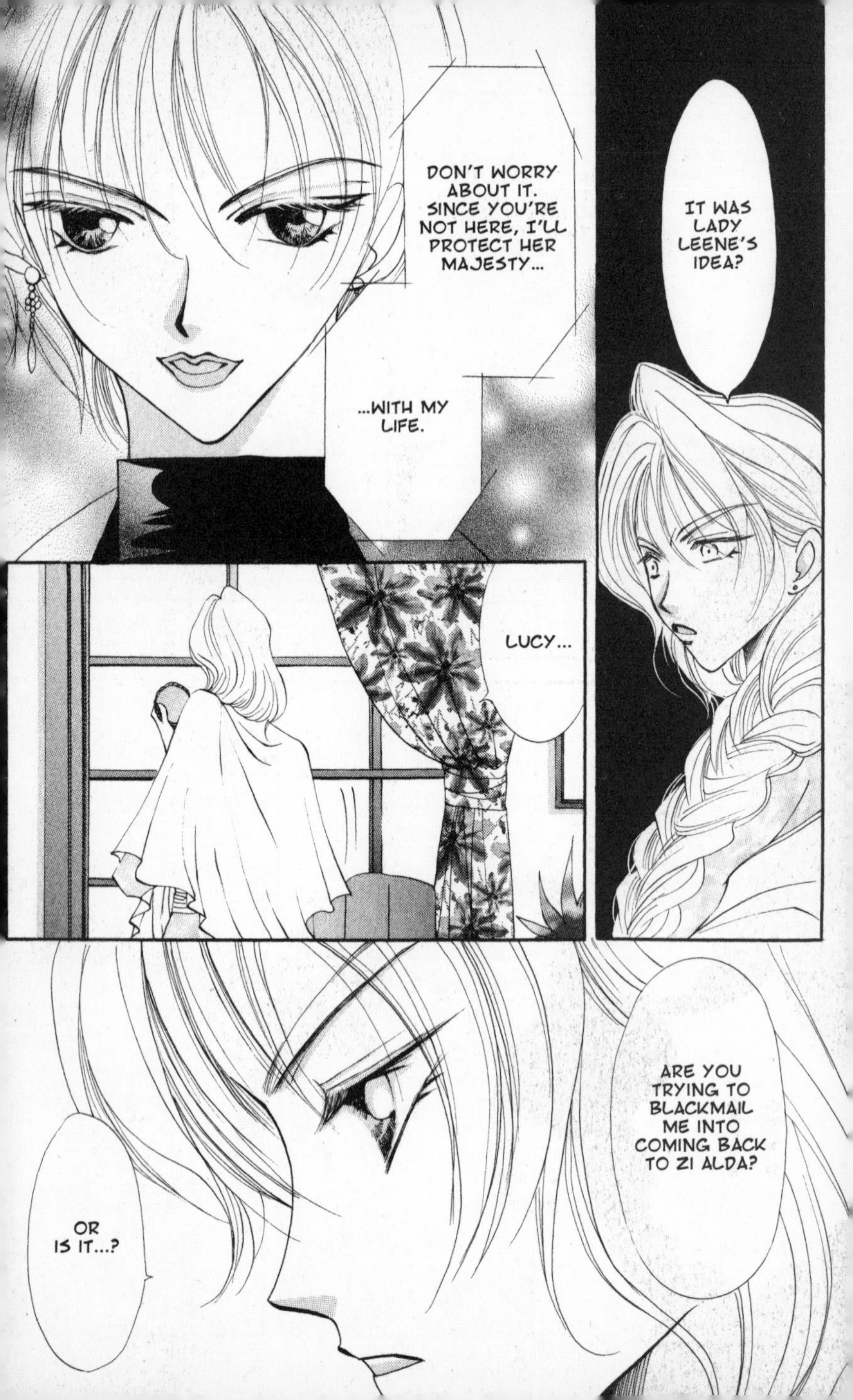
IT WAS LADY LEENE'S IDEA?
DON'T WORRY ABOUT IT. SINCE YOU'RE NOT HERE, I'LL PROTECT HER MAJESTY...
...WITH MY LIFE.
LUCY...
ARE YOU TRYING TO BLACKMAIL ME INTO COMING BACK TO ZI ALDA?
OR IS IT...?

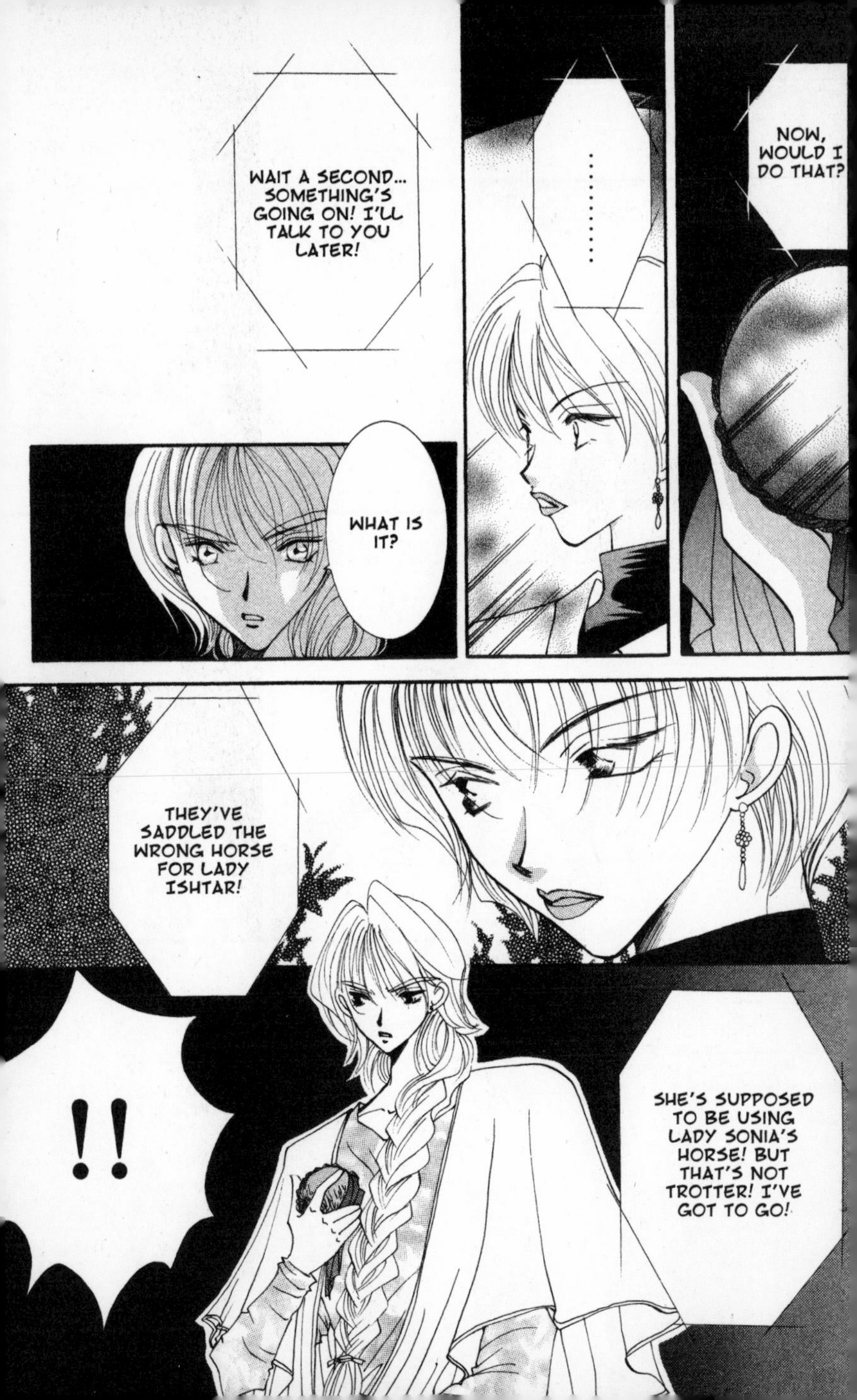
NOW, WOULD I DO THAT?
......
WAIT A SECOND... SOMETHING'S GOING ON! I'LL TALK TO YOU LATER!
WHAT IS IT?
THEY'VE SADDLED THE WRONG HORSE FOR LADY ISHTAR!
SHE'S SUPPOSED TO BE USING LADY SONIA'S HORSE! BUT THAT'S NOT TROTTER! I'VE GOT TO GO!
!!

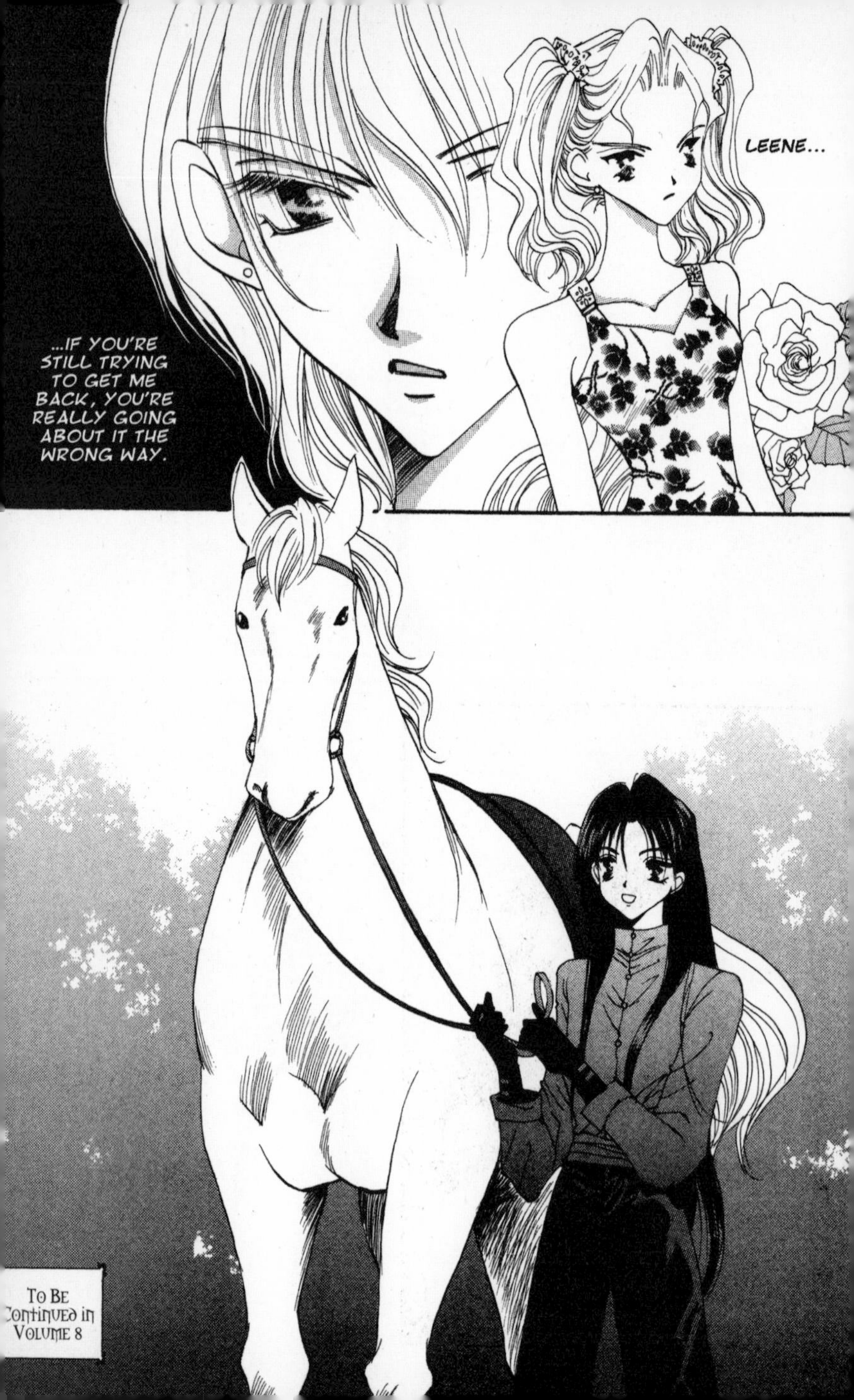
LEENE...
...IF YOU'RE STILL TRYING TO GET ME BACK, YOU'RE REALLY GOING ABOUT IT THE WRONG WAY.
TO BE CONTINUED IN VOLUME 8

In Place of a Postscript...

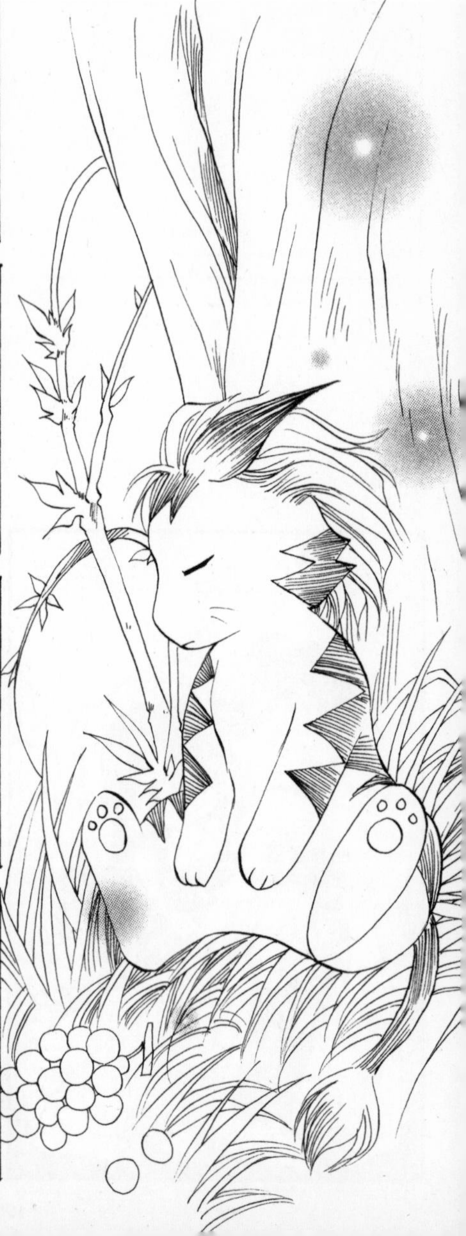

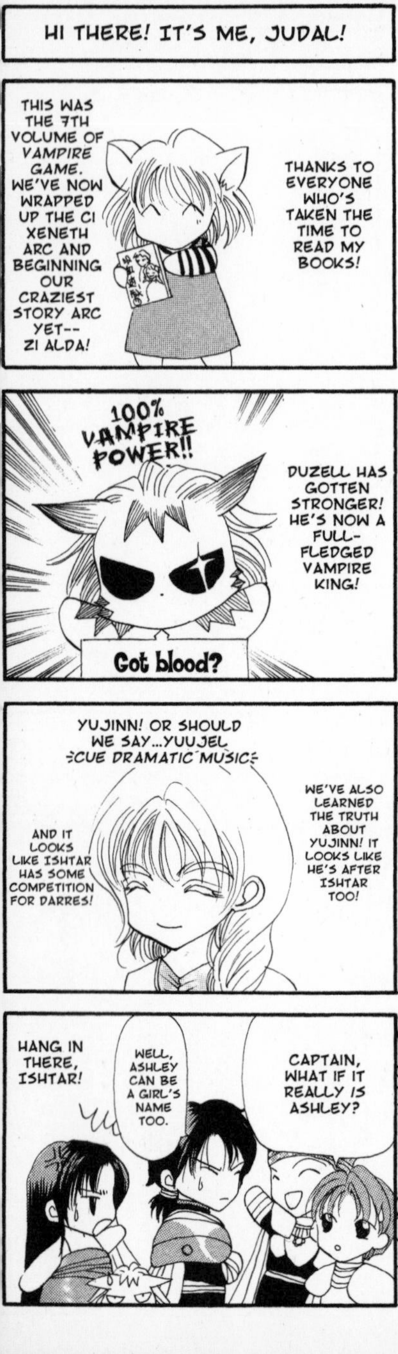
HI THERE! IT'S ME, JUDAL!
THANKS TO EVERYONE WHO'S TAKEN THE TIME TO READ MY BOOKS!
THIS WAS THE 7TH VOLUME OF VAMPIRE GAME. WE'VE NOW WRAPPED UP THE CI XENETH ARC AND BEGINNING OUR CRAZIEST STORY ARC YET-- ZI ALDA!
DUZELL HAS GOTTEN STRONGER! HE'S NOW A FULL-FLEDGED VAMPIRE KING!
100% VAMPIRE POWER!!
Got blood?
YUJINN! OR SHOULD WE SAY...YUUJEL
CUE DRAMATIC MUSIC
WE'VE ALSO LEARNED THE TRUTH ABOUT YUJINN! IT LOOKS LIKE HE'S AFTER ISHTAR TOO!
AND IT LOOKS LIKE ISHTAR HAS SOME COMPETITION FOR DARRES!
CAPTAIN, WHAT IF IT REALLY IS ASHLEY?
WELL, ASHLEY CAN BE A GIRL'S NAME TOO.
HANG IN THERE, ISHTAR!

ANSWERS TO QUIZ 1

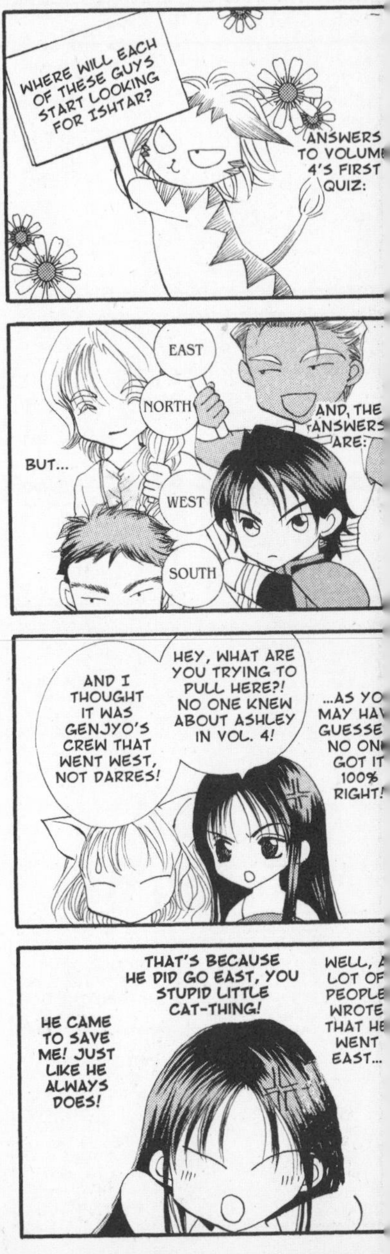
ANSWERS TO VOLUM 4'S FIRST QUIZ:
WHERE WILL EACH OF THESE GUYS START LOOKING FOR ISHTAR?
AND, THE ANSWERS ARE:
EAST
NORTH
WEST
SOUTH
BUT...
...AS YO MAY HA GUESSE NO ON GOT IT 100% RIGHT!
HEY, WHAT ARE YOU TRYING TO PULL HERE?! NO ONE KNEW ABOUT ASHLEY IN VOL. 4!
AND I THOUGHT IT WAS GENJYO'S CREW THAT WENT WEST, NOT DARRES!
WELL, LOT OF PEOPLE WROTE THAT HE WENT EAST...
THAT'S BECAUSE HE DID GO EAST, YOU STUPID LITTLE CAT-THING!
HE CAME TO SAVE ME! JUST LIKE HE ALWAYS DOES!

ANSWERS TO QUIZ 2

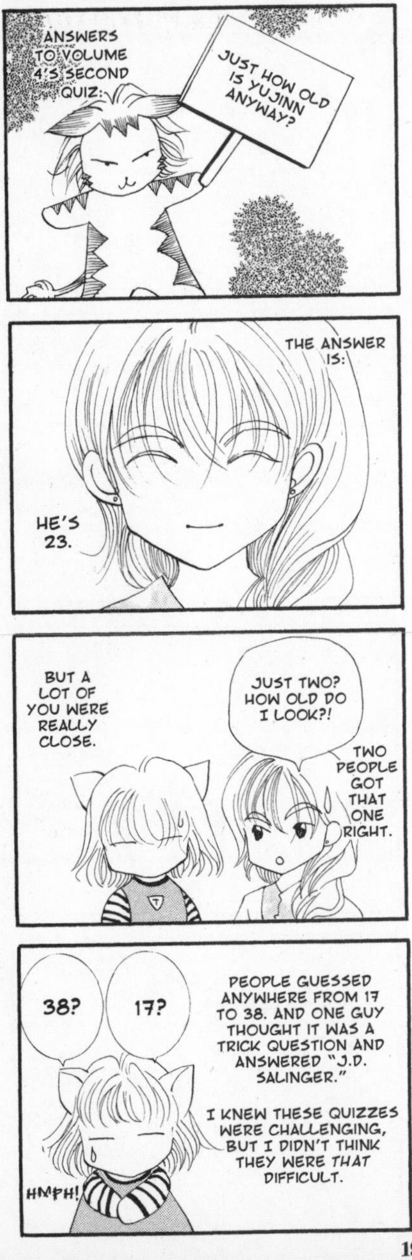
JUST HOW OLD IS YUJINN ANYWAY?
ANSWERS TO VOLUME 4'S SECOND QUIZ:
THE ANSWER IS:
HE'S 23.
TWO PEOPLE GOT THAT ONE RIGHT.
JUST TWO? HOW OLD DO I LOOK?!
BUT A LOT OF YOU WERE REALLY CLOSE.
PEOPLE GUESSED ANYWHERE FROM 17 TO 38. AND ONE GUY THOUGHT IT WAS A TRICK QUESTION AND ANSWERED "J.D. SALINGER."
I KNEW THESE QUIZZES WERE CHALLENGING, BUT I DIDN'T THINK THEY WERE *THAT* DIFFICULT.
17?
38?
HMPH!

ANSWERS TO QUIZ 3

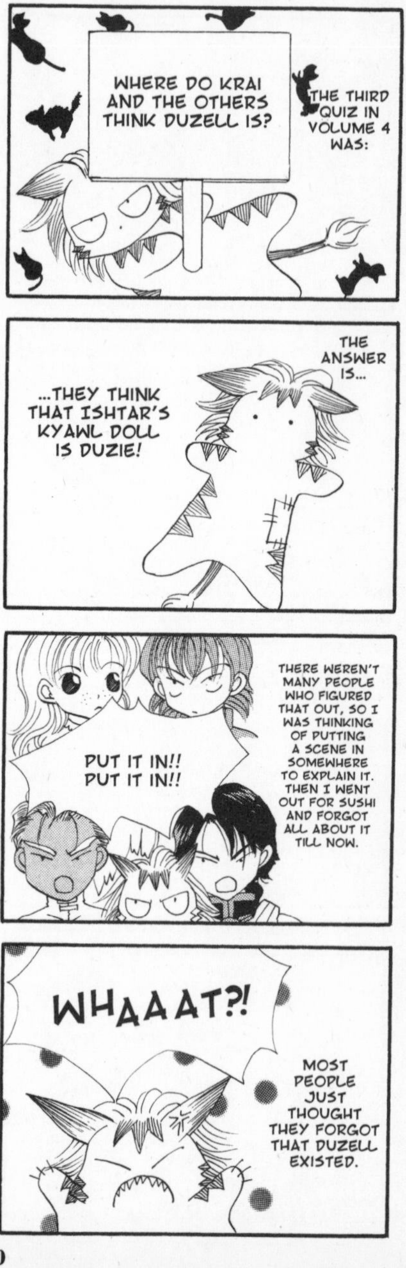
THE THIRD QUIZ IN VOLUME 4 WAS:
WHERE DO KRAI AND THE OTHERS THINK DUZELL IS?
THE ANSWER IS...
...THEY THINK THAT ISHTAR'S KYAWL DOLL IS DUZIE!
THERE WEREN'T MANY PEOPLE WHO FIGURED THAT OUT, SO I WAS THINKING OF PUTTING A SCENE IN SOMEWHERE TO EXPLAIN IT. THEN I WENT OUT FOR SUSHI AND FORGOT ALL ABOUT IT TILL NOW.
PUT IT IN!! PUT IT IN!!
WHAAAT?!
MOST PEOPLE JUST THOUGHT THEY FORGOT THAT DUZELL EXISTED.

LETTERS, PART ONE

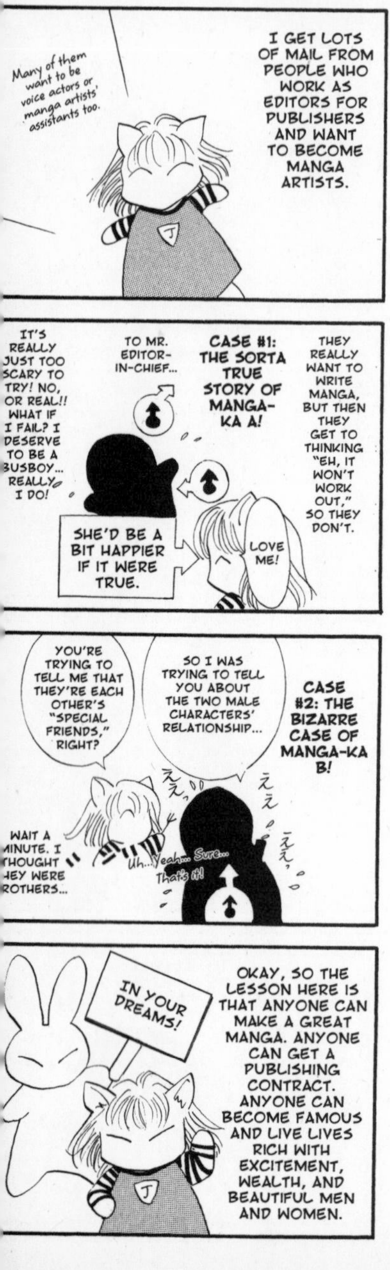
I GET LOTS OF MAIL FROM PEOPLE WHO WORK AS EDITORS FOR PUBLISHERS AND WANT TO BECOME MANGA ARTISTS.
Many of them want to be voice actors or manga artists' assistants too.
THEY REALLY WANT TO WRITE MANGA, BUT THEN THEY GET TO THINKING "EH, IT WON'T WORK OUT," SO THEY DON'T.
CASE #1: THE SORTA TRUE STORY OF MANGA-KA A!
TO MR. EDITOR-IN-CHIEF...
IT'S REALLY JUST TOO SCARY TO TRY! NO, OR REAL!! WHAT IF I FAIL? I DESERVE TO BE A USBOY... REALLY, I DO!
LOVE ME!
SHE'D BE A BIT HAPPIER IF IT WERE TRUE.
CASE #2: THE BIZARRE CASE OF MANGA-KA B!
SO I WAS TRYING TO TELL YOU ABOUT THE TWO MALE CHARACTERS' RELATIONSHIP...
YOU'RE TRYING TO TELL ME THAT THEY'RE EACH OTHER'S "SPECIAL FRIENDS," RIGHT?
ええっ
ええ
ええ
Uh... Yeah... Sure... That's it!
WAIT A MINUTE. I THOUGHT HEY WERE ROTHERS...
OKAY, SO THE LESSON HERE IS THAT ANYONE CAN MAKE A GREAT MANGA. ANYONE CAN GET A PUBLISHING CONTRACT. ANYONE CAN BECOME FAMOUS AND LIVE LIVES RICH WITH EXCITEMENT, WEALTH, AND BEAUTIFUL MEN AND WOMEN.
IN YOUR DREAMS!

LETTERS, PART TWO

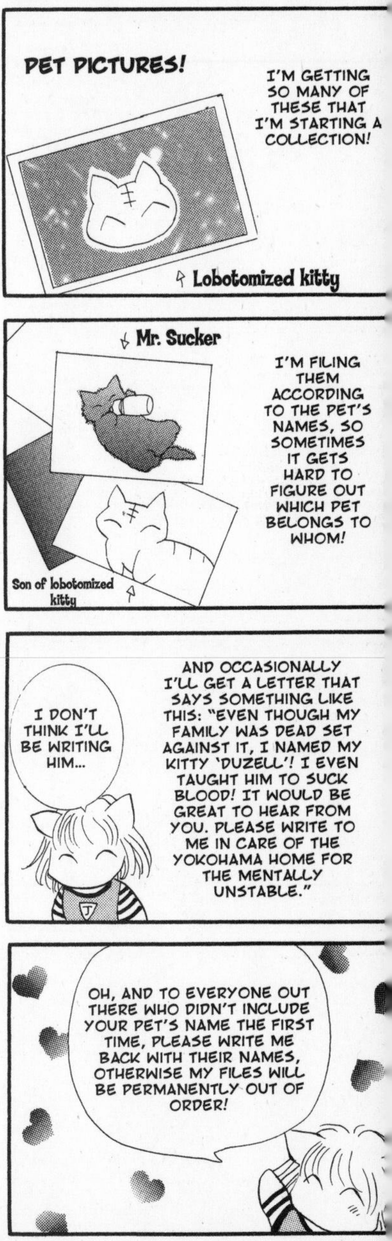
PET PICTURES!
I'M GETTING SO MANY OF THESE THAT I'M STARTING A COLLECTION!
Lobotomized kitty
Mr. Sucker
I'M FILING THEM ACCORDING TO THE PET'S NAMES, SO SOMETIMES IT GETS HARD TO FIGURE OUT WHICH PET BELONGS TO WHOM!
Son of lobotomized kitty
AND OCCASIONALLY I'LL GET A LETTER THAT SAYS SOMETHING LIKE THIS: "EVEN THOUGH MY FAMILY WAS DEAD SET AGAINST IT, I NAMED MY KITTY 'DUZELL'! I EVEN TAUGHT HIM TO SUCK BLOOD! IT WOULD BE GREAT TO HEAR FROM YOU. PLEASE WRITE TO ME IN CARE OF THE YOKOHAMA HOME FOR THE MENTALLY UNSTABLE."
I DON'T THINK I'LL BE WRITING HIM...
OH, AND TO EVERYONE OUT THERE WHO DIDN'T INCLUDE YOUR PET'S NAME THE FIRST TIME, PLEASE WRITE ME BACK WITH THEIR NAMES, OTHERWISE MY FILES WILL BE PERMANENTLY OUT OF ORDER!

A DAY IN THE LIFE

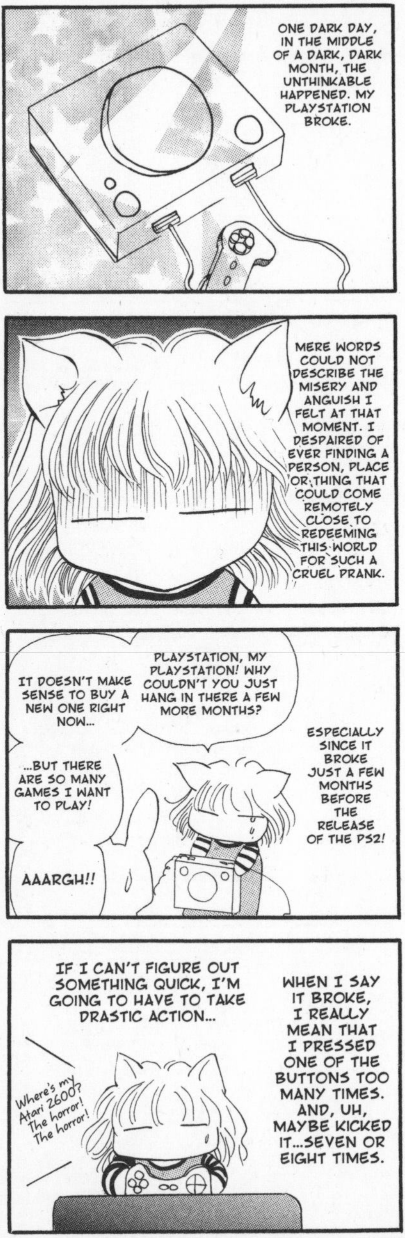
ONE DARK DAY, IN THE MIDDLE OF A DARK, DARK MONTH, THE UNTHINKABLE HAPPENED. MY PLAYSTATION BROKE.
MERE WORDS COULD NOT DESCRIBE THE MISERY AND ANGUISH I FELT AT THAT MOMENT. I DESPAIRED OF EVER FINDING A PERSON, PLACE OR THING THAT COULD COME REMOTELY CLOSE TO REDEEMING THIS WORLD FOR SUCH A CRUEL PRANK.
PLAYSTATION, MY PLAYSTATION! WHY COULDN'T YOU JUST HANG IN THERE A FEW MORE MONTHS?
ESPECIALLY SINCE IT BROKE JUST A FEW MONTHS BEFORE THE RELEASE OF THE PS2!
IT DOESN'T MAKE SENSE TO BUY A NEW ONE RIGHT NOW...
...BUT THERE ARE SO MANY GAMES I WANT TO PLAY!
AAARGH!!
WHEN I SAY IT BROKE, I REALLY MEAN THAT I PRESSED ONE OF THE BUTTONS TOO MANY TIMES. AND, UH, MAYBE KICKED IT...SEVEN OR EIGHT TIMES.
IF I CAN'T FIGURE OUT SOMETHING QUICK, I'M GOING TO HAVE TO TAKE DRASTIC ACTION...
Where's my Atari 2600? The horror! The horror!

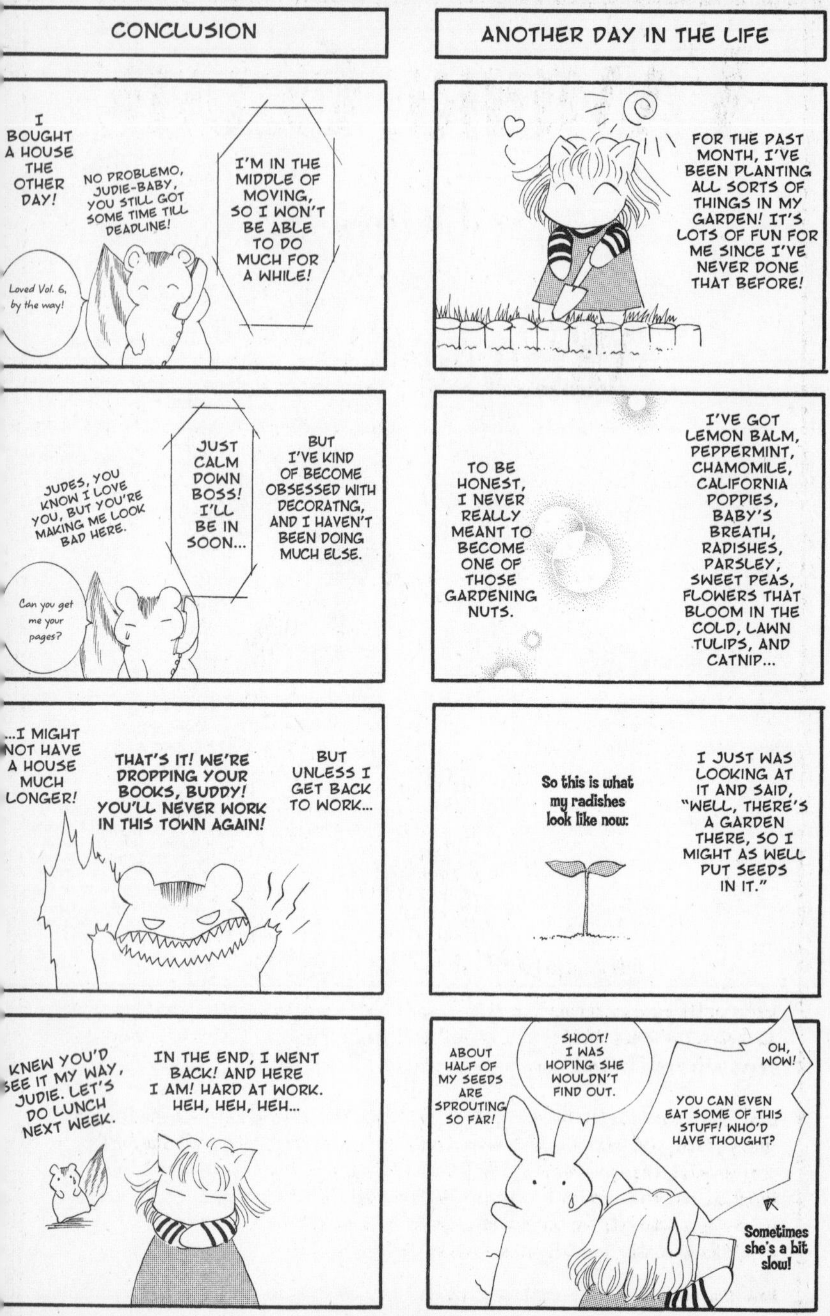
ANOTHER DAY IN THE LIFE
FOR THE PAST MONTH, I'VE BEEN PLANTING ALL SORTS OF THINGS IN MY GARDEN! IT'S LOTS OF FUN FOR ME SINCE I'VE NEVER DONE THAT BEFORE!
I'VE GOT LEMON BALM, PEPPERMINT, CHAMOMILE, CALIFORNIA POPPIES, BABY'S BREATH, RADISHES, PARSLEY, SWEET PEAS, FLOWERS THAT BLOOM IN THE COLD, LAWN TULIPS, AND CATNIP...
TO BE HONEST, I NEVER REALLY MEANT TO BECOME ONE OF THOSE GARDENING NUTS.
I JUST WAS LOOKING AT IT AND SAID, "WELL, THERE'S A GARDEN THERE, SO I MIGHT AS WELL PUT SEEDS IN IT."
So this is what my radishes look like now:
OH, WOW!
YOU CAN EVEN EAT SOME OF THIS STUFF! WHO'D HAVE THOUGHT?
Sometimes she's a bit slow!
SHOOT! I WAS HOPING SHE WOULDN'T FIND OUT.
ABOUT HALF OF MY SEEDS ARE SPROUTING SO FAR!
CONCLUSION
I'M IN THE MIDDLE OF MOVING, SO I WON'T BE ABLE TO DO MUCH FOR A WHILE!
NO PROBLEMO, JUDIE-BABY, YOU STILL GOT SOME TIME TILL DEADLINE!
I BOUGHT A HOUSE THE OTHER DAY!
Loved Vol. 6, by the way!
BUT I'VE KIND OF BECOME OBSESSED WITH DECORATNG, AND I HAVEN'T BEEN DOING MUCH ELSE.
JUST CALM DOWN BOSS! I'LL BE IN SOON...
JUDES, YOU KNOW I LOVE YOU, BUT YOU'RE MAKING ME LOOK BAD HERE.
Can you get me your pages?
BUT UNLESS I GET BACK TO WORK...
THAT'S IT! WE'RE DROPPING YOUR BOOKS, BUDDY! YOU'LL NEVER WORK IN THIS TOWN AGAIN!
...I MIGHT NOT HAVE A HOUSE MUCH LONGER!
IN THE END, I WENT BACK! AND HERE I AM! HARD AT WORK. HEH, HEH, HEH...
KNEW YOU'D SEE IT MY WAY, JUDIE. LET'S DO LUNCH NEXT WEEK.

VAMPIRE GAME

Next issue...

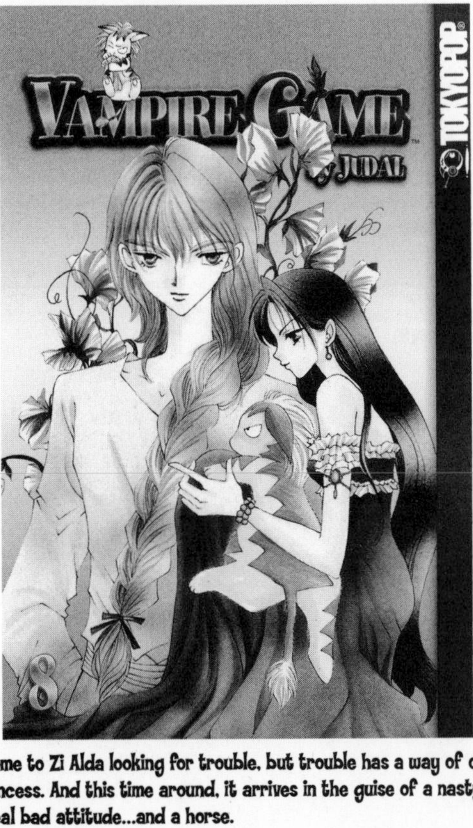

VAMPIRE GAME
by JUDAL
TOKYOPOP
8

Ishtar didn't come to Zi Alda looking for trouble, but trouble has a way of catching up with our beloved princess. And this time around, it arrives in the guise of a nasty-tempered beast with a real bad attitude...and a horse.

Lady Leene was once the fairest girl in all of Zi Alda. Then Princess Ishtar came to town. Young, pretty, and powerful, Ishtar would make any woman feel threatened. But for the very jealous Leene, the princess is more than a threat, she's the enemy. Enter Backbreaker. Untamed, wild and completely unbroken, Backbreaker is a hurricane made equine. And he's got a riding date with the unsuspecting Ishtar. Will our princess prevail?
Or will Backbreaker take Ishtar on a ride to die for?

Note: Judal wishes it to be known that no horses were hurt in the drawing of this manga.

ALSO AVAILABLE FROM TOKYOPOP®

For more
information visit
www.TOKYOPOP.com

03.30.04T

ALSO AVAILABLE FROM TOKYOPOP®

MANGA

.HACK//LEGEND OF THE TWILIGHT
@LARGE
ABENOBASHI: MAGICAL SHOPPING ARCADE
A.I. LOVE YOU
AI YORI AOSHI
ANGELIC LAYER
ARM OF KANNON
BABY BIRTH
BATTLE ROYALE
BATTLE VIXENS
BRAIN POWERED
BRIGADOON
B'TX
CANDIDATE FOR GODDESS, THE
CARDCAPTOR SAKURA
CARDCAPTOR SAKURA - MASTER OF THE CLOW
CHOBITS
CHRONICLES OF THE CURSED SWORD
CLAMP SCHOOL DETECTIVES
CLOVER
COMIC PARTY
CONFIDENTIAL CONFESSIONS
CORRECTOR YUI
COWBOY BEBOP
COWBOY BEBOP: SHOOTING STAR
CRAZY LOVE STORY
CRESCENT MOON
CROSS
CULDCEPT
CYBORG 009
D•N•ANGEL
DEMON DIARY
DEMON ORORON, THE
DEUS VITAE
DIABOLO
DIGIMON
DIGIMON TAMERS
DIGIMON ZERO TWO
DOLL
DRAGON HUNTER
DRAGON KNIGHTS
DRAGON VOICE
DREAM SAGA
DUKLYON: CLAMP SCHOOL DEFENDERS
EERIE QUEERIE!
ERICA SAKURAZAWA: COLLECTED WORKS
ET CETERA
ETERNITY
EVIL'S RETURN
FAERIES' LANDING
FAKE
FLCL
FLOWER OF THE DEEP SLEEP
FORBIDDEN DANCE
FRUITS BASKET
G GUNDAM

GATEKEEPERS
GETBACKERS
GIRL GOT GAME
GIRLS' EDUCATIONAL CHARTER
GRAVITATION
GTO
GUNDAM BLUE DESTINY
GUNDAM SEED ASTRAY
GUNDAM WING
GUNDAM WING: BATTLEFIELD OF PACIFISTS
GUNDAM WING: ENDLESS WALTZ
GUNDAM WING: THE LAST OUTPOST (G-UNIT)
GUYS' GUIDE TO GIRLS
HANDS OFF!
HAPPY MANIA
HARLEM BEAT
HONEY MUSTARD
I.N.V.U.
IMMORTAL RAIN
INITIAL D
INSTANT TEEN: JUST ADD NUTS
ISLAND
JING: KING OF BANDITS
JING: KING OF BANDITS - TWILIGHT TALES
JULINE
KARE KANO
KILL ME, KISS ME
KINDAICHI CASE FILES, THE
KING OF HELL
KODOCHA: SANA'S STAGE
LAMENT OF THE LAMB
LEGAL DRUG
LEGEND OF CHUN HYANG, THE
LES BIJOUX
LOVE HINA
LUPIN III
LUPIN III: WORLD'S MOST WANTED
MAGIC KNIGHT RAYEARTH I
MAGIC KNIGHT RAYEARTH II
MAHOROMATIC: AUTOMATIC MAIDEN
MAN OF MANY FACES
MARMALADE BOY
MARS
MARS: HORSE WITH NO NAME
MINK
MIRACLE GIRLS
MIYUKI-CHAN IN WONDERLAND
MODEL
MY LOVE
NECK AND NECK
ONE
ONE I LOVE, THE
PARADISE KISS
PARASYTE
PASSION FRUIT
PEACH GIRL
PEACH GIRL: CHANGE OF HEART
PET SHOP OF HORRORS

03.30.04T

SUKI™

A like story...

by CLAMP

TOKYOPOP®

T TEEN AGE 13+

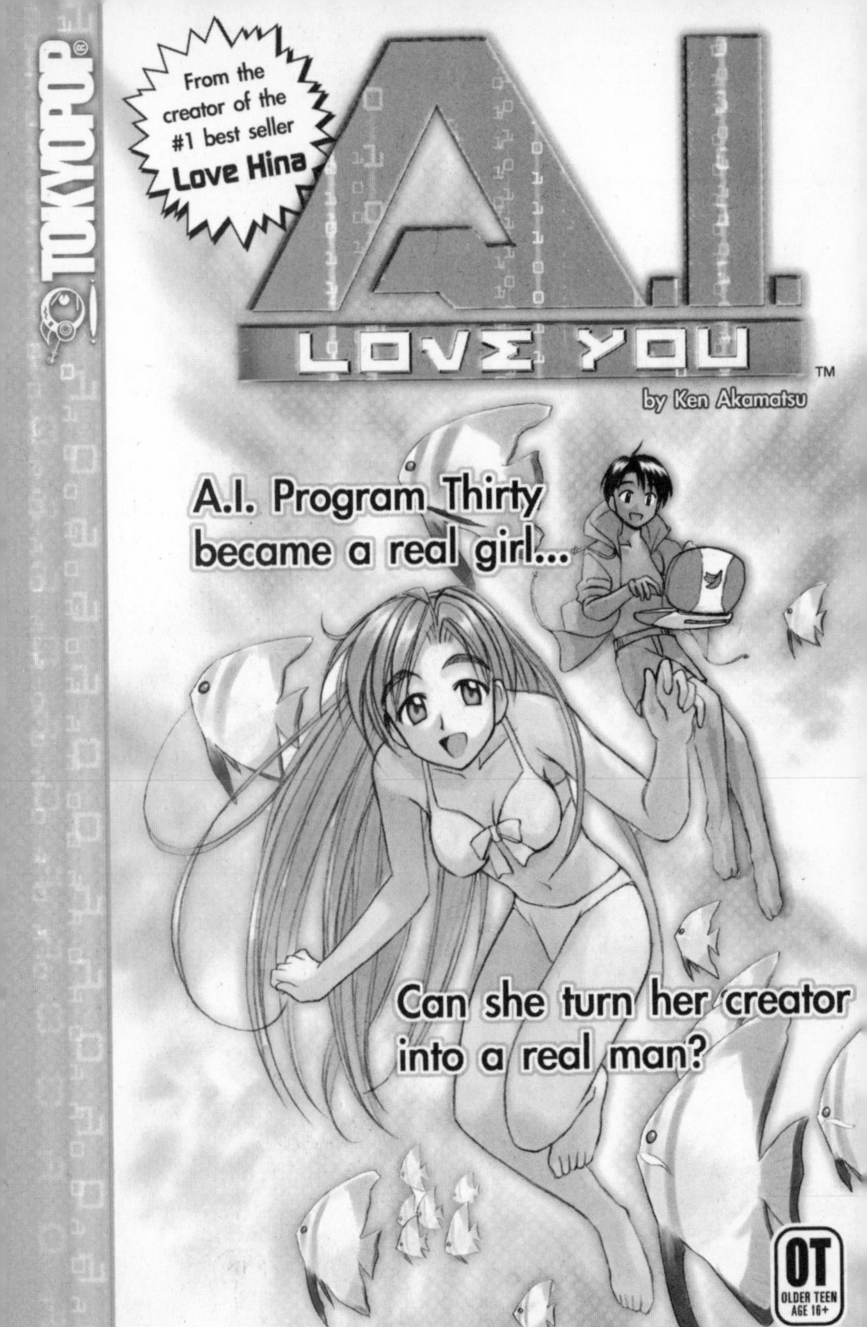
TOKYOPOP®
From the creator of the #1 best seller Love Hina
A.I. LOVE YOU™
by Ken Akamatsu
A.I. Program Thirty became a real girl...
Can she turn her creator into a real man?
OT
OLDER TEEN AGE 16+

STOP!

This is the back of the book.
You wouldn't want to spoil a great ending!

This book is printed "manga-style," in the authentic Japanese right-to-left format. Since none of the artwork has been flipped or altered, readers get to experience the story just as the creator intended. You've been asking for it, so TOKYOPOP® delivered: authentic, hot-off-the-press, and far more fun!

DIRECTIONS

If this is your first time reading manga-style, here's a quick guide to help you understand how it works.

It's easy... just start in the top right panel and follow the numbers. Have fun, and look for more 100% authentic manga from TOKYOPOP®!